# ANCIENT, VAST, AND INFINITE

## A MYTHIC FANTASY OF DEATH AND STAR-CROSSED SOULS

### CAROLYN ZED

Bad Axe Press

To B.H. – You have been with me since the garden.

# CONTENTS

# PREFACE

In summer of 2023, I was weeding my overgrown vegetable garden one evening. My gardens are prone to becoming overgrown, so I am prone to sudden bouts of "I really should do something about that" weeding sessions.

But we're not talking about my shortcomings as a gardener. We're talking about this story.

While I do any monotonous task, I let my mind drift to the wealth of random scenes and stories that fill my head. Some I've been visiting since I was a kid. But on this particular evening, I started monologuing to myself: muttering under my breath to the ragweeds and dandelions I was trying to vanquish. In a flash that I'm still trying to wrap my head around, I uttered this snippet of dialog:

"I am dead."

"Yes. Quite."

What came to my mind next was a flood of questions:

Who was dead? How did they die? Why did they *know* they were dead? Who were they talking to?

Weed by weed, I answered those questions, each point flowing effortlessly into the next. The main character had been murdered, and they knew who had killed them. They were talking to a Greeter, a bureaucratic member of the numberless ranks of dead souls. They were in the realm of the dead. But something was wrong. Something was *unusual* about how the main character had died. Something that neither of them understood.

I've experienced inspiration before, but nothing quite like this. Over the course of the next hour I forsook the weedy garden and took myself on a long rambling walk while I worked out some of the mysteries in this storyline. The plot came to me in a steady stream, like I was opening door after door into strange new worlds. I have certainly heard of creative people experiencing such strokes of inspiration, but a story had never come to me so suddenly and so completely. Never ever. This was new.

In November of 2023, I set out to actually write the story. I didn't officially participate in National Novel Writers Month, but my goal was the same: 50,000 words by the end of the month. I've tried to challenge myself to write like this before, but have never gotten close to 50,000 words on a single story.

That year, I smashed the goal.

But the story wasn't finished. By February 2024, after three months of dedicated evenings, I had finished my first draft.

I gave the story it space to breathe. Some trusted eyes have read it, and I have revised it heavily. But through it all, the plot from the garden stayed as a golden blossoming thread throughout; the foundation of the story that had come to me all at once.

Now, it is finally time for the story to be out in the wild. There's drama. There's trauma. There's love and passion and loss and friendship and joy and heartbreak. And some really big trees. It is not the best book, but it is mine. My first pancake, imperfections and all.

As I am writing this preface, the final piece of writing I will do for this novel, I am reflecting on what it means to be a creative. For me, it's not about selling thousands of copies of a book or achieving any sort of notoriety. It's about making something out of nothing. Taking a story that came to me in the garden and putting it to words and putting those words on paper. It's about enjoying the process of writing and seeing where the story goes.

I am honored you would spend you time reading my debut novel. I hope you find entertainment and joy amidst these pages, the same way I did when writing them.

With gratitude,

Carolyn Zed

# I.

I knew I was dead before I opened my eyes. It was the kind of thing you couldn't debate. I knew I had died and I knew who had killed me.

I opened my eyes. This wasn't the living room of my tiny, dirty apartment.

Soft ground.

Soft ground. Darkness.

Soft ground. Darkness. Thunder.

Thunder?

I moved myself to a sitting position and gasped as I was overcome with a rush of electric shocks. It was like being crashed into by a wave of static. The outline of my body was crackling and snapping. I was a terrified, frenzied animal.

There was hardly any time to adjust to that terrible sensation when the distant thunder turned into a raging storm. Thunder boomed and lightning struck violently but I saw no flashes of light. No rain fell either, or if it did I could not feel it. The unnerving static sensation was the only thing my body was registering besides the sounds of the storm. I looked around, trying to make out where I was. The space was vast and almost completely dark. I could sense there were tall pillars looming around me. The ground was covered in moss. Was I in the woods? The pillars were certainly tree-like.

I had only been conscious for a split second, but I could tell something was rushing towards me. In the darkness I saw an even *darker* mass hurling through the towering trees in my direction. The frenzy in me rose higher. Fight or flight doesn't care that you are already dead. I remained frozen on the soft ground as the shape gathered itself into a thin pillar of absolute darkness unlike anything I had ever seen before. It was like a gash of infinite blackness. It boomed with the sounds of thunder - the storm seeming to come directly from it. The buzzing of my skin reached a new intensity as the column of darkness loomed over me.

I stared into its depth and became mesmerized. The blackness writhed like a dark ocean, like the fastest moving clouds I had ever seen, and thunder continued rumbling. Despite how terrified I was, I was overcome with a sense of longing and desperation and a boundless joy I had never felt before. That made no sense. I became aware that the darkness I was staring into was...watching me. My abdomen lurched with panic, and yet there was an unexplainable feeling of familiarity. And relief.

*"Do I know you?"* My voice was distant and fragile.

Thunder echoed back, followed by a new surge of longing and confusion. I started to see things in my mind, things I didn't recognize. Flashes of trees and hills and sunlight and people with faces I did not know:

*A windswept cliffside.*
*Trees so tall they touched the clouds.*
*Running down a forest path.*
*Lying under a tree in the sunshine.*
*A face, at the edge of my vision.*
*It was like looking at someone through tear-filled eyes.*
*The taste of something sweet in my mouth.*
Then fire.

Fire. Fire. Fire. Engulfing trees and hills. And pang of anguish like a knife being driven into my chest. A sound that sent ice through my whole body. Fear won out and I faded into blackness.

*I was standing on lone, bare rock in a dark sea. Waves crashed around me, and I had a growing panic that I was going to get swept under. I tried to call out, but my voice was lost in the sound of the increasingly angry water. A huge crack of thunder exploded overhead.*

I woke up in a sweat, screaming. Rain was pouring down the window next to my bed.

"Hollis! Hollis!" Lights turned on in the hallway.

"It's nothing! I'm fine." I gasped, untangling myself from my sheets. My door burst open.

"You scared me, baby." My mother sat on my bed and smoothed back my hair. The astringent scent of alcohol wafted off her as she fussed with my sweat-soaked hair.

"Sorry, it was a dream."

Thunder rumbled outside, rattling the old panes in my bedroom windows.

"You used to get these same nightmares when you were a little one. Every time it would storm, you would cry." My mother kissed my head. "You used to say you missed someone. I never knew what you were talking about."

"I'm fine." I rolled over and pulled the blankets over me. I was eighteen. This was ridiculous.

The memory faded.

# II.

I woke up in a warmly lit room. It was comfortable, with sunlight filtering in through a hazy window to my right. I slowly sat up. I was in a luxurious bed, ornately carved from dark wood. The room was normal in most respects except for the fact that each piece of furniture looked like it belonged in a museum or castle or something. It was not at all like any of the dingy spaces I had called home when I was alive.

Hazy memories came back to my mind. The memory of my mother, the windswept cliff, the blurred face I could hardly make out. The visions I had seen were fading, but I distinctly remembered a storm. So, the visions weren't over now that I was dead. *Why?* Why was I still crazy

I jumped at the sound of rustling papers. A delicate looking man was seated at a desk to my left. He seemed to be very involved in whatever task he was working on as he wrote rapidly. I observed for a moment. His hair hung in effortless bronze waves that somehow looked tidy and messy at the same time. His shoulders were angular, and he had excellent posture. His hands glided across the paper so quickly I wondered how he could possibly be writing anything legible. His skin was fair but flushed with a healthy glow. He certainly didn't skip any step of his skincare regimen. As if sensing my scrutiny, he paused in his writing, looked straight ahead at the wall and said:"You are awake."

His voice made me jump again. It was quite a normal voice, fairly boring and inoffensive, except for the low sound of rustling leaves that accompanied each word. He turned to face me slowly. He inspected me unblinkingly for a moment while I continued to do the same to him, my mouth hanging open stupidly. He wore gold framed glasses. His eyes were warm, hazel and inquisitive, and as I suspected his complexion was unnervingly flawless. He was beautiful. I could not tell how old he was and I struggled to gather my thoughts.

I knew I was dead. So, what was this then? I knew that fucking asshole had killed me. I could still feel the clench of his fingers against my neck. I had left my body. I had seen myself on the floor of our grungy horrible apartment: my brown eyes glazed and red, and my full lips tinged blue. I had watched him slump back and stare at his bloodied hands. Then things had faded to darkness. And then the storm had come."I'm dead." I broke the silence with the only thing I knew was a fact. Twenty two years old and already dead. Just fantastic."Yes, quite." He smirked slightly now as he spoke, "And it makes my job easier that you know you are dead already. What year did you die in?"

"2010. Do people not know? Do they not know that they are dead?" I stretched my hands out in front of me, suddenly inspired to look for signs of the struggle that had caused my death. They looked normal, but somewhat cleaner. My nails were long and healthy, not chipped and coated in flaking paint as they had been. My hair, too, normally a tangled mess of brown waves felt clean and full. Certainly not the state I had died in.

"People do not always quite know what has happened. You on the other hand seem to have a clear grasp of where you are and when you joined us. That is a wonderful start." The man was now standing. He was wearing a dated but classic navy blue suit with a silk pocket square he adjusted carefully as he spoke.

"Some folks die so suddenly and unexpectedly they are quite surprised to learn what has happened. Others are waiting to die so they certainly know a bit better, and some-"

"I was murdered."

The last scene of my life was playing in my head. The way that asshole had looked at me with his face contorted in rage and effort.

"Yes, quite." The man stood facing me, seeming to hold space for me to say some other profoundly obvious thing.

I didn't know what to say next. I felt like I would either cry or scream if I opened my mouth again. If I were alone I would have done both, but with this strangely proper little man I didn't want to do either.

"Do you want to know where you are?" He offered.

Still concerned I would start screaming at him if I talked, I nodded.

He broke into a wide grin. It was a little off putting how enthusiastic he was, suddenly breaking his cool and collected demeanor with a burst of giddy energy. I drew back as he rushed to sit on the edge of the bed.

"Where do you think you are? Oh, humans have such an interesting and complex relationship with death. I have looked at your life, I cannot wait to hear where you think you are and what you think-"

"You *looked* at my *life*?"

"Oh yes, excuse me but circumstances," He motioned to himself and then to me, followed by a grander flourish to the whole room, "being what they are."

"And what *the fuck* are they? Where *am* I?" I asked, climbing out of bed. Had I not been teetering on becoming irate I would have found amusement in the ridiculously modest floor-length linen nightgown I was wearing.

"Where do *you* think?" He repeated, as if he were coaxing a child to do their homework.

"Heaven? Hell?"

"Precisely."

"Which *one*?"

"Well, it is not so simple. I would like to take the explanation much slower so that-"

"Just fucking explain it!" I spat. The man's smile widened slightly but his eyes were no longer warm and kind.

"Please." He motioned to a set of chairs near the window.

I stomped over and sat. This pompous nerd and his self righteous attitude were grating on my nerves. What was his game, anyway? Did he get off from explaining stuff to angry confused dead people? He certainly liked being the smartest one in the room.

"Where are we and what was that storm thing last night?" I demanded, listing the first unexplained thing that came to my mind. I shuddered at the recollection of the intense feelings that had overcome me as I had started into the depths of the darkness.

"Oh! That is much easier to explain." He sat in his chair with absurdly good posture, "The *storm* you met was our benevolent host. These are his rooms and home that we are in. I suppose...." he trailed off and muttered, "...this is not the easiest thing to explain either."

"Is this hell?"

"No. There is no such thing."

"*What?*"

"You were not very religious in your life but you do seem keen to latch on to those typical human ideals. Hell is not real, no. Humans struggle to understand forgiveness so they invented the concept of hell."

"Humans, what?" My mouth was back in its previous state of hanging open stupidly, "Are you not human?"

"I was, a long long long time ago." He folded his hands and stared at me, irritated as he waited for follow-up questions.

"I....so what? So like, hell isn't real? Just heaven? What is here? Where are we?"

"Well, matter is neither created nor destroyed, right?"

"What the fu-"

He waved his hand at me. "Science taught you that."

"If you watched my life you'd know science wasn't *my thing*."

"Well. Of course. But it is the law of nature. Life decays to make new life."

"Sure."

I was flooded with mental images of spiders weaving webs and mushrooms pushing up through the forest floor and flowers blooming and dying in cracks of stone. Death into life into death into life. It was too much too fast, like one of those image recognition tests where they flash pictures on a screen. I blinked rapidly as the episode ended and took a shaking breath. The nerd looked at me quizzically before continuing.

"The same is true for your soul. There is so much energy contained in a human that can not just become nothing. It has to be spent or absorbed someplace. That place is here. And by human standards the energy of the soul is fairly boundless. It is quite hard to wrap your heads around what comes after death. So it seems like eternal life."

"What? I-"

"Can I please explain more? I feel that I will answer many of your questions if I finish the basic explanation. I did not want to get into this yet but you seem so dissatisfied."

I snorted, glaring at him.

"Dissatisfied? Do other people have *no* questions?"

"They have fewer. Or at least they are far better listeners."

I rolled my eyes. "Go ahead *professor*."

He adjusted his glasses, like the absolute caricature of a studious little pencil pusher. I rolled my eyes again. I had hated school when I was alive. School had been full of jerk teachers looking down on me because of who I was and where I lived. I could still hear my mom in her sober moments nagging at me about my poor grades in every class besides literature and computer science. Everyday there had been a nightmare at that prison of a school. How could hell not be real if I was stuck here with this academic twerp reliving that feeling of being looked at as stupid and inferior?

The man had sensed my brooding and waited to speak until I refocused on him. He cleared his throat and began:

"When a human dies their soul is a tremendous ball of energy. That energy field almost immediately leaves Earth's plane and comes here. It is a sort of dimension beyond Earth. And from this is where all the heaven and various afterlife stories come in. Humans used to be so much more observant and perceptive of these things. But well," He eyed me judgmentally over his glasses, "Humans have become less focused on things they used to understand quite clearly."

As he spoke, the gentle sound of leaves was ever present. I felt no breeze and could not see outside through the frosted window to determine if there were nearby trees or not.

"Regardless," he continued, "This Otherworld plane has existed since the formation of the planets. It is an energetic field both tied to and separate from

Earth. As a life with a soul dies on Earth, their soul comes here. To make new life on Earth is a divine act, and pulls from the core of non-soul energy on Earth."

He frowned at my confused expression.

"When humans make a new human, that new life is given a soul energy made up of parts of the energy of their parents. Just as their body is composed of pieces of their parents' bodies. In addition to the soul energy of the parents, a new soul draws energy from the Earth itself. Animals, plants, and the like. Sometimes it takes a while to deliver that energy. So that explains why babies do not enter the world fully aware, no?"

He acted as if I was going to be wowed with that particular revelation but I was growing even more impatient. I hated being lectured at.

"Okay so what then? We die and our soul comes here and we just," I waved my hands around angrily, "Chill out?"

"No. Well, yes. You *can* do that. Most humans take a great deal of time doing that at first when they arrive. But there is a great deal of power you can expend here that you could not on Earth. In this place you can engage in the act of creation as you thought only possible by *gods*. Render buildings, pull up mountains, raise seas and all of that. Where you are now is our Host's domain. A space they created when they first arrived. Often humans spend time after first arriving here mimicking Earthlife. Living out their joys and dreams in a way they could never have previously imagined. In these more Earth-like spaces we often occupy more human-like forms."

He gestured to his own appearance with pride. Was I supposed to be impressed by his little blue suit? So far the afterlife was irritating beyond belief.

"Life here is more similar to Earth." He continued, his tone icy at my bad reception of his educational rant. "When you move deeper into this plane you will see things beyond Earthly understanding and will be able to express the true power of your being."

He paused, looking suddenly uncomfortable before adding, "Well. Perhaps."

It was my turn to speak, because he had trailed off into a concerned silence. His eyes were distantly gazing across the room. We were quiet for a while.

"So, can I see my family then? The ones who are here?" He jumped at my sudden breaking of the silence, "Are they here? My Grandpa? My Aunt?"

"Oh yes, well, everyone is here. Yes. But you cannot see them yet." His eyes flicked over me with concern. "But every human who has ever lived is here in some form."

That was shocking.

"Even *shitty* people?" I blurted.

Each time I uttered an obscenity he flinched or narrowed his eyes. It made me inclined to swear even more profusely than usual.

"Oh certainly. Even people who performed true atrocities on Earth."

"*Hitler?*"

"Humans really have been asking about that one a lot lately. Yes Hitler *was* here. You know, we have had to make special policies to explain this one. It seems like everyone knew him."

"He was Hitler...I mean, like, yeah we all know about him. But he's here?"

"He *was*. This is hard for many humans to understand, but every soul that comes here gets the same choice. Enjoy this Otherworld in peace and tranquility or give your soul's energy up to be dissipated. Some humans cannot or will not give themselves over to peace and joy. Those souls often elect to be unmade. The most powerful among us, the ones who have been dead the longest whom we call the Old Dead, are able to cleanse and disintegrate a soul. That soul's energy then becomes available for reuse here or on Earth as new souls if needed."

"So Hitler?"

He sighed, exacerbated with my fixation on the subject.

"Did not want to live in peace. But, funny enough, Stalin did."

"What?"

"Yes, Stalin opted to stay and is quite the scholar on rose plant genetics. He has made some really interesting discoveries that have been sent to Earth as new breeds."

For the first time since dying I laughed.

"It is true! One of particular note is Genus-"

"I believe you." I rubbed my face in my hands while still laughing dryly. "No hell and Stalin loves roses. What the *fuck* is happening?"

I let out a short scream-like laugh into my hands. I was going to spiral out of control soon and start smashing windows or ripping my hair out if I couldn't pull myself together.

"It certainly can be difficult for humans to understand that there is no hell. The power of the Old Dead keeps any of the souls who would elect to stay but may misbehave in check. It is also why we so heavily regulate contact with Earth. No need to stir up trouble down there. We can observe but we cannot intervene."

"So, why can't I go see my Grandpa?"

The man grew terribly uncomfortable at my return to that topic. He smiled, started to speak, faltered and went back to his fake smile. The struggle he was undergoing to regain his composure was very visible. He was hiding something. My panic rose. I wanted nothing more than to see a familiar face. Something familiar. *Anything* familiar. A smell, a taste, a person, a place - *anything* I knew from before.

"Well. That is a rather...unique...situation. And something I am not totally able to or rather *allowed to* explain."

"What the *fuck* does that mean?" I stood up, making him flinch at my abrupt movement.

Static crackled across my skin. The frosted window nearest me cracked, then shattered. I jumped away from the glass shards as they scattered across the chair I had been sitting on. What the *fuck* was that? Had I just...? Virgil looked just as startled as I did, confirming that the property destruction had indeed been my fault.

"I-I'm sorry I didn't mean to do that!" I stammered.

He looked at the window intensely for a few moments, then waved his hand as if it was the most casual thing he could be doing. The glass reassembled itself seamlessly. I stared at the window, not quite sure what I had just done.

"I will explain what I am able to, but you will have to be satisfied with that for now." He was speaking slowly, inspecting me closely as he spoke.

"Get to it," I said shakily, trying not to seem horrified at breaking the window. I paced across the room over to the desk. I was tired of being stared at so intensely.

"Something unique has happened here. And I was hoping that you would be willing to discuss what led to your detainment here with the Host of this dwelling."

"Detainment? What? Like, I'm stuck here?"

"You and the Host appear to both be detained here."

I was not comprehending what he was saying.

"Something happened on Earth that resulted in you and the Host being bound to each other in a way that well, is quite unique."

"This doesn't happen to other people?" I felt static creeping up my spine. He sighed.

"No. No it does not."

"What happened? Why is it like this?" I walked back over to where he was sitting.

"Well it is *quite* the mystery, Hollis. One that I hope you will help me solve in due time." He held up a hand to stop my next question, then gestured at the ornate wardrobe in a corner of the room. "Enough question and answer for now. Get dressed and let us explore this lovely domain and go meet your Host."

The Professor left me alone to change and hyperventilate in peace. I dug my nails into the flesh of my arm and tried to breathe as deep as I could. The static feeling slowly receded a bit, and I decided I could try to get dressed. The ridiculousness of my nightgown was beginning to dawn on me and with a fresh wave of rising panic I walked to the wardrobe, dreading what I would find inside. Humorously large ballgowns? A pantsuit to match his?

I prayed for something better than the ratty jeans and sweat soaked t-shirt I had died in, but less presumptuous than the formal wear the Professor had on. I turned the latch and swung the door of the wardrobe open to find a set of fairly normal looking khaki joggers and a bland grey linen shirt.

"*Not too scary.*" I mused, getting myself dressed.

As I joined the Professor outside the bedroom, I gasped. The space was an enormous, expansive hall with vaulted stone ceilings and pillars as far as I could see. The floor was glassy smooth marble inlaid with a twisting, twining pattern of black stone. The whole hall was flooded with light and shining.

"I believe you may recall this part of the dwelling." The Professor took off walking along the wall that the bedroom was situated on.

"I, uh, don't?"

"You passed through here when you arrived."

"Oh it was nighttime. It was dark." I could only remember the enormous trees and the moss-covered ground. And the storm.

"Mh. Yes. There are no days and nights here. You are still perceiving things with your human sensibilities. That is normal." His pace was quick and I struggled to keep up. His movements seemed effortless, as if the slick footing did not deter him in the least. I, however, was sliding around in the simple, leather shoes that had been left for me.

"It was dark then because our Host willed it. It is light now because I advised him to give a sense of normality to the rhythms to you."

"He's making it light?" We turned abruptly through an opening and found ourselves outside of the hall.

"Holy shit."

The scene that lay before me was like a garden in a kid's fairytale book. Flowers like I'd never seen, birds singing, animals grazing serenely on grass too green to be real. Every space was shimmering with vibrant color and light. Somewhere in the distance a fountain splashed.

"He has done a lot of work in this area again, I see." The Professor shielded his eyes from the sun.

"Do you know him?"

"Well, not really. I have just become acquainted with him since we arrived. I was assigned to this case, so I have taken some time to get to know him as well as you."

"This case?"

I was hardly listening. A hummingbird zipped by my head and hovered for a moment in front of me. I held out my hand curiously and taking the cue, the bird rested in my palm. My eyes widened and I inhaled in disbelief. This was like magic. I had never been so close to a bird so gorgeous before. It was tiny and shimmering and jewel-like. Nothing like the pigeons and crows and sparrows of the city; all drab and grey and brown.

"Oh yes. Well, there is *always* someone to meet the newly dead soon after they arrive and explain the Otherworld to them. Somewhat like a guide. You can just call me Virgil." He laughed awkwardly, looking over at me to see if I found the name amusing. Disappointed that I was not laughing and was also much too enamored with the bird in my hand to be actively listening he cleared his throat.

"The gardens and dwelling stretch on for many human miles." He continued dryly, "Our Host has been dead for quite some time in Earth years, so he has had a lot of opportunity to build and explore here."

The hummingbird was looking directly into my eyes. I became uneasy with the very intense eye contact, and stretched my arm out away from me. The bird took the hint and flew off, zooming over some flowering bushes and into the distance.

"This is amazing." I walked deeper into the garden.

"Yes yes, many create their own paradise when they arrive here. As I said, these types of spaces are much more similar to Earth life as the newly dead create dwellings that mimic grandeur on Earth." He sounded rather annoyed with how impressed I was.

"So, where is this Host?"

"I am not sure." The Professor frowned slightly, holding up a hand so that I would remain hushed. He closed his eyes and the sound of rustling leaves once again intensified. I looked around to try and discern where it was coming from before landing on the obvious conclusion that somehow, he was making this noise.

"How do you-" He waved his hand at me to shut me up. As I was about to protest, a distant clap of thunder echoed from inside the hall behind us. I jumped at the sound.

"Ah." He turned quickly on his heels and set off in the direction of the noise. I stumbled after him, struggling once again to navigate the ice-like sheen of the marble floor.

"That was him last night? The storm?" I said, trying to keep pace.

"Oh yes. That was our Benevolent Host. Just as shocked and confused as you were, I imagine. He was quite confused to have a guest after all of his solitude."

A thousand questions came to my mind but I couldn't ask any of them. Virgil was crossing the hall at an alarmingly quick rate. How could he walk so fast? He cut between rows of columns and headed towards the wall that ran perpendicular to the wall that my room and the entrance to the garden were on. Reaching the distant wall, he waited for me to catch up with him. When I got to his side he looked half amused and half irritated at my very pitiful walking skills.

"You have yet to release your human limitations on movement." He said casually, "That will come with time. Now, let us meet our Host."

"What-" He was off again before I could form my next question. I growled in irritation and set off after him. He walked along the wall, looking over his shoulder often to see if I was keeping up with him. After a few minutes of brisk walking in silence, we arrived at a grand arched entrance with two enormous wood and iron doors. The Professor or Virgil or whatever the hell he wanted to be called looked at me. He raised his eyebrows as if to ask *"ready?"*, then opened the door.

Inside was another vast room, though not quite as seemingly endless as the hall of columns. The ceiling was vaulted and crossed with wooden beams that were ornately carved in flowing, organic shapes. The floor itself was covered, thankfully, in an intricately woven rug depicting vines and flowers and birds. Grey stone dominated the walls and spaces between the beams. Each stone was carved into some sort of flower or plant or other natural-looking design. The wall to our right was solid stained glass windows overlooking the garden, and the wall to our left housed a monstrous fireplace. Most impressively, across the room on the wall opposite us were floor to ceiling shelves filled with books.

"It's like Beauty and the Beast." I murmured. Virgil shot me a deadly look.

"Hmph. He was *just* in here." He muttered, looking around the empty space.

Gentle thunder sounded from behind us. I yelped and leapt forward, turning my head to see where it was coming from.

"Ah." Virgil turned himself around slowly. "Yes. It did take us some time, please remember that our guest is unable to travel as we are."

In the entrance of the library was a figure. Well, sort of a figure? It was very difficult to comprehend what I was seeing. In the general shape of a human there was a darkness that occupied the center of the entrance to the room. From it the soft sounds of storms and thunder emanated. There were no discernible features that I could make out on this figure, beyond human-ish and taller than I was. Quite a lot taller than my respectable five feet nine inches, actually. His frame was near at least eight feet in height.

Seeing him again made my chest tight. I felt that same surge of longing and confusion I had felt when I first saw him. My body crackled all over with static energy. Again? No, keep a hold of it, stay awake. The last thing I heard before I blacked out into another vision was Virgil demanding to know what was happening to me.

*On a windswept cliffside, trees towering behind my back.*
*Under a fruit tree in the sunshine, smiling, laughing.*
*Running down a path through trees impossibly tall, as a child.*
*A man calling to me from across the field.*
*Sunlight glinting off the beams of a well worn loom.*
*Purple cloth, so dark and rich.*
*Picking a tiny, perfect flower from the crevice of a stone.*
*Hiding, jumping, playing.*
*A face, just at the edge of my vision.*

I strained to see the face as my vision faded.

# III.

My window was dim when I awoke. When I remembered where I was, I let out an irritated groan. How long had I been out for this time? I remembered what Virgil had said about our Host being the one who set the light and darkness in this place. I clicked my tongue at myself in irritation. It was strange to know the truth of being dead but still be unable to truly understand the workings of this place.

"*Fuck.*" I thrashed under the luxurious bedcoverings. How was it that I felt like I was about to go get some answers and I fainted or whatever again? Back to square one. Some sort of dumb Groundhogs Day trap. I always hated that movie.

What *was* this place? And what was *I?* I felt so disconnected from myself, like there were big empty rooms inside my mind that had just opened up. Rooms I'd never been into before. It was like knowing there was something else there, but not being able to see it without turning on the light. And god, was I fumbling to find the light switch.

I shook my head to clear it. This line of thinking was not helping me. I looked at my hands again in the dim light. Then kicked off the blankets to reveal my legs. I looked like me, sort of. It struck me how clean I felt. How lacking my skin was of its normal variation of color and texture.

"*I need a mirror,*" I thought, standing up and crossing to the window. I touched the glass with a finger lazily, then screamed.

The pane was suddenly shot with silver veins, emanating from where my finger touched. They raced across the surface until the whole pane was a shimmering mirror, reflecting my own stupid horrified face back at me.

But was it my own face? I breathed deeply and looked at the reflection. It seemed like me but also *not* me. My hair color was the same, and the general shape of my face was the same...but it seemed more fluid. Perhaps a trick of the mirror? A warped pane? A magic spell? The bad lighting? I looked like myself and a stranger all at once. I leaned in closer to the mirror to see the color of my eyes. As I watched my pupils dilate, I got my second shock since waking up: My eyes went from my typical warm brown to being solid pools of black. No whites, just endless blackness.

Screaming again, I fell backwards. The window snapped back to a normal pane of glass as I hit the ground. However the pane was not glazed over as before, but clear glass that revealed the garden outside.

I sat on the floor for a few moments, allowing myself to regain some sort of calm. My hand that had touched the glass tingled with that electrical feeling again. I flexed it wide, trying to relieve the sensation. It began to fade. I stood up, and went back to the window.

"Don't touch it this time." I muttered to myself, clenching my hands behind my back. The garden was much more enjoyable to look at than my own face anyways.

The light all over the garden matched the dim twilight-esque level that was in my room. There were no birds or animals to be seen. Far beyond the paths and bushes and fruit trees and flowers that were closest to the dwelling was a rolling meadow. Beyond that stood a tall line of trees.

In the middle of the meadow, a light was glowing. It was blue and cold looking, and it wavered in its intensity. Bored of my room and being alone, I decided to go investigate. I was still dressed in what I had been wearing when I had blacked out in the library. I shivered at the memory. So annoying. What was the *deal* with that? Fainting spells? Did I need to go to the seaside for my ill humors? What was the Otherworld, a Jane Austen novel? What was *wrong* with me?

Pushing that persistent question from my mind, I walked myself right out of the room and along the wall to the entrance to the garden.

Nothing seemed to be stirring in the garden. The air was still and warm, but the silence made me shiver. I walked resolutely towards the blue light, which I could still see quite clearly beyond the hedges. I reached the edge of the meadow and stood in the shadows of a tree. Which felt stupid, because I was quite certain that whoever was out there with the blue light would be able to see me no matter how I hid. But still I hid and observed.

Noises were reaching my ears now, there were sounds of rocks grinding and trees creaking. The sounds came from where the blue light was brightest. I listened for a few moments before I heard the sound of wind making leaves shiver. Virgil. His voice came from the blue light as well but I could not see him. Nor anyone else, for that matter. I was craning my neck around the tree and squinting my hardest to try and see where he was and who was with him when a hand went over my mouth.

My vision went red with rage and electricity crackled down my spine. I bit and screamed and kicked and flailed as hard as I could. My hands clawed at the hand that was clamped resolutely over my mouth, stifling my noise completely. I was drug backwards through the garden and back into the hall before my assailant turned me to face them.

"Host." He said softly, putting his free hand to his own mouth, "No scream. Host."

I wrenched his hand away from me, most likely because he finally allowed me to, and spat at him. He stood, looking utterly confused at my reaction.

"Why?!" I shouted, shaking with rage as invisible electricity cracked around me, "*Why did you touch me?!*"

He frantically put his hands over his own mouth and looked in panic at the blue light. It still shone brightly in the meadow.

"No scream, no scream." He put his hands on his chest, "Please, *please.*"

The desperation in the last "please" and the look on his face of utter regret made me stop shouting. The currents of electrical charge that flowed across my skin subsided slightly.

"*Don't touch me.*" I hissed, spitting on the floor.

My hands shook and my breathing was shallow. Without thinking I touched my neck. In the panic I had felt someone else's phantom grasp closing in. My breath burned as I took it in short ragged gasps.

"Not touch." He said softly, taking a step away from me.

"Good." My voice was less bitter, but still not kind. Breathe, breathe.

"Good." He agreed.

I looked him over, trying to focus on anything besides my own trembling. So, he had a human form. He was still tall but a slightly more normal human version of tall. He had long hair that shimmered like wet ink as it flowed over his shoulders in glistening curls. His face was angular, with warm sepia skin and a short, well groomed black beard. His eyes were solid pools of jet, flickering over my face in continued concern. I would have been much more startled by his eyes had I not just seen my own turn black. He was wearing loose pants, like mine but more billowy. His torso was bare.

"You are the Host?"

"Host." He held his arms out and took an additional step backwards, showing off his full height and frame.

"This is your human form?" My chest was still tight with panic. *Breathe.*

He smiled at me and watched my reaction with curiosity laced with concern.

"It's...tall." I offered. His smile intensified. He bowed. I was still trembling with rage and confusion, but he was amusing.

"What's the light out there?" I turned back to the garden. Without seeming to move, he flashed to stand in front of me and the entrance. He inclined his head and I could hear soft sounds of thunder. He was muttering to himself, searching for words in his own language.

"I heard Virgil."

"Virgil." He repeated. Then without warning he was striding across the hall away from me. I took off to follow him, cursing the icy smooth surface yet again.

"Hey, what's Virgil doing out there?" I asked, barely able to keep up, "Who is he talking to?"

"Virgil." He motioned upwards, to the ceiling, "Virgil talks."

So helpful.

We reached the door to the library and went inside. The fireplace crackled to life as he waved at it, pacing back and forth.

"*Who* is he talking to?" I asked again, my skin had nearly stopped tingling before he had waved the fire to life. When he made that motion, a faint static sensation returned to my arms. I wrapped them around myself, squeezing to try and stop the feeling of blind panic that was beginning to replace the fury of being dragged back into the dwelling. What the fuck was happening?

The Host stopped pacing and looked me over. I must have been particularly pathetic looking, because his face was pure pity. I broke his gaze and stood in front of the fire.

"You can't understand me anyways."

"Some." He said, staying the same distance away from me but walking to the side of the fire. I sighed.

"This whole thing is fucking stupid."

We stood for a few moments in silence. The fire crackled merrily, making the whole room come alive with shifting shadows. I squeezed my arms tighter. My vision started to blur. Crying? Now?

The Host was creeping nearer to me, I could feel his presence grow closer. I turned my shoulders to face away. Crying felt so pointless. Why mourn for my own death? There was nothing I could do to change that fact. Stupid fucking idiot, getting myself killed by that worthless piece of shit. I was twenty two years old and dead. The anger and confusion and sadness boiled over all at once and I let out a gasping sob.

"*Why?*" I wailed, unable to contain the anguish. I put my hands on my face, dragging my fingers across my eyes and mouth, rubbing the tears away forcefully. "Why? Why me? Why now? Why? So fucking *stupid*."

"Not touch." The Host had moved to stand in front of me. He held up his hands to show me that they were not moving towards me. That just made me feel guilty. It wasn't him who deserved the rage I had delivered earlier. The Host was dead too. And much, *much* longer than I had been. He hadn't killed me, and somehow my dying had gotten him trapped here. Or something.

"It's all my fault." I choked, lowering myself to the floor and curling up into a weeping ball. The feeling of static was coming back to my arms. I dug my nails into my biceps, trying to stop the sensation as my body continued to heave with sobs.

"To mourn your own death is to begin to expand your life." Virgil was standing in the doorway to the hall of columns, surveying the scene with cool indifference. I suppose it had to look somewhat comical: me, on the floor crying uncontrollably and the Host standing over with his hands raised as if he was surrendering, looking terrified.

"It is good to mourn and feel despair." Virgil walked to a chair along the wall near the fireplace, still in my line of sight, "That despair will help you live a greater life here."

"Fuck you." I hissed, wiping snot on my hand.

"Anger is to be expected as well."

"You aren't a therapist!"

The Host sat on the floor in front of me. He was looking back and forth between Virgil and I as we spoke.

"Perhaps now is *not* a good time to relay what I have learned," Virgil mused, looking at me out of the corner of his eye to see if I would take the bait. I didn't and he fell into silence.

Tears continued to flow onto the cool stone floor, but most of my hysterical display had stopped. I sniffled and closed my eyes. After a few moments I heard Virgil and the Host speaking to each other. It sounded like a distant storm moving into woods full of dry leaves. I gave in to curiosity.

"I want to know what's going on. Why can't I go anywhere else? What did I do wrong?"

"Nothing is wrong, nothing is wrong. Nothing like that." Virgil's tone had gone from lecturing to soothing, pity taking hold of him as I continued to be a pathetic lump on the ground.

"Then why am I *here?*"

"That is what I wanted to tell you. I have learned some information on that topic." I sat up slightly and peered over at him, "I was speaking with the committee that has formed on your case. There is an inquiry being made into the...situation. As such, they will need to know more about you and your current state."

I laughed coldly. Current state of absolute shit show.

"As such I have been tasked with assisting you in this adjustment period. I will guide you towards a more complete understanding of what your abilities are in this place."

"Abilities?" I wiped at my face again, sniffling still as my nose and eyes continued watering. Virgil looked at me, disgusted.

"Yes. Whatever they are, it stands to be seen." He offered me a square of cloth and I blew my nose loudly.

"So like, training? To see if I have powers?"

"Not training, no. And you most certainly do have abilities, or as you say, *powers*. Everyone does."

The Host said something to Virgil.

"Our Host wishes to say again that he is very sorry. For something I am not sure I understand, but he asserts that you will know."

I looked at the Host from my position on the floor. He was eyeing me apprehensively.

"It's fine."

"Fantastic. With that settled, I would like to begin the exploration of your abilities as soon as possible. But being in a volatile emotional state is not conducive to that sort of an experience." Virgil said condescendingly. Whatever conversation he had been having out in the meadow had clearly left his patience with both the Host and me quite thin.

"So what, I should just calm the fuck down and we can start?"

"More or less."

The Host spoke to Virgil again, for my benefit Virgil replied so I could understand him.

"Yes certainly. But that might not be the most helpful."

"What might not be helpful?" I demanded, sitting up fully. I was feeling a mild sense of preference for the Host's suggestions at that moment. Virgil's snippy attitude was wearing me out. The pompous prick.

"Oh well, our Host suggested that since you seemed to have enjoyed recreational substances on Earth that maybe a similar experience here would help you but I disagree. You are not ready for any such-"

I was on my feet with my fists balled at my sides.

"*Drugs?!*"

"Well not exactly-"

"You suggested *drugs?!*" I stepped towards the Host who was still sitting on the floor. He fumbled backwards away from me, scooting awkwardly with his hands up again.

"Both of you know everything about my life, huh? You think you know me? You think you know my life? Just some drug addicted wreck who got herself murdered? HUH? Tell me? What am I supposed to do to calm down here with two fucking angel assholes speaking in riddles and not telling me why the *fuck* I can't go do the rest of the normal Otherworld shit?" My head snapped back and forth between the Host and Virgil. One of them looked horrified and remorseful, the other was cleaning his glasses absently on a second handkerchief.

"Are you done?" Virgil asked coolly, returning his spectacles to his face.

"Done?! I'd say this is a pretty normal reaction to the circumstances. You know what? *Fuck you both!*" I shrieked and stormed out of the room.

I tore across the hall of columns away from the library. Tears were pouring down my face again and I was still shouting a rage-filled tirade when I made it out of the hall and into a passage I had not been down before. It opened into a moss-floored room with tall stones. I continued my rampage through that room and down several more passages. As I was finally coming off my renewed rage and sinking once again into despair I found myself in a room of water.

The part of the room that I had entered had a distinctly indoors feeling. The space was massive again, and this part of the room was decorated richly with tan marble on the walls and floors that was inlaid with ornate plant patterns. In the walls behind me there were alcoves that held burning torches. I could smell the heat and ash from their ever-burning flames. In front of me stretched a pool of water. Ornate fountains on either side fed it and sent calming ripples across the water's surface. It was beautiful, but what was at the opposite end of the room made me momentarily forget my anger.

The high vaulted ceiling became arched beams that were open to the sky about half way down the length of this vast space. And after that, the arches became trees. It was as if the dwelling was melting seamlessly into nature, and the two spaces were in absolute harmony with one another. At the far end of the space, mirroring the placement of the entryway I had just come through, there was a breathtaking waterfall. It toppled over the ledge of a cliff, then ran down a steady incline of smooth black rock and gray boulders before splashing over another sheer face about ten feet above the surface of the pool.

Walking along the edge of the pool, I saw the inlaid stonework shift into actual plants and vines as I made it to the halfway mark. It all blended so beautifully, I could not keep from wandering closer and closer to the falls. Here, where the stone arches gave way to massive trees, there were also water plants. Lily pads floated serenely with their white and pink and yellow blooms. Instead of torches at this end of the pool, the water lilies seemed to glow softly. The atmosphere was still twilight, but I was not finding it difficult to see.

With the fit I had just thrown, my body had gone back to feeling like one big static shock. I wondered if it would hurt, jumping into the water. Would I electrocute myself? Were there fish in here I was going to barbecue? I pondered for a moment. I realized how badly I wanted to swim.

I took a deep breath, exhaling with a shudder. It felt ridiculous to be so mad in a place like this, but here I was, still incensed at Virgil and the whole purgatory situation I seemed to be in.

"Purgatory!" I said out loud. That's what it was like. Being not in a bad place, but not a good one either. What was that book? Dante's Inferno? I groaned, suddenly remembering that Advanced Lit class from high school. The only thing I had been advanced at ever: understanding tortured whiny authors and their stupid books. Well, that and finding trouble. And running my mouth. And being an enabler for my alcoholic mother.

"Just call me Virgil!" I mimicked, bending down to touch the mossy forest floor. "Fucking stupid. Dante's fucking Inferno. Fuck."

I still had Virgil's handkerchief clutched in my hand. I wiped my eyes and blew my nose. Really, what was the sense in being enraged in such a grand and stunning place? The Host's dwelling would doubtless provide me with endless entertainment and exploration.

"And Virgil is supposed to train me or whatever. And then the Old Dead or whoever was making the calls on what was happening will eventually make some sort of decision and we can all move on. Clearly Virgil isn't excited about being here with us. And the Host doesn't want to entertain guests. Better stuff to do, right? Right. Yeah. None of us want to be here."

Lost in thought, I kicked off my shoes and started taking off my pants. I really wanted to swim in this gorgeous pool. My static feeling wasn't fully dissipated and I was curious to know what it would feel like in the water. Once undressed, I walked between the trees to the cliff where the waterfall was crashing down. I had always dreamed of swimming in a waterfall.

I had loved swimming on Earth, jumping into Lake Michigan off the crowded bike paths downtown in the city. The sting of the water was always so cold even in the heat of summer. I missed that feeling, I realized with a pang of longing. Swimming always made me feel calm. It always quieted the voices in my head. When was the last time I had done that? Right after I graduated high school? That summer, maybe? It had been years since I had been swimming, I realized, and that made me sadder still.

That sadness solidified my decision. I jumped as far and as hard as I could.

The water enveloped me and killed all my senses besides my mind. I could not hear bubbles or the waterfall once I was submerged. I was too terrified to open my eyes. The static intensified to the point that I felt like I was going to combust. Each bone in my body was charged with a raw ache.

I saw visions.

*A hazy bar where terrible music played.*
*Purple flowers growing in the cracks of the sidewalk.*

*Someone laughing at me.*

*Wind whipping my battered body as I waited for a train.*

*Purple flowers growing in the cracks of rocks.*

*My mother's face the first time I came over with a black eye:*

*Disappointed.*

*A train whipping past me and blowing my hair across my face.*

*Voices in my head whispering advice.*

*Purple flowers on my bedside table.*

*A glass shattering.*

I was aware of each inch of myself, and then some. There was a space around where my body ended and my awareness continued. The feeling was impossible, as if I could move and manipulate more than just my own body. I thrashed, but could not feel the water even though I knew it was there. I realized then that I wasn't desperate to breathe. How long had I been underwater? I tried moving my arms up to see if the terrible electrical current would subside if they broke the surface. Whether they did or not I could not tell. Everything was now a hot, stabbing, searing pain.

The visions returned.

*I saw his face. His horrible face twisted with rage and effort as I laughed at him for the last time. My throat burning as he forced me to stop laughing.*

I tried to scream but nothing happened. My mind reeled. It felt like dying all over again, except in a silent and lonely struggle. I resisted the pain and tried to remember what happiness felt like.

*A sunny day.*

*Warmth.*

*Laughing, running down a path in the woods.*

*The taste of a sweet warm fruit in my mouth.*

*Sitting beneath a tree in the sunshine.*

*Thunder echoing off the hillsides.*

*Warm wind whipping my hair into my face.*

*A face at the edge of my vision, coming into focus.*

*"Do I know you?"* I whispered to the vision.

# IV.

"Please." The sound of thunder boomed behind the word. I felt a hand on one of my wrists, then the other. I was being hauled out of the water. I could feel air on my arms as they came slowly, painfully above the surface. When my face broke the water I heard myself screaming. Inch by inch I was lifted and dragged to the shoreline. It was as if I was made of cement.

"Please."

"You!" I gasped.

I was still too scared to open my eyes, so I reached wildly towards the voice of the Host. My body convulsed with pain, making me stop in my blind reaching.

"Why does it hurt? I'm already dead, why do things hurt?" I wept into the moss, "I just wanted to go swimming."

"Yes, dead. Yes, feel." I tried to find him again with my outstretched hand, but the Host wasn't near enough for me to reach him. "Please. Not touch."

"Why not touch?" I was amazed I still had tears to shed after all the ridiculous wailing I had been doing.

I heard his struggle to form words. The sounds of thunder soothed me and I tried to calm my breathing. My pain was subsiding slowly, but my bones still ached and burned.

"Pain," His voice was tense.

"Pain?" I opened my eyes and looked in the direction of his voice. He was sitting on the ground, slumped against a tree. The skin on his arms was blackened. From his hands to his wrists was completely charred, and his forearm and shoulders were laced with angry black lashes that fanned out like roots. I gasped.

"Was that me?!" I crawled backwards away from him in panic.

"You, yes. No fear, please. Please. See?" He passed his hands along the markings. They faded slightly as he moved his hands over them.

"What is happening?" I wailed again.

"Do I know you?" He asked, repeating the question I had whispered to my vision.

Then the Host smiled at me with a wicked, knowing smile. What was this? It sent unpleasant shivers through me. I heaved and choked as my chest tightened to the point that I could not breathe.

"What happened?!" Virgil demanded, appearing in front of me.

Sounds of wind whipped and thunder rumbled quietly in response. I watched Virgil's face become more and more terrified as he looked at the Host's arms and back to me. I looked at the Host.

He was staring directly at me still smiling devilishly, his eyes solid black. My vision failed and the last thing I heard before I collapsed was thunder.

I was five years old, running through the woods, and I was very sure I was not supposed to be there. Smoke snaked around the trunks of the enormous trees. I knew the fire was far away, but the wind had brought it here to warn us. We were getting ready for it. I was definitely supposed to be at home.

I kept running down the familiar path. I did not want to be at home. I was being pulled into the woods. The voices always told me where to go. They always kept me safe.

They had told me about the battle. They sent me visions of the fires long before the smoke arrived. I had heard the sounds of death and screaming. They told me to go to the woods, among the sacred trees. They said my destiny was going to meet me there. What the voices foretold was always true.

I slowed down, hearing something on the trail in front of me. A shape separated from the thickening smoke. A child my age walked towards me. I smiled.

# V.

I awoke in my room with light pouring through the window. The memory of the vision was still clear in my head. I could smell the smokey, earthy perfume of the woods. I shivered and tried to force myself to focus on where I was. Fucking Groundhog's Day.

"I'm in three places at once." I muttered, getting out of bed and going to the window. Chicago. Some ancient woods. And here: dead.

I was plagued by memories of my pathetic life on Earth: my addict of a mother, that shitty house, school, my job and how I'd thrown it all away. Things had been going so well and I couldn't keep myself out of trouble. I couldn't resist that horrible asshole. I had detested him, and he had killed me. Why had I let him get so close?

But those weren't the only things I saw when I closed my eyes. The visions showed me memories as well as things I had never seen. Never? The scenes in the woods and hillsides felt strangely familiar. It was an upsetting feeling, like I was being shown things I had forgotten. I had never in my life been to any place with trees that large. The biggest ones I had ever seen were here in the Host's dwelling. I shuddered again, recalling the trees in the smoke of my last vision. I tried to push it from my mind as I looked out the window.

Through the glass I could see a black form passing through the garden accompanied by a blue sliver of light. Through the pane I could hear thunder and wind deep in conversation. I went out into the hall of columns. I needed to stop thinking. I buried the urge to go look for the drugs Virgil had mentioned. Nothing good ever came from quieting the voices that way.

Virgil and the Host came in from the garden. They had returned to their human forms, but were still talking in their own language. I stood waiting for them to say something I could understand.

"Ah, you are awake. Are you quite calm?" Virgil said, eyeing me judgmentally.

"I guess." I was about to tell him how shattered and fragmented I was feeling. I had never mentioned the visions and memories I saw when I was unconscious, but I was certain he would take great interest in them. I opened my mouth to speak, but before I could he continued buoyantly:

"Superb. Come along!" He strode across the hall in the opposite direction of the library. A route we had not traveled before. I hesitated and looked at the Host, who seemed to have tweaked his appearance slightly. He was still monstrously tall, with red-brown skin and kind dark eyes, but it seemed he had added some sort of patterning to his arms. Almost like a barely visible tattoo or patterned scar. The skin there caught the light differently, and gleamed slightly. My eyes widened in recognition.

"Are those from yesterday? From-from the pool?" My voice was pinched.

"Nothing." He waved his arms and pulled a flowing tunic out of nowhere. Covering the scars, he smiled at me. Was this funny to him? It was almost as if my concern amused him.

"Come. Now." Virgil snapped from across the hall. I sighed and turned to follow. I crossed the floor easily to reach him, and found myself able to keep pace easily.

"New floor." The Host said, suddenly at my shoulder.

"What?" I looked down. It was indeed different. No longer did the glossy surface reflect me in its mirror-like finish. Instead, the floor was a more worn stone and easier for me to navigate.

"Wow, it's-" I began to apologize for him having to make so many changes to his dwelling, but Virgil cut me off.

"We will be exploring what your abilities are in the context of the general state of your mind." Virgil began in a droning voice, "To do this, you will be put in a state of senselessness, and our Host and I will perform some small tests. Your little swim gave us the clue on how to best test you."

We passed out of the hall and into a narrow passage.

"Small tests like what?"

"Oh, it does not make sense to explain that part as you will not be participating in the administering of the tests." Virgil waved away my concerned interjection, "I will however explain what you will experience."

We walked outside into a small courtyard, surrounded by tall leafy trees. The light filtered through them pleasantly, and gave the whole space a soothing green hue. At the center of the courtyard there was a small pool made of dark gray stone. It was a hexagon shape only a few feet across, with a few fallen leaves floating across its surface serenely.

"You will go into the pool, but this time we will be present to prevent your tantrum." Virgil explained, handing me a silken robe.

"When you enter the pool, you will lose your connection with your body again. You may feel vast, or you may feel quite small. You will likely begin to feel a desire to stretch, expand, and extend. We will temper this, preventing you from extending too far too fast."

Virgil motioned for me to get undressed and put on the robe. I shook my head no, my throat dry.

"Yes." He asserted.

"Can you go? I don't want to, uh, get changed in front of-"

"Oh for the love-" He disappeared from view. I shakily undressed and put the robe on. It felt nice against my skin, but I trembled nonetheless.

"Please. Be calm." I screamed when the Host spoke. I wheeled around to see him leaning calmly against a tree.

"*Were you here the whole-*"

"Not ask *me* to leave." He shrugged.

"I forgot you were here." My whole body flamed in humiliation, "I-I-"

"Enough." Virgil was back, "You are going to need to be less fragile about your human form. It is not something we see as any sort of...*opportunity.*"

Virgil sounded disgusted at the thought. The Host continued to smirk his unnerving smirk and I stammered furiously, which he ignored. I hated him. I hated them both. This was infuriating and it made me feel like a stupid child, but my curiosity overcame my ego. I wanted to see what would happen next.

"Now then. You will need to be much more calm for this." Virgil waved the Host over and motioned for me to sit on the ground. I sat obediently, but could not stop my hands from shaking. The Host knelt in front of me.

"Hold hands." Virgil ordered tiredly, seeming to be dreading this entire ordeal.

I stared at the Host. His eyes were kind, but glinted with something I couldn't figure out. I felt like I was on the outside of a joke, about to get pranked by two cosmic bullies.

"Not touch?" He asked.

"Yes, touch." I whispered, offering my hands to him. He took them gently and I immediately static crackled as our skin met. I sucked in a nervous breath and tried to wriggle my hands away.

"Sh. No, not fear this." The Host was staring directly into my eyes. He breathed deeply, and our connection strengthened. When he spoke again, to my surprise, he spoke fluently. He was drawing on my knowledge through our connection. I could feel our minds entwining with each other; becoming a single tapestry of synapses.

"Do not look at him, look at me. You will not hurt me."

The static gained power and my whole body shook in fear. I remembered the pool, the visions I had in the water, his face contorted in pain when he pulled me out.

"But your arms-" I choked. The sensation of the unseen energy coursing between us unnerved me. What was going to happen when we went into that water?

"You are in control this time. You will not hurt me." The Host's voice gathered its thunderous undertone and he closed his eyes. When he opened them, they were all black.

"You will not hurt me." He repeated. I could not tear my gaze from his. I stopped blinking. He seemed to observe a change in my eyes and smiled softly. Satisfied, it seemed, or as though he had been proven right.

I had no idea what Virgil was doing. There was only the Host and me. Nothing in the world could have pulled my focus away from him. Something was building.

"Are you sure?" I whimpered, terrified of the feeling that was gaining even more intensity where our hands met. The roaring thunder pounded all around us and his grip tightened. All I could feel was the sparking charge that raced up and down my skin and his hands on mine. Every other feeling faded away.

"I am sure," he said firmly.

He stood slowly, leading me to stand with him. Sounds of wind rushed past my ears, answered by thunder and the sizzling snap of energy coming off of me as we moved slowly forward. I was no longer shaking. We moved together, completely synchronized as he backed towards the pool. He paused at the edge, his piercing black eyes inspecting my face to see if I was ready. I nodded. I longed for the abyss I knew was waiting in the water for me.

His grip tightened so extremely that I felt like my hands might shatter. Suddenly, in a fluid movement he flung himself backwards, dragging me into the water on top of him. As we sank, he wrapped his arms around me and locked me in a tight embrace.

The visions came faster than they ever had before.


*Waves crashing.*
*Thunder roaring.*
*Fireworks lighting up the backyard of my childhood home.*
*Towering trees burning.*
*Sun filtering through the leaves of a fruit tree.*
*I was smiling.*
*I was crying.*
*Someone hit me hard across the face.*
*Purple flowers growing in the cracks of sidewalks.*

*Someone was under the fruit tree with me.*
*I could not see their face.*
*As I strained to see it, the vision changed:*
*Running with other kids down the sidewalk.*
*Running with other kids down a forest path.*
*I was laughing.*
*I was screaming.*
*Someone touched my cheek gently.*
*Purple flowers growing in the cracks of rocks.*
*The whole forest was on fire.*
*Sun filtering through the leaves of a fruit tree.*
*Warm wind whipped my hair across my eyes.*
*A name whispered in my ear.*
*Another name I whispered back.*
*Someone was under the fruit tree with me.*

"I saw you!" I sputtered and gasped, spewing water everywhere.

I lay on the ground at the edge of the training pool. The Host was on all four over me, dripping water into my face. I scrambled to a sitting position and grabbed his face. He looked shocked, but put one of his hands over mine.

"I saw you, it's you in the visions, under the tree-" I pulled away and coughed more water up.

"Visions?" Virgil was at my shoulder, frowning, "What visions?"

"I see things when I'm not awake, it happened on Earth too," I babbled, turning back to the Host, "I could never see the face before, the person under the tree, and now I did and it's you."

The Host smiled, still half crouched over me. I saw new scars on his arms and shoulders and knew I had caused them. Again. Remorse washed over me.

"What tree? You will need to describe this vision in great detail so I can-" Virgil blathered.

"A fig tree." The Host's voice was a low growl. He was smiling again. That smile that terrified me. I became suddenly aware of how close our bodies were. I scooted away slightly. His wicked grin continued.

"You saw the vision as well?" Virgil asked him in shock.

The Host didn't answer, he was too busy staring at me with his pitch black eyes. I was sure mine were black too.

"Please, Hollis, explain what you saw-"

"Her name is Arga." The Host said firmly.

Arga!

Hearing him say the name that had been whispered to me in the vision sent my shivers down my spine.

Arga!

The name that was always at the tip of my tongue.

Arga!

I had never loved my mother's name for me, Hollis, and had asked my friends to call me something better. Something that was more *me*.

"*So, what should we call you instead?*" They had jeered when I couldn't come up with something right away. Why was I even friends with any of them?

But there was a name. There was a name so close, *so close* but I couldn't find it.

"*Ari, I guess.*"

Arga!

The name I had been hunting for all along. Hearing the Host say it was delicious beyond belief. My body burned with joy and I could not stop smiling.

Virgil looked from the Host to me and back again.

"Her *what?*" Virgil hissed.

"He's right," My voice was barely a whisper, "That is my name."

I shivered again. I was collecting myself, remembering parts of the vision. A dawning realization crept over me, filling me with a new thread of giddiness: *I knew the Host's name.*

"Your name was Hollis. That is on your birth certificate and that is what your mother called you. And you went by Ari for a while with friends. Your stage name was-"

"No, I...I was called Arga, before all of that." I interrupted Virgil, but my eyes were locked with the Host's. I couldn't break his gaze.

I knew his name.

"Before? What do you mean, *before?*" Virgil demanded, his voice gaining pitch the more irritated he became.

The Host's smile intensified and he actually laughed. It was a beautiful sound, accompanied by gentle thunder. My eyes welled with tears as I stared at him. It was all so familiar.

*It was like looking at someone through tear-filled eyes.*

"What is so *funny??*" Virgil was irate.

"You saw the flowers?" The Host was speaking directly to me.

"Yes." I breathed.

"Those are your flowers. You are named for them. Their color."

"How are you speaking fluently? Did you *gain knowledge* from her during the vision?" Virgil was frantically trying to interrupt us.

"How do you know?" I could hardly speak, my chest was one big knot of joy and confusion and relief and an unending list of questions I tried to push away.

I knew *his name.* And he knew mine. He was the face in my visions.

"I know you." The Host stood and reached out to help me up. Virgil got between us.

"Enough!" His voice boomed with the sound of violently rushing wind, "That is enough! You!"

He pointed at me.

"You will tell me everything you saw. And you!" Virgil pointed at the Host, "Please give us some privacy!"

The Host glared at Virgil, his eyes hostile.

"As you wish." He growled, bowing mockingly.

"No," I said suddenly, panic in my voice, "No, Iskur don't go."

Virgil and the Host looked at me in shock, then at each other.

"What did you just do?" Virgil whispered, wide eyed.

"Nothing? *What?* I didn't do anything!" I scrambled to my feet awkwardly.

"You stopped me from leaving." The Host said slowly, awe painting his face.

"I-I didn't mean to! I just-"

"What is *Iskur?*" Virgil demanded before rounding on the Host, "And why are you suddenly *fluent*?"

"It's, uh, it's him. Iskur is him." I pointed at the Host.

The tiniest of smiles played at Iskur's lips. Virgil inhaled sharply.

"His *name?*"

I nodded, trying to avoid Iskur's gaze.

"*How?*" Virgil said in a measured but terrified tone, "*How* do you know his name? That name has been lost for centuries, millenia...you have no way of..."

Virgil trailed off. Iskur was smiling wildly now, his eyes filled with a feral light.

"I know you." Iskur's voice was low and dangerous. My throat constricted and I couldn't talk. But I smiled. And a couple stray tears fell. This was the kind of thrill I loved. Something unknown, a spark and the feeling of being on the edge of going too far.

Iskur took a step towards me. I did not back away. My whole body crackled with the destructive static energy. He reached his hand out to me, but I shrank away from that. I couldn't risk touching him and striking him with this energy again. I did not want to cause him pain. My thrill dimmed. That's all I was good for on Earth: hurting people I cared about.

"No," I whispered hoarsely. My vision was blurring. I felt the familiar pull of the visions as I slipped away from consciousness.

He lunged at me suddenly, catching me in his strong arms as I fell. Virgil was shouting, wind was roaring, and thunder was echoing. I hardly heard it as I sank into blackness. Again? Really? I couldn't fully be annoyed because my newfound knowledge was feeding a tiny spark of joy:

I knew his name.

# VI.

I was seeing visions again:

*A hazy bar where terrible music played.*
*Purple flowers growing in the cracks of the sidewalk.*
*Someone laughing at me.*

I was in a memory, back in Chicago. It was 2008, two years before I died. Someone was laughing at me. I walked towards the laughter. I'd seen him in this shithole so many times. Wearing fucking sunglasses. Inside. At night. What an asshole. He would do nicely. I was compelled to talk to him, finally. I had seen him and felt drawn to him for weeks, but I couldn't resist it any longer. Who cares if I'm getting my life on track? The pull was too strong. This must be what deer feel like when they see headlights.

"Well well well, you finally got brave enough?" His voice was dry from smoking too many cigarettes.

"What does *that* mean?"

"You aren't sitting sulking in your corner tonight. You are coming up to sit at my bar."

He opened a beer and slid it down to the regular waiting at the opposite end.

"I don't sulk."

"Sure you do." He mocked my sullen expression.

"Fuck you." I stood up.

What was I doing here? This fucking loser didn't deserve my time. I was getting my life back in order. Mom was back in AA and holding a job. I had just started working in the office at the hospital last month. I was proud. I had gone from CNA to office lady all because someone took notice of my ability to always fix the nurse's station computers. The pay was good. Things were *good*. I was edging out of the cycle of destruction mom and I kept getting ourselves into. So, what was I doing here talking to this asshole?

"Wait." He grabbed my hand.

I gave him a furious stare before yanking myself free. He lifted his sunglasses up to rest on top of his head. His watery blue eyes glinted dangerously. I liked his smile. And his curly blonde hair. He looked like he wanted to be a surfer, but I knew he had never left the city.

"I see you look at me."

He was whispering now. Without thinking I leaned closer to hear him against the terrible music playing. His breath smelled like smoke and beer.

"You always look like you want to ask me something. What do you want to know?"

My head was whirling.

*Do it now.*

I reached into my pocket. I stared him in the face as I took his hand and pressed a folded paper into it. I said nothing. I walked out of the bar.

"Are you happy now?" I asked the voices in my head, "Will you finally shut up about him?"

Maybe mom had this too. Maybe that's why she drank and smoked so much: to shut up those demons in her head. I couldn't blame her. The visions and voices were so disruptive.

Every time something was going well, an invisible thread and whispered voices would pull me off my path. The voices always told me where to go. They always kept me in trouble. Double trouble when I ignored them. They kept me on a path that felt like my ruin. Every time I got my life on track, the voices got worse. Darker. More sinister. Since getting the new job, that nagging feeling had pushed me to dark bars and alleys and into my worst behavior. Just a couple drinks before bed to silence the voices. Or something stronger to take off the edge.

I craved the abyss, and it craved me.

*I was smiling.*
*I was crying.*
*Someone hit me hard across the face.*
*Purple flowers growing in the cracks of sidewalks.*
*Purple flowers withering where they grew.*
*Waves crashing.*
*Thunder roaring.*

I woke up in my ornately furnished room. Again. Immediately I remembered what had led to me blacking out. Again. For fucking serious? I flung the blankets off and leapt to my feet. I rushed to the door with a singular focus and goal: I had to find Iskur.

I hurled the door open and ran directly into him.

"Ow, *fuck!*" I shouted, rubbing my head where I had slammed into his torso.

"Sh. Sh." He pushed me back into my room and closed the door.

"What are you-"

He pointed out my window. A blue light flickered in the meadow.

"Virgil," I whispered.

"He is speaking with the Old Dead. We must hurry."

Iskur turned, opened the door slowly, and led me out into the hall of columns. The dwelling was dark. We crept across the hall silently, heading to the passage opposite my room. Iskur motioned for me to keep quiet. I nodded. We rushed down the passage, through the room with stones and around the twists and turns that led to the room with the pool and waterfall. As we passed the arched entrance, Iskur waved his hand and it filled in with stone. Static passed over me when it happened.

"Come." He held out his hand. I took it hesitantly.

He led me faster than I could have gone on my own. We sped along the pool, past the waterfall, and into the towering trees. The memory of my vision of running as a child through smoke in trees this tall came back to me. I could almost smell the smoke. Iskur slowed down and looked at me inquisitively.

"You know this place?"

I stopped.

"Can you...see what I am thinking?" I asked awkwardly.

"Not always. Only your visions if we are touching. You were remembering one just now."

"Yes," I looked at the trees in wonder, "These trees, you know them?"

"I lived among them. They are sacred."

"Where are they? On Earth I mean."

"Arga," Shivers went down my spine when he said my name, "Have you not been where they are?"

"How is that my name? I mean I *know* it's my name when you say it, but nobody ever called me that on Earth. Ever." I reached out to touch one of the enormous tree trunks. Their shaggy red-brown bark was pleasantly spiky on my hand. It felt ancient. Alive. I withdrew my hand, "And how did I know your name?"

Iskur walked to my side.

"We have many questions to ask each other that Virgil will not want us to ask."

"Pft. Virgil," I muttered, "He'll be here in a second to interrupt us."

"It will take him a while to find us. This space is unkind to him. He does not like to come here. It takes very much effort for him to enter here, even without the entrance blocked." Iskur explained. He sat on the soft, mossy ground, "Everything about this is hard on Virgil. Being here with us wears him out. He has a job to do and it is not easy. Not easy at all."

I was surprised to hear pity in Iskur's voice. I didn't know what to say.

"What are these trees?" I asked. Anything to change the subject.

"Cedars, you call them."

"Cedars. They are huge."

"Yes. They are modeled after the ones you see in your visions."

I sighed, sitting with him.

"I don't understand the visions. Why are we linked? Bound? What does any of that mean? Virgil seems like he doesn't have any clue."

"He does not. We are a mystery to him." Iskur waved his hand and a small orb of fire floated in the air between us. It cast spooky shadows over his face as it flickered.

"What does that mean?" I rubbed my head, "nothing since I died makes any sense. There's no hell. I can't go see my family. You and I are somehow connected? I know things I shouldn't know. You can see what I'm thinking."

I covered my face with my hands. The destructive, static energy was building back up. I felt it in my shoulders and neck and spine as I grew more tense.

"Not touch?"

I laughed sadly, peeking between my fingers at him. He was holding out a hand for me. I took it slowly and inspected his face as I did. He closed his eyes as the burden of the pain split between us.

"How do you do that?" I asked as the anxious energy subsided. He kept a hold of my hand, tracing my knuckles gently with his thumb.

"I just do."

I sighed.

"That's not very helpful."

"I do not know how to do it. I just can do it. It is like breathing."

"Breathing? Do we even need to breathe here? I guess breathing is pretty pointless when you are dead."

"No, we do not need it. It makes us seem more human, so Virgil suggested that we breathe and blink and look more human. He does not breathe, normally. I have always liked to breathe. In all the ages since I have died that is the one human thing I cannot forget to do."

I smiled at him.

"I don't think I could forget to breathe," I whispered, enjoying how he was tracing his thumb along my hand, "I don't think I can forget how to be a human."

He nodded in agreement.

"You said you know me?" I asked sheepishly.

"Hm?"

"Before, by the small pool. After you said my name you said: *I know you*."

I glanced at him. He was smirking at me. His eyes were still human, but I had a feeling they wouldn't be for long.

"I do. And you know me."

"I saw you in my vision, under the fruit tree." My face burned at the memory as it flashed in my mind again.

*His face filled with joy, sunlight dappling him with golden blotches as the wind played with the fruit tree's leaves. He leaned towards me.*

My body flushed with heat. Fuck. I shook my head, forcing myself to return to the present moment.

"Yes. A fig tree." Iskur leaned towards me. I pulled my hand out of his.

"I've never sat under a fig tree."

"I have," Iskur leaned forward and propped his head on his arms while staring at me intently. He blinked and his eyes were black, "I sat under a fig tree many times. With someone I knew."

"Who was it?"

"Arga," His voice made me shiver, "what do you mean who was it? Think. You saw the vision. Who did you see?"

"I saw you." I stood up and took a few steps away from him.

"And no one else?"

"No."

"So, who was I with?" Iskur asked softly.

He was grinning devilishly again, and stood to follow me. I backed further away, bumping into the trunk of a tree. He stopped a pace away from me, but I still felt the warm rush of some strange emotion flowing through my chest.

"I-I don't know?"

He took a step closer.

"Yes you do."

"I-"

I knew my eyes were as black as his.

"Arga," He breathed. I shivered again. It was a *good* name.

"What?" My voice cracked.

"Who was I with?" He asked softly.

He leaned an arm against the tree next to my head. I could not breathe. My chest was tightening so much that I thought my ribcage would crack. Did I even have bones?

"I-" I knew the answer, but how was that even possible?

Stone grated against stone, making me cry out in distress and cover my ears. Iskur straightened himself with an exasperated sigh.

"It was you, Arga. I was with you."

A second later a very angry Virgil appeared between us.

"What is the meaning of this?" Virgil shrilled, "What are you two discussing so secretly?"

Iskur eyed Virgil with cold contempt.

"What were *you* discussing with the Old Dead?" His voice was quiet and antagonistic.

Virgil whipped around to stare at him.

"It is my *duty* to report to them the developments here." He snapped, listing important things he had to report on, "Your shared visions, your sudden *knowledge share* mind link and learning to speak fluently from her, the name thing-"

Iskur was right, this space made Virgil very irritable. Cranky, cranky. I smirked. I couldn't keep from laughing at his absurd anger.

Annoyingly, they stopped arguing in a language I understood. Wind and thunder took over. I rolled my eyes and sulked off through the trees, letting them bluster and storm. It made me so *angry* when they talked like that. All the amusement of Virgil being pissy was gone in an instant. Iskur appeared at my shoulder.

"You two make me feel so stupid when you talk like that!" I snapped. He held up his hands defensively. His eyes were still black.

Virgil appeared at my other shoulder.

"Hollis, do not walk away from us," He said sternly.

"It's *Arga*," I shouted in his face.

To my surprise, Virgil's eyes were black as well. Hadn't seen him do that before.

He snorted.

"Fine. *Arga*," He mocked, "Do not walk away from me when I am speaking to you. And both of you, do not try and lock yourselves away from me."

"Speaking to me? I can't fucking *understand* you two when you talk with the wind and thunder voices," I started walking deeper into the woods. Iskur followed me dutifully, but Virgil hung back.

"Please." His voice was labored and strained.

I turned slowly to face him.

"I cannot go further, it is too exhausting. Please. Let us retire to the library and talk."

The begging struck a chord with me. Iskur gave Virgil his most evil smile.

"The Great Greeter Virgil cannot stand to be among my trees?"

Iskur disappeared then reappeared directly in front of Virgil. He bent down to look him in the face patronizingly. Virgil looked physically drained, as if his appearance was diminished.

"You know how these trees affect me." His tone was acidic.

"Iskur, stop," I said firmly. They were both so irritating with their argument.

Iskur stood up straight and let out a breath. He turned to look at me with a mix of confusion and awe on his face. Virgil perked up slightly and leaned around Iskur to look at me.

"Curious," he muttered suspiciously.

Had I just controlled Iskur again? My chest tightened like it was in a vise.

"Did I just...?"

"Let us *please* go to the library," Virgil whined.

I walked over to Iskur, touched his arm and walked past. He followed me, and Virgil trailed behind him.

The library was somewhat rearranged since the last time I had been in it. There was still the huge fireplace and wall of thousands of books, but the middle of the room was now a hexagonal pit, sunken about four feet into the stone floor. A set of steps were carved out, leading down into the pit which was littered with pillows.

"What is this?" Virgil looked over his glasses at the new addition to the room.

"For more comfortable talking." Iskur came to my side, "We seem to need to do so much talking."

Virgil muttered and wind sounds whispered along with him. Iskur winked at me again and I smiled back, stifling a laugh as Virgil begrudgingly strode down into the conversation pit. We followed dutifully. Virgil being crabby was funny again.

He set himself to work clearing a space of bare floor amidst the sumptuous silk and velvet pillows. Then Virgil waved a hand and a straight backed chair appeared. He sat, still mumbling acid-laced retorts about the absurdity of this arrangement. Iskur and I situated ourselves comfortably onto the pillows.

"It's like storytime!" I said, hardly able to contain my laughter at the image of Virgil sitting stiffly in his chair while Iskur and I reclined at ease before him.

"Tell Arga about what you told me. How the Old Dead wish to meet her," Iskur cut right to the chase with a competitive smile, "Go ahead, *Virgil*, guide us through this."

They wanted to meet me? A jolt of panic went through me. When? How?

"They *what?*" I demanded, snapping my head around to look at Virgil.

Virgil adjusted himself nervously.

"Yes. Well. Arga will need to be able to control her energies more before they will meet with her. It is very obvious she is able to control you, Iskur. And you can share visions when touching which is very peculiar."

"So peculiar. Yes. And how," Iskur used an incredibly condescending tone, "Will Arga learn to control this?"

"Both our Host, sorry, *Iskur.* Both Iskur and I will assist you in learning-"

"How long will this take?" Iskur cut Virgil off entirely, "Hm? How long will we all be trapped here?"

I enjoyed the way Iskur's newfound speaking flowed. His voice had always been deep and powerful, but it was so much more enjoyable to hear him speak in longer sentences. Whatever control of language he had learned from our connection in the pool suited him just fine. The timbre of his voice stirred something in me that I didn't understand, but also did not hate. That delicious spark of danger again.

"Like I said, it is not time that the council measures in: it is *progress* they care about."

"So what," I joined the conversation peevishly, "I reach some secret level and I unlock a meeting with them?"

"Essentially, yes." Virgil sighed, "It is not ideal for any of us. But this is the situation we are in."

"What level do I have to be at? What do I have to do?"

"I am..." Virgil glanced at Iskur nervously, "I am not sure."

"How are you not sure?"

"The Old Dead are a cryptic bunch." Virgil explained, "They do not always share what they are looking for. I am to assist you in your management of your abilities, and when you reach a certain point, they will take you into their presence."

"Great. So my life is a video game now? And I'm playing against some final boss that doesn't tell me the rules?"

"Nobody is *against* anybody in this, Arga. It is simply a process in order to-"

"You must be *honored*." Iskur's eyes were human again, but still filled with rage, "Such an *important* job."

"It is a duty." Virgil stood up calmly, "I will perform my duty."

I eyed Virgil suspiciously. Iskur had previously made excuses for Virgil, saying it was his job to be the way he was. He had pitied Virgil, it seemed, being stuck here with us. But now? The pity was gone from his voice.

"And you will assist me in this, correct?" Virgil asked over his shoulder as he was retreating up the stairs, "Can I rely on you?"

Iskur bowed his head slightly.

"Of course." He intoned hollowly.

Virgil made a satisfied sound and walked up the stairs, vanishing as he reached the top. I turned to Iskur.

"I'll work hard. We'll all be out of here in no time."

Iskur looked back at me with sadness on his face.

"I am sure you will work hard. But," He sighed deeply, "There already is no time."

# VII.

The next era of our imprisonment passed peaceably enough. I began to lose grip on the rhythm of day and night. It was a pleasant feeling, being able to lie in the library and read the ancient books for endless periods with no breaks.

"Who's Enkidu?" I asked Iskur lazily as I flipped through a copy of Gilgamesh.

These were rare moments when we weren't supervised by Virgil. He was out talking with the Old Dead in the meadow, leaving Iskur and me free to laze around without his omnipresent babysitting.

"What about him?" He laid next to me, creating various plants and vines and twining them up the beams on the ceiling.

"The character. Enkidu."

"I never got along with any of them." Iskur snorted derisively.

I sat up and looked at him in shock.

"Did you *know* him?" I asked, astonished. He looked at me blankly, brow furrowed.

"Is this a joke?" He asked defensively, narrowing his eyes at me.

"I- no! I just thought, you said you didn't get along with Enkidu or Gilgamesh or whatever so like I don't know I thought maybe you knew them?"

"Stories like that are a collection of real events retold poorly."

I laughed.

"Fine. Keep your secrets."

He snorted and continued adding more violets to the plants twisting around the library. Earlier Virgil had made him close off all the passages and halls with pools, and afterwards he had become very sullen.

I tossed Gilgamesh aside, "What were the names you had on Earth again?"

"Hadad, Haddu, Adad, and eventually people called me Iskur. There were other names, but I forsook those."

"Well, I really like Iskur." The name still brought slight joy to me every time I said it. Not as strong of a thrill as the first time I had said it, I still chased that high.

"I am glad you like it." His voice was monotone.

"Do *you* like it?"

"I do not plan to use my own name much."

"Why not? Like: *Hi I'm Iskur!*" I faked his deep voice and held out my hand to him for a handshake. He reached over and took my hand in his absently, still crafting plants from thin air with his other hand.

"So pouty." I flopped back down on the pillow beside him, "Is it about the pools?"

"Yes it is about the pools." He said darkly, "He is not letting you try anything."

"I am trying!" I yanked my hand out of his, "Hey, I'm progressing!"

The plant he was making withered in midair and turned to dust. He rolled over to face me.

"Arga, I know you are trying. It is not you, it is *him*." He said, bitterly.

I had been through nearly a dozen training sessions with Virgil at this point. We worked on my focus, on my deferment of the anxious energy, and on my ability to safely start a shared vision with Iskur. I still had not done the latter. The last attempt had ended when Virgil pulled me out of my trance-like state because I seemed to him to be getting too close to spiraling. Iskur had disagreed, snapping on Virgil and accusing him of being overly cautious.

"He doesn't want things to get any more fucked up." I still felt salty about the situation myself.

"He does not want you to try and fail. He only wants to report small progress. Only victories. We still have not had another shared vision-"

"Well, I don't blame him. Failing means all that!" I waved at the scars lacing Iskur's arms. The wounds from my first two experiences exercising my powers were the worst ones, but he had a few new small marks from the last session. It was his job to hold me in the training and balance my precarious control a bit further. It was terrifying still, the way that Virgil and he both grew panicked about the scars. Iskur tried to hide it but I wasn't stupid.

You're supposed to be able to heal yourself fully when you die, and control every aspect of your appearance. Your physical form is totally up to your own imagination. From the fear it caused them both, I gathered that being able to permanently scar someone was not a normal newly dead person type of activity.

"These are nothing," Iskur shrugged.

"What if they are worse? What if you can't stop me?"

"You are worse in the water, and the pools are closed off." He muttered spitefully.

I rolled my eyes.

"I'm going for a walk." I left the pit in the library with anxiety brewing in my mind.

I glided across the hall of columns towards the garden. One thing I was quite proud of was my movement. In some of the earlier sessions, Virgil had shown me how to hone my awareness and move with more grace and speed throughout the dwelling. I still could not disappear and reappear in a different place, but to be able to stride faster and with more precision was a definite improvement.

In the garden I saw Virgil in his light form out in the meadow. I groaned and wheeled around to go back into the dwelling. Iskur was directly behind me and I slammed face-first into his chest. So much for renewed gracefulness.

"Stop *doing* that!" I yelped.

"Arga." His voice was serious. I looked up at him.

"Yeah?"

"I am really glad you like Iskur."

"Oh, uh, good. It's a good name."

"And Arga?"

My hands clenched at my sides as my face grew hot. The way he said my name. Oh, it did something to me that I adored.

"Yeah?"

"You are working hard. You are learning so much. I am anxious to…" He trailed off thoughtfully.

"To leave?" I offered.

"No! No. Not to leave. To see you reach your true strength." He held out a hand for me. I stared at him.

"Why?"

"Why? You seem nervous."

"No, not *why the hand?* Why are you so desperate to see me wielding power?" He did not answer.

"What?" I goaded, "Why do you want to see what I can do?"

"Because, Arga," He dropped his outstretched hand, "You showed me things. That shared vision, it was wonderful. There were so many things that made sense to me. There are mysteries unraveling between us."

"Us. *Us.* We've been over this, Iskur," I whispered, glancing at Virgil's blue light nervously. We had kept things from Virgil. I never shared all the details of the vision I had seen, and I certainly did not tell him that Iskur believed we had been alive at the same time, "You died thousands of years before I was born. There's no way you knew me, alright?"

"No. We knew each other. That is certain."

I snorted.

"Of course you can't see how fucking insane this is." I tried to walk around him but he shifted to block me further, "*Stop it.* Let me through."

I talked myself out of the vision we had shared every chance I got. There was no way that we knew each other. There was no way we had been alive at the same time. Right? It defied logic. Easy to explain: it simply did not happen. But it wasn't that simple. No matter how many times I went over it in my head, I knew that I *knew* him. It had me frantically reading ancient text about reincarnation and gods and life and death whenever I had a spare moment.

We could never talk about it, not with Virgil always watching us. And when we were alone I could never find the words to ask what it meant.

"Arga." His voice was tinted with a warmth that made my chest tight. He had always sounded kind, but this? I could not handle it.

"What?" I refused to look at him.

"Come with me."

I looked up at his face at last. His eyes were deep black, burning with something I didn't want to understand. Don't look at me like that! I blinked and looked away, regretting making direct eye contact. He didn't ask me to come with him again, and he didn't have to. We both already knew I was going to go with him. He took my hand and led me across the hall.I trusted him implicitly. No matter how angry I was. No matter how much I tried to convince myself otherwise, I had seen his face in my visions. I knew his name. He knew my name.

Virgil and his poindexter mannerisms had grated on my nerves since our very first interaction. Even though I knew that both Iskur and Virgil had calibrated their human appearances to be more acceptable to me, Iskur's felt more genuine. His hilarious miscalculation of the average height of humans and his refusal to correct it. Virgil had loudly complained about it, and Iskur had shrugged it off. He owned his mistakes and didn't pretend to have all the answers. Even if, terrifyingly, his past *did* hold all the answers.

We passed over a colorful bridge made of glass and out into the night air. Iskur had darkened the ambient light after closing off the pools earlier. The sky was a black void awash with waves of light. It looked like the Northern Lights, or what they were supposed to look like. I had never seen them on Earth. I thought eventually I would stop gasping at each new and astounding thing I saw, but apparently I had not reached that threshold of amazement yet. It was gorgeous and I loved it.

"What is it?" I murmured, entranced.

"It is the galaxy." Iskur stopped to watch me be filled with wonderment.

"Wow." I whispered.

"It is beautiful."

"Yeah. Gorgeous." I walked further into this open space. The dwelling often wove from structure to nature and back again, combining elements of both as it faded into nature or as nature gave way to building. The way the glass bridge faded into the mossy forest floor was seamless as anywhere else. As moss overtook the flooring, patches of glass were visible; like tiles of a jewel-paved pathway that was being overgrown. We followed it until it faded completely to moss.

"Wait here." Iskur said, disappearing suddenly. I heard distant sounds of rock and earth rending itself and assumed he was filling in some lake or pool he hadn't buried yet. I sighed. He certainly loved a water feature, and here I was making him have to destroy all his hard work. Wrecking everything, like always.

"Come." He returned as abruptly as he had left. We set off at a blistering pace through the trees. They were enormous here as well, towering ancient cedars. Iskur was teaching me the differences between trees and plants as we lazed our time away together. I noticed how with my improved ability to move about the dwelling quickly, I was still able to discern details of things as we passed. Nothing looked blurred or distorted as we moved swiftly beneath the trees.

We came to a clearing where a small stream bubbled pleasantly. I made a concerned noise when I saw it.

"Arga, it is fine," Iskur walked to the stream. He waved his hand and expanded part of the stream bank, creating a shallow pool. The familiar crackle of static passed over me, like every other time I was near him when he made some change to our surroundings.

"What are you doing?" I asked nervously. His smile was dangerous and he seemed motivated by a manic energy.

"I want to show you a vision *I* have had."

"I don't know..."

"Pff, Virgil is busy and you know how he hates the cedars. It will be short, please. Let me show you a piece of the mystery you have resolved for me."

He motioned for me to crouch on the streambank and look into the water. He shifted into his light form, black and ominous. I shivered slightly to see it again.

I looked into the water as Iskur hovered above it. He lowered himself into the stream, not disturbing the surface as he went underneath. The surface of the stream glowed faintly, and a scene began to reveal itself.

I assumed I was seeing things from Iskur's perspective. He was standing in the cedar woods, among the tall trees. "Iskur!" A voice shrieked from down the path.

He ran to the voice. A woman robed in purple threw herself into his arms. Her face was obscured as she wept bitterly.

"Anaid, what has happened?"

"My father he-" Her voice broke. Iskur comforted her and led her off the trail into the woods.

"What is it?" He sat her on the soft forest floor. She was shaking with rage as she cried in his arms.

"My marriage," she choked.

"Who, Anaid?" Iskur's voice was somber.

She didn't answer.

"Anaid, *who*?" Iskur asked again.

"That murderer."

"No."

She let out a scream of anger and pounded her fists on his shoulders.

"Anaid, no. We will not allow this."

"He'll kill me." She whispered, "He knows who you are, he knows about us."

"*I* will not let that happen." Iskur took her face in his hands. He tipped her head up and I was looking into my own eyes.

Everything went black.

I was running through the cedar woods, face burning with rage. I knew if I opened my mouth I would scream or cry, neither of which I wanted to do just yet. I had to find him. I had to tell him what my fool of a father had done. As I came to a curve in the trail, I saw him walking towards me.

"Iskur!" I shrieked, grabbing at him in panic.

"Anaid, what has happened?" His eyes were troubled but his voice stayed calm.

"My father he-" my voice broke. Iskur comforted me and led me off the trail into the woods.

"What is it?" He sat me on the soft forest floor. I shook with rage as I cried.

"My marriage." I choked. I could have cut him down when he had told me. I *loved* my father. I never had imagined he would trade my welfare for the safety of the village.

"Who, Anaid?"

We had known my marriage would come. We were not fools. We knew it would not be Iskur, the nameless orphan who fled to our village when he was a child. The boy I had found in the woods in the smoke when we were both seven years old. My father loved Iskur as a son and valued his cunning mind, but Iskur was not a match for the daughter of the chieftain. Iskur was a genius, a seer, a healer, a kind hearted and generous man. He was beloved in the village. But he was an orphan and a refugee. All his people were slaughtered, his family's possessions burned and stolen. Everything he had was ours. We stood to gain nothing from a marriage to him.

I knew it could never be him, but the suitor my father was choosing instead? Despicable.

"Anaid, *who*?" Iskur asked again.

"That murderer."

"No."

I let out a scream of anger and pounded my fists on his shoulders.

"Anaid, no. We will not allow this."

"He'll kill me." I whispered, "He knows who you are, he knows about us."Iskur took my face in his hands. He tipped me head up to force me to look at him. His eyes were deadly serious.

"*I* will not let that happen."

"Unacceptable! You are working against everything we are building!" Virgil boomed uncharacteristically loud as I came back to the present.

Thunder roared as Iskur yelled.

"Nothing happened!"

"Was there water here?"

"No!!"

Wind and thunder battled against each other as I tried to calm myself down. What had I just seen? My perspective of Iskur's vision? How was that possible? I died in 2010. I had never gone to the sacred cedar groves that Iskur had roamed thousands of years ago. This was impossible. I felt like I was going to combust. The destructive energy was taking over again.

"Arga," Iskur was at my side, hands on my shoulders, "Stop resisting me. Please. Give it to me."

My chest felt like it was being crushed by a boulder. I wanted to claw my skin off and dive into a bottomless lake and never surface. I wanted to scream and cry. I couldn't make a sound. I couldn't move. I felt Iskur trying to draw the destructive energy off of me but I refused to let him. I refused to hurt him again. This was my fault. I was losing control, he didn't need to be punished.

I pushed him away violently and jumped to my feet. Virgil was shouting, the sound of wind and thunder was deafening. I fled, feeling the ground beneath my feet cracking and rending itself away from me. I was carving a path of destruction.

I knew Iskur would find me first. I was in the room with the great pool and waterfall. I stopped running and waited. He appeared beside me. I held up a hand to him.

"Stop," I ordered.

He obeyed. I let the dark thrill of being able to control him run through me. Indulging in bad behavior felt delicious.

"Arga," He put his hands up in surrender and took a step towards me.

"Iskur. I saw it. I saw what you showed me. But it was me. My view. From my eyes. I was there."

He raised his eyebrows in amazement.

"You saw that same vision?"

"From my perspective. Close the room. Hide us from him."

It wasn't a *Command*, but Iskur waved the stone entrance shut obediently.

"Fill the pool."

"Arga…"

"You said he was moving too slow." Static whipped across my body. I was in agony, but I needed to see what we could see together.

He looked around anxiously.

"Are you scared?" I grinned savagely. I wanted that pool filled with water. I waved my hand.

The pool filled with water. I knew it was filled without looking. In my mania I had the utmost confidence that I was going to get what I wanted. I was fixated on my singular desire: to be in the water with Iskur. It was like being on Earth again when I had resisted the voices too long. I would give in to their path and every obstacle would move out of my way to bring me the destruction I was craving.

Iskur inhaled sharply when the water appeared in the pool. There was no time to waste being amazed. I strode to where he stood. He looked into my eyes, searching for something.

"I will hurt you," It was true and it made me sad. Remorse in the middle of destruction? How human of me.

"I will not feel it," His voice was a deep rumble as he took my hands. He grimaced and tried to hide his pain.

The stone door screeched against itself as Virgil forced it open.

Iskur gave me a dangerous smile. I returned it. This was my natural state: ruining everything I had been working towards.

"No!" Virgil bellowed like a hurricane.

Iskur winked at him. We plunged into the water.

# VIII.

"My daughter," My father was not the type of many who would tremble, but there he was, on his knees in front of me: trembling in the light of the flaming hillside behind me, "Forgive me."

"For what?" My voice was a cruel hiss. I wanted to hear him say it.

"For not believing you. Both of you."

I laughed coldly. Iskur took my hand.

"You believe us now." Iskur said evenly, "That is what matters."

I glared at him. *That* is what matters?

"Yes yes, oh holy ones. I am humbled by your presence."

"Our coming was foretold." I motioned to the Seer who cowered among the crowd of our people, "Though the one who bore the message does little to acknowledge that now."

The events of the last few days had left me bitter and resentful. Somehow, the last couple hours had absolved everyone's guilt in Iskur's eyes. I was not so easily placated.

"We were wrong to ignore the signs. Please, forgive us." My father bent his face to the ground.

"We forgive you." Iskur squeezed my hand, "We know that you will not make this mistake again."

Later, after we extinguished the fire to the combined wonder and horror of the tribe, I took Iskur aside.

"What was that?" I asked in a pained whisper.

"What was what?"

"Forgiveness? After what those monsters did to you? To us?"

"Your family are not monsters. The guilty ones are gone and will never be back."

"More will come." I muttered, kicking a smoldering tree branch. The air was thick with aromatic smoke.

"Would you come challenge us after we brought a god down to smite your betrothed and his warband?"

I smirked.

"He really did look terrified when I stood over him, that stupid Prince Aatazaz."

"Yes he did." Iskur agreed with a laugh, "Your darling betrothed is gone. I would say your wedding is off."

"I still cannot forgive my father. They arrived with a *warband* and he was going to continue with the negotiations as if they had only come with emissaries."

"Arga," He pulled me into him, "They are gone."

"So is Qateel." I murmured, a sudden pang of guilt coursing through my body at the thought of our friend Aleyin's brother.

Iskur was silent for a while, then kissed my head.

"We all knew there was risk."

"Yes." I agreed, "We did."

"We need to speak to Aleyin." I added, after a pause.

"In time. He needs to grieve with his family."

"What must they think of us?"

Iskur drew me back to look at my face. I could not get the image of his eyes turning black out of my head.

"Arga, they think their son and brother died to bring a prophecy to fruition. And if they don't, they will depart from here in fear of us."

"You say that like it is nothing."

"Some will leave in the coming days. Some have already fled. Does it bother you?" Iskur searched my face.

"No." It wasn't a lie. I was glad that there would be fewer judgemental faces in the crowd each day. Fewer people who looked at us with fear and hatred rather than admiration.

"Everything is changed now," Iskur put his hand under my chin, "You have changed us all."

"We did this together." I took his hand from my face and kissed it, "Now we have a bond between us unlike any other."

He kissed me then, overcome by the implication of what we had accomplished. Speaking with our ancestors among the dead was one thing. Speaking to a god? Cleaving our souls to each other in the golden light of that great power? Indeed, everything had been changed. Whispers on the edge of my hearing disrupted my focus on our passionate embrace. I was used to the voices, but these were new. Strangers. I pulled away from Iskur and listened. He waited patiently, accustomed to staying silent so I could decipher the messages from beyond.

"New voices." I breathed, exhilarated by this development, "I need to try to hear them more clearly."

Iskur's eyes were black as the darkest night when I looked at him. He smiled that impish smile I loved so much and took my hand. We raced through the blackened trees, not caring as the lingering smoke clogged our noses and eyes.

There were prophecies to fulfill.

The pain was so excruciating I thought I would die. But, no, you can't die again when you are dead, can you? My body felt like it was being torn apart. Were we still underwater? I felt nothing but agony. Agony and guilt. Pulling Iskur in had been a mistake. I felt him reaching for me, taking whip after whip of the destruction I was flinging as I tried to escape the pain. How many new scars would this be?

Everything stopped.

I was in my room again when I awoke. My whole body ached and I did not want to open my eyes. Someone stirred next to me.

Iskur?

I cracked an eye open. I was right. He was draped over the edge of the bed to my left, barely on the mattress.

"You are going to tell me everything you saw."

Virgil was hollow with exhaustion. He spoke slowly, meticulously. I sat up and looked at him. He looked as horrible as he sounded. His eyes were still jet black, flashing in the dim light of my room. I had never seen him without his suit jacket, but it was nowhere to be seen. His shirt was wrinkled, and his sleeves were rolled up. He peered at me over his glasses like a vulture.

"What *happened* to you?" I breathed.

"What *happened* to me?" He repeated mockingly, "What happened. *She* wants to know what happened."

His maniacal laughter caused Iskur to jump to his feet. He looked around for a moment, confused, before his gaze landed on Virgil. His eyes went black.

"Must have been difficult to bring us here," Iskur said with venom. Thunder rumbled behind every word.

"Very," Virgil stood and strode over to Iskur, standing directly in front of him confrontationally, "Very, *very* difficult."

The sound of wind rushed through the room aggressively.

"Can you shift to your lightform, Virgil? Did the effort wear you out? You look terrible, you must not be able to change your suit." Iskur goaded, baring his teeth in a cruel grin.

"You *fools!* If I had not drained the pool and drug you out of there-"

"You drained the pool?" Iskur interrupted, sounding even more offended, "Why? Agra filled that pool herself!"

Virgil opened his mouth to say something, but stopped. His mouth hung open comically as Iskur's statement registered with him.

"Agra did *what?*" He looked at me in confusion.

"I filled it," I squeaked, feeling completely overrun with guilt and shame at my behavior. This was the worst kind of hangover: the emotional reckoning I always got after giving in to my destructive impulses. Wasn't this supposed to all stop after death? Did existence ever become less messy? Couldn't I stop being so stupid?

"You?" Virgil squinted suspiciously at me.

Iskur was still growling in his thunderous voice as he sat on the bed in front of me, blocking Virgil's penetrating stare.

"Yes, *her*," He retorted, "She filled the pool."

"*How?*" Virgil walked around the end of the bed, trying to look at me without Iskur blocking him. Iskur moved across the bed to continue shielding me from Virgil.

"Call off your dog, Arga, this is *important!*"

"He's not my dog, he's not my anything!" I stood up, head spinning. How *had* I filled the pool? I had just wanted it. Willed it and it happened.

"Oh, I am your dog, Arga," Iskur jumped to his feet again and began backing Virgil into the corner of the room, "You have seen the visions. I am many things but I am your dog *above all else*. Loyal. Bound to you. Subservient until my undoing. My broken oath demands it."

What the *fuck* was he talking about?

"Stop it!" I shouted.

Both Virgil and Iskur looked at me in surprise.

"Iskur. Leave him alone," I walked over to where they both stood and shoved Iskur back. I put myself between the two of them.

"He's right, you know. That was fucking stupid of me to do."

Iskur frowned at me.

"You wished to do it," He said, sounding hurt.

I groaned in exasperation.

"I *know* I wanted to do it but that doesn't mean it was fucking *smart* does it? You saw my life on Earth. Dumb shit. All the time. That's what I do."

Virgil made an agreement noise.

I glared at him. Shut the *fuck up*, professor asshole.

"You two both suck," I sputtered, "I don't know what is going on or how I'm doing things and all you do is fight. I'm fucking sick of it!"

Iskur and Virgil looked at me, then at each other. They spoke to each other in thunder and wind. It sounded much calmer, but the fact that I couldn't understand them made me grind my teeth in irritation.

"You are right, you are right. I will- ahhhhggg!" Virgil made a hand gesture then groaned in pain.

"What's wrong?" I was even more confused, "What happened?"

Iskur chuckled.

"Virgil attempted to create his notebook he has been using to keep his spy notes in, but he is still too exhausted from stopping us."

I glared at Iskur, then walked over to Virgil.

"This is good. This is very very good," Virgil panted slightly as he slumped back into a chair.

"On that, we can agree," Iskur stood at my side.

"What's good?" I was still frowning, not at all following their enigmatic train of conversation.

"She can wound you, she can create water-" Virgil was listing things on his fingers.

"She is right fucking here," I added, counting on my hand too.

Virgil snorted derisively.

"You would certainly not be here had I not stopped your idiotic display in the pool."

I sighed.

"Thank you."

Virgil seemed shocked and uncomfortable at my gratitude.

"It is my duty to keep you from...damaging things," He glanced at the silvery scars that laced Iskur's arms.

"Would I have, I don't know, actually ended myself if it had gone further?" I sat on the edge of the bed. Iskur sat with me.

"I do not know what you are capable of, which is why we are all here," Virgil took off his glasses and rubbed his eyes. They had shifted back to human after I had thanked him.

"Virgil," Iskur's tone was diplomatic, "Are you able to contact the Old Dead and tell them of these *developments*?"

"I must, but I am too worn at the moment. Your dwelling is not easy from which to communicate," Virgil put his glasses back on, "I will retire. When I am refreshed I will be in touch with them. They will be most interested in everything that has happened."

Virgil stood and drug his chair in front of the door.

"What are you doing?" I asked.

"Arga, we are all too exhausted to function. You two should rest as well, and I do not feel that I should leave you out of my sight considering how cavalier you have been lately regarding logic and common sense."

Iskur raised his eyebrows.

"Would you not prefer to lie down with us?"

Both Virgil and I shouted incoherent protests, much to Iskur's amusement. Iskur laughed and laid himself on the far edge of the bed with his back to Virgil. Still slightly uncomfortable by Virgil being so parental, I eventually laid awkwardly on the bed as far from Iskur as possible.

I wasn't sure what I was supposed to do.

"Uh..." I started awkwardly, "Do you sleep here in the Otherworld?"

Iskur looked over his shoulder at me.

"Yes. You have slept many times."

"Only after blacking out."

"Hm." Iskur rolled over to face me, "You have not just laid to relax and sleep?"

"No."

"It is just like on Earth," Virgil said impatiently, "Pretend you are asleep until you fall asleep."

I closed my eyes. I thought about the visions, the pool, and filling it with water. I thought about the agony I had felt and wanted to ask Iskur how bad it had been for him. I opened my eyes and looked at him. The tunic he wore left his forearms exposed. There were definitely more scars there. I sighed.

"Just breathe," He didn't even open his eyes as he whispered to me, but he did smile slightly and offer his hand. I took it and let him calm me.

After ages of silence, I started to feel the pleasant pull of sleep on my mind. I allowed it to fill me with its inky blackness. Then, I was gone.

I awoke to a comfortable twilight-like darkness in my room. Iskur was still lying at my side, unmoving. I felt so well rested that I smiled. I closed my eyes again and tried to drink in the feeling of peace.

"Awake at last."

I shrieked at Virgil's words. He appeared at the end of the bed. Iskur lazily sat up at my scream and glared at Virgil.

"In a rush?" Iskur asked, bitterly.

"What the *hell*, Virgil?" I roared. Virgil smirked back at me.

"Yes, well it seems that we are in a bit of a rush." Virgil said, tipping his head condescendingly, "We have some work to do."

His outfit was back to its normal state of spotlessness and he seemed much more peppy than before I had fallen asleep. Clearly he was feeling restored as well. Virgil disappeared and reappeared at the door.

"Do not delay!"

I rolled my eyes and tried to calm the shakes of panic that still traveled through my body.

"He says I'm supposed to fucking stay fucking calm and then he does shit like that?" I fumed.

"Yes, that was unkind." Iskur seemed preoccupied. As I crossed the room he came to my side and grabbed my hand, "Breathe."

I obliged, looking at his face. His eyes were black.

"What is it?"

"Mh. It is...unclear."

"Great." I pulled my hand away and followed Virgil across the hall of columns.

Virgil led us through the dwelling to the room we had been using to do my training in. It was another massive space off of a winding hall that split from the hall of columns. The room was lit with floating orbs of fire that bobbed around the ceiling. In the continued darkness, it gave the space a really eerie atmosphere. Virgil turned to Iskur.

"More light, if you please." Virgil commanded.

Iskur obliged, and the ambient light slowly increased until it appeared to be midday. I sighed involuntarily at seeing the space more clearly again. The room was a large, square hall with rows of pillars that flanked the walls on each side. The center of the room was a few feet lower than the rest. The columns were situated atop the two steps that led down into the center of the room. In the very middle was where we would do my training or testing or whatever else. What was seated in the middle of the room varied. Most often it was a single large cushion, other times a chair and table with objects for me to interact with on it. Today there was an empty vase.

"So." Virgil strode with purpose to the middle of the room, "Let us see if you can create something again."

"What did the Old Dead say about me filling the pool?" I asked, following him.

"Oh, they were quite intrigued."

"They believe it was me?"

"Certainly. They were able to determine that it was indeed you," Virgil shot a glance at Iskur, "Who did it. But as I was not able to observe this happening, they would like a first hand perspective. So, please."

Virgil waved at me to proceed.

"Uh...You want me to just fill the vase?"

"Yes. Do what you did before. I will watch, and that will be all for today."

Iskur stepped towards me.

"No no, I would like to see her attempt it alone." Virgil was even more uptight than usual, if that was possible. It freaked me out.

Iskur shrugged and gave me an encouraging smile. His eyes had remained black, which was way harder to read. Was that concern on his face? Fear?

"Okay." I said, slowly exhaling and closing my eyes. I focused internally, and shut out all other thoughts. One of the many unnerving things about Iskur and

Virgil was their freaky ability to stand silent and unmoving for endless periods. As they watched me, there was no sound. It was as if everything was waiting and holding its collective breath.

I allowed the silence to fill me as well. My breathing continued and I became even more aware of it. In and out, slowly. I focused my energy on recalling the feeling I had experienced when I was filling the pool. I had wanted it so badly then. But I didn't now. I didn't want to make water. I wanted to make *life*.

A fluttering sensation started gathering in my chest. My mind leapt excitedly. I focused my attention on collecting that feeling. I nurtured it like a flame, asking it to grow, and grow it did.

"*Okay, stay calm.*" I ushered the feeling to flow from my chest and down my arms. I moved my hands intuitively, slowly letting the feeling stream through my hands. Heat gathered in my palms this time and I felt strangely in control. I opened my eyes.

Hovering before me and continuing to grow was a beautiful sprig of a cedar tree. I could see the twigs braiding themselves together as I gave it my power and focus. My face broke into a huge grin. I let the energy flow faster in a rush of exaltation. The sprig stemmed into a full tree and grew rapidly. A tree! I laughed gleefully, and brought my hands towards the ground. The stone floor cracked open as I motioned with one hand, leaving the other hand to uphold and continue growing the tree. With dirt exposed, I carefully lowered the still growing tree. Roots shot out as the tree neared the soil, and buried themselves rapidly. I moved my hands once more up and across the tree, which now stood at my height. As I moved my hands up, the branches thickened and the trunk stretched upwards. I laughed again, my smile not fading as I released the tree from my control and allowed the feeling of creation to subside.

The high of this success was incomparable. I felt like my chest would undo itself with joy as I looked over my shoulder at Iskur. His face was aglow with pride and joy as well, black eyes shimmering wildly in the light. I peeked around the spiked needles to see Virgil. His face was utterly bewildered, which brought me even more glee.

"So?" I gushed, walking around my creation to stand proudly before him, "How's *that?*"

"That is..." He said slowly, trying to regain his composure, "That is certainly... impressive."

I whooped in celebration and turned back to take in the tree in all its glory. This was what I needed: a solid win. After so much frustration and stress, the tree was a huge release. I babbled excitedly about how it looked. I could not believe how well I had done. Me! The complete and total fuckup who helped her mother drink herself into an abyss. Me! The girl guaranteed to destroy every good thing that ever happened to her. I couldn't believe it.

"Tell *that* to the Old Dead!" I proclaimed to Virgil, boastfully. When I turned to look at him again, he was gone.

"He left already." Iskur walked over next to me and gently touched the lowest branch of the tree.

"Oh. Well, what do you think they will say?" I asked in a rush of nerves. This was certainly bound to get their attention.

"I think they will want to see you." Iskur sounded strange. Like his voice was strained by some emotion. I looked at him, examining his face to try and better understand what he was feeling.

"Arga," He said, stepping closer to me and placing a hand on my shoulder, "You have done so well. How did it feel?"

"It was amazing." That word didn't hardly cover the joy I had felt. The release of tension and pain and fear, the way the act of creating the tree had both drained me of energy and filled me at the same time. It was indescribable. Iskur smiled in understanding.

"Mh. It is a beautiful thing, no?" He took his hand off of my shoulder. I grabbed his hand in both of mine and held it tight.

"It's so good," I agreed. What a terrible way to describe it. *So good?* It was the best feeling I had ever experienced.

He placed his other hand on top of ours and looked at the tree with a smile.

"I can feel you in this tree." His eyes blazed with happiness when he looked back at me, their black depths shining. My body grew giddy again, and my chest whirled with awareness of the deep pool of power to which I now had access. As my smile broadened even further, and I did something quite impulsive: I reached for Iskur's face, pulled him towards me, and kissed him.

The sensation was like falling into a warm silken bed. Heat and passion continued between us as another tension I didn't know I had been holding uncoiled itself. I could see nothing, feel nothing besides the lack of space between us. Endless moments passed in an outpouring of bliss. We were entwined in a way that transcended our physical forms. I felt the welcome snap of static that we shared and embraced it. The energy surrounded us and pulled me further away from my understanding of what space I was supposed to occupy. I was leaving my body.

In that space beyond the physical, I felt him. Iskur was still with me, as a pillar of darkness. His presence pulled me and calmed me, and I met him in my own form of gold and white. As we collided again, I heard thunder and the sound of rushing water. Stormy depths unexplored. My voice! It felt like singing and shouting and crying out in pleasure as the sounds of the waves crashed.

We were spiraling upwards. No dwelling existed, nothing in my sight but him. I was shedding layers of doubt and confusion as we entwined and broke apart, and met again. This was all that mattered. This was everything. The sky could have rained fire on us and I would not have felt it.

Blue light abruptly pierced my euphoria, bringing despair and a terrifying shrinking feeling. My form retracted rapidly and I regained my sight and sense of the physical space. I was on the ground at the base of my tree. I could smell its resinous sap and the freshly turned dirt. As my senses grew more clear and adhered themselves to my body once more, I became aware that Iskur was beneath me, and we were still tangled around each other. I met his eyes, certain that mine were as black as his. This was paradise. A slight warmth returned as he smiled at me, but my body froze at the sound of an unwelcome voice.

"Enough!" At Virgil's hissing and disapproving tone I leapt to my feet.

"Are you *satisfied?*" Virgil continued in a tirade, storming past me to loom over Iskur.

Iskur was still half reclining on the ground, a pleased smile on his face.

"Hardly." He said. "You are quite rude."

"*Rude?* Oh well, pardon me for my *rudeness*."

"You forced us back into our bodies. No doubt you know how painful and disgusting that feels." Iskur was on his feet now, "She was able to leave her human form! At her own will! And you forced us back."

"Really. At her own will? Hm??" Virgil's tone was shrill and accusatory, "You had *nothing* to do with coaxing her out of her form? No?"

"She kissed *me*." Iskur roared, indignant, "There is no forcing here. How *dare* you suggest-"

"How *dare* I? Let me think. How dare *you* be leading her on, building up this fantasy for her that there is something between you two-"

"There is!" Iskur boomed.

"There certainly is something *you* want from her, and you are manipulating her to get it!" Virgil howled, jabbing at Iskur with his fingers as he spoke.

"*I am not manipulating her*!" Iskur's voice threatened to shatter my ears, "And you are being incredibly rude still, you know she cannot understand us. Stop leaving her out. Sling these accusations so she can hear you!"

"I am the only thing standing between your unquenchable desire for power and her delicate state of mind and *you* keep *pushing*-"

"I....uh....I can hear you." I stuttered as I cut Virgil off. I was flushed from listening to this whole exchange unfold. That was a lot of insight to gain all at once about the two of them. Virgil seemed so fraternally protective of me, and it was weirdly endearing. I would have found this sort of nice if his assertion of Iskur manipulating me hadn't made me uneasy. Both of them wheeled on me. Iskur's face was one of joy and triumph, Virgil's was awash with fresh horror. He stammered helplessly while Iskur broke into a fit of laughter.

"I, uh, sorry." I was coming down from the high and was starting to fear the crash. Iskur stopped laughing and looked at me with an unmasked tenderness and care. He walked to my side and took my hand in his. My downward spiral slowed and my panic plateaued at his touch.

"You did nothing wrong." Iskur lowered himself to meet my eyes directly, "I do not regret this."

My chest swirled again, warmth returning. I'd know if I was being used, right? If for some reason I was just the key to more power or something for him, like Virgil accused, I would know, right? I always knew when I was being exploited on Earth, but I just let it happen. I looked over his shoulder at the tree again and swelled with pride. I had done that all on my own. My progress was rapid now. First the pool, then the tree, then leaving my body and gaining my voice. I had no idea if I was speaking like a human or with the sound of lakes and oceans and rivers, but I could understand the other two at the very least.

"Nothing wrong indeed," Virgil intoned, regaining his composure at last, "Arga. The Old Dead will see you."

The last thing I saw was Iskur looking terrified against the backdrop of my tree.

# IX.

When I became aware of my surroundings again, I was in an endless, formless hall. The ground beneath my feet was solid, but there were no walls or features to be seen beyond the darkness that encircled me. I was rooted into my body. It was the most human I had felt since the night I had arrived. There was an oppressively large power all around me, as if something was squeezing my very soul and confining it to this human form.

"Iskur?" I called shakily, "Virgil?"

"Arga." A voice boomed, coming from everywhere at once and also sounding like it was being whispered directly in my ear. I shivered. Freaky.

"Yes?" What were they doing, trying to terrify me? My hands shook violently.

Light began to grow in the far edges of the space, gathering intensity like a sunrise that was happening on all sides at once. The space became more visible and it was unsettling. It looked vaguely like a building, but as if a building had been built by aliens who didn't understand what buildings were used for. Which, I supposed, was sort of the case. There was no solid roof. Where Iskur's dwelling's structure would have melted into nature, this structure melted into space. Pieces of stone and glass that were wrought into intricate, abstract shapes floated aimlessly above. The arm of the galaxy was closer here: it dominated the entire sky.

Stone stairways to nowhere, various impossible arches, and towering columns dotted the expanse at random intervals. It was like standing inside one of those trick drawings, where structures sort of fold into themselves infinitely. Everything seemed pointless, but placed with great intention. All of the elements were elaborate. The space walked the line between natural and futuristic, and was unlike anything I had ever seen before.

"Arga, you are here to discuss what is to be done."

I jumped at the voice's uncanny everywhere-and-right-here manner again.

"Okay? What do I need to do?"

"You are the product of a powerful oath made ages ago on Earth. You do not recall this oath?"

"Uh....no? I wasn't alive then?"

"You were, but you do not remember."

I was silent. Keep your mouth shut and don't give them anything.

"You have been so far unable to remember the oath, but you have recently created life and shed your human form."

"Yeah. I, uh, made a tree." I looked in every direction for the source of the voice. It was impossible to tell where it was coming from. The voice was rather female sounding. Not kind, but not terribly harsh either. It was stating facts in a dull tone and waiting for my responses. There was no hint of emotion in the voice at all. I hated it.

"Yes. A cedar tree. Does this mean anything to you?"

"Iskur likes cedar trees?"

"Indeed."

"Is that bad?"

"It is neither good nor bad. It merely *is*."

"Okay? Uh...where are you? I can't see you?"

"Would you prefer we take human form?"

"Sure?"

I wasn't sure if I was about to regret that statement or not. In a flash, a woman and two men appeared before me. They were hovering twenty feet off the ground and bathed in a piercing blue light that made Virgil's seem dim. They were enrobed in fabrics that seemed to swirl around them of their own volition, like living scarves entwining themselves over and over again on their bodies.

The woman spoke, her voice much more human.

"Is this preferred?"

Their light was so bright I shielded my eyes from it.

"Uh, sure."

They were even taller than Iskur. Their height and luminosity and the fact that they were floating in front of me made them an imposing trifecta. The woman continued.

"You have been informed of the basic realities of this realm, but there is much more you do not yet know. What questions do you have before we proceed?"

"*What?*"

"Do you have questions for us?" The man on the right spoke for the first time. His voice was warm and soothing, like honey. He smiled as he spoke.

"What's going to happen? Can I go see the rest of the world now? Is Iskur free to go?"

The woman now smiled at me. I was feeling more at ease. The Old Dead were not so scary after all. All that Great and Powerful Oz stuff was just for show.

"Iskur. It is wonderful that you gave him back his name." She said, with kindness lacing her voice finally.

"Yeah, so like, now that I have control of stuff, can we go?"

The man on the left floated downwards and touched down on the stone floor gracefully. The other two followed him. As they did this, their lights became less blinding. They still kept their distance from me.

"We have much to discuss about this." The third man said. His voice was gravely, like stone being ground against itself. The woman nodded in agreement.

"Arga, you and Iskur have a strange bond that we do not understand. We have never seen such a thing before. It requires us to observe you closely, and move with caution." She said soothingly.

"What do you mean, observe me closely?" My chest tightened again.

"Our faithful servant, *Virgil,* you call him, reports your progress to us. We form hypotheses based on these reports," She explained.

"And what's your theory now?" I asked, trying to seem brave and calm. Like I do this sort of conference call with ancient powerful dead people all the time.

I was slightly hopeful that Virgil did not know enough about the visions both Iskur and I had seen to share the theory I was secretly forming: that against all logic, I had somehow lived two lives. Reincarnation? One soul, two lifetimes? It didn't seem possible, but it was starting to become the only unspoken theory I could form that explained any of this insane circumstance.

"We believe that you were once one of the most powerful beings on Earth. And somehow, you forgot." The man with the sweet and gentle voice spoke, "For some reason we do not understand, you have gained immense ability since death. It seems you are a very volatile being."

"I'm *what?*" *That* was a bit different than my crackpot theory, "I'm sorry, you think I was some sort of freak superhero on Earth and just didn't know it?"

"That is...one way of explaining it." The gravel-man said, sounding unimpressed with my way of putting it. He and Virgil were two peas in a pretentious pod.

"Okay, so what's the problem? I'm figuring things out now. Easy fix. I just stay calm and have a peaceful afterlife and nothing bad happens."

"When a soul dies and comes here, they come into their power over time. The longer they are here the more they can control and express the immense power every human has within them," the woman intoned.

I nodded, Iskur and Virgil had explained that.

"It seems your soul died thousands of years ago and was tied in part to your ancestral line, traveling as a silent companion, unable to ascend here due to the terms of your vow with Iskur." The woman explained, walking to stand a few feet before me.

I remembered what Iskur said when he got in Virgil's face in my room after my pool-filling fiasco:

*"You have seen the visions. I am many things but I am your dog above all else. Loyal. Bound to you. Subservient until my undoing. My broken oath demands it."*

So they *did* have more figured out than they were letting on. Panic constricted my chest.

"When you were killed, it broke the vow and allowed your soul to travel here at last."

"I...don't understand," I fumbled for words. Anxious energy roared inside my head.

"There has been bestowed on you a wealth of power and knowledge that has been building up over centuries." The sweet-voiced man explained, "This has never happened before. As I said, you were among one of the most powerful beings on Earth and as such were able to do unfathomable things."

"I don't think that is possible," I asserted, "I was a terrible disappointment on Earth. Ask Virgil, he'll tell you how bad I did in school. And did you see how I died? Not very good at picking men either."

"It is a lot to take in." The gravel-voiced man came to my side, "And you must understand that we are learning about much of this alongside you."

"So then what? I am a puppet to the ancestor that made a vow with Iskur? My life isn't real?"

"No, not at all. You are the person you experienced on Earth *as well as* Arga. You have a duality. Two things are true at once." The woman floated to stand directly in front of me. I had to bend my neck upwards to look at her face.

"I don't get it."

I didn't know which was a worse reality: reincarnation or being possessed by some bitch who died ten bazillion years ago. My throat was raw and my palms were hot. There was no way what they were saying was accurate.

"That is nothing to worry about. But do you understand that the depths of your power is something of a concern?" The kind man spoke and joined the woman in front of me.

"I-I'm learning to control it."

I clawed at the palms of my hands as the heat in them reached a new height. The feeling of being confined into my body had been intensifying this whole time, and as it did so did my fear. Iskur had said he would be here with me when the time came. Where was he?

"Yes, yes you are but, there are...dangers." The woman's voice was soothing but it did not stop my static panic from spreading.

"What dangers?" I asked. My voice shook as I spoke.

Virgil appeared as if summoned. He was in his human form, avoiding looking directly at me.

"Virgil, as you call him, has shown us that you can wound Iskur in a manner that defies healing." The woman said in a measured tone.

"I didn't mean to-" She stopped my excuses with an abrupt slicing motion of her hand.

"We know. That is the danger." She said, her voice suddenly icy. She motioned to Virgil who bowed his head and faded into his light form. Scenes flashed within him, playing back all the times my energy lashed out and inflicted pain onto Iskur. My fearful shaking turned to rage.

"Stop it! I didn't mean to hurt him!" My voice boomed loud across the expanse. Virgil snapped back to human suddenly. He looked shocked to find himself back in a body. The Old Dead exchanged knowing glances then turned to me.

"As you can see, you are able to induce your will onto others who *should* be much more powerful than you." The women spoke in a calculated tone.

"I didn't-"

"You pulled him into his human form to stop him relaying the things he observed." The warm-voiced man explained gently.

"I-I didn't mean to. I just-"

I was frantic. The force that was pressing down on me was becoming too much to bear. I looked to Virgil for help, his eyes finally met mine. He looked horrified. I wanted to run, to scream and rip and kick and claw and flee. I was feral, but I was frozen to the spot.

"Arga," The man with the stone-like voice was speaking to me now, "This is why we have brought you here. To ask you to protect this realm from the powers you cannot control and we do not yet fully understand. We are the bringers of balance to the Otherworld. It is our duty to protect all present and future dead."

"You are like a weapon, Arga." The woman's voice had grown mighty again, seeming to come from all corners of the vast space, "A weapon that no one can control. We have studied your power and know that what you are capable of-"

"I'm not a weapon!" I exclaimed, "I'm not going to hurt anyone! Please, where is Iskur?"

Tears were streaming down my face. Crying? Again? Really? Could I do something less pathetic?

"What are you going to do to me?"

"We know you are inside somewhere, full of memory and dominance. Reveal yourself!" The kind-voiced man stopped sounding so kind. His voice grew deep and commanding as he stepped towards me. The stone-man held out his arm to stop his comrade.

"I do not think she has reached awareness." Stone-man said.

"What the fuck are you talking about?! *Where is Iskur?*"

I had reached my breaking point. Pain ripped through my body as I lunged at them. They called me a weapon? I'd show them a fucking weapon. Effortlessly the three disappeared and reappeared floating above me in what I assumed were forms they had adopted to terrify me. It worked.

The woman was vast and violent, her eyes empty pits and her teeth sharp and lion-like. Her hair flowed in a mane around her head and she stood before the other two in a position of defense. The once-kind man's appearance had become more like that of a bull than a man, with horns atop his head. He stood stoically to the woman's right. On the left the third man screeched. He was an enormous eagle, gnashing his beaked face in the air. I fell backwards in terror.

All three still had vastly human forms with the exception of their animal-like faces. They were still clothed in the writhing bands of cloth, which whipped more rapidly about their bodies. On each of them were three sets of wings, with brightly illuminated feathers flashing aggressively. Virgil was on the ground beside me, face down in fear or reverence. Same thing, I guess.

Besides the three main speakers, I became aware of a swarm of other blue figures in a ring above us. For a moment they were visible to me, each individual field of energy appearing as a flashing blue ring of light conjoined with the next. That was what was keeping me in my body. There was an entire army using all their might to force me to stay in my human form. I blinked and couldn't see them anymore. But oh, did I feel them. The army beat down on me with a mighty pulse of energy, sending me sprawling to my knees.

Bringing my attention back to their great and terrible appearances, the three speakers flashed their brilliant light. I couldn't look away, I was a tiny moth in their blazing flame. The three spoke as one, in ghastly unison that shook the stone beneath me.

*"Your power is outside of your control and will cause endless harm if you are allowed to wield it. On behalf of all those who have come before you and all of those who will come after, we ask you: will you submit to us in peace?"*

Despite the quaking ground and his obvious terror, Virgil's head snapped up at this request. His movement drew my eyes for a second and as I looked at him, it was as if he was about to speak. Instead he shut his mouth tightly and stared at me. Was he confused about something? I looked back at the Old Dead.

"If I submit, what will happen?"

The two creatures on the flanks looked to the lioness. In a blaze of light, the three diminished slightly and became less vast and less terrifying. They retained their animalistic looks, but returned to a more human scale. I felt crushed and small, but I was not willing to blink and break their gaze. Stupidly stubborn even in death, I glared at them.

"You will be bound to a fixed space within this realm. Or, you can elect to submit your energy for reuse among new populations. You can be unmade and reformed into a multitude of new lives." The woman spoke alone. I stood up again to face her.

"Kill myself?" I asked bitterly.

"Be unmade." The bull replied. I glared at him.

"Suicide."

"Or, be bound to one fixed space in this realm." The eagle spoke plainly, "A dwelling of your own, as Iskur has chosen. A paradise you alone inhabit, never to leave."

"Never to leave?" I asked, hot, angry tears continuing to spill over my cheeks. Virgil shuffled, stood up, and slunk to my side.

"It would be thus." The three said as one.

My mind raced, Iskur was bound to his dwelling? Trapped there like a prison? Why hadn't he told me?

"Iskur and I, he said we are bound by this vow. Could I see him? Could we stay together?"

"No." The unison voice intoned.

My tears came faster now. I got off my knees and leaned towards them in my best attempt at looking menacing. They were scared of what I could do, right? Good. I was quaking with a dangerous cocktail of fear and anger and confusion. I felt destructive energy threatening to snap my spine. What kind of afterlife was this? No hell my ass. An eternity alone would be the worst hell I could create for myself.

"Kill myself or spend eternity alone? *Those are the choices?*"

"You will be given time to decide." The woman spoke and held her hands up. I was being dismissed. I raged against the force of energy they were blasting me with, but it was no use.

I ripped through blackness and cosmos and an unintelligible sea of colors and lights. Virgil and I tumbled ungracefully to the stone floor as we arrived back in Iskur's dwelling in the hall of columns. I leapt to my feet and took off through the hall at breakneck speed. I screamed for Iskur, my voice louder and more powerful than it had ever been. In my wake, cracks formed in the stone floors.

*Where was he?*

Iskur was not in the training hall with my tree where I had last seen him. I flew through the halls, with Virgil appearing in front of me at various points to try and slow me down. Each time I fled past him, howling in blind panic and rage. No way I would let Virgil stop me. I had to find Iskur.

*Had the Old Dead taken him?*

I used my destroying energy and ripped open the stone closures to the waterfall pool, tore through the passages and raced through our favorite forests to try and find him. It felt so good to let the energy lash out freely. Was this what they meant? That I would *like* to wreck things? The more I looked for Iskur the more violent my outbursts became, until a deep sorrow welled up in me.

Iskur was nowhere.

Electricity and fear coursed through my body as my panicked flight slowed. My frenzied search had reached its peak. This was the downward part that I feared most. I walked and the rage began to boil away, leaving just fear in its wake. I shouted and shouted and begged and pleaded as I wandered. My path took me back to the hall of columns. I was a zombie. Nothing mattered. My vision blurred. I collapsed in the library and let grief pour over me in wretched waves.

The destroying energy from my rampage had not vanished, but since I wasn't spending it ruining Iskur's house it had nowhere to go but me. It hurt fiercely, but I refused to let it lash out again. I'd done enough. What a cosmic tantrum. I wept and ground my teeth together. I couldn't force the feeling to stop. I hated it. I hated it. Where was Iskur?

"Arga?"

Virgil. He crept into the room.

"Where is he?" I sobbed, clutching my ribs in agony, "What did they do to him?"

"Arga, he is with them. He is making a case for you to them. He was summoned as we were sent away. He spoke to me as we passed. You *must* keep yourself together, Arga."

Making a case for me? I lifted my head off the floor. That sounded good. Virgil came to my side and touched my shoulder hesitantly. I tried to keep my snapping, biting electrical charge to myself and not pass it to him. The parts of me I could see were still human, but hardly. I was glowing white hot and gold lightning raced across my arms as I tried to contain the destruction.

"You need to give me some of this energy, Arga. You lose control if you do not."

"I've already *lost* control." I cried weakly, "I don't want to hurt you."

"Too late for that." He winced as some escaped my grasp and flowed into his hand. He took it as calmly as he could.

"Breathe," He gasped. Was he telling himself or me?

We took a dozen ragged breaths in tandem. The glow of my skin lessened, until I looked more like an ember in a fire than an overpowered lightbulb. The lightning stopped. Virgil released me and stood up.

"Thank you," I murmured.

I was embarrassed. Freaking out for nothing while Iskur was making a case for me. Surely he was more trusted by them, right? Surely they would listen to him, right?

"What will he say to them?" I scooted awkwardly to sit with my arms wrapped around my legs tightly.

"I do not know, but I know he *is* respected by them. Please, Arga, try not to embarrass yourself. This is very strange. Very strange."

Virgil started pacing around the room. I tried to breathe deeply and help disperse the remaining tension I was harboring. Iskur would change their minds. He was powerful like them. He understood the vow. The oath. Whatever. He could fix this.

"Virgil." I snapped, "I'm supposed to be calming down can you stop fucking pacing?"

"It is just so strange."

"Yeah? It's strange that some gods want me to die?" Panic again. I sniffled pathetically.

"It is never...it is never like this. They do not give choices that are so *extreme.*"

"But what about Hitler, huh? You said he opted to die. Didn't they tell him to stay in prison or die?"

"Well, no. It was more of a 'learn and be reformed' or cease to exist. There is always a path for redemption. Always. That is how this realm thrives. There has never been a case of eternal isolation."

"Except for Iskur." I said brokenly.

"I did not know that he was in isolation until they said it. Very strange." He muttered tensely. Virgil was growing more and more frantic.

"This does not make *sense.*" He blurred between his light and human form.

"What are you *doing*?" I demanded.

"I am trying to see if I can reach Iskur. I cannot."

"Isn't he with the Old Dead?" My voice was shrill, "Virgil, where is he??"

"He is likely with them but...this is not how things work. You should be allowed to train and grow into your powers, however long that takes." Virgil was pacing again.

I felt darkness encroaching and I fought against it. I shakily tried to calm myself and make a flower or twig or something, but only sparks and static would come. I could not call on the life-giving core of energy within myself. Figures. Self destructive in life, self destructive in afterlife. Virgil was muttering to himself and I was hearing a mix of words and wind. Was my ability to decode his Otherworld speech fading? A cold wave of fear washed over me and I stood up slowly.

"Virgil." It was someone else's voice that spoke, wasn't it? No. I was hearing myself like a guest. Like a stranger outside my own body.

Virgil stopped pacing and stared at me in rising alarm.

"Arga, no." He breathed, "You have to fight-"

I felt the walls within me break and the destroying energy poured forth again. Virgil vaulted towards me, a blend of bright light and his human form. He collided with me as the charges broke free of my control. I left my body and the room and all of existence. This was something entirely different than my previous fit. I was hurtling through space while being burned alive. I could see the galaxy unfolding around me as I sped through it. Colors and lights blurred in my vision. Not good. Not good. Not good. Fear and terror screamed in my head and I just wanted to be safe, was that so much to ask? Make me safe, let me be safe. That's all I ever wanted when I was alive, anyways. I was in a kaleidoscope of visions and sounds and feelings and places. It was so hot that it was ice, and I was moving faster than light.

Then there was nothing.

*"Why are you with him?"*
*"You know this only ends in tears."*

*"Has he hurt you?"*

*"Why are you doing this to yourself?"*

*"This is because you never had a father."*

*"He'll do it again."*

*"It'll be worse."*

*"You are being self destructive."*

*"Do you WANT to die?"*

# X.

Where was I? Everything felt vast and empty. Slowly, I felt the vast empty expanse of where we were. I reached out with my mind. Where was I? Had I erased the dwelling? Had I gone nuclear and destroyed all of Iskur's hard work?

Darkness.

Darkness. Nothingness.

Darkness. Nothingness. Blue light.

But, how could there be a blue light when there was nothing?

Virgil was with me. I could not see anything beyond the light that was Virgil. I was outside of my body and didn't feel like trying to gather myself back into it. I should have felt much more concerned, but being able to let go of all the tension and fear and panic had released me from a self-made prison. I was floating and at peace for a time before I decided to try and talk to Virgil.

"Did I kill you?"

"I am already dead, Arga."

The retort brought me a small bit of joy. He seemed fine. I was still feeling high from the release of all that pent up anxious energy, so I didn't press the matter further. I felt safe. What a funny realization.

"Where are we?" Virgil asked.

"You don't know?" My peaceful state dissipated slightly. That little know-it-all should know where we are. I was new to this whole realm of the dead thing. He was the expert.

"Do *you?*"

"No." I admitted.

Way to kill the vibe entirely, Virgil. I explored the space with my mind. Vast. Empty. Devoid of life. No discernable up or down. No light sources. No stars. No galaxy.

"How did you *do* this?" Virgil sounded awestruck, which was very weird to hear. I expected a lecture.

"I really don't know."

"I cannot feel any of the rest of the Otherworld." Virgil's voice was still full of reverence and awe.

"You can't?"

"Arga, you have taken us to a void." Virgil gasped, "I do not think they will be able to find us here."

"That's good, right?"

"Hm. For now, while we figure out what you are. Arga?"

"What?"

"Try and make something."

"But-"

"Just try."

I started to pull at the feeling of creating, but stopped cold.

"Iskur!" My wave-voice echoed across the nothingness.

"Yes I know. We left him in the lurch, really. This will likely be quite confusing for everyone else."

"Virgil," Fear was building up again, "Virgil, we have to go back!"

"Arga, I am going to explain everything to you. *Every single thing.* Everything they told me *not* to tell you. There is something terribly wrong with all of this and we need to figure out your past and get you back to Iskur," Virgil floated towards me, gathering himself into his human form as he did, "But for that to happen I need you to make this space into something we can use to explore your past."

"Can't you make anything?" I was starting to pull myself into my human form again as well.

"I can not do it here. I have tried. I need *you* to try."

"It's not like, you are tired and can't do it?"

"We have been here a while now. I should be rested. I cannot make anything."

That was concerning. We floated silently in our human forms for a few moments. I sighed.

"Alright. Let me try." I closed my eyes.

It was even easier to find the power to create this time. Virgil was going to tell me everything. I was going to know everything and we would find a way to get back to Iskur. I moved my hands and opened my eyes. My hands glowed with a pleasant golden light. Virgil looked awestruck again, his glasses sliding down the end of his nose.

"What do you want me to make?"

"Anything." He breathed, sounding more impressed than he had so far. Which was really saying something, as his tone had been atypically reverent since I had torn us out of space and time.

Right. Make something.

I wanted an up and a down, the lack of orientation of the void was making me feel dizzy and small in my human form. I placed my hands below me and sent my creative energy flowing across the space. Beneath us suddenly felt like there was something *there*, but we still couldn't see it. My glowing hands did not illuminate much.

"What did you make?" Virgil asked.

"Uh, ground I think?"

"Perhaps some *light* would help."

I nodded in the dim light and began to focus again. I pushed the golden glow that surrounded my hands into an orb shape and put all my effort towards separating it from me. It split easily and bobbed satisfyingly in the air between Virgil and I.

"Fascinating." Vigil leaned in and inspected the glowing light. It wasn't fire, like Iskur would make for us. It was...just light. I lifted my hand and it levitated upwards, shedding a bright glow across the void. We were floating above what looked like an infinite ocean.

"There's nothing here but water?" I observed, feeling stupid.

"Interesting. You made an endless sea for us."

"Where is the rest of the galaxy?" I looked around us as if I had just misplaced the gleaming mass of stars that typically split the sky. The floating light was offering greater visibility but above us was still a blanket of black.

"I do not know. Make something else." Virgil commanded, cutting off my rising panic.

I breathed slowly. Creation came easily for me here. Next I tried to make a cloud, and sent it upwards with the floating light above us. At Virgil's behest, I increased the luminosity of our light and pulled up a modest stone platform for us to stand on. At the creation of the stone, gravity took a gentle hold on us and affixed us to the ground. I was exhausted.

"Rest." Virgil said, "I will try to make this space a bit more functional."

I reclined on the uncomfortable slab of stone I had made, cursing the fact I had not thought to make pillows. My whole being ached with the exertion of making so many things so quickly. I was tired, but satisfied. It pleased me greatly to be making things, despite the desperation of the situation I had gotten us into.

Virgil sputtered in frustration.

"I *still* cannot create anything!"

"Maybe it's because you are in my dwelling now." I mused, half awake in the warm light.

"Hm. Perhaps you have some sort of omnipotence here." He continued muttering to himself in annoyance.

"I'll make you some more land when I wake up." I murmured in exhaustion. I heard Virgil make one last indignant noise before everything faded away.

I was standing on the charred hill at the edge of our village. Our people went about their daily lives, fewer in number since last evening. Everything had changed then.

"The ones who remain are beyond loyal," Iskur was watching them too, guessing my thoughts.

I kicked at a smouldering chunk of wood.

"For now," I murmured.

When my father had arranged my marriage to that murderous demon of a prince, he had sealed our destiny. That wretched prince was the son of the warlord who had slaughtered Iskur's entire tribe ten years before. They had arrived with a warband to treat for my hand in marriage. A warband! And my father displayed detestable cowardice and agreed to their terms.

Well, I couldn't have that. Not when that monster, my betrothed, revealed to me yesterday that he and his father knew Iskur was not only my lover, but also the last surviving heir to the tribe they had usurped. My father may have sealed our destiny, but my future husband signed his name to it in blood when he threatened me that night.

"You're my bitch now. I'll drink out of that dog Iskur's skull on our marriage night. You'll give me strong sons, and I'll slit your throat."

I smiled at him then. And started laughing. He looked at me with stupid confusion. I kissed his cheek, lingering to whisper:

"You're a fool. You will never see another sunrise."

He had been too drunk and dumbfounded to do anything besides hit me hard across the face. I laughed harder, and walked swiftly into the night. We had been near the edge of the village. I disappeared into my woods.

When Iskur found me on the hillside that was covered in our violets, I was seething with rage. The voices in my head were always quiet here, unlike when I was near the great stone in the village. The stone was where I'd go to hear our ancestors' wisdom. Here on the hillside was my place for silence. The place where Iskur and I had discovered that there was a power beyond the ancestors' voices and beyond the gods of our ancestors. There was something more, and we had met it once before.

In that silent place, I told Iskur my scheme. He got our most loyal friends: the brothers Qateel and Aleyin. They stood witness on the hillside as Iskur and I called to a power we had only ever seen glimmers of on one other occasion. Nobody had believed us before. Not the Seer of our village, not my parents, nobody. Even Qateel and Aleyin had been skeptical, but they loved us fiercely and stood by us that night. They all thought it was one of *our* gods. A known divinity that was blessing us. But we knew better, Iskur and I. That fateful night, I reached out with every part of my soul, begging the great and powerful being to bind our oath. On our knees we made our vow and were given the gift of the tiniest piece of power unfathomable.

I got lost in the memory again: Golden light splitting the sky and that indescribable voice that spoke to us. How my own voice had seemed frail and woeful as I asked the thing to give me the power to destroy the ones who threatened us. Iskur's voice had seemed like a distant thunderstorm as power was granted to us. Iskur's oath. How my heart had leapt with joy as Iskur spoke his oath:

*"I vow to prevent her betrothed from killing her, or let my fate be endless servitude to her in this life and the next. For love and for duty. Loyal. Bound to her. Subservient until my undoing. My oath demands it."*

I remembered how our souls felt as they were binding in that white hot light. All I could see was Iskur on his knees in front of me. Qateel and Aleyin on their faces in reverence or fear. Same thing, really. I remembered the way the light of that ancient power faded away with a rumble of thunder. The sickening realization that Qateel was lifeless on the ground behind us. The screams of terror from the warband's camp. Flames. Flames and smoke.

My father cleared his throat awkwardly, breaking my recollection and bringing me back to the present moment.

"Fear not, my beloved child," my father stood at my side, surveying as I surveyed the people I had once called friends and family and neighbors.

"I am not afraid," I glared at him. Iskur made a warning noise.

"My child, these are our people...*your* people," my father said emphatically, "What you have done brings joy and blessings to us all-"

"*Murderers!!!*"

My father's encouraging speech was cut short by the agonized wailing I had been waiting for. Iskur tensed.

"*Beyond loyal*," I whispered venomously, scowling at Iskur.

"Anaid..." My father's voice trembled. My eyes must have turned black again.

"My name is Argamannu now, father," I strode purposefully away towards the source of the continued accusatory screams.

"We all knew the risks," Iskur said, "He participated willingly-"

"What happened?" My father struggled to keep up.

My mother was attempting to soothe the tormented, shouting woman. She looked at me with a mix of confusion and disbelief on her face.

"Aleyin says Qateel is dead. Is it true?" My mother's voice cut through the weeping of Aleyin and Qateel's mother.

"No, it cannot be true," My father looked at me, "It cannot, can it?"

I stared back at him, trying to look brave. Trying to forget the sound the omnipotent being had made. Trying to forget everything about that night.

"*No,*" My father backed away from me, "*What have you done?*"

When I awoke, I was shaking. Where was I, even? My void. My stone. Alone. Well, alone with Virgil. All I could remember from the vision was smoke and golden light. And Iskur being there. And fear. I shook my head to clear it. Was that more of my ancestor's life? The smoke? The golden light?

It was all fractured. I was a broken glass.

Virgil was currently standing over the water's edge, peering deeply into it.

"What do you see?" I walked the four paces over to him and pushed the vision the rest of the way out of my mind.

"Water, as you have learned, has power here. And you are particularly receptive to its properties. We were not expecting that. We truly had no idea what to expect with you. I fear we planned poorly. But, here we are now." He sighed, "The water will show you things that have been. I can use myself to reflect what I know to you. I believe Iskur did this for you?"

"Yeah, he did."

"We could try that now. Or..."

"Or what?"

"Or you could look into the water and try to pull up memories of your past."

"I don't *want* to remember my past. Earth sucked shit. I had a shitty life and I fucking got killed, or did you forget?"

"Yes yes I know *that*." Virgil waved his hand in front of my face in annoyance, "I am saying your true past. The *rest* of it."

"Virgil, the rest of my past? You cannot believe the Old Dead's theory." Images of my last vision flitted into my mind. I didn't understand them, and I didn't want Virgil to start analyzing them. I longed for Iskur; he could tell me what all this meant.

"Did you not hear the Old Dead try and call up your recollection? They distrusted you and thought that you were playing the fool with them."

"Why would I be faking this? I don't know what I am doing or how I know this stuff!"

"Arga." Virgil's face was gravely serious, "Arga your soul...it is...it is not new."

I blinked at him vacantly. I recalled how the Old Dead had spoken to me:

*"We know you are inside somewhere, full of memory and dominance. Reveal yourself!"*

"*My soul is not new,* what does that mean?"

Virgil sighed again, laboriously.

"I do not wish to...*influence* your memories of your full past," Virgil said cautiously, "Perhaps before I explain further you should look into the water and see if you can recall anything on your own. But please. Do *not* touch the water. I cannot pull you out."

I nodded shakily and knelt at the edge of our stone dais. I looked into the water and willed it to show me something.

I saw the chamber of the Old Dead.

"Iskur, you are called again. Your name returns."

"It is so."

He was a pillar of blackness and the multitudes of Old Dead were an encircling chain of blue light and energy. The threefold voice was speaking from everywhere and nowhere all at once again.

"It is well that she named you thus. She knows you, it seems." He said nothing.

"Where is Arga?" They asked.

Iskur was agitated, the shape of his black form was undulating rapidly. At times it looked like a cloud, other moments nearly like a tree. Its edges were jagged and raw now, then faded to smoky ripples. "

We have given her a choice. It is not a choice that is easily made. We rely on you and the one she calls Virgil to both help her in seeing the dangers she could create if she is allowed to continue being."

"Continue *being?* You force her to choose a new death?"

Thunder resounded in the space, the blue field of Old Dead convulsed slightly.

"To call it a death is inaccurate. She would be made into new lives. Multitudes immeasurable. We are able to do that much with her consent."

"She has only just begun to live again!"

"You know the risks better than any other knows."

Iskur snapped into his human form with a shout of rage.

"How dare you suppress me! What do you fear? That I would fight you? That *she* would fight you?"

"We have no fear except for the fear of the fates of the unnumbered current and future dead. If she were to lose control and you were not able to stop her, she could tear the very fabric of time and space. You know this. You two have done this before."

"Do not lecture me on my own past! You have no understanding of the things you are speaking about! Your vision is limited and you do not see your own blind spots."

"Iskur, you are beloved among us. We do not wish to cause you harm, we seek your counsel."

"Then *why* are you not listening? Why have you forced me into my human form? And *why* will you not let her live?"

"She will live on, as an endless sea of human life."

"That is not the same and you know it."

"What is it that you would have us do? She cannot control herself."

"*Yet!*" Iskur raged, "You have not given her a chance!"

"She scarred and wounded you. She could destroy this place and all the souls in it. She is a danger."

"She is not! Nothing has been done to give her favor or help in this insurmountable task you place on her. Allow me to share this burden!"

"You do share it. For you will have to help in her undoing when she consents to it. It is only you that can deal the final blow."

Iskur's face. The look of horror and pain that contorted his expression made me reach out towards the reflected scene and gasp. Virgil clasped my hand to keep it away from the water and did not let go.

"I know that." His voice was a deep, sorrowful rumble, "I do not ask this for my sake, though the pain of that would be unbearable. I ask for her, who has been blameless in all of this. Please. Banish her with me into the most remote and protected of places. Let me help her control this curse. Please. Do not make her choose this."

The water rippled and the vision disappeared. Virgil and I had both our hands wound tightly around each other. Electricity snapped between us.

"I....I did not know you would be able to see him." Virgil's voice was a hoarse whisper.

"They are going to make him kill me?" I whispered back.

"I think he is the only one who can."

"Did you know that? That they would ask me to-? That he would be the one to-?"

"No. No, I truly had no idea." Virgil stood and pulled me up with him. He led me to the center of the stone and kept a hold of my hands. The sorrow that was welling up in the very core of my being felt like it would drown me. The sea around us began to shift slowly and sway with gentle waves.

"Arga, you will need to remain calm. We cannot go into the water." Virgil said softly, looking with concern at the sea.

"What will they do to him?"

"They will not do anything to him." Virgil let out a heavy breath, "They need him to deal with you."

I fell to my knees and let go of his hands. Just fucking great. This was what we needed.

"Arga, we do not know what they said to him. Your vision ended before they replied. They could have honored his request."

"Yeah but," I started to cry harder, "But then I freaked out and landed us here."

"Yes, that does not look good, all things considered."

"They probably think I was like, faking it and had control over my powers or the old me woke up or something and went evil and crazy."

"They certainly might think that."

Great. Besides wrecking the pretty dwelling spaces, I also fucked up my chances at redemption. The waves were becoming increasingly ferocious.

"Arga, I think you should try to make something else."

"What?"

"Make a plant. Yes. A plant. Can you make us some vegetation? This rock is so dull and lifeless."

I knew he was trying to distract me, but I also was not excited about the idea of falling into the water and giving the Old Dead the satisfaction of being right about me losing control any further.

"Alright."

I focused my mind on the feeling of creation. That small fluttering felt weak in my chest, but it was still there. I coaxed it, encouraged it, and moved my hands. I watched a sprig of cedar slowly take shape. I smiled sadly, and grew it into a small bush. I cracked the rock and made dirt fill in the crack so the tree could root. It felt good, and cleared my head. The waves had settled back to stillness when I was done.

"It is beautiful." Virgil smiled, touching one of the branches cautiously. When he outstretched his arm I noticed many small shining scars across his palms and the back of his hand. My doing, yet again. I sighed. My chest felt like it was going to crack open in sorrow.

"Virgil, we need to get back to Iskur."

"Yes, I agree." Virgil looked at me with a sympathetic gaze, "The Old Dead are unlikely to be pleased with our disappearance. But, Iskur is a wise and old being himself. He has a lot of power when he is within his own dwelling. Like you here, he has much more control of that place. He easily shielded his mind from me. I am trained to be able to explore the innermost memories of all the dead besides, of course, the Old Dead. And yet I could not penetrate his mind."

I smirked, remembering how proud Iskur had been when he had told me about how much he enjoyed keeping Virgil out.

"It would have been helpful now to know exactly how you and he ended up in the state you are in," Virgil sounded mildly bitter.

"So, do you think if he gets back home he can stop the Old Dead from hunting him down or something? Or keeping him captive?"

"I do." Virgil seemed very certain, "The Old Dead are the most powerful beings in our realm, but their power is in their ability to act as a single unified force. It is especially amplified the closer they are to the center."

"The center?"

"The place you were with them. That is the center of the realm. The nearest point to the middle of the galaxy that you can reach without ending up in a blackhole."

"Oh!" I stood up excitedly, "And Iskur's dwelling is much closer to Earth!"

"Precisely. His dwelling is actually quite proximal to Earth, and he derives his power from that proximity. Well, at least he did while your soul was still on Earth. Even still it *should* be a place where he can remain unharmed."

"But like you said, they don't want him hurt. They *need* him to deal with me." I started expanding our platform, growing it from a stone slab into a more natural island shape. I did it slowly while still speaking with Virgil, my mind racing to make fresh connections.

"Correct. Though they could detain him and keep his power diminished, in order to seek you out on their own."

"Hm. Could they find us here, do you think?"

"I think if they *could* they already would have."

"True." I looked up at my floating light. It was acting as the sun, keeping us in perpetual midday.

"It does not sit well with me at all that they would suggest you be imprisoned or unmade."

"Yeah me either." I laughed sharply, making a soft sandy beach on one side of our growing island.

"Arga, it is not funny. This is a completely unprecedented act on their part."

"What nobody has ever fucked up an oath this bad? Come on, surely someone has made some sort of promise that backfired."

"No. Not like this. Not one that results in the Old Dead fearing that someone would rip a hole in time and space and put the future of our realm at risk. They are unable to do much besides thicken and thin the veil between Earth and here, let alone tear it."

"I guess that would make me pretty fucking scary if they think I could do that. I wouldn't even know *how* to do that."

"You would not even know how to transport yourself to an uninhabited plane either, would you?" Virgil said mockingly. I threw a handful of sand at him. He held up his hand to deflect it, but none of the sand disappeared. It hit him directly in the face. I snorted.

"Still no luck with your magic, huh?"

"Obviously." He wiped his glasses on a handkerchief.

"How are you able to be a human, then?"

"I am not able to change anything about this form, I have discovered. Unfortunately."

"Why? What's the problem? Want to be taller?"

"No. I would like a clean suit."

"Wait, you just changed your human appearance by using your mind before?"

"What did you *think* I did? Laundry?"

An unexpected round of laughter broke loose between us. It was the first time I had heard him laugh.

"Well, we're stuck here and you can't change your clothes. Better be nice to me so I make you some new ones."

Virgil wiped his eyes with his sand-stained handkerchief.

"I suppose I must."

The island was now fifty yards wide with a soft sandy beach on one side that sloped up to a grassy meadow. The space was vastly crescent shaped, with a small still lagoon along the sandy shore. In the middle of the sandy beach was our original rock dais, standing like a jetty into the water. I walked out onto it and peered off the edge. The water there was clear blue, but empty. I waved my hand and a small school of silvery fish appeared. They floated together momentarily, transfixed in their own sudden appearance, then darted off together to the deep. Virgil, who had walked out beside me, snorted.

"Fish?"

"The water looked empty."

"Do not fatigue yourself with trifles. A shelter would be ideal."

I gave him an irritated look and waved my hand. A hummingbird appeared hovering above my palm. It let out an indignant squeak in his face before darting off to the grass.

"Glad to see you are in such high spirits."

"You said I need to stay calm, so I'm staying calm."

"So I did. And so you are. But, that shelter?" Virgil motioned to the flat grassy patch.

"Mh. As you wish."

I bowed teasingly as he rolled his eyes and stomped back up the tiny beach. Within a few more moments, I had erected two small stone rooms that shared a central courtyard. I put a fire pit and pillows in the middle of the courtyard, and furnished Virgil's hut with a bed and pillows before doing the same to mine. The structures were incredibly rudimentary; nothing at all like the opulence of Iskur's dwelling. I felt a pang of sadness and appreciation for how beautiful he had made the place and how hard he must have worked on it.

"It will do. You should rest again. I do not like the idea of you wearing yourself out on frivolity."

I was making flowers and cedar trees and hummingbirds around our little patio between our huts. Virgil was right. I was growing tired again. Creating things was not wearing me out like it had that first day. Perhaps the exertion of ripping us away from Iskur's home and into this limbo state had been too much? Or maybe I was just getting better and better at calling up creative energies. Whatever it was, I was finally tiring out after the day's island improvements.

"I should rest, yeah." I agreed, heading towards my room, "Do you need anything?"

"I do not need anything."

"Okay bye." I waved and the light of my world dimmed into a glorious orange hue, like a vibrant sunset. I left the ambient light partially on so that Virgil could move about and inspect all the little flowers and creatures I had made, if he wanted to. I was especially proud of being able to create the small animals and fish and bugs.

I tried not to think about Iskur or my impending doom or the fact that we were trapped in this purgatory without any idea how to get back. Instead I listened to the crickets and the hummingbirds I had just made and closed my eyes and tried to pretend everything was fine.

# XI.

*The pain was unbearable.*
*I kept laughing in his face.*
*Make him do it.*
*Make him finish it.*
*Then I could go home.*
*I could be free.*
*Purple flowers growing in the cracks of rocks.*

We were on the stone dias looking into the water again. I had woken up in a panic that Virgil had soothed by asking me if I wanted to see if I could call up a vision. On the surface of the water, I was seeing what looked like Virgil's blue light form in the center of the Old Dead's chamber. The Old Dead were asking it questions:

"*Do you understand your role?*"

"Is that you?" I whispered to Virgil while we watched together. He shook his head no, frowning.

"Who is it then?" I asked.

"Just watch the vision, I do not know." He hissed. I turned my attention back to the water.

"*I understand,*" The blue light replied in a generic, unisex tone.

"Then go. You are tasked with a duty of great importance."

"*It is an honor.*"

The vision faded and I turned to Virgil.

"Are you sure that wasn't you in the past?"

"Yes I am sure. That was not how I was tasked with your case."

"Who was it then?"

"That was a short one. Nothing was made very clear. I do not think it was the past, I think like before we are seeing things somewhat as they happen. Just catching parts of scenes."

"Yeah it seems like it."

I was lying on my stomach to get a better view into the water, Virgil was on his knees next to me.

"Virgil?"

"Yes?" He looked concerned that my voice was so shaky.

"I was alive when Iskur was, wasn't I?"

He looked at me with a soft expression for a long while.

"Arga was, yes I think so."

"And Hollis. Hollis is Arga, I think." I sat up and looked at him intently. My voice was still shaking. I hated putting my theory into words.

"I do not know." Virgil's voice was kind, "I do not understand you or Iskur."

"I see things. Things from when Iskur was alive. And it was a *long* time ago. But I was there. I remember it. I see it, I hear it, I can smell it sometimes."

"Did you have visions of his time before you two had your first shared vision? When you were Hollis, did you see things?" Virgil kept his eyes locked on mine, but took one of my hands. The sea had started to heave again with my rising anxiety.

I remembered my nightmares during thunderstorms when I had been on Earth as Hollis. I remembered the sadness and longing and heart-breaking desperation that always flooded me when thunder sounded in the distance. My mom had always said it was like I was grieving. I guess I had been.

"Yes. I saw things from then. And I felt things. The thunder it always-" My throat constricted. Virgil nodded and looked out over the water.

"I want you to show me everything you have seen, once you are calm of course." Virgil glanced nervously at the growing waves.

"I will but, what do you think I am?" My voice cracked. Really, getting emotional. Crying? About not understanding anything? Ridiculous.

"I think you are unique," Virgil smiled sadly, "And I think it is a pity that there is so much pressure on us to understand you."

"You must have some theory or something about how any of this is possible." I tried to keep my voice even.

"Well, yes, I do. But it is just a theory."

"Tell me."

Virgil looked at the waves again.

"I'm fine." I lied. He gave me a skeptical smirk.

"I will tell you my theory. Can we retire to the patio?"

I nodded. We walked hand in hand up to the stone patio and stood for a moment looking at each other's jet black eyes.

"This is only a theory." Virgil asserted.

"I know. Please?" I wanted to know what he thought had made me into this shattered, fragmented creature.

He proceeded with another heavy sigh:

"You and Iskur both lived on Earth at the same time, thousands of years before you died. As you know, souls are made of energy and cannot be created or destroyed. You and Iskur, you were both very capable humans. You were able to commune with the dead, speak to ancestors freely, and gain knowledge of the past and present far outside of what a normal human could. The Old Dead spoke with you often. I am not sure of what, but I know that at least Iskur as a human was known to them when he was alive."

"At some point, you two decided to push further than merely speaking with the dead. One or both of you wanted something more. As you searched for that *something more*, a vow was made between you. I do not know the terms. I do not know if it was related to your search for abilities or not. I do know that in a very unfortunate event, you died. Your soul was separated from your body, but bound to your lineage and unable to pass into the Otherworld."

"Why?"

"I do not know. The inability to pass into the Otherworld can sometimes happen. Souls will remain on Earth for a short time due to unfinished business, like wanting to wait for a spouse or loved one to make the journey with them. Or because they made some sort of exchange. But those are all relatively temporary."

"What do you mean, exchange?"

"Well, some humans will forsake the afterlife in desire to protect something. Their own tomb, perhaps. Their home, their country. Humans call it haunting, we call it Remaining. Souls that Remain on Earth do not grow in power or ability in the way that souls in the Otherworld do. They have some abilities, but the results of Remaining are varied and limited."

"These are ghosts, yeah?"

"Yes. Often that is how they are interpreted."

"So like, when psychics are talking to the dead, are they talking to remaining souls?"

"Psychics very rarely speak to anything anymore. Oracles and prophets used to be common and revered. Their ability to predict the future or see the past was due to them being people like you and Iskur. Ones who could reach out to ancestors in the Otherworld and ask for guidance. They were not really seeing the future so much as they were tapping into the wealth of knowledge of all those who died before them. But that skill became less and less common as the Old Dead tightened up the connections to Earth. The veil is much less porous now, and humans have much less desire to try and correctly converse with the dead."

"You keep saying people like Iskur and me, I wasn't born thousands of years ago."

"Technically, your soul was. And then, we shall call whatever happened to kill you *The Event*. When The Event happened and your soul was stripped from your body, it did not get the option to come to the Otherworld. Instead, your soul immediately latched on to one of your line. A relative, perhaps. And your soul continued to travel with them until they died. The part of the life that they lived left, and you remained. Attaching to the next in line and so on and so forth until we come to modern times. And you."

"What happened?"

"That is the strange thing. When you died on Earth, the piece of the soul that had been traveling in your family for centuries merged with you. You and your ancestor and all the lives she lived are one because of the way you died."

"Because I was murdered? Was nobody else murdered?"

"Apparently not in the *right way*."

"What's the right way to get fucking murdered, Virgil?"

"Whatever way you did. I suppose."

My mood grew foul. Outside of the sheltered harbor of our little island lagoon, the sea was starting to boil even more.

"I am not trying to upset you, Arga."

"I know. It's just upsetting no matter what." I muttered, "I hate him."

"It is not ideal to be murdered."

"No shit. How did you die?" I asked bitterly.

"Tuberculosis." He said, looking like he surprised himself at how quickly he had answered.

"Oh." I didn't really know what to do with this information, "I'd take that over strangulation, I guess."

"It was not fun, either. Dying rarely is something a human desires."

"Yeah." We paused for a moment, lost in our own thoughts.

"Virgil?"

"Mh."

"Do you have family in the Otherworld?"

He made the saddest face. I was not expecting that. I was about to apologize and tell him to forget I asked when he spoke:

"Well, no. My life on Earth was sordid and lonely. I did not know my family well. I chose instead to pass my time here by being the first friendly face that the new dead see in the Otherworld. As soon as I was able, I requested to become a Greeter. Being greeted into death was one of the most kind and welcoming experiences I ever had. After the lonely life I led and the slow painful death, it was such a joy to discover something so vast and paradise-like existed. I wanted to offer that to others. It was one of my greatest accomplishments."

Fuck. My chest clenched with anguish. I squeezed his hand tightly.

"You should still be proud of that. You will get to greet people again."

"No Arga, I have the feeling I will not be greeting any more dead for a long time."

"We'll get out of here! We can figure out how, I know we can."

"It is not that, Arga. I am breaking the codes and oaths I swore to uphold by telling you all of what I am telling you. The Old Dead are acting strange. There is something very suspicious about all of this. I have been dead for long enough to understand the natural order of this realm, and what they are doing flies in the face of all that is established and safe and good in this place. We are all dead. We do not force anyone into an eternity of isolation or certain unmaking. No, even if there were a future in which I would be allowed to be a greeter again, I simply do not think I could do it while knowing that it is built on injustice."

"You mean if the Old Dead were to reward you for turning me in, you would never forgive yourself?"

"Yes. Exactly that."

I released his hand and sat down in the grass along the patio. The sea had calmed. I made some butterflies. Virgil watched me work with a sad smile on his face.

"I'm really sorry I fucked everything up for you."

"Arga, we have all just ended up in the middle of something I do not think any of us fully understand. I think you and Iskur made mistakes thousands of years ago, and over the centuries those mistakes have somehow compounded in a way neither of you intended. The soul you inherited or absorbed gave you great power. A power that Iskur and you are both bound to. And the only way that the Old Dead see fit to make this realm safe from that unintended outcome is to destroy it. Which is what I cannot figure out. Why would they need to destroy it?"

"They are scared of it?"

"They are the most powerful of all the Dead. They have been dead the longest, and together wield the most power. They have nothing to fear."

"If you are dead for a certain time can you join them?"

"What?"

"Like, is there a constant addition to their forces? Are there more and more Old Dead?"

Virgil frowned.

"No, I do not think so."

"They are a fixed number?"

"Yes, as far as I know."

"So, if Iskur and I together overpower them, couldn't that be a threat?"

"Hm." Virgil rubbed his forehead, "But why would strength be a concern if you abide by the rules of the realm and do no harm?"

A sinking feeling grew in my chest as a realization dawned on me.

"What if we had tried it before?"

"What do you mean?"

"What if," I was on my feet, pacing nervously across the patio, "The thing that fucked my soul over and passed the powers down over the generations, what if *The Event* was Iskur and I trying to do something to the Old Dead? Something they didn't like?"

Virgil started pacing opposite me.

"That could be something."

"And when Iskur died and submitted to be a good boy, they thought it was over? Because my soul never came up here?"

Virgil was nodding vigorously.

"Arga, I have something to show you. I think you are ready to see it."

I felt a nervous flip inside of me as Virgil looked at me intently.

"Come with me to the water, but when I show you this, please do not touch the water." Virgil instructed as we hurried back to the beach. I nodded obediently and knelt down at the edge of the stone.

"They are really going to hate me showing you this." He muttered as he entered his blue light form. The sound of wind rushed as he plunged into the water.

His memory reflections glowed on the mirror-like surface of the water. Virgil was walking with the gravel-voiced eagle Old Dead man. They were alone in a hall filled with ornate basins of water.

"You are being shown this in case she assumes this form." The man spoke dryly, "Or if she is able to project her dreams and visions and share this image with you."

Virgil nodded. They stopped at a basin.

"Animdugud, thank you for showing me these. She is at rest in the dwelling now. I have been unable to see any dreams she is having or has had since arriving. She had shielded herself from me, like the other one has."

Animdugud nodded slowly, moving his hands over the basin.

"Urgula has predicted as much. The dwelling on the ancient one does not allow us for ease of exploration of their minds."

The waters of the basin churned and a small, glowing figure about a foot tall emerged. It was like a statuette, small but detailed and showing the full form of a woman. Color flooded the figure slowly, filling it from the feet upwards. She wore a sumptuous purple cloak, wrapped about her body and belted at the waist. Her hair was jet black and plaited intricately. Her face was fierce and serious. Her face was my face.

"This is the ancient one, the one whose powers have fused with this new dead. She was known to the one whose dwelling you are in. Iskur he was called. Though he has forsaken that name. This new dead may know him as such if she retains the memories of the ancient one. See if she calls him by that name."

"I have not seen if she knows him, as he was not in human form."

"Request that he enter a human form that is similar to how the ancient one would have known him. It may help to remind her. Observe her reactions to him closely. And his reactions to her."

"Yes, Animdugud."

"One more thing before you return."

"I am your servant, Animdugud."

"Do not trust them."

The memory faded and Virgil reappeared at my side.

"So you weren't suspicious then when that asshole was all like, *don't trust them?*"

"Arga you have to understand, it was terrifying for everyone when you appeared. Iskur was confined to his dwelling by his agreement to the Old Dead. None ever visited him, and you *appeared* there when you died. I was the nearest Greeter and was dispatched to care for you immediately, and the Old Dead were shocked that any of this was happening. Nothing shocks them. They have seen everything."

I snorted in disbelief.

"Yeah, because I'm so scary."

"Arga. His dwelling was rife with repellant for other souls. What I understand now is he agreed to be isolated when he died, and the Old Dead left him alone. You broke through all those protections and wards and barriers and arrived in *his dwelling* without any knowledge of how to break down those walls. Once you were there, the Old Dead had to exert considerable effort to even dispatch me there to care for you."

"Really?"

"It is true. That place is so exhausting to be, and you just thrived there. Your arrival made it incredibly difficult for me to leave as well. You had an extremely strong pull on the two of us. And you saw how several times you have been able to impose your will on Iskur."

"So Iskur couldn't leave either? The Old Dead kept him there as part of their agreement?"

"Before you arrived, it seems it was more of a self-imposed, agreed upon exile. He might have been able to leave, but we never pushed it very hard. He said he felt such a strong pull from your presence that leaving would have taken a great deal of strength. We were not sure what would happen, so we focused the training instead on stabilizing you."

"Wait wait wait, hold up, do you think that since I'm gone he can feel me? Is there still a pull?"

"I do not know. Maybe?"

"Could the Old Dead feel a pull from me?"

"Not that they ever mentioned to me."

"So if I try to reach out to Iskur do you think he would feel it?"

Virgil considered this for a moment.

"I don't want to try and travel back to him since like, to travel here I was super fucking pissed off and upset but I *could* try to get him here instead?"

Virgil put a hand to his forehead as he thought intently.

"Reaching out to him across the void might be something to try," he said.

I whooped, jumped up quickly, raced up to our huts and into the long grass behind them. I wasn't going to wait around and let him change his mind. Virgil followed slowly behind.

"What are you doing?"

"I'm going to try to connect with him."

"You should be closer to the water."

"I want to try it up here."

"Fine." Virgil drug one of the chairs I had made for our patio over to the edge of the meadow and observed me nervously.

I settled myself in the grass and listened to the chirping and humming of all the little beasts I had made. I spent a long time focusing inwardly, trying to find the connection between us that I knew was somewhere inside me. The longer I searched the more dismayed I became. It wasn't coming easily. I wasn't feeling any sort of pull or call.

I focused on my memories of him. His face, twisted in fury and pain, yelling at the Old Dead in the vision I had. My anxiety sizzled across my shoulders.

"Whatever you are doing, Arga, do not do that." Virgil suggested.

I gritted my teeth and shifted my focus.

Iskur's face, pulling me out of the pool the first time. More pain, but mixed with pride. The way he had beamed with pride when I made my tree. His face as he was admiring my tree. The kiss.

My body flushed with a ghost of the euphoria I had felt in that moment. I knew I was shifting out of my human form, and I let it happen. It was a calm experience, a steady fading out of the solid and into the ethereal. I needed this, it felt so soothing.

I fixated on that warm euphoric feeling. How our bodies had first physically met, then shifted and collided together in what had felt like an infinite dance. I reached for the parts of the memory where I felt him strongest: the moment our forms met each other and were mingling in temporary ecstasy.

Trapping that feeling, I shifted myself slightly back into my human form, but didn't transition all the way. I felt fuzzy around the edges, but the connection to that glorious feeling was strongest when I was outside of my human shape.

"To the water." I said, my voice sounding like a swelling sea. Virgil nodded and followed after me dutifully.

On the stone, I lowered myself to the edge of the water. Unsure what to do next, I paused.

"Try placing your hands over the water, but do not touch it," Virgil offered.

I obliged and focused that feeling downwards, pushing it from my chest to my arms to the very tips of my fingers. A hazy energy field bloomed around my barely-formed hands, like heat rising in waves off the hot pavement in summertime. I released the haze and it descended onto the water. Pulling myself fully into my human form, I peered over the edge with Virgil to see what appeared on the water's surface.

The surface of the water undulated slightly, then smoothed over again. At first nothing appeared and my heart began to sink. Why didn't it work? Impatience flared up inside me. Then the water clouded over and turned black, followed by silvery grey. We saw the galaxy unfolding rapidly in the reflection, zooming ever inward through gas and light and dust.

In an instant, we were seeing the view from high above the dwelling, careening closer and closer. Then, through stone and brick to the room in which we had done my training. I saw my cedar tree in its entirety for a moment, before the vision settled amongst the branches. Its spiny, needle-like leaves laced the edges of the reflection like a frame. The room was empty.

"What now?" I whispered to Virgil.

"I am not sure, I have never done something like this before."

"Can he hear me?"

"Try speaking. Try calling him."

I dug deep inside myself and tried to find our connection again. Grasping at the spark, I spoke:

"Iskur."

The water trembled at my words.

"Iskur. Are you there?"

A resounding crack of thunder made me jump backwards. Then I saw his face.

"Arga!" His voice sounded strained and fearful.

"Iskur!"

He faced the tree.

"Where are you?" He looked suspiciously at the tree, "Is it you? I cannot see you."

"It's me! Iskur, I'm with Virgil. We're-"

"Arga. Stop. I-I must be sure it is you. Things have happened and I must be sure."

My chest wrenched in fear.

"Iskur, it's me!" Why didn't he trust it was me?

"It is both of us, how could anyone else reach you in this way?" Virgil snapped.

Iskur smiled a thin smile.

"Hello Virgil. Certainly it would be difficult to reach me here. Especially now. But I cannot be too sure. Arga, tell me something only you know."

"I-I don't know." My face felt hot. Virgil was staring at me.

"When was the first time we touched?"

I kept my eyes glued to the water, refusing to look at Virgil's judgemental stare.

"Uh, when you pulled me from the pool. No. No, I was in the garden. I was in the garden watching the blue light. Watching Virgil talk to the Old Dead. I didn't know that then. But you, you came up behind me and took me back inside."

"Arga," he breathed with a sigh.

I smiled, tears welling up in my eyes.

"Iskur, come find me," I begged.

"Are they detaining you? I have felt you since you left. Distant but pulling at me. I have tried to reach you and call you back to me but-"

"No, I'm safe. We're safe. Someplace else. I have not heard you or felt you, I think I need to call you to me."

He nodded.

"When you speak I feel you but you are still so far away. Somewhere I do not think I can go unless you show me the way." He closed his eyes and shifted into his black light form.

"Show me, Arga. Bring me to you."

His voice sent shivers down my skin. I looked at Virgil. He shrugged.

"Try." He said, continuing to observe closely. His eyes were black.

I shifted out of my body easily this time, like sliding out of a heavy coat. I looked at Iskur in the water, and latched onto the connection between us. I felt him, even over the endless expanse between us. I felt him calling now, I could hear his thunder rolling through me and resounding across the oceans. I called back and the connection intensified. Virgil drew back up the beach and shifted out of his human form as well.

I hovered above the stone as the ocean seethed and boiled with my efforts. Our light went out, only Virgil and I glowed. The sea raged and crashed as I shouted across the void to Iskur.

"*I am here.*" I cried. I heard him calling back distantly. The churning waters made the vision choppy and impossible to make out. I kept calling and gathering power to feed to the connection between us.

But it wasn't enough.

I could feel the connection fading. It wavered despite how hard I clung to it. I screamed and roared like an animal in pain, binding myself to the now feeble connection in anguish. I needed to amplify my power. I was frantic as my being floated above the ground, levitating higher and higher with the continued effort of keeping the connection.

I knew what I had to do.

I heard Virgil's wind voice howling in protest as I rocketed downwards towards the waves. Without heeding his warnings, I plunged into the water.

The water instantly deadened the violence of the storm that was still raging above me. I felt electricity like fire crackling through every part of my vaporous state. This was the first time I had been outside of human form in the water. I felt the expanse of my power unfold at a frightening speed. Before it could slip out of my grasp, I muscled the energy and applied it to the connection between Iskur and I. It felt like I was wrenching a door open against a hurricane, but it slowly gave way. All at once I felt the full intensity of Iskur's call to me. It was a powerful current I was not ready for, but welcomed hastily. He was singing and calling across the cold expanse of space, and I sang back to him. I could do this. I could bring him here. He was on his way.

As our voices combined, I felt myself shrinking back into my human form. Above me a bright light split our sky. I saw it distorted in the heaving waves that I was far below. Hold on to it, hold on to the connection. Hold on. I was sinking faster, losing my ability to control the enormous weight of power I had been wielding.

Darkness clouded my vision and it felt like lightning was striking me over and over. No, not darkness, not now. Had I done enough? The pain was unbelievable. I faintly saw a comet cut through the light in the sky and plummet into the ocean above me. Down it sank, and I could feel it being besieged by the whips of power radiating off of me. I closed my eyes. Something held me.

He was here.

# XII.

Lightning danced around them as the sudden storm enveloped their group. With hands raised, they sang together. The harmony wavered, straying as each individual sang their own refrain. It was chaos and resolution as the song came together. Wind began to whip the hillside, and a lightning bolt caught a tree down the hill on fire. The flames engulfed the tree, but nobody noticed. They were all looking upwards.

A golden light was glowing in the cloud that had gathered above them. The light seemed to writhe and boil, gathering intensity as the group continued to concentrate their energy and focus above. In a flash there was a golden beam piercing from the cloud to the ground in the center of their circle. It swirled and brightened, becoming a blinding flash.

Everything went dark.

"-certain you were not followed?"

"Silence!"

"This is important! Were you followed?"

Thunder and wind screamed at each other as Iskur and Virgil argued bitterly.

"*Will you leave us alone?!*"

I peeked through heavy eyelids. It was dark. We were lying in the sand, Iskur and I, entangled and battered. Virgil was somewhere nearby, blustering away in panic.

"You're here." My voice cracked pathetically as I grabbed Iskur's arms. I had done it. I had brought him to us. I thought my chest was going to crack open from the happiness that filled it.

"Sh. Sh. Yes. I am here. You did it, you did all of this. You are so strong. So strong." He pressed his face against the top of my head and breathed raggedly. The journey had clearly not been an easy one for him either. I cried in relief and let myself fade back to darkness.

*I was smiling.*
*I was crying.*
*Someone hit me hard across the face.*
*Purple flowers growing in the cracks of sidewalks.*
*Purple flowers withering where they grew.*
*Waves crashing.*
*Thunder roaring.*
*A golden light that blinded us all.*

When I awoke again, I was in my bed. It was still dark. I sat up slowly, and cautiously tried to make some light. I felt a searing pain when I tried to call the creating forces, and shrank away from the task. That sucked. I was not up for that yet.

"Arga," His voice was warm and rumbling.

He was sitting in the dark across the small room from me. I leapt from the bed and flung myself at him, wracking sobs instantly taking a hold of me. I didn't feel any shame in my tears. He was here.

"You're here, you're here," I kept crying.

He held me tenderly and ran his hands down my back. I tried to look at his face but could hardly see it in the darkness. I reached up and touched his cheek. He was smiling tearfully. I pressed my cheek against his and let our tears mingle.

"You brought me here."

"You were in the water." I said, recalling the last few moments of the effort of bringing him here.

"I was. So were you. Do you remember?"

"I do."

"You are so brave. So strong."

"Iskur, at the end it hurt me so bad. Did I hurt you again? The power, I-I couldn't hold on at the end."

"Sh. Sh. No, you did so well."

"Did I hurt you?" I asked again, fearing the answer he was avoiding giving. I must have hurt him.

"I am here. You brought me here, that is what matters."

"How bad is it?"

"Arga."

"No. Tell me. Can you make a light? Can you show me?"

Iskur put his hands on my face. I enjoyed the warmth for a moment before resuming my line of questioning.

"Can you make a light?"

"I can."

"Please?"

"No."

"Is it that bad?" My voice squeaked in sorrow, "Iskur?"

"Arga, I would endure this a thousand times over to be with you."

"Show me."

He took my hands and placed them on his arms.

"Feel." He instructed.

I traced his features slowly. I felt the scars I knew of, the way his skin was more glossy in those places. I reached up and put my hands on his face. Nothing seemed different. My heart grew lighter, maybe I hadn't destroyed him so utterly.

His eyes closed as I traced over them, down his cheeks and followed the lines of his tears. His ears, his jaw, his mouth. He was smiling as I felt his lips carefully. I smiled too. Then I moved down his jaw again and to his neck. I tensed, finding a new wound.

This scar was a welt, unlike the others that laid flat on his skin. The old ones only offered a different, shining texture where I had whipped him with my lashes of energy. This one was a raised ridge as thick as one of my fingers. My breath caught as I traced it downwards from his neck to his chest. He was wearing a shirt, but I could feel the injury radiating beneath the thin linen. He put a hand over mine to stop my trembling.

"A price willingly paid." He whispered in my ear.

"I'm so sorry." I shook and sniffled back a sob, "How far does it go?"

He moved fluidly, shrugging out of the shirt. He took my hand and replaced it on his chest. The scar ran outwards like a starburst from the base of his neck. Tendrils like roots wound across his chest and down his torso. I traced it lower as it crossed itself and twined around to his back.

"Show me." I breathed, pulling my hand away slowly, "You said you can make light here."

Iskur waved a small flame into existence and sent it floating above us. The light cast the scars into high relief and sent gnarled shadows across us both. The old and new scars gleamed in the light. I saw that the new scar wrapped up across the underside of his chin and around his neck and into the back of his hairline. I reached up to the back of his neck and followed the scar through his hair. It crossed his scalp, and emerged at the edge of his forehead.

"I'm so sorry, Iskur."

"Stop." He took my hands and brought them in front of us, "Arga, stop. I did not want to show you for this reason."

I leaned forward to rest my head on his scarred chest. We sat for a few moments like that, breathing together.

"Why was Virgil asking if you were followed?" I asked softly, fear seeping back into me.

"He is scared. I was not followed."

"Who would follow you?"

"Mh. There are some."

"What do you mean?" I looked up at him.

"Arga, we both need to rest before we discuss this." His voice was strained and exhaustion was pulling at me again as well.

"Fine." I stood up and pulled him with me. He followed obediently, "But when we wake up, I want answers."

"Of course." Iskur let go of my hand as I climbed into bed. I reached for him again. He climbed into the bed next to me. We slept together, breathing as one.

The dwelling looked horrible. There was rubble and debris everywhere. The hall of columns looked like an ancient ruin. The only thing that stood unharmed was my cedar, alone in the training hall. The floor was singed and charred.

A lone blue light bobbed through the destruction.

"Arga or Iskur: is one of you well enough to give us some significant light yet?" Virgil asked in an impatient but forcefully polite tone from the patio some time later. Iskur must have woken up first, he was tracing shapes in the blankets against my back absently. I looked up at him and he smirked, closing his eyes to feign sleep as Virgil came to the door. I clamped my eyes closed tightly as well.

"I know you are awake," Virgil said accusingly.

I rolled over to look at him. Iskur's fire orb was still bobbing around the room.

"I don't think I can." I said, too afraid to try to create anything still. The searing pain was not something I wanted to revisit.

"And I cannot make a light such as was in my dwelling, to illuminate the whole sky." Iskur did not turn to look at Virgil, "But I will make you many fires when I awake."

Virgil snorted indignantly and walked back toward his hut.

Iskur drew me closer. I traced the scar on his neck.

"Leave it." He murmured, looking at me through half-opened eyes. I withdrew my hand.

"Virgil told me more of what he knows about us."

"He has decided to be helpful?" Iskur opened one eye and raised an eyebrow in surprise.

"He doesn't like the choices the Old Dead gave me. He thinks it's strange and unfair."

"It is. He is correct."

"I saw them talking to you."

"You did?" Iskur opened his eyes fully and rolled onto his side to face me.

"I was able to see visions in the water. Two of them, both in the Old Dead's chamber. I saw you and heard what they said."

"I have never been their favorite son."

"Their son?"

"Not like humans think. No, we are all more or less their children. That is how they see their role. To be protective of us all. When someone threatens the whole pack..." He trailed off.

"So, they don't like you?"

"Arga, I made some very serious mistakes on Earth. What does Virgil know? What has he told you?"

"Well, he was pissed off that you shielded most of your past from him."

Iskur was very pleased with this. His self-satisfied smile made me smile.

"He knew nothing specific?"

"He has a theory. That we shredded my ancestor's soul and sent it down my family line and that for some reason all the powers that had been growing for thousands of years got given to me."

"That is putting it very kindly. I am glad he is being so generous with his explanation."

"What does that mean? Do you know something?"

"Arga, I have seen much. No, I have seen *all*."

"I don't understand."

"I apologize, there is much we need to discuss, but you must regain your strength."

"How am I going to understand why the Old Dead want to kill me if I don't know what happened on Earth?"

"When I heard your voice in the tree, Arga. I was so happy." He stopped and closed his eyes, "Arga, I was sure that they had kept you when I came back to the dwelling."

"I didn't mean to leave."

"There was so much destruction. The floors, the walls, cracked and crumbling. It looked like they had fought you and taken you."

My chest tightened with guilt. I ruined everything like always.

"I was looking for you, I didn't mean to destroy your house, I'm so sorry."

"No no, that can be rebuilt. I was certain that they were keeping you. That they had brought me to speak with them in order to separate us and trap you."

"No, I just freaked out and came here."

"How did you do it?"

"I really don't know. I just lost control."

"Well, I am so happy that you did. It is a good place to be. They cannot feel you here, that is for certain."

"Why did Virgil think someone could follow you?"

"What was your second vision?"

"Answer my question." I would not be deterred. He was deflecting and I hated it.

"No, Arga, tell me the vision." He was very serious, and his face was intense.

"Uh, it was short. There was a blue light with them. They were telling it that it had a job."

"What was the job?"

"I didn't see that."

Iskur nodded gravely.

"Mh. And you only saw a blue light?"

"Yeah, what was it?"

"A hunter."

My breath caught in my chest.

"A hunter? What does that mean?"

"Yes. A hunter has skills bestowed by the Old Dead. They are very clever. Virgil saw this vision with you?"

"Yeah, why does that matter? Can the hunter find us here?"

"Did he tell you anything about the vision?"

"No, he seemed just as confused as I was."

Iskur snorted and stood up.

"You think he knows something?" I stood with him.

"I think he *should* know something."

We walked out of my shelter. Iskur began lighting more floating fires and sent them hovering about the island. Virgil walked up from the beach when he saw us on the patio.

"Arga, that was incredibly foolish and impressive." Virgil said in a slightly complimentary tone.

"Wow, thanks." I glared at Virgil. He and I had been getting along so well before, why was he being an asshole again now?

"To be able to call Iskur to us-" Virgil continued cooly.

"The second vision." Iskur interrupted, crossing his arms at Virgil.

"What about it?"

"Do you have any idea who they are sending?"

"I did not recognize the hunter, no."

"You *knew* it was a hunter?" I rounded on Virgil.

"I was suspicious."

"Why didn't you *tell* me that the Old Dead had hunters?" I stepped at him. That fucking little jerk was *still* keeping secrets.

"Arga. What good would it have done? You are fragile as it is and to share frightening revelations about which I was not certain would have done *nothing* to improve your stability."

I rolled my eyes. Firelight flickered across the three of us.

"Did the hunter come to your dwelling?" Virgil asked Iskur.

"Yes. But it could not enter. When I saw you two were gone I put up further protections."

"Good." Virgil nodded approvingly, "Your dwelling is hard on them. They are not suited to do much in the far reaches of our realm unless they properly prepare."

Iskur nodded.

"Much in our favor."

"So, what do we do now?" I asked.

Both Virgil and Iskur looked at me.

"We stay here." Iskur said, sounding confused, "What do you think we are going to do?"

"I wasn't sure if we needed to go back-"

"No!" Both Virgil and Iskur said in unison.

"Okay! Sorry." I put my hands up in apology.

"Arga, this is a place far from the view of the Old Dead. We can remain here and help you gain control of your skills before we ever consider going back."

"On this Virgil is right," Iskur said, placing his hand in mine, "You have made us a safe refuge."

"Okay, yeah." I looked around the island, "It's uh, not much right now."

"We have time to expand the place and work on your skills." Virgil said understandingly, "I am somewhat frustrated that I seem to be the only one here who cannot *create* anything."

"My creation is limited. I cannot make a large light, it seems. But I can make the smaller things you need while Arga recovers." Iskur offered.

"Wonderful. I would like a notebook, pen-" Virgil continued listing small items and Iskur began making them for him. I walked over to one of the chairs and fidgeted with its woven back impatiently.

"So this hunter, what is it? It can't come here, right?" I asked as Iskur finished the last colorful handkerchief for Virgil.

"No. Only someone with a very intense connection with you can feel you in this place. I doubt if Virgil were outside of here that he could feel you." Iskur wagged his eyebrows teasingly, "It is just me that you can call through the emptiness of space to your secret paradise."

I smiled. That was a relief. Finally something was going right.

"It seems that the connection to get here must be a strong, two way connection. And for others to sense it, you must be exerting yourself a great deal. Iskur could not fully feel you until you tried to contact him with all your strength." Virgil was hurriedly making notes in his new journal.

"Good."

"Yes, Arga. This is a very good thing you have made." Iskur came to my side and looked at me intently, "Do you need anything?"

"I just want to talk with you," I shot a look at Virgil who was completely absorbed in his note writing.

Iskur nodded and we wandered to the grass field. The island somehow felt even smaller with three of us here. Iskur made another orb of fire for us. It followed as we walked through the small meadow. Hummingbirds flew out of hiding in our wake. Iskur gasped in surprise.

"You made these?"

"Yeah! And crickets and butterflies and some fish!" I added excitedly as Iskur held out a hand for a hummingbird to land on.

"Arga, your powers are wonderful to behold."

"You make hummingbirds all the time."

He laughed.

"I have had countless eons to practice. You have had seconds in comparison."

"Maybe I'm just better at it than you." I bantered back.

"That is what I am saying."

"Well, thanks. Does it make you sad? That I am so much *better* at it than you?" I teased.

"Yes."

Iskur's sudden tone shift took me by surprise. The look on his face was pained. That was not the reaction I was expecting. What was this?

"Oh, I'm sor-"

"Arga, I am sad that you have the burden of centuries of power and have not had the chance to learn to live under the weight of it all. But," His tone turned lighter again, "It is a joy to see you creating beauty from this struggle."

I didn't fully understand him but I smiled, and he smiled back. I held out my hand for him and he took it in both of his. Turning my palm upwards, he delicately traced the lines across my hand. A shudder ran through me at his touch. He smiled wider, looking mischievous. He squatted so he was closer to my height and continued to hold my gaze.

That look in his eyes, what was that? What was he doing? Nobody ever tried to seduce me when they'd already *had* me. And Iskur had had me, hadn't he? There hadn't been much time to think about those moments after I made the tree. Passion I was used to, but this? All romance left any of my other dirtbag lovers on Earth as soon as we had been intimate. Iskur bent down and brought his mouth to my palm, kissing delicately. I put my hand on his head and pushed it back so he was looking up at me.

"What are you doing?" I asked quietly.

He grinned and moved his head back down to my hand, kissing it more forcefully.

"Not touch?" He asked in a tone that made my skin flush. He continued to kiss my hand, my wrist, my arm.

"Iskur-"

He lowered himself further until he was on his knees in front of me. He released my hand cautiously and tipped his head to one side with a playful smile.

"Not touch?" He asked again.

"I don't understand this." I said hoarsely.

"Which part?"

"Any of it. You knew my ancestors right? And the one that my power comes from. Who was she? Who was she *to you?*" Why was he making me ask this?

Iskur smiled and nodded in understanding.

"Ah. You think I love a memory. Arga, no. It is not so easy to explain. But, I knew you then. I have known you in every lifetime you have lived. I will know you across every star, in every form, no matter where you hide. The ancestor of yours that has been spoken of is not an ancestor how humans think of it. I saw many visions in the water when you brought me here. I have gained knowledge that some," He looked to where Virgil was sitting, "Would do unspeakable things to obtain."

"What do you mean?"

"You are not a fragment of a soul that was inherited. It is not a line of blood. The one from whom your powers were gifted had no children."

"But the Old Dead and Virgil, they all said it was an ancestor of mine that knew you and whose soul had been passed down through centuries. What were they talking about?"

"Arga," Iskur's eyes were gleaming and his smile had a hint of danger to it. He came close to my ear and whispered, "We are not human. We made ourselves into something new."

My skin prickled. I saw the flash of golden light in my mind again. Fire. Smoke. The sound of waves and thunder.

"What do you mean?" I whispered back, flushed with an excitement I did not understand. Iskur looked back towards the patio where Virgil sat lost in his writing. He put his face against mine again and spoke in a hushed tone.

"We made ourselves into gods."

"Gods?!" I could not whisper. Iskur put his hand over my mouth and laughed quietly. I swatted him away.

"I thought we failed. But we did not, Arga. You are here. After so many ages, you are here at last." I hadn't seen him this giddy before.

My eyes widened and my breath caught in my chest.

"*Gods*?" I hissed.

"I will tell you everything, Arga. But," He straightened up and spoke louder, "We need to make a bigger island."

"I could not agree more!" Virgil was striding across the grass towards us.

Virgil began listing his suggestions for how to improve the space but I could not hear him. Gods?! I stared at Iskur with my mouth opening and closing like a fish. He winked at me. Good thing Virgil was too busy with his home improvement planning to notice me. He took off walking towards the beach, describing some sort of walking path. Iskur winked at me again, took my arm and pulled me along to follow behind Virgil.

Gods?

I needed to get time alone with Iskur as soon as possible. He had some serious explaining to do.

# XIII.

I skur and I spent time expanding and improving our island. I could only work in short sprints at first, but my recovery progressed nicely. Iskur deferred to me on every creation. I grew weary of his constant requests for my thoughts on some new shoreline or tree or part of our house but he insisted that the space should be exactly how I want it.

"It is your dwelling." He repeated for the millionth time as I rolled my eyes.

"But I *like* what you make! You can just make whatever you want."

He waved his hand across two palm trees and a woven hammock appeared. He ushered me over and demanded I lie with him. Exhausted, I obeyed. Not long before I had finally remade the light that illuminated the whole expanse. Virgil was very pleased.

I rested my head on Iskur's bare chest. The terrible scar had healed over to a less raised state, but it still gleamed brightly against his undamaged skin. He was so proud of it and had shown me how it could be seen even in his non-human state. When he was a black pillar of light, it showed as a silvery streak that flashed like lightning. He loved it, but it still made my chest tight if I thought about it too hard.

"How do you feel?" He asked, running his hand through my hair.

"Tired."

"Mh."

Virgil was not far from us. He was sitting just up the sandy beach on the original stone dais.

"What's *he* doing?" My eyes were closed. The hammock rocked soothingly.

"He's writing."

I sighed. We hadn't dared to talk about the past since Iskur had first revealed our secret to me. That felt like ages ago. Even with the island being larger now, and our rooms being much more private and house-like, Virgil was always near. There had been no easy way to wander off too far. He was always seeking us out to have this or that made for his rooms.

"Does he *never sleep?*" I was so tired of waiting to talk.

"Not yet. But he will." Iskur observed Virgil through half opened eyes. "We will have time soon."

"I hope so," I said, trying not to sound too bitter.

Iskur kissed the top of my head delicately.

"Are you going to sleep?" He asked.

"I may."

"Would you like to go home?"

"Here is good." I said lazily, looking out over the ocean.

"You did so well. A light is no small thing to make."

"Thanks. Yeah, it takes a lot of effort doesn't it?"

"Mh."

"Why do you think you couldn't make a light here besides the fire?"

"It is your realm. The light has to come from you."

"Is that how all dwellings are? Only the one whose dwelling it is can make the light?"

"I have never been to any dwelling but my own until now. I do not know if it is the same everywhere."

"You agreed to be confined to your place? Or did the Old Dead force you into it?"

Iskur leaned back to look at me.

"Where did you hear that?"

"Virgil."

"Of course." He laughed, "They certainly would give him as many points against me as they could. Yes, I agreed to the confinement. They did not force me, I suggested it. When I died they did not know what to do with me. I was the most powerful soul to cross into the Otherworld then. Until you, of course."

He glanced over at Virgil.

"You should get some rest." He laid back and closed his eyes. "We will be able to talk soon."

There was no point in asking more questions. Might as well give in and get rest. We swayed gently in the hammock as I drifted off to sleep.

*Wind whipping through oak trees.*
*Thunder echoing against rocks.*
*A golden light blinding everyone.*
*Someone hit me across the face.*
*I was smiling.*
*I was laughing.*
*Waves crashing.*
*Purple flowers growing in the cracks of rocks.*

"Arga." Iskur had his hand on the side of my face.

"*What's wrong?*" I gasped, suddenly awake and staring at him tensely.

"Sh. No," He laughed, "Sorry, no it is nothing bad."

"What is it then?" I slapped his hand away. Embarrassing. Panicking all the time.

"Virgil went back to his rooms." Iskur grinned wildly.

"Oh!" I sat up too quickly and dumped us both out of the hammock and into the sand.

"Sh! He has not been gone long. He left us to sleep."

I let out a giddy laugh and climbed on top of him, pinning his shoulders to the sand. He let me do it, smiling wickedly.

"Tell me everything." I demanded.

In a whirl he flipped me off of him and onto my back in the sand. I caught my breath as he bent forward and kissed my neck.

"Tell me!" I tried pushing him away as I laughed.

"It would be so much faster if I could *show* you." Iskur looked longingly at the sea.

"No, no. It would make so much noise."

"I know. I know." Iskur backed off of me and lifted me up from the ground. I closed my eyes and forced all the sand off of me. The grains fell away diligently. Iskur did the same and sat back in the hammock. I paced in front of him.

"What did we do? And why don't I remember it? How did I live like a human when we-"

"Slow down Arga!" Iskur laughed and pulled me towards him. I collapsed into his lap, "One question at a time."

I looked up at him and smiled. Whenever my mind had turned to questions about our past, our present became so confusing to me. As we had been working on the island and waiting for time to speak privately, I had tried my hardest to push it all from my mind. There was no denying the connection between us. I was utterly devoted to him, and he to me. It was like nothing I had ever experienced before, and if I thought too hard about it it terrified me. Nothing else on Earth came close to this.

As if sensing the conflict in my mind, Iskur began:

"You are so fragmented because you are far smarter than I am. As it was all falling apart, you forced yourself to forget. That was your idea from the beginning if things were to go wrong. We had agreed to forget in order to protect each other. We were torn apart and put back together. Well, *I* was put back together. I awoke a stranger to everything but my new power and the longing to find something I had lost. I could not forget everything, but I did not understand it until I saw that last vision when you brought me here."

"I don't think I forgot everything either." My voice was warm as I sat up and leaned into his arms.

"No? What do you remember?"

"I used to always dream of thunderstorms, when I was on Earth. Of lightning and rain and dark clouds over the sea." The dreams came flooding back, "I saw faces and just thought they were dreams. Virgil said that I might have repressed my visions on Earth. I think I was remembering things."

"Mh. Likely you were."

"So, we became gods?"

"We were foolish."

"What did we do?"

Iskur shook his head.

"We were powerful on Earth. In our time we could easily speak to the dead and it was considered a gift. In your most recent time, those who actually could speak to the dead were so rare it was a joke."

"Yeah." Psychics, mediums, that one shop down the street from my last apartment where that lady read tea leaves, palms, and cards. Laughable.

"We were not a joke. You and I. We found each other through fate or chance, and our skills increased. We learned from each other and from the dead. The Old Dead favored us above other humans. They loved us. But we wanted more. It was not greed. Well. Maybe it was a bit of greed. But we had a theory. You wanted to know how our Earth came to be and the Old Dead had no knowledge of it."

"Seriously?"

"Yes. They did not know how Earth or the Otherworld came to be."

"How is that possible?"

"They are only the first humans. Their knowledge is all of human existence but nothing further. We wanted boundless knowledge."

"So, what did we do?"

"This is the part I am not proud of."

"Was it bad?"

Iskur closed his eyes.

"I said I would tell you all. So yes. It was bad. But we did not intend it to be so."

"What happened?" My chest tightened, recalling the partial memories that had come to me in the visions.

"We called out to something more powerful than the dead and it answered."

The golden light. A sound I couldn't quite remember.

"What was it?"

"I am still not sure. We hid ourselves as best we could from the Old Dead and reached this...*being*. It was as if it were the center of the universe. The being kept us out of view of the Old Dead, and we asked it our questions. In the face of its raw power, we stood brave. I am not sure why, but it spoke with us that first time very briefly. We called on it later in desperation to have our oath to each other be sanctified. There was a cost for that, and it bound our souls together. Then a third time we called on it, it was amused by us. We asked to be given even a fraction of its power. To our shock it obliged. I could not hold the power, but you took it with ease. As I was breaking apart, you came to me and took more than your share of what we had received to lighten the burden on me. It sent you into oblivion."

"I can see the light." I saw it in my mind, a golden cloud boiling with fury and fire, "I remember the light when it happened."

My skin crackled with energy at the memory.

*White hot light like fire, turning blue and gold and black.*
*Voices screaming in unnatural pain.*
*The feeling of grabbing blindly for someone, something.*
*Iskur's face shifting from human to black like the darkest night.*
*Grabbing him, screaming.*
*Taking his face in my hands and pulling his burden from him.*
*Forcing him to return and feeling myself fade.*
*Undoing myself, shredding my own mind to pieces as I lost control.*

"I can see it, Iskur." His arms were around me, sharing the electrical charges that coursed through my body.

"Sh, sh. No, it is over now, you are here."

"I know I am here, I know." I sniffled, "But how did I get here? How did I live a whole life with you back then and then another whole life again?"

"The vow, Arga, I made a promise to you. Humans make promises and vows all the time. Oaths are of great importance. Some vows bind people beyond Earth, but most do not. Our vow was infused with the weight of the power of that great being. It tethered our souls together. It banished me from so many things once I died, and it kept you trapped on Earth until-"

"Until what?"

"I think you found a way to come here by becoming a human again."

I blinked at him.

"What do you mean?"

"What was left of you existed trapped on Earth until you found a way to join me here. The way you found to join me here was to force me to break our vow."

"What was the vow?"

Iskur shifted uncomfortably.

"Arga, I-"

"You told me you would tell me everything. Don't break another vow." I regretted saying it as soon as the words left my mouth. What a cruel thing to say. He looked away over the water with hurt plainly on his face. His black eyes glimmered with tears.

"I'm sorry," I croaked.

"Arga, I promised you that I would keep you from being killed by your betrothed." He said wretchedly.

My chest constricted and I remembered his words:

*"I vow to prevent her betrothed from killing her, or let my fate be endless servitude to her in this life and the next. For love and for duty. Loyal. Bound to her. Subservient until my undoing. My oath demands it."*

"I-I remember." I choked. *Subservient.* That word grated in my head. Did that mean Iskur had no choice in the matter anymore? Had he bartered his freewill with those words? Was his love a matter of fulfilling a vow?

"I do not know how you figured out that you had to live out breaking that vow to get here, but you did. You gave your soul human form. Lived. Died in a way to break the oath. And came here."

I wrapped my arms around myself tightly.

*Someone hit me across the face.*

"But life was so real and I remember so much of it. So many things. I really lived them."

"Yes, of course you did."

"That life was real, that's who I am. Or was."

"Arga, I know. You are both now."

"But I can't fully remember the me that you know!" I choked back a sob and felt the anxious energy building rapidly, "I can't remember anything besides bits and pieces! I see my father and you and fire and a golden light and purple flowers and the woods and someone named Aeylin and his mother and my mother and there seems like there is always crying and screaming and fear-"

"You are remembering so much. And you will know more with time." Iskur stood and held his arms out for me. I came to him.

"Iskur I-I know you, but I don't *remember you.* Not all of you. Not everything we were." I wept. I felt more lost and out of place than ever.

"I am glad that you know me now. That is enough."

"Is it?" I looked up at him.

"More than enough."

"*How?*"

"How? What do you mean?"

"How is it enough?"

"It is *more* than enough. Arga, I have waited for you through the centuries not knowing who I waited for. I have felt your presence on Earth and have known that I unfairly burdened someone. It was my punishment, to know that somehow I was excluded from the same suffering: That I continued living and died and got to come to the next plane while I left someone I could not remember behind. That was *torture.* I knew there was someone who was unable to make this journey and unable to escape an endless empty wandering in a place not meant for them. I did not understand it all as I do now, but, seeing you here? That first night, when you were lying gasping in my dwelling you called me to you with such ferocity. I was ripped against my will to stand over you. It was the most joy I have ever felt. Everything else is added bliss."

His eyes were still black but his expression was reverent and loving.

"It is more than enough." He repeated.

"Did you love me on Earth?" I asked quietly, still shaking in his arms.

"I did."

"Did I love you back?"

"You did. But there were other obstacles."

"My fiancé?"

Iskur laughed and thunder rumbled loudly.

"He was something we feared at first, but he was easily dealt with."

"Dealt with?"

"You killed him."

I remembered that too. I remembered the sick satisfaction of keeping my promise to that bastard: "*You will never see another sunrise.*" I heard the screams and smelled the fire and saw the golden cloud receding into the dark night sky as Iskur and I descended the hill after sanctifying our vow.

Unease threaded through my mind. All the dark deeds I had done to keep Iskur and myself safe. Our friend had died in the face of that *thing* we had called on to give us power. Had we sacrificed him? Did I care? I couldn't remember his face. I remembered his mother screaming at us, spitting and crying and cursing Iskur and I. I remember thinking she was pathetic, and I remember thinking she was right when she called us monsters.

"We were villains."

Iskur waited a moment to speak.

"And heroes, Arga. Everyone is both."

We stared into each other's eyes for a long time.

"I felt our history the first time I saw you as a human." I said, reaching for his face. He bent down to let me caress his cheek, "I was so mad at you for touching me. You terrified me when you grabbed me. But when I saw you, my heart, it...it was like seeing an old friend. I used to cry every thunderstorm. My mother always said I was mourning something."

He kissed my palm.

"I wept at the sound of the ocean when I heard it after you were gone. Rivers too. I never understood it until I heard you gain your voice. We both moved through grief we did not comprehend."

He dropped onto his knees so he could better reach my arm to continue kissing it. I let him trace up one arm, across my shoulders and neck, and down the other. As he reached my other hand, I took his face in it and brought it to my face. Our lips met and I shifted out of human form. Iskur joined me swiftly and we danced across the sand in ecstasy. We twined and wove ourselves around each other. Being with Iskur in my realm was paradise. As I clung to him I reached new heights of bliss. We had not been together like this since I first made the cedar tree back in his dwelling. Iskur never tried to do anything besides caress, kiss, and hold me while we were in human form. I had no desire to be with him in that way, and he sensed it. I was afraid it would have paled in comparison to being with him in our light forms.

My laughter and pleasure resounded like gentle waves on a calm sea. We raced back up the beach, swirling and colliding pleasantly as we rose high above the island into my endless sky. We were locked together in rapture for what felt like hours. Until a voice shouted across the sand. Ugh. Virgil.

"Sleep well?" He said loudly, uncomfortable at the sight of us entwining across the beach. Begrudgingly, I shifted back to human form.

"I slept very well. Have you tried it lately?" I asked sarcastically. Iskur stayed in his lightform, writhing around me playfully. I tried to wave him off and laughed as he dodged my blows.

"This is unbecoming, you two."

"Prude." Iskur boomed jokingly at Virgil. Iskur shifted slowly back into his human form, coming together to stand behind me.

Virgil scowled.

"You have been awake a while, I heard the thunder a moment ago."

"Yes we woke up shortly before that." Iskur put his arms around me.

"What *are* you two?" Virgil asked indignantly. My chest tightened and my mind raced. Had he heard us talking?

"What are we?" Iskur asked calmly

"What is all of this?" Virgil waved at our embrace.

"Oh Virgil, are we leaving you out?" Iskur asked, his voice filled with mock pity.

Virgil blustered and sputtered in disgust. I jolted at the joke too and made a horrified face at Iskur. He found my disgust hilarious.

"Absolutely not!" Virgil stormed off, steaming about the ridiculousness of it all.

"We are divine lovers, Virgil!" Iskur called after him.

"Oh, is *that* it?" He shouted sarcastically over his shoulder at us.

How enjoyable, irritating that little nerd. I laughed. Iskur took off walking after Virgil.

"You can stay here, but I should probably see what he came looking for us for in the first place." Iskur explained, kissing the back of my hand as he passed me.

"Another handkerchief, probably." I trotted after him up the sandy path towards our home.

# XIV.

It was indeed another handkerchief that Virgil wanted made, as well as several more notebooks and pens. Virgil had been using his time to make as many notes as he could about his knowledge of the Old Dead, us, and the connections between Earth and the Otherworld. Not being able to create anything grated on his nerves, but he seemed to be warming up to our new routine. As Iskur finished making the last few items, Virgil thanked him. He remained lingering awkwardly on the patio.

"Yes?" Iskur said, eyeing him suspiciously.

"I was wondering." Virgil sounded uncomfortable.

"What is it?" I asked impatiently. I was hoping to get some more time with Iskur now that Virgil had all the notebooks he desired.

"Would you two be opposed to...well, oh nevermind." He grumbled, turning away.

"What, Virgil?" I asked. He spun around, looking even more flushed and embarrassed than he had on the beach.

"I was wondering if you would like to dine!" He snapped.

"To what? Dine? Eat?" I asked, incredulous.

"It has been some time since I have truly just enjoyed a meal. At Iskur's I dined alone. I enjoy eating, it is a pleasure unparalleled in this realm. And well, I miss eating with company. Foolish. Stupid I know. Forget I said anything."

"No wait!" Iskur called, rushing after him, "Virgil, it is a lovely idea. I will make us a feast."

"Nothing so extravagant is necessary," Virgil blustered, "A simple meal, I do not want any such excessive frivolity. Some fruits, perhaps. And good wine. I have missed the taste."

I was grinning. I had not eaten anything since dying. I never felt hunger physically, but now talking about food made me miss the taste and act of eating.

"That would be really nice." I agreed, "Do things taste better here?"

Both Iskur and Virgil looked at me.

"Have you really not eaten since arriving?" Virgil asked in shock.

"Uh...no...there wasn't really food around the dwelling and I never thought about it until now."

The two of them exchanged a glance, then looked at me with giddy grins.

"You need to try fruit first-"

"No! The herbs. Mint is so-"

"Oh! What about peppers?"

"*Peppers?* No. Fruit first!"

The two of them were arguing playfully, overrun with the excitement of having me try food. "I cannot *believe* we did not think to have you eat before!" Virgil exclaimed.

Iskur set off back down towards the beach, producing plates of bronze, cups, carafes, and various blankets and pillows. The goods followed him obediently, levitating towards the beach. Virgil issued a long string of suggestions and commands and I followed behind them, laughing at their antics.

On the beach, Iskur lowered all the goods to the sand and Virgil busied himself arranging everything. For my part, I dimmed our light and turned its hue orange and purple. Iskur whistled at the light change, and winked at me approvingly.

"It is like an Earth sunset!" He proclaimed.

Virgil waved us over. The blankets and pillows were arranged in a comfortable half circle, and Virgil was pouring wine. Iskur had created baskets and bowls of fruits of every kind. Berries spilled over from ornately decorated wooden bowls. Peppers strung in garlands were strewn across the ground in snake-like braids. There were melons and tomatoes and coconuts. Trays of herbs and greens glimmered in the warm light. We all settled onto the plush quilt that the feast was spread on and took our glasses of wine.

"Do not drink yet!" Virgil was borderline silly with anticipation, "You have to eat something first."

"What will be your first taste?" Iskur was lounging to my left watching me excitedly.

"I don't know, what is it like? Is it different from Earth? Does stuff taste the same?"

"Oh it is different. It is all the tastes you remember from Earth, but in their best form." Virgil grinned, "You will not forget the first thing you taste."

"What did you try first?" I asked Virgil, eyeing the spread indecisively. What could I possibly choose from this dream picnic?

"A fig."

"As did I." Iskur added.

"A fig?" I wrinkled my nose, "I never had a fresh one on Earth."

"Never?" Iskur sounded shocked.

"Never." I said.

"Grapes are a good first taste." Virgil offered, looking about for them.

"Here." Iskur produced a small bunch of bright crimson grapes and held it out for me. I took the bunch and carefully pulled one off the vine. It was gorgeous, like a small, round jewel. Nothing at all like the oblong grapes I remembered from the grocery stores.

"This is the kind that I would eat on Earth." He explained, "It may be different from yours."

I popped the grape into my mouth and let the flavors explode across my tongue. It was shockingly intense: rich, floral, tart. It was exactly how Virgil had described: the most perfect flavor of a grape had been taken and intensified. My eyes widened and I let out a satisfied groan.

"It's so *good!*" I exclaimed, popping more into my mouth.

Virgil and Iskur took turns making me try different things and watching my reaction. Apples, pears, olives, and bitter herbs were all as sensational as the grape. Iskur finally offered me a fig.

"You had dried ones on Earth?" He inquired, eating a pepper with his other hand.

"I had fig jam, I think. It has a lot of seeds, right?"

"Mh. But the most wonderful flavor."

"Figs are delicious." Virgil was reclining in a very un-Virgil-like relaxed fashion, sipping his wine.

"Alright, let's see what's so good about these then." I took the fig from Iskur and took a bite. The skin gave way and sent a wave of juicy flavor into my mouth.

*I was on a windy mountainside in the blazing midday sun. Iskur was with me, and we were under a gnarled tree. He reached up and plucked a fig from the tree, looking into my eyes the whole time. I took it from him, it was still warm from the sun. I took a bite and reached up to kiss him. The taste of figs mingled between us.*

The vision faded.

Iskur was watching me lovingly as I mentally returned to the beach. He smiled, seeming to know what I had been seeing. Virgil peered over my shoulder to see how I had liked the fig, but his expression shifted from comfortable to suspicious when he saw my face.

"Your eyes are black." He said with a scowl, "Why did a fig do that?"

"Do what?"

"Make you have a vision. What did you see?" He demanded.

"Figs are delicious." Iskur said casually, "It is nothing. Try a pepper, Arga."

"It is *not* nothing!" Virgil hissed, "Her visions are important. What did you see, Arga?"

"I-I saw a fig tree."

"And?"

"A fig tree." I repeated. Virgil squinted at me, suspicion increasing.

"Virgil, leave it. She saw a fig tree." Iskur sipped more wine, but fixed an intense gaze on Virgil. Virgil, in turn, affixed his suspicions on Iskur.

"You know that her visions are critical, correct?"

"Yes of course." Iskur sipped some wine and handed me a pepper. I bit it and savored the delightful fiery feeling that warmed my whole body.

"Then *why* are you being so dismissive?" Virgil accused.

Iskur squared his shoulders towards Virgil and gave him a vicious glare.

"Stop it." I scolded the two of them, "Virgil, I saw a fig tree. What does that mean, hm?"

"You said you had never eaten a fresh fig on Earth, but eating one here sent you a vision of a fig tree. It makes me wonder," He glared at Iskur, "If you are perhaps remembering pieces of your ancestor's life."

"Is that possible?" I asked. Play dumb. *Play dumb.*

"I am not sure, but I have been hypothesizing that based on what the Old Dead said to you in their chamber that they believe they can communicate with the one who died long before you. Or that whoever it was is still within you, suppressed."

I felt nervous at how close he was to the truth. Why didn't Iskur trust Virgil enough to share the whole truth with him? He was annoying, sure, but I trusted him way more than I had at Iskur's dwelling. But, I *did not* want to be the one who revealed something that Iskur wanted to keep hidden. I took another bite of the pepper and shrugged.

"Hm. I'm sorry that it wasn't more than just a fig tree. It was a damn good fig though."

"Eat another one." Virgil was scrutinizing me intently. I put my defenses up further. If Iskur could stop Virgil from being too nosy, maybe I could too.

I waved my hand and made another fig appear. I faked confidence and took a huge bite. No vision. I tried not to appear relieved. I felt Iskur relax a tiny bit behind me.

"See? It's fine. Delicious fig." I said, munching happily.

Virgil shook his head slowly.

"I apologize. I want to understand this mysterious circumstance we find ourselves in and your visions are our most helpful assets." Virgil went back to drinking his wine and eating olives.

"We all do." Iskur leaned over me to touch glasses with Virgil, "We are in this together."

"Together." Virgil affirmed, lifting his glass to touch mine as well.

"Together." I said. I was wracked with guilt. I never was good at keeping secrets.

The guilty feeling faded as we talked and laughed and ate for a long period. Iskur showed me how to juggle apples. Virgil wanted us to all try different wines and complained hilariously when Iskur was unable, or perhaps unwilling, to produce anything besides the delicious red wine we had been drinking. The wine I produced upset him even further.

"If only I could make us some! Then you could try some real delicacies!" Virgil moaned dramatically, falling over in a slightly exaggerated anguish. We laughed at his absurdity.

I dimmed our light further, feigning twilight. Iskur sent orbs of fire floating around us. I curled up against him, feeling utterly satisfied and at peace. Virgil asked for a book of poetry, and began reading to us in the flickering light. Words of love and heartbreak, peace and destiny. Iskur kissed my shoulders and neck gently. I tried not to shift out of my human form but it was a difficult impulse to resist. I held strong and closed my eyes, smiling. *This* was bliss. Warmth spread through me as I willed myself to engrain this feeling into the core of my being.

Safe. Happy. Loved.

In a subdued tone, Virgil turned the subject away from his poetry reading and to more serious matters.

"I think we should continue to explore your capabilities, Arga. Now that Iskur is here it will be much safer to test things."

A spike of nerves. I let out a breath slowly. Iskur gave me an encouraging squeeze.

"It would be good to learn what else you can do. And to hone the skills you already have." He said enthusiastically.

"Sure." I said hesitantly, "Is there some sort of endgame?"

"Endgame?" Virgil asked, pouring more wine in his glass. None of us were drunk, despite the gallons we had collectively consumed. It seemed only to warm our bodies and taste delicious.

"Yeah, like, is there some goal to training me?"

"Well, it might be nice to have a bigger island for one thing." Iskur said, rolling onto his back. "I can build faster with you, if you build up your strength."

"Or," Virgil said in a calculating tone, "We could perhaps demonstrate your skills to the Old Dead if we ever are to return to that realm. Showing them that you have the utmost control would likely make them reconsider their previous ultimatum."

I stared at him. It hadn't really occurred to me until that moment how badly he must want to go back. Despite all the potential trouble he was in, it had to feel utterly maddening to be here with no idea how we had gotten here and no abilities of his own. I knew that feeling well. That was me when I arrived. I grabbed his hand. He stared at me in confusion.

"I didn't think about how hard this must be for you. I'm sorry Virgil. You didn't ask to be here and you must feel really trapped."

He opened and closed his mouth several times in shock.

"Well, yes it is all a bit much for me. I am sure you two are very comfortable here and it is growing more and more lovely but at some point-"

"You'd like to go back." I finished for him.

"No, I would like to see justice served, I think is closer to how I feel."

"Justice?" Iskur sat up in a flash and looked at him, "What *justice?*"

Virgil withdrew his hand from mine.

"Fuck. Iskur. Calm down!" I scolded.

"Our realm has always held some similarities to Earth, but there are certain rules and balances that are kept. The whole purpose of the Old Dead, their entire reason for existing, is to arbitrate in situations where the fate of the current and future dead is at stake. That is what they do. And, to me, it seems that there is something else at play when it comes to you and Arga. Something they are not revealing. Something perhaps you two understand better than I do, or perhaps not. The point is, I want to see this mystery unraveled and a justified ending reached."

I looked back at Iskur. His eyes were black and unreadable. I wondered if mine had shifted too. Judging by the way Virgil was adjusting his glasses and observing us, I was guessing that they had.

"Virgil. I do not trust you." Iskur said. His voice was ice. I felt like I was caught in the middle of a firefight as the two of them stared each other down.

"The feeling is mutual." Virgil said in a clipped tone.

I sat up slowly and scooted back away from the two of them to better watch the conversation unfold. Where was this going?

"How do I know that *if* we return, you will not hand us over to win favor with the Old Dead? You have revealed some of their secrets to Arga, they are unlikely to be very happy with that."

"*Why* would I reveal those secrets if I wanted to turn on you two?" Virgil's voice became shrill. He was genuinely hurt.

"I do not know but-"

"*Enough!*" I shouted and the sea began to rumble. They both looked at me, startled, "Iskur, he was so distraught by the whole way the Old Dead had treated me after we got back to your dwelling. It was him that told me how fucked up the choices were that they gave me. While I was busy *destroying* your house looking for you, he was trying to stop me and tell me that none of this was normal! He tried to diffuse my freak out and take off some of my energy. You know how *that* feels. Would someone who wanted to have me destroyed do that? Hmm? Cut it out. He's not going to turn on us. We *need* to trust each other."

Iskur looked from Virgil to me rapidly.

"You tried to take her destroying energy?" Iskur asked quietly.

Virgil looked highly uncomfortable.

"Unsuccessfully, obviously."

"Did she...?" Iskur trailed off, looking nervously at me.

"Did I scar him? Yes. Show him." I snapped impatiently.

Virgil sighed and unbuttoned his shirt cuffs. He rolled up his sleeves to reveal several thin jagged scars on both forearms.

"Nothing like your badges of pride. I could not withstand much."

I glared at them both in turn. *Idiots.*

"Now *stop it* with this pointless arguing. Virgil wants to figure out what the fuck is happening, and we want to figure out what the fuck is happening. And none of us want any sort of punishment from the Old Dead. Right? Right."

Iskur smirked at me. He looked proud. Then he turned to Virgil with his hand outstretched. Virgil took Iskur's hand slowly but clasped it tightly when their hands finally met. His sleeves were still unbuttoned and both his and Iskur's arm scars gleamed in the firelight. Iskur pulled him closer and smiled wickedly.

"Is it time to tell you what we did?"

Virgil looked shocked at the sudden intensity in Iskur's face. There was a wild energy about him that thrilled me, but it was making Virgil increasingly uneasy.

"Wha-what do you mean?" Virgil asked.

"You want to know what I was keeping from you, do you not?" Iskur let go of Virgil's hand.

Virgil's eyes narrowed.

"What are you going to confess to me?" He whispered tensely.

I stared at Iskur, feeling my own anxiety heighten. I didn't like the secrets game, but what would happen after Virgil knew the truth? Would he hate us? Hate me? Turn against us, repulsed at what we had done?

"This is a gesture of trust that I share this with you. This which the Old Dead do not yet know or understand."

Virgil stood up.

"Iskur, stop." He said, wind rippling across the beach as he spoke, "I have my suspicions but please, stop. I do not want you to reveal anything to me until you feel like you can truly trust me."

Iskur looked at him inquisitively, then stood up as well. Calmly he held out his arm and motioned for Virgil to do the same. Virgil put his arm next to Iskur's. Iskur traced the scars that laced both of their arms.

"You know what I endure gladly for Arga. You have felt it. You know that it is but a fraction of the pain she feels." Iskur and Virgil locked eyes, "You have my trust. Do you wish to know why I take what she gives so gladly?"

I was holding my breath, watching the two of them stand locked in a staring match. Their eyes were both searching each other's intently, looking for any hint of danger or deceit.

"Because you love her?"

"Mh, and so much more. It is the least I can do after what she has endured for me. Virgil, we saw that which is only a whisper in human imagination and it bestowed us an unimaginable gift."

Virgil sucked in a breath in shock.

"I *knew it*. I knew it." Virgil took off pacing across the beach. He started shouting over his shoulder at us, "I *knew* you were something different. You both! HAH! I knew."

I stood up with Iskur. That was not the reaction I was expecting at *all*.

"Is he...okay?"

Iskur laughed quietly.

"He has been on to us for so long. It was driving him crazy at my dwelling." Iskur laughed again, then called out to Virgil, "Was it not, Virgil? I could keep you out of my mind, and so much of Arga is unexplainable."

"It was making me absolutely mad! And *you* being so protective. It was a wild thought, an impossible thought. These are things that seem absurd even with all of the wonderful impossibility of the Otherworld. I felt like a human again, running up against logic and coming up short."

Virgil was giddy.

"So it is true? Is there something *beyond* the Old Dead?"

Iskur smiled proudly.

"Indeed." He said, picking up his wine glass again and taking a dramatic sip. The man loved theatrics.

"Hah!" Virgil whooped and raced across the sand, "And you, Arga, you were there?"

"I only remember pieces of it. Iskur remembered everything when we were in the water here after I brought him."

"Oh, how fascinating. So he had forgotten his past as well? Hm curious. I have so many questions. So much I want to know. But! There will be time for that." Virgil rushed back to us as giddy as a child in a candy store, "Another toast!"

I laughed as Virgil thrust my glass into my hand.

"A toast to what, Virgil?" I asked, shaking my head. I couldn't keep from smiling at his exuberance.

"A toast to being right. A toast to the unexplained." He sighed happily, "A toast to the stories being true. A toast to humans not being alone!"

# XV.

"Humans have always told stories of life and death and what comes after," Virgil was talking to Iskur and I while the three of us lounged on some mossy stones Iskur had just created.

It was some time after our beach picnic. Virgil had ushered us off to bed immediately after his toast. When we reconvened after our rest, Virgil had an entire notebook filled with his questions for Iskur. Iskur had put him off, saying that perhaps it would be better for him to explain to us first what he knew about powers beyond the Old Dead.

I had brought the light back up to a midday shine, Iskur had built us a shaded retreat under some palm trees near a new lagoon I had dredged. Waterlilies bobbed pleasantly on the surface, and hummingbirds darted around the blooms. We were taking turns peeling and sharing oranges.

"These stories, you learn when you die, are often based on the connections that used to be so much stronger between our realm and Earth. The Old Dead make up so many of the mythos and images of deities throughout the history of humanity. However," Virgil paused dramatically, "There is a natural curiosity that we do not leave behind when we die. As humans we wonder what is after death, and once dead some of us..."

He put his hand on his chest to indicate that he was referring to himself in particular, "Wonder if there is a power even beyond that of the dead."

"What do the Old Dead think about this?" I asked, peeling another orange and handing Iskur and Virgil pieces of it.

"They do not trifle with these curiosities. It does not concern their duty, which is to keep the balance of peace and tranquility in the Otherworld, so they do not think about it at all."

"Who thinks about it then?" I took another bite of orange and savored the intensity of the taste.

"People like me. The dead who study the human realm. We who watch Earth closely and see what happens with humanity. Greeters especially need to know what humans are experiencing when we are working with the newly dead. It takes time to work with one dead soul, so there are times when you complete your task with one soul and an entire generation has passed. Earth time and Otherworld time are not congruent, so keeping track of events is very difficult, but important."

Iskur peeled an orange and handed segments to us all. We paused for Virgil to eat a few pieces.

"To the matter of powers beyond the Old Dead, this is something scholars occasionally explore. It is often waved off as frivolous study. Most gods and deities can be attributed to the Old Dead's early involvement on Earth or to the general connection between the two dimensions. Prophets, oracles, and the like are ones who can talk with the dead more easily. But some scholars say there is something more, that humans in ancient times had dealings with powers outside of the Otherworld. Powers none have been able to contact or prove."

Virgil peeled us an orange and shrugged as he carried on talking.

"That is all I know about the power beyond. There is no name for it, only occasional debate between us dead scholars about ancient human experiences and whether or not those experiences can be attributed to the Otherworld or *something else*."

"Well," Iskur tossed an orange into the air and caught it, "Now you have met two humans who survived meeting something beyond. Or sort of survived."

"I still cannot get over the fact that my wild suspicions were right." Virgil had such a pompous expression on his face it made me laugh aloud. He scowled at me, "You do not understand that these are very fringe beliefs. The theory of a power beyond is not interesting to most souls. I felt like I was losing my mind!"

"You might be." I threw a peel at him. He snorted indignantly.

"No thanks to you two. Are you satisfied now? May I ask my questions?" Virgil brandished his notebook.

"Mh. I think there is more research you have done on the power beyond, but we can look at those notes later." Iskur tossed an orange at me. I started peeling it.

"Oh yes, there are notes on various stories and instances that *could* be some additional power, but how does that compare to a first hand account? Two accounts, in fact!"

"I don't remember it really. Like I told you." I said with a sigh, "Just parts of it. Lots of screaming."

Iskur slung his arm around me.

"I can show you, Virgil. I remember everything." Iskur looked at me and winked, "Then you could see it again, too."

I felt uneasy. The fragmented memories I had of the event were not pleasant at all. I wasn't sure if I was going to enjoy the full knowledge of what I had done. And yet there was a compelling desire to see what Iskur and I had seen so long ago. My love for danger was a defining trait. I wanted to peer over the edge into the abyss of my past transgressions.

"Wait, first, one question," Virgil flipped through his notebook vigorously, "Arga is your contemporary, correct? You were alive at the same time?"

He looked up at Iskur expectantly.

"Mh. Yes."

"And how then did she live and die so recently?"

"That is more than one question." Iskur teased, standing up. He looked down at Virgil with a cunning smile.

"Please explain that, and then you can proceed."

"Unfortunate for us all, I do not know how she did it," Iskur held his hand out to me, "But somehow, she stayed on Earth until she figured out some way to become human again and die."

Virgil shuddered uncharacteristically and looked at me sidelong.

"You do not remember how you did it?" He asked.

"No, I don't remember much of my ancient life. Just tiny pieces."

Virgil inspected me for a few moments. A staring contest, I didn't look away. Iskur clapped his hands eagerly and broke Virgil and I out of our reverie.

"So!" Iskur proclaimed, "Are you ready to see?"

We followed Iskur to the edge of the mossy stone we have been resting upon. The three of us peered into the water for a moment. Iskur waved his hand and the lily pads all bobbled to the far edge of the lagoon leaving the water's surface clear. It reflected the three of us back at ourselves in an unearthly green cast.

"Arga, can you make the sky dark?" Iskur asked, kissing my hand as he shifted out of human form.

I obliged, my chest contracting as he hovered above the surface of the water. Virgil was staring at me intently.

"I am going to show you the third and final time we spoke to the power beyond." Thunder rumbled as Iskur spoke.

"If this becomes too much for her," Virgil said to Iskur's form, "I will disrupt the surface of the water and you must stop."

"Agreed." Iskur rumbled.

My chest felt like it was being smashed by a boulder. Iskur plunged beneath the water, and the scene began to unfold on its undisturbed surface. To my surprise, Virgil took my hand. He tried his best to disguise his grimace of pain as he shared the nervous energy that was already building. He *tried* to hide the grimace, but I saw it. I steadied myself with a breath then looked at the water as the scene unfolded:

We were on a mountainside overlooking a valley. The whole place was covered in cedar trees too big to comprehend. Their towering trunks flanked us on the cliffside. We were seeing the scene from Iskur's point of view, and he abruptly turned from the cliff and walked back among the trees. It reminded me of the forest in Iskur's dwelling with the trees so old they felt alive. The place I had arrived the first night. Obviously the likeness was intentional. The forest looked ancient, and the trees' branches dimmed the bright sunlight that had been shining on the cliffside.

Iskur walked quickly along a path he clearly knew. The memory blurred, seeming to show the passing of time. Iskur was still walking through the woods. He was slower now, much more careful about how he walked. It was very quiet, and dusk was setting in.

Someone stepped into his line of sight a few yards ahead of him. He let out a pleased noise, something like a murmur of relief and growl of pleasure. The figure stood still, enrobed in a dark purple cloak that covered its face. Iskur walked briskly towards them. When he reached them they stood a moment in front of each other. Then the cloaked figure suddenly leapt into his arms.

"They told me-"

"No, my love, I am here-"

"They said-"

"I am not."

The two of them clung to each other and wept.

I could feel Virgil's eyes boring into me. It was like watching a movie with someone who only cared about seeing my reaction to it. I kept my eyes on the water and the scene that played out.

Iskur pulled the cloak away from the head of the other person and I was staring at my own face. I was still young, but not a child. My eyes held an indisputable knowledge and I was the image of strength and confidence. My skin was a gorgeous umber color and glowing from days out in the sun. My eyes gleamed with tears and my smile- oh my smile! It was the absolute outpouring of love and joy that I had felt when I woke to see Iskur with me on the island's beach. I was looking at myself through a lover's eyes, and I was radiant.

"*You.*" Virgil breathed.

"Yes." I tried to breathe evenly, feeling anxiousness creep over me again. Virgil squeezed my hand.

"You know that my father found out," Past me said, wiping my eyes.

"I know, Arga." Iskur touched my hair delicately.

"He said you were willingly banished and agreed to never return." I closed my eyes, enjoying the feeling of his touch.

"I am here. And you. You clearly did not believe him that I was gone. You still came."

"No. Hah!" I laughed, "I can still feel you. I think I would know if you had died."

I put my hand on Iskur's chest and he covered it with his.

"I know. I am glad you came."

"*Enough!*" A third voice roared raucously from a tree branch above. Both Iskur and I burst into laughter as the voice's owner jumped down. "I know it has been six months but can we wait for the romance until after?"

"Aleyin!" Iskur wrapped the man in a hug. Aleyin was tall and lanky, and wore a purple cloak like mine. His eyes were fierce and mischievous, but filled with joy when he looked at Iskur.

"Who else, my brother?" Aleyin pushed Iskur back, "I would not miss the chance to save your life again."

"I think," I wrapped my arm around Iskur, "It is my turn to save someone." Iskur sighed and kissed my head.

"None will need saving." He said resolutely, "Is it we three?"

Aleyin smiled impishly.

"No, Iskur, we are all here." He said, pointing up the hill.

"All?" Iskur asked.

"We have grown in mythos since that night, my love." I said, taking him by the hand and leading him upwards, "Our fellow Seers have joined us from afar."

We three walked up the mountain and entered a clearing. We were nearly at the mountain's peak and the vista that spread out before us was stunning. The moon was full and its light shone down on the rest of the forested peaks and valleys beyond. The trees were bathed in moonlight and glimmered like dark emeralds on the hillsides.

In the clearing stood nine more people, clothed in various purple garments. However, none had cloaks so fine as me or Aleyin. Aleyin led Iskur around to the gathered individuals and introduced him to the few he did not know.

"If you did not come tonight, we were still going to try," I explained to Iskur. A woman offered Iskur a purple cloak embroidered all over with leaves and flowers and interlocking geometric patterns. He took it and bowed deeply to the woman.

"Thank you, sister in sight, it is beautiful." He said to the one who had given him the cloak as he put it on. She nodded to him reverently.

All who were gathered looked like they had the weight of immeasurable understanding on their minds. They were a range of ages, the youngest looking no more than ten years old. A boy with a crooked smile and a missing front tooth.

"You honor us with your presence," Iskur said to the gathered group. They murmured returned acknowledgements in response. "It is this night that was prescribed to us all in dreams, in visions, in signs and in portents."

He nodded or motioned to select individuals with each word, identifying who had predicted the date in which ways.

"It is well that you are all willing to come. You know the great peril we will endure. You have heard of what happened when last we..." He trailed off. I took one of his hands, and Aleyin the other. Aleyin had lost his jester behavior and was the most serious of all.

"When last the great powers came to us, we were not ready to meet their glory." I continued for him, "But now, we have made ourselves worthy of such a gift. All of us have sanctified ourselves. We have prepared for this night in constant consultation with our ancestors. We are ready to speak to the Nameless Ones."

The assembled group nodded somberly. Some smiled expectantly, but they all seemed very aware of the intensity of the situation.

On the water's edge, Virgil was clutching my hand with such a ferocity I almost withdrew from his grasp. But what happened next made me forget the constriction of my fingers:

Everyone's eyes turned black.

Thunder cracked and the Seers formed a circle. No one spoke, but all moved with instinct and intuition. Or perhaps they had rehearsed it? Something told me that they were now bound by their singular mission, and were moving together towards their purpose with little past planning. I grew nervous watching the scene. Tension was mounting.

Lightning danced around them as the sudden storm enveloped their group. With hands raised, they sang together. The harmony wavered, straying as each individual sang their own refrain. It was chaos and resolution as the song came together. Wind began to whip the mountain top, and a lightning bolt caught a tree down the hill on fire. It was barely out of Iskur's line of sight, but still Virgil and I gasped when we saw the fire. The flames engulfed the tree, but nobody in the vision noticed. They were all looking upwards.

A golden light was glowing in the cloud that had gathered above them. The light seemed to writhe and boil, gathering intensity as the group continued to concentrate their energy and focus above. In a flash there was a golden beam piercing from the cloud to the ground in the center of their circle. It swirled and brightened, blocking everything else from Iskur's view. His eyes were affixed on the light and the endless shimmering surging power it was gathering.

Galaxies split open in the light's depths, as if a door had been ripped open into the cosmos. The tension of the gathering of the light seemed to shift and time seemed to slow. The glare from the golden portal that had opened was illuminating the whole lagoon as Iskur stared into the glimmering shape.

"*Who asks?*" It was the sound of everything at once.

I remembered that sound. I had heard it thousands of years before. I had heard whispers of it the night I died. I remembered it now. *How* could I have ever forgotten that sound? That sound was on the edge of my hearing in every vision and every dream. Never clear, always muddled. How could I have forgotten it?!

It was thunder and lightning and every storm that had ever raged. It was children laughing and babies crying and lovers moaning and screams of terror. It was eagles and song birds and wolves and lions. It was trees groaning and oceans crashing. It was all. Rock, fire, water, rain, wind, animals, humans, plants. Everything that had ever grown and lived and died. Every song ever sung. Every tear ever cried. Everything. It was not one thing, though it spoke with one voice. I could see how someone merely hearing the noise would think there was one power we were speaking to, but I understood it all over again. This power was each individual power. It was one and many. It was an unending reserve of all life.

"Iskur asks." His voice was thunderous against the screaming wind.

"Arga asks." My voice was as deep and booming as the sea.

Nobody else spoke.

*"None have asked before. None that can hold it. Will you hold it?"*

On the stone with Virgil, I writhed in terror at hearing the voice but was utterly transfixed by the scene and how it reverberated in my psyche. I knew this scene I knew this scene. I knew the voices. I knew what was coming next.

"We can hold it." They said in unison.

"No!!!" I screamed, clawing out of Virgil's grasp. I had to stop them, *now*. I had to try. Virgil clamped his arms around me and pinned me down on the rock to prevent me diving into the pool.

The scene blazed white. I heard the screams of anguish and I wept bitterly. I could remember it now. My soul bending under the weight of the gift we had asked for. I remembered looking at Iskur in that circle and seeing him fail to hold it. His soul, bound to mine, untethering and slipping away. Not to death, no, but to join that unending chorus of all that had been and will be. He would go to a place I could not follow him. I would lose him. I remembered how hard I had fought. How I had clung to his soul and pulled it back to Earth. I took the gift he could not carry and let it undo me.

*"You will hold his power, too?"* The scene in the water still only showed a searing white hot light as the voice spoke.

*"I can hold it all."* My voice was broken in grief and agony, but confident.

*"You will walk this path alone."*

More screams of anguish, this time from me specifically. I screamed with my past self, feeling the anguish wash over me. Virgil was on my back, using every ounce of his strength to keep me from throwing myself in the lagoon. In the back of my mind, I knew I could overpower him and dive into the water with Iskur, but I let myself be restrained and only fought enough to keep him holding me down. I knew the moment he had a chance he would splash the water and make Iskur stop, but I needed to see it. I needed to know what he saw when the Nameless Ones left.

The vision reopened and the whole forest was ablaze. Iskur stood, groaning in pain. He retched violently for some time, spitting blood and bile into the grass. Slowly, he stood, and from his perspective we saw the carnage in the clearing of our sacred hillside.

Our fellow Seers were lifeless corpses littered across the ground. They were not bloodied and torn, there was no gore, but the scene was disturbing nonetheless. They did not look peaceful in death, they were lying as if they had been struck down in motion, their limbs splayed. Their faces were frozen in masks of fear and surprise.

Iskur began screaming as he registered what he was seeing. He flung himself on each of their lifeless forms in turn, ignoring the inferno that was growing in the trees around him. He begged and pleaded and screamed and retched and clawed at his face until he was bleeding. He clung to Aleyin especially and sobbed bitterly for what felt like hours. The fire entered the clearing and he stood up at last, his display of grief having left him a hollow shell. He lovingly laid all the bodies out across the grass and watched as the fire began to burn them. His movements were slow, as if he was weighted down. He removed his regal cloak and laid it delicately over Aleyin.

"What have I done?" He whispered, holding Aleyin's hand. He kissed the top of our dear friend's head, then covered it fully with the cloak.

The flames at last had gotten close enough that he had to move away from the clearing. Striding towards the trees, Iskur waved his hand at the flames violently. A passage of ash and smoke appeared in the wall of flames. He passed through it and into the forest.

"I did not see your body. Someone is missing. *Where are you?*" His voice was haunted and tinged with fury. The crackle of the flames increased and the vision faded.

I ground my cheek against the rock and continued to weep. So selfish, so foolish. I remembered it all now, I remembered waiting for Iskur in the clearing. Knowing full well that he would come. My father had sent Iskur away in the weeks after the murder of my betrothed and had told me he had killed himself. I remembered knowing very clearly then that he was lying to me. I had waited. Kept quiet. We had already made our plan.

I remembered the murmur of voices when I had told all the gathered Seers that Iskur was near. I could feel him. Our souls were tied by our earlier vow and the mess we had made of that. Memories flooded back and I cried and cried. I heard someone crying with me.

*"Iskur!!"* It was Virgil, and he was wailing in pain.

I felt Iskur emerge from the water in the darkness and come to my side. I could not stand it anymore. I snapped out of my human form with a whiplike crack of destroying energy. He met me as I rushed out of Virgil's grasp. We collided and he did his best to wrap me up, but I was too far gone. I felt myself surging and I didn't want to hurt him. Not another scar, not another ruined life, not another selfish act because I couldn't control myself. I fought him.

It seemed to shock him, because I found it easy to repel his attempts to embrace me in this state. He called to me, begging me to return to his grasp.

*"How could we?!"* I shrieked across the island. The sea boiled with my misery, *"How could we be so stupid?!"*

"It is the past," Virgil was a streak of blue light, in pursuit of me as well.

*"We murdered them!!"* I cried, waves breaking over the beach as I careened across the sky.

"Arga, it cannot be changed! Please, I have borne this pain for you already. I have paid for this for us! In the thousands of years since we died I have suffered for this!" Iskur intercepted me at last, wrapping me in his presence and cleaving himself to me. I withheld my pain from him, trying to bottle it in.

How could we have been so selfish? So power-hungry? Calling the Nameless Ones had killed Aleyin's brother the first time we had done it, where was our remorse? We called it again and brought even more destruction onto those we loved. I wanted to crawl to the bottom of my raging sea and burn alive. Burn dead?

"Stop keeping it away. Let go of the destructive power. Share the burden with me." Iskur was whispering in my consciousness. I felt like a stone being broken under a hammer, such was my grief. I held out a little longer before finally giving over and letting the electricity whip and snap and crackle across us both. I knew it was hurting him and it added to the ache of sadness I was already feeling.

Virgil swirled around us, watching and waiting to see if I would escape again. Iskur and I sank down to the sand above the tideline. The waves were slowing and calming along with me, and they had receded back down the beach.

"Come back to human form with me," Iskur cooed, beginning to gather himself into his human shape, "We can breathe together."

I obliged slowly, feeling the sad ache turn into sobs as I became human once more. Virgil joined us, kneeling at our side looking heartbroken.

"Breathe, Arga."

"Why did we do it?" I wept.

"Arga, it is the past. I knew I had done something on Earth that had resulted in the deaths of so many that I loved. I had visions before you came of the ending of the one I showed you. I knew their names, I saw their bodies. I knew I had killed them. I mourned and grieved for centuries, not knowing how or why they had died. I have paid the price for them, this is not your punishment to bear." Iskur held me in his strong arms, never flinching at the sparks of energy that kept flaring back up intermittently.

"Not my punishment? I was there with you! I called them all! I arranged it! *Why*? Why did we bring all those people there? Why did we think we could do that?"

"My love, we had done it before. We had met the Nameless Ones and taken some of the power with ease. It had been an accident when we made our vow. We thought it would be just as easy to do it intentionally. And we liked the power. Others looked to us as leaders and after a life of being unwanted it was intoxicating to me. For you, I cannot say what the motivation was. But we pushed each other to explore more and try harder. Together we were so much more powerful. We wanted to become gods, to have the power of creation in our hands."

"You said we did it! You said we became gods! You said we succeeded. It doesn't feel like success to me!" I spat, anger swelling in my chest.

Killing murderers who wanted to kill us was one thing. Deleting an entire warband from existence could even be construed as heroic. But this? This was too much. Too far. How could we?

"Arga, we did. We held what was given to us, though in unequal shares. You have so much more in you than I do, since you saved me from being consumed by the Nameless Ones. We became a separate thing from normal dead souls. Virgil knew it, and the Old Dead do too, though none of us fully understand what it means."

"I hate it. It's a curse and we killed people to get it."

"We did not know they would die."

"Oh yeah? What did we *think* would happen, huh? I remember telling them when we gathered in that clearing. We waited for you and we talked. They didn't know if you would come, and everyone agreed to try it without you, and I told them it could kill us all if we didn't have your power to add to ours. So yeah. I *knew* the risks."

"So did they, Arga. Please, I beg you, let the pain and shame and guilt of this be mine."

"We did it *together!!*" I wailed.

"Iskur..." Virgil was still kneeling near us, looking up.

"Virgil, wait." Iskur snapped, then continued compassionately, "Arga. It is so hard to understand, I know. I punished myself endlessly for the atrocities I committed, though I did not understand them. Please, the guilt you are feeling I have borne for you. Do not despair. I paid that burden for you in my thousands of years of waiting. A small price to pay for the gift you gave me."

"Iskur!" Virgil leapt to his feet and pointed at the black sky in terror. We both looked up.

A silvery blue comet was splitting the sky and plummeting closer and closer to the sea. I also sprung to my feet and watched in horror as it crashed into the water. No, no, no. The waves engulfed the blue light and surged towards us with a ferocity that horrified me. Beneath the water, the blue light was rocketing towards the beach. Virgil jumped in front of Iskur and I, starting to shift into his blue light form.

"*The hunter,*" Virgil whispered in a tormented and desperate voice, "Run!"

Iskur grabbed my arm and started to shift to his light form but it was too late. I was rooted to the spot and the light was upon the shore, gleaming brightly as it shifted into a solid configuration. Iskur and Virgil came to my sides and held my arms tightly, both having returned to their human shapes. My skin felt like it was on fire and two terrible things happened in rapid succession:

I recognized the person in front of us.

And I ripped a hole in the universe.

I could distinctly feel the four of us being flung through the reaches of space as my entire being reeled from the fact that the last person I had seen on Earth had been standing on my beach. The man who had killed me was hunting us.

# XVI.

"We wished to speak to you first, before any Greeter," The woman's voice came from everywhere at once.

"Speak then."

"You are Iskur. What is Arga?"

"I do not know," His voice was sad.

"Iskur, you are blessed among the dead. One of the most powerful seers to have walked the Earth. The first word on your lips as you died was 'Arga.' And you do not know why?"

Silence from Iskur. Stones rumbled in annoyance.

"You have ties on your soul that connect with Earth. Have you any unfinished deeds?"

"Many."

Thunder growled distantly.

*Arga. Arga. Arga.*
*Who is Arga?*
*Purple flowers growing in the cracks of rocks.*
*A golden light that blinded us all.*

# XVII.

I tried to rub my eyes, but moving my arms was absolute torture. I couldn't bring myself to do more than lift them slightly. Agony. Had I been hit by a truck? The ground was coarse, dry, and stony. I saw nothing else besides stone and sky and didn't care to try and turn my head. I was in human form and I was in the worst pain I had ever felt. I closed my eyes. Maybe I was dreaming. Maybe I was dying?

I was already dead.

Red stone.

Red stone. Blue sky.

Red stone. Blue sky. Sunlight.

Sunlight?

I heard a groan to my left, then a shuffling sound. Painstakingly, I turned slowly towards the source of the noise.

"Iskur!" I choked, panic coursing through my body.

I struggled to my hands and knees and crawled towards him. He was covered in dust, coughing and sitting up. I flung myself onto him, sending him backwards onto the ground again.

"Sh, sh. You are here. I am here." His voice was hoarse.

A shadow passed over us. I looked up to see Virgil standing above us, glasses cracked and suit torn to shreds. He stared down at us, breathing heavily. I opened my mouth to ask him what had happened when someone else spoke.

"Gang's all here, huh?" That familiar voice croaked, coughing as he sauntered towards us.

"*You!*" I shrieked, launching to my feet.

Rage replaced the pain. How often had I fantasized about being stronger than him and being able to hurt him like he hurt me? How dare he show up on my island and ruin my safety. Virgil didn't even turn to see who I was lunging at. He threw out a scarred arm and caught me. Iskur was on his feet with his arms around me a millisecond later.

"Do not bother, Arga." Virgil wrestled with me tiredly.

"*What did you do?!*" I screamed, my voice reverberating across the desert. I fought against Virgil and Iskur, who were restraining me very successfully.

"Me?" That asshole dared to laugh casually, "This was aaaaalllllllll you, Ari."

"Don't *fucking* call me that!!" I continued to struggle against Iskur's iron-like grip.

He held up his hands in apology, continuing to smile that sick smile and laugh. His golden wavy hair was long and shaggy like I remembered it, but coated in desert dust. He had the beginnings of a black eye.

"Okay! Okay! Hah. Geez. You look so different now, without all the makeup and stuff. It's nice."

"*Fuck* you Travis. Why the *fuck* are you here?!"

"Hey, hey, calm down calm down." Travis said with another quiet laugh, "Geez, they just sent me to talk with you, alright?"

To my shock, Virgil turned and launched at Travis. It must have shocked Travis too, because he was knocked flat onto his back with a thud. Iskur dropped his hold on me and rushed over to where Travis and Virgil were grappling in the dirt. Virgil dodged each of Iskur's attempts to separate the two of them. I was frozen where I stood.

"*Talk?* They sent you to *talk?* Talk to me, you murdering swine!" Virgil landed an impressive punch on Travis' jaw. The sound of the blow snapped me out of my stunned paralysis. *I* wanted to hit him. Why let Virgil have all the fun?

"You fucking *killed me* you fucking *god damn asshole!!*" Iskur stopped trying to pull Virgil off of Travis and caught me instead. He locked his arms around me, but I could see over his shoulder. Despite the fury that was dominating my mind, there was a tiny realization dawning on me. Was he shorter?

"Arga. Sh. Sh." Iskur whispered soothingly.

"Get *off me* you fucking *nerd!*" Travis flung Virgil backwards and scrambled to stand up. "Ask her! *Ask her!* She *wanted* me to kill her. *Ask her!*"

I screamed, my body convulsing with rage. Iskur lifted me laboriously and began to walk away from Travis with me slung over his shoulder.

"Arga? That's the new name? Fucking weird. But yeah. We need to talk." Travis was following us, but Virgil blocked his path.

"I highly doubt that you have anything worth saying." Virgil's voice was sinister as he stood his ground.

"Hey little buddy, aren't you supposed to be kind and accepting of all souls?"

Virgil whispered some incoherent venomous reply. Iskur took me to the shade of a large rock formation and set me down gently.

"Arga, sh, sh, I know, I know." He had his hands on my face, "I need you to breathe with me, Arga. You need to be calm. We are somewhere else, yes? We need to be calm and figure this out together."

"Why is he here? Where are *we* here?" Pain flooded my body again.

"I do not know." Iskur said, looking deeply into my eyes.

"Maybe we could *talk* and-" Travis offered from where Virgil continued to block his approach.

"Stay back!" Virgil swung and hit Travis with an impressive upper cut that sent Travis stumbling backwards. I let out a cruel laugh. I loved this new side of Virgil.

"Hey! *Fuck!* I'm not going to hurt anyone, *Gabriel.* Back the fuck off! It's *her* you have to worry about!" Travis stumbled towards Virgil again.

"*Stay back!*" I had never seen Virgil so feral. He wound up to punch again.

"Fuck me. They didn't tell me that you and your boyfriend had a guard twink, Ari." Travis rubbed his jaw.

"What do you want to talk about? What can you explain that I have not already figured out, hm?" Virgil's tone was acidic, "You are a hunter. You were the last person to see Arga on Earth *and* you were her lover *and* you murdered her, so you are the one most connected to her in the Otherworld. Thus the Old Dead sent you to find her when she fled. Am. I. Wrong?"

"Uh no, that's pretty much it." Travis stuttered stupidly.

"He is *dead*." I breathed, eyes widening.

Iskur nodded and smiled sadly.

"So *Virgil*, then where are we?" Travis brushed dust off his arms.

"That I do not know. But we are *not* going with *you*." Virgil concluded emphatically.

"Yeah, come on buddy, you know none of us are going anywhere. You've already tried, right?"

Virgil's silence made my panic kick up a notch.

"What does that mean, Virgil? Tried what? What's wrong?"

"Arga," Iskur tried to keep me down but I pushed past him and went to stand at Virgil's side.

"Virgil. What does he mean?" I demanded.

"We are unable to travel in this place." Virgil said in a measured tone.

"Unable? Like, what? Like we are still in my realm?"

"No."

"You and me both got a hunch on this one, right?" Travis punched at Virgil's shoulder playfully, but Iskur caught his fist before it landed.

"I do have a working theory of where we are, yes. I could not say if it is the same as *yours*." Virgil's voice was full of detestation.

"Virg, where are we?" I asked, trembling. I put my hand on his shoulder and turned him towards me, forcing him to break eye contact with Travis.

"Where?" I asked again.

"I think we are on Earth." He said reluctantly.

"Earth?" My voice broke.

"Damn girl, I can see why the Old Dead were concerned about you. This whole transportation thing you got going on is pretty intense. And you can't control it, huh? Typical. You bipolar freak."

Virgil lunged at Travis, but missed. I wasn't registering the scuffle. I was walking away, looking in stunned horror at our surroundings.

Red stone. Towering rock formations. Brilliantly blue sky. The sun. That was the give away. In the Otherworld, the light just *was*. It never felt like the sun, it didn't give off heat. It was just ambient light from an unseen source. But here? There was heat. Dust and grit and heat.

Virgil was screaming at Travis still, but Iskur was calling my name.

"Arga?"

"Earth." I whispered, falling to my knees.

How? I remembered being on the beach after my rampage from seeing the Nameless Ones. I remembered seeing the comet, Travis, enter my realm and take shape in front of us. The recognition of him, the searing blinding panic that took hold. The way we had all rocketed across space together. It had felt so similar from when Virgil and I had transported to my realm and yet different. What had been different?

We had all been in our bodies when I took us.

The realization made my skin crawl. When I had taken Virgil and I to my realm, we had been mostly in our light forms. When I had brought Iskur, he had been in his lightform. Travis had arrived in my realm in *his* lightform, too.

But on the beach? Right before we left? All humans.

I put my hands over my face. I had to stop the pounding in my head. Virgil and Travis sounded distant. Even Iskur, who was now at my side again, sounded muffled and far off. My vision was blurring and I felt sick.

I was on the ground, hunched over my knees. My breath was razor sharp in my chest. I felt Iskur's hands on me, and I became aware Virgil and Travis had come over as well. The last thing I heard was that fucking asshole click his tongue and say:

"Not *that* much has changed then, huh?"

*Loud music blaring.*
*Sweat pouring down my body.*
*I was sighing.*
*I was running.*
*The other dancers ignoring my black eye.*

*I was crying.*

*I was smiling.*

*It was working. I felt it. I was close to what I wanted.*

*A ring sparkling on my hand.*

*Running through the halls of an apartment building.*

*Running through the paths of my village.*

*Wind rattling the leaves of an oak tree.*

*Thunder booming.*

*Waves crashing.*

*Someone touched my cheek gently.*

*Purple flowers growing in the cracks of rocks.*

*The whole forest was on fire.*

*Sun filtering through the leaves of a fruit tree.*

The sun had set when I awoke. A fire crackled near where I laid, and Iskur was sitting to my side. I stirred and he leaned over me, smiling sadly.

"Where is he?" I growled, bristling as I remembered where we were and who was with us.

"Virgil is holding him."

"Where? How?"

Iskur nodded behind us.

"A cave."

I snorted.

"What's keeping him in there?"

"Virgil." Iskur let out a dry laugh.

"You had a fit, trembling all over. The hunter was unsympathetic. Virgil hit him with a mighty punch."

"Again?"

"Quite hard."

"He knocked him out?"

"Yes. It was impressive." Iskur was smirking and rubbing my back.

"So what, then? Virgil just beat the shit out of him again and now Travis is trapped in the cave?"

"Yes, that is somewhat how it went. We tied him up as well."

Iskur was shirtless, so I assumed that was where the bindings had come from. The scars across his chest gleamed in the dancing firelight. Another reminder of past failings. I sighed.

"I'm so sorry this is all so messed up again."

"No, none of that. It *is*. That is all. It just *is*. And we will find a way back together."

I stared at him. His face was placid, but looked worn and tired.

"We can't leave, can we? We can't go back to my realm?"

"Traveling between Earth and the Otherworld is impossible. *Was* impossible. You can do it, as we have learned. But because of the trip here we are all very exhausted."

We were quiet for a few moments.

"Do you think we will recover our abilities? Soon?" I asked, fear gnawing at my insides.

"I do not know when, but if we were able to come here we will be able to go back." He answered the question I wasn't asking directly.

"I had to become a human and fucking *die* to do it last time and I don't even remember how I did it." I said.

"I do not think that is the way it will be, Arga. We have human form now. You were a wandering spirit. A wandering *god*." Iskur pulled me to him tenderly.

The fire crackled merrily as we stared in silence.

"How did you start the fire?"

"Like a human."

"There aren't any matches though."

"Matches?" His brow crinkled in confusion.

"Iskur, how did you start this fire?"

"Arga, like a human. I have no powers here right now, I am too exhausted from traveling."

"How does a human light fire? Like you just rubbed *sticks* together?"

"Yes? They are very dry, it seems not to rain here. How would *you* start a fire?"

In spite of all the unease I was feeling I burst into laughter.

"Iskur when I was alive there were matches and lighters and things that lit fires. Like, nobody did the stick thing. That's like a survival skill that nobody knows how to do, at least nobody where I lived."

He was so charming when he was confused. His brow furrowed.

"I had not given much attention to how humans made fire in your time. I watched much of your life with Virgil, but there were so many things I did not understand," He paused for a moment, "But I did wonder about the lack of fire."

"Oh my god, Iskur. There is so much for you to see."

I laughed at the absurd thought of him riding in a car, shopping for groceries, using a phone, typing on a computer. The images suddenly disgusted me. Imagining Iskur navigating the modern world I had inhabited made my chest ache intolerably. My laughs turned to panic.

"We have to get back. You don't belong here."

"Sh, sh, Arga, we will. We will."

Virgil trudged into the clearing where we were sitting. I sniffled and tried to gather myself.

"Care to switch, Iskur?" He asked, sounding utterly drained.

"Is he awake?"

"Yes but he is quiet now." Virgil plopped on the ground next to us with a groan, "I just cannot stand to look at him any longer."

Iskur kissed my shoulders.

"Will you be alright here with Virgil?" He asked.

"Yeah, I'm good. Go ahead. I'll be alright." I took a shuddering breath again, not convincing anyone that I was calm. I held his hand tightly before letting it go to allow him to leave.

Once Iskur had reluctantly walked up the path, I turned to Virgil.

"Thank you," I said quietly.

Virgil was an absolute mess. His hair was dusty and unkempt, his suit was shredded and torn. I realized his suit jacket had been placed on the ground under where my head had been. His shirt sleeves appeared to have been sacrificed to be restraints for Travis as well.

"Thank you for what?" He said grumpily.

"For beating the shit out of Travis."

Virgil let out a hollow laugh.

"That monster," He spat into the dust.

I could not help laughing at how spiteful Virgil was about Travis. It warmed me to think that I was not alone in my loathing.

"You look like shit, Virgil." I scooted closer to him. I tried to dust his hair off, but he ducked out of my reach.

"So do you."

"I feel like shit," I admitted, rubbing my head.

"I can imagine. That was quite a seizure."

"A seizure?"

"Yes. It seems that your destructive energy, the parts that you struggled to control in the Otherworld, manifested in a seizure here instead of the normal electrical fit. Which would be fascinating if this was not all so distressing to be here."

I sighed and continued rubbing my head.

"Well fuck. Where are we anyways?" I asked.

"Earth. That is certain. Other than that I do not know."

I looked over at Virgil. His hands were folded in front of him. I saw the blood and bruises on his knuckles in the firelight. He caught me staring and smirked.

"Holy *shit*, Virgil." I breathed.

His eyes glinted devilishly in the firelight.

"I will not tolerate him abusing you further. I am your guardian angel, after all."

"What *happened?* I know he's a fucking asshole but like, you don't seem the ass kicking type."

"When we arrived he and I awoke first. That *brute* made a most contemptible suggestion which he repeated during your seizure. And, well, I will not tolerate him abusing you further."

"What did he suggest?"

Virgil snorted and clenched his hands tighter.

"That we should perhaps not assist during your fit. That perhaps this would be an ideal time to leave you and escape." Virgil's voice was a vicious snarl.

"Escape? *From me?*" I jumped to my feet.

"Virgil!" Iskur shouted from up the hill behind us, "Do not *upset* her!"

Virgil shook his head, and stood up in a huff.

"I better switch with him, I have no mind for keeping calm right now."

"Virgil wait, what did he mean, *escape* from me?"

Virgil sighed and rolled his eyes.

"The Old Dead are quite convinced that all of your abilities are well within your control and they have told him as much. To him, you are a great deceiver. He feels that you tricked him into killing you. And he believes that Iskur and I are entrapped by your powers. He sees himself as a liberator-"

"A liberator? He's a *murderer!*"

But Travis' voice echoed in my head: "*Ask her! She wanted me to kill her!*"

"Virgil!" Iskur's voice boomed across the valley.

"I am on my way!" Virgil shouted back as he stomped up the path.

Iskur reappeared in less than a minute.

"He is not good at being a calming voice of reason right now."

Iskur collected me in his arms. I was still bristling indignantly at the information Virgil had just shared. Liberator? From me? The monster?

"I am not faking this! I cannot control it! And first they say I'm a danger to everything and out of control and need to be kept separate or killed and now they are telling *him* that I'm a witch? Like a sorceress who can just do this stuff and pretend I have no idea how it's happening?"

"Oh Arga, I know, I know. The Old Dead are powerful, but our power is something they do not understand. With me they thought I was just a superb human. Once in a milenia. One with a deeper connection to the Otherworld.

There have been such humans before and after us. They were the prophets, seers, and oracles. They were the ones who could know more than was possible for others.

"The Old Dead did not suspect much with me when I died. I was under scrutiny, yes. But they did not think my power and ability was from something non-human. I even suggested I remain isolated. Just to be safe. I was very compliant. But you? You had so much more of the gift from the Nameless Ones. That baffles them. I have kept what little I remembered of our past a secret in these many thousands of years."

"But, what about the other Seers?" I asked, "The ones who died that night on the mountain? Couldn't the Old Dead see from them what had happened?"

Iskur smiled a knowing smile.

"Ah Arga, that was your greatest discovery. There are places on Earth where it is easiest to talk with the Otherworld. And there are places that are furthest from the sight of the dead. Those sacred places that are far from the sight of the Otherworld are where things can be done that the Old Dead can never see. If I were to show that vision to the Old Dead, they would not see it. What happened on that mountain has been veiled to them eternally."

"I discovered that? How?"

Iskur pulled me closer to him.

"You have the skill of speaking with the dead. You could hear them at all times and often sought out places of quiet when their voices became too much."

I remembered in my past life trekking to that hill whenever I wanted to be free of the voices. It was quiet there, I loved it. The stone in our village was loud. The dead all spoke at once in my head when I sat at the stone.

"I don't hear them anymore. I didn't hear them when I was a human again. Well, at least not specific voices. It was more like, impulses. Like a devil in my head. Why can't I hear ancestors now?"

"Mh. The Old Dead and living humans have done their best to close those connections between the living and the dead. None wish for those conversations to flow freely."

"Why?" I asked quietly. The fire snapped as Iskur tossed another stick onto it.

"Oh, because of us. And others. There was much knowledge being shared between the Otherworld and Earth. The shared knowledge sometimes resulted in unfair advantages among peoples who had better seers. The Old Dead like balance. So."

I shook my head, feeling exhaustion wash over me again.

"I really cannot remember most of our life." I picked up a stone. It bothered me immensely that I could not remember.

"You will. You remembered the mountain."

I shuddered at the recollection. The scene was seared into my consciousness now. The golden light, the screams, the fact that I had known the risks and allowed the other Seers to attend. Travis wasn't entirely wrong about how much of a monster I could be.

"We are evil."

"And we are good. Everyone is both. You will remember more."

How was he so sure of that? What other atrocities had I committed in that life? I hoped I had seen the worst. You know, killing a warband with fire and later using all my friends as human sacrifices to gain favor from an ancient power. All those great choices I apparently made. We watched the fire burn for a few more minutes in silence.

"Iskur?"

"Hm?"

"How did you die?"

For a moment I thought his eyes had turned black, but it was a trick of the light.

"I looked for you and...well. Things were not as easy. My arrogance caught up to me."

"Did you know who I was? Who you were looking for?"

"No. Never. Which led me to make poor choices and poorer friends. And I died. Very soon after you."

He *did not* want to discuss this. Why was that? Did it even matter? We were here together now.  I tried to release my curiosity and stopped pressing him on the subject. My mind wandered, trying to think of something else besides his mysterious death to talk about.

"Where do you think we are?" I asked.

Iskur looked up at the sky, "I recall these stars. They do not change. It is Spring. The first day, or near it."

"You can tell the date by looking at the stars?" I asked, incredulously.

"They are the same as when I lived. Stars do not change much. But," He looked around, "The land is not ours. It is someplace else."

"Where on Earth did we live back then?" I asked, leaning against him sleepily.

"The land of the cedars." He sighed, sounding dreamy, "There was no other name then. We were people of the wood and hills. Others like us were of the sea, and of purple."

"Purple?"

"Oh yes, the most holy of colors. The most beloved and demanded. Our land was beloved by all, and we were skilled at making things."

"I have no idea what you are talking about, Iskur," I said with a yawn.

I closed my eyes and started to drift off to sleep. Just as I was nearly gone, Iskur tensed and hissed quietly. He darted to the fire and stamped it out.

"What are you-"

He put his hand over my mouth. I slapped him away. I *hated* when he did that.

"*There are others near.*" He breathed into my ear.

# XVIII.

I heard the voices. People were approaching from across the valley. Their voices were echoing off the rocks behind us. My skin prickled and a cold sweat broke over me. Iskur took my hand and pulled me up. We raced up the path towards the cave. Virgil was crouched at the cave entrance, looking like he was going to spring at us like an animal.

"It is us." Iskur whispered. Virgil relaxed only slightly.

"Who are *they?*" He hissed motioning out across the valley.

The moon was full and shining brightly onto the landscape. Even if the moon had not been full, I felt like my night vision was quite better than it had been previously on Earth. The other people were still a quarter mile or so away, but we could hear them as if they were only a hundred yards off. A trick of the valley? The way the sound carried? I could make out four figures, all dressed in flowing garments and speaking amongst themselves jovially. None of them carried lights of any kind. They were making their way by moonlight alone. What were they *doing?*

"Did they see the fire?" Virgil asked, his voice barely a whisper.

Iskur shrugged. We watched their slow progress intently for a while.

Go away. Turn around and go away.

They did not go away. Instead they paraded themselves straight for the clearing Iskur and I had been sitting in. Iskur backed the three of us into the cave with Travis used the brush to obscure the entrance slightly. Virgil kept peering out from among the twigs and updating us on the strangers' progress.

"They are in the clearing," He hissed in distress.

"Who are they?" I asked, trying to get a look. Virgil waved me away in irritation.

"They look absurd." He muttered.

"Absurd *how?*" A frightening thought dawned on me and I gripped Virgil's shoulder violently, "Virgil, what year is it on Earth?"

He put his hand up to my mouth to shush and I smacked it away just as I had Iskur's. When would they learn?

"Don't shusshhh me," I breathed, "What year is it?!"

"How would *I know?!*" Virgil hissed back at me under his breath, "I have no idea where or *when* we are."

I peered out between the sticks with him. The four strangers had made themselves very comfortable in our clearing. They were dumping canteens of water onto the embers of our fire, but overall seemed joyful and celebratory.

"We must have scared someone off in a hurry!" A woman with a melodious voice said tartly as she emptied her canteen onto the coals.

"I do hope they come back, it would be lovely to have more souls with us. Don't you agree, Deena?" Another woman, this one sounded like she was high out of her mind. Her voice was airy and slow.

Deena, the first woman, murmured in agreement. She sounded satisfied that the fire was out as well.

"Not very safe, lighting a fire." She said more to herself than to her companions.

"Oh the *moon!*" A man said with a groan of pleasure, "What glory! A full moon on Ostara!"

Virgil looked at Iskur and I in turn.

"*Ostara?*" He mouthed.

Iskur and I shrugged.

"I don't know. They are speaking English though." I whispered.

Virgil shook his head.

"They are but you will be able to understand any language now." He said into my ear, "It will all sound the same to you, you will just know it."

Before I could express my shock at this revelation, Iskur jostled his way in to look at the clearing below.

"It's a delight. We are so blessed. Oh thank you Mother, thank you." Another man with a pitched, sing-song voice began to hum. The other three joined in their own fashion.

I couldn't see them too well if they moved out of the entrance to the trail up to our cave, but they all began pacing and passing around the clearing meditatively as they hummed. I could briefly observe each of them in turn.

The one called Deena was the youngest, maybe in her thirties? She was short-er than the others, with a rather sharp ear-length haircut. She wore a long tunic over hiking pants and boots. The other woman was languid and wavy. Her hair fell in grey ringlets all down her back. She moved around like she was swimming through the air and was wearing countless shirts and shawls and scarves. She was older, near sixty. The first man who seemed to have quite a lunar fixation never took his eyes off the moon. He paced around with a sidestep to keep his face affixed on it. He was dressed in cargo pants and boots, and what appeared to be a long open front tunic. The other man, who had started all the humming, was tall, wiry, and carried a stick. He gave off the air that he thought himself the leader of this group. They all seemed modern enough, contemporary to my last time on Earth as a human at least.

A group of white hippies in the desert speaking English and doing some weird ritual in the middle of the night at the beginning of spring? I knew where we were.

"Oh my god," I breathed, "We're in *fucking* Sedona."

Iskur and Virgil looked at me in confusion.

"Arizona." I was able to speak a little louder, as the humming and singing was reaching a greater volume below.

Virgil's eyes widened.

"Sedona? In *America?*" He said incredulously.

"I think so." I looked back down at the clearing.

The group seemed to be finding their own spaces in the clearing and were not passing by the trail as much. Their chants were competing, like they were all trying to be more loud or authentic or rhythmic than each other and draw the rest of the group to follow their lead. It was an absolute din.

"You said it was the first day of spring, right?" I asked Iskur, using nearly my normal speaking voice.

"Mh. The stars seemed that way. What is this they do? A ritual?" He looked utterly perplexed.

"New age spiritual garbage. I had a friend who was into this shit. She used to go to Sedona or Mount Shasta every equinox to do some weird celestial *thing* and smoke a bunch of weed and fuck outside."

Iskur continued to stare at me.

"Smoke what? And do what outsi-"

"Nevermind. I think we are in Sedona." My face flushed red.

"Weed is a colloquial term for the plant that makes what you would have called *charas*, Iskur." Virgil explained.

"Charas?" Iskur's eyes glinted with mirth, "These people think they are seers?"

"Yeah pretty much." I took a step away from the cave's entrance. Their singing was becoming too much for me.

"If we *are* in Sedona," Virgil retreated into the cave with me, "That is very interesting indeed."

"Why?" I asked, observing the cave in more detail now.

It was about twenty feet deep and ten feet wide with a sloping ceiling that I could stand up comfortably in towards the entrance, but would have to crouch at the back if I went back to where Travis was flopped unceremoniously on the floor. There were no other tunnels or entrances.

"Well, Sedona is a very interesting site..." Virgil was getting lost in thought.

I waved my hand in front of his face.

"Hey!" I snapped, "Explain. The more we all know the faster we can figure this out and get out of here!"

"Well, have you ever been to Sedona?" Virgil glared at me.

"No. Not like, as a human no. Not that I remember."

"Precisely."

"Virg, that explains nothing." I slumped against the wall. Iskur was still watching the hippies with confusion.

"You have never been here and yet you *brought* us here." Virgil was pacing now.

"So? What does that *mean* Virgil, I have no patience for this right now."

"Sedona is a site of great power."

I snorted derisively. "Yeah sure. Powerful bullshit maybe."

"No, it is." He asserted, "The folks who congregate here may not be able to truly connect with the power but it *is* here."

"I don't believe this." I muttered, rubbing my head, "You mean to tell me that these fucking hippies hang out at some sort of celestial highway for real?"

"Yes, a highway is a good analogy. Maybe a bit more like a station on the highway."

"A truckstop." I groaned, "We're at a fucking interstellar truckstop."

"Well, I do not fully understand all of the particulars but there are sites on Earth that humans could converse more easily with the Otherworld, and then there are sites that humans reportedly could reach out to the, well, the Nameless Ones as you say."

Iskur joined us and sat next to me.

"Is this an Otherworld place or a Nameless Ones place?" I asked, rubbing my head.

"Unsure, but if I had to guess I would say Otherworld. Many of these sites were closed off by the Old Dead over time as things became unbalanced, so humans may still be perceptive enough to feel those closures. Or they may flock to the sites out of tradition."

Virgil stopped pacing and sat with us.

"This is a good discovery. Sedona is good."

"Is it, though?" I motioned to the cave's entrance and the horrific singing-wailing that was now occurring outside.

"I do not understand the ritual." Iskur said with a furrowed brow, "I feel nothing from them. They are not chanting with any sort of intention. They are just making noise. I think they are confused."

"Yeah that about sums it up. But it looks like we didn't go *back* in time or anything."

Virgil let out a surprising laugh.

"Oh no, Arga, no. You would not be able to take us back in time onto Earth. It is just a matter of how *much* time has progressed since you died."

"Well I don't know how any of this works, for all I know we could have time traveled back to when Iskur was alive!"

I was getting louder. Iskur's hand flashed up as if he were going to cover my mouth and I fixed him with a withering glare. The voices below trailed off slightly. One or two of the singers had paused in their song. In the brief interlude, a bellowing shout rang from the back of the cave.

"*HELP!*" Travis seized his opportunity to get the attention of the hikers below.

Iskur and Virgil scrambled to stifle further shouts, but the sound had definitely gotten the worshipers' attention. They had all stopped singing and were murmuring to each other in hushed tones. I flew to the cave's entrance to peek out and see what they were doing.

"Yes, I heard it too."

"Up there?"

"I hear something now."

Travis was putting up a fight against Iskur and the shuffling noise echoed in the cave. Virgil had shoved another wad of cloth into Travis's mouth but the muffled shouts were still audible enough. The struggle had drawn the hippies' attention to the trail. They were all congregated at the bottom of it.

"A flashlight?" I heard one of the men whisper.

"No, we didn't bring any technology." The airy woman said.

There was a moment of deliberation, then the two men filed up the path first followed by the two women.

"Hello? Does anybody need help?" The moonlover called. The man who had seemed to so desperately want to be the leader before was shrinking behind the much shorter, bare chested moon-obsessed fellow. The scuffling continued at the back of the cave and I motioned to Virgil and Iskur violently to try to get Travis under control. The posse was making their way slowly up the trail towards the cave entrance. Great, just spectacular. This was what we needed.

"Hellooooo friends?" The airy lady sang, "We can help, we are all friendssss."

I made a sudden decision and pushed aside the brush hiding the cave.

"Heyyy!" I called back, coming out onto the trail and waving slightly, "Hey sorry! Yeah we're good, it's-it's my...cousin. He's having a bad trip."

The moon man walked up swiftly to me and looked me over.

"Hey wow, yeah okay, no worries friend. Was that your fire we put out?"

"Yeah it was sorry w-we were hiking earlier and got split up and he was tripping pretty bad when we found him so like, we were just going to stay out and help him sleep it off but like," I had no idea what had come over me, I was pulling backstory out of thin air and had a flood of worried girl tears on my cheeks, "I don't know it got really scary he's been really violent and we don't have phones and-"

"Oh honeyyyyy," Airy lady was holding me now.

"How many of you are there?" The wanna be leader was pushing himself back in charge now that he saw there was no danger.

"It's me and my boyfriend and my cousin and my brother," I sniffled, "You can come out now, guys."

Virgil was the first one to edge out of the cave. He was giving me the most irate and confused glare he could muster without outright asking me what the hell I was doing.

"This is my brother, Vee." I said, giving my voice a fake shakiness, "And this is my boyfriend, Isaac."

Iskur smiled nervously at the assembled audience as he came out of the cave with Travis in tow. Travis looked like he had been freshly battered by Virgil and was somewhat delirious.

"And my poor stupid cousin Travis." I cried harder, "I don't even know what he *did* earlier but when we found him he was so beat up and just he's just he's been so fucking high all day and he must of gotten a bad batch or something we were so scared."

"Shhh, shhhhhh honey it's okay now you are with friends!"

"Did you try to report him missing earlier today when you got split up?" Mr. Boss asked.

"No of course not, we were out here all day looking for him and didn't bring our phones." I sniffled into the silk hankie the woman had handed me.

"Wow you all look really rough," Deena was eyeing us all suspiciously.

"Yeah, we've been trying to get him back but he's been so violent. He got a swing on all of us a few times." I explained, "And we all slid down a trail at one point."

Deena was inspecting Travis. Iskur had untied his legs but not his arms. Travis was muttering to himself deliriously.

"He seems like he's coming down." Deena observed.

"I'm *not high*," Travis roared suddenly, making the other four jump, "They are imprisoning me!!"

"Easy, pal." The moon man put his hand on Travis's shoulder, "Hey buddy, we've all been there. It's no fun to have a bad trip. Amiright, Clive? Hahaha!"

Moonman slapped the shoulder of the tall man, Clive apparently, in recollection of some past bad trip they had shared. Clive nodded solemnly. Travis settled back down and mumbled to himself.

"We should get you all back to town. Where are you staying?" Deena asked.

"Uh, nowhere yet," I floundered, "We just got to town today. For the solstice - I mean Equinox. Sorry. I'm just-"

"No, honey, angel, baby, no it's okay you have been on a journey today, sweet soul. Come stay with us. We have a beautiful Earthship not far from the park. Plenty of space for weary travelers."

"Thanks," I gave the lady's hand a squeeze, "Uh, I'm H-H....Heather."

"Hello beautiful and brave Heather, I'm Celeste." The woman gave me a surprisingly bone-crushing hug. *Of course* she was called Celeste.

"Hey, I'm Martin." Moonman reached his hand out towards Iskur. Iskur took it slowly, unsure what to do. He clasped Martin's hand and smiled absently.

"Itzak," He said slowly, looking at me for confirmation.

"And I am Vee." Virgil shook everyone's hand rapidly so he could break Iskur's awkward grasp on Martin's hand, "And, again, he is Travis, and he is having a very, *very* bad trip. Can we take him to a hospital, please?"

"Oh no, is it that bad?" Celeste asked slowly.

"Yes, very, very, *very* bad and he needs a doctor. It is urgent." Virgil was speaking in a clipped and frantic manner.

Martin and Clive looked over Travis who was mumbling to himself still.

"Yeaaah he doesn't look good. Let's get him up. Can you walk, friend?" Martin asked Travis amicably.

"I'm *not* tripping." He slurred.

"Sure you aren't, friend," Clive said patronizingly.

He motioned for Iskur and Virgil to come heave Travis up. They obliged and we began to parade ourselves down the trail. Clive led the way, then Deena and Martin, followed by me and Celeste who would not let go of my hand. Iskur and Virgil dragged the weakly thrashing Travis at the rear of our procession.

In the clearing, Clive and Deena gathered up the bags they had brought with them and we paused for a moment. Martin grabbed Travis's feet to help speed the process and got swiftly kicked.

"I'm so sorry, he's such a fucking asshole." I said as Martin reeled backwards.

Virgil dropped Travis with a thud and held him still with a foot on his chest.

"Could I trouble someone find two large branches and a blanket?" He asked in an acidic tone.

"Oh, I brought a blanket!" Deena said triumphantly.

Clive clutched his walking stick preciously.

"We need to make a sling to carry him with." Virgil said, glaring at Clive, "There is no way we can just drag him like this."

Clive sighed and gave over his stick. Martin found another in the brush and Iskur quickly fashioned a sling and rolled Travis into it. Virgil had re-bound Travis's legs and, while nobody was looking besides me, had given him another blow to the head. Groaning slightly but not putting up a fight anymore, Travis was carried between Iskur and Martin in the makeshift sling.

We paraded slowly across the desert in the moonlight. Celeste offered us an endless supply of granola bars, dried fruits, and nuts from her multitude of pockets. My human form still was not requiring food, but I took what she offered. Be normal. A regular human would be starving after such an ordeal.

Virgil came to my side when Celeste went to offer food to Iskur. I heard him exclaim with joy when she produced dried figs for him. I smiled tiredly.

"*What are we doing?*" Virgil asked in a hush.

"Taking Cousin Travis to a doctor. That was *your* idea, darling *brother.*"

"Well yes, I know *that*. I mean," He glanced around, "*After that.*"

"I presume you wanted to *leave* him in the care of a doctor while we..." I trailed off and stared at him expectantly.

"We need to know what year it is." Virgil mused.

"I mean it can't be too much longer after I...you know. Can it?"

"I have no idea."

That thought unsettled me. How long *had* it been? We had reached a much more groomed trail and were making much easier progress across the terrain.

"Is this your first time in Sedona for the Equinox?" Deena had dropped back to match pace with Virgil and I. She was speaking directly to him, ignoring me.

"Oh, well. Yes." Virgil fumbled.

"Oh such a shame that it's been going so poorly for you all so far. It's such a powerful time. The energy it is just so raw." She sighed happily, looking at him for confirmation.

"Oh indeed. I can feel...how...raw it is." Virgil shot a cold glare at me as I stifled a laugh.

Despite the insanity of the situation, things were going well. These folks were going to get us to a hospital, we'd ditch Travis and go clean up somewhere. Then the three of us could figure out what to do next. Maybe after a *true* rest our powers would return and yes. Yes. That would be good. Then we could go back to my realm and live in peace. Forever. Maybe?

But then there was still the looming crisis of the Old Dead. Could they find my realm? Travis found it, could they? Or was it just because he was so connected to me? I felt my anxiety begin to prickle up. I took a deep breath and released it in a shuddering sigh. Instinctively, Virgil grabbed my hand to try and dispel the destroying energy. Deena was still chattering away at him, pelting him with questions about where we were from that he was struggling to answer.

"Oh you would not know our town it is...small." He floundered.

"What state do you live in? Here in Arizona?"

"Oh no, uh no....we live in....uh...Chicago." He was relying on what he had learned from my life as Hollis to construct a backstory.

Deena laughed.

"That's not a small town, jeez! I know Chicago, I live in Milwaukee!"

Virgil let out the fakest laugh I'd ever heard. The comedy of his struggle broke my rising panic and I let the worries of our future slip away. One step at a time. Figure that out later.

"Oh yes! Mill Walky. That is...a place," Virgil struggled.

Celeste saved Virgil from further strain by gliding back into our midst and taking my other hand.

"Vee, is it? Martin is feeling weary and has a bad shoulder. Could you switch with him for this last bit of the journey? I know you must be so tired already. I'm so sorry to ask." She asked kindly.

"Oh of course, yes." Virgil squeezed my hand and went back to take Martin's place at the back of the sling. Once he was situated, we all took off walking again. I could see a road in the distance with a single van parked along it.

"Our chariot awaits!" Clive said boisterously as he motioned at the distant van.

"Oh good it's still here." Deena laughed, "Wouldn't that have been just your luck today, Heather? If our van was missing?"

I frowned at her. This lady was annoying.

"Yeah. It would have been." I said sourly.

"Deena, do not invite negative thoughts to our space. We are guiding our friends out of a time of trouble." Celeste rubbed my shoulders. I tried to casually get her to stop touching me.

"I'm sorry." Deena said sheepishly. She walked on in silence for a bit, then picked up her pace to catch up with Clive.

"Deena is young in the ways of spiritual energies." Celeste explained quietly when we were alone, "Unlike your wonderful soulmate, Isaac. He is such a wonder. I feel such a depth to him unlike any other. You too, Heather. Have you been practicing as a seer for very long?"

"*What?* I uh, yeah. Sort of. I have always...felt things. Seen things. But I'm still figuring it out."

Celeste nodded understandingly and hummed a little.

"I am saddened for you to not have gotten to spend this night in peace, but I feel that our meeting is an important piece of our paths that we do not understand yet."

"Mh. Yes. For sure."

I looked at Celeste with renewed interest. Was she actually perceptive to our differences, or was she *wanting* to see something in us? Neither thought was comforting.

# XIX.

A t last we reached the road. Travis was shuffled into the back of the van and the rest of us piled in. Clive sat in the driver's seat. Iskur seemed perplexed, touching the outside of the van in reverence. Virgil murmured something in his ear and shoved him into the van. I clambered in after them and shoved myself on the bench seat at the back of the van between the two of them. It was, of course, a beat up Volkswagen bus from the 60s. Virgil was struggling to keep Iskur from touching and inspecting everything. I grabbed his hands.

"Later." I said firmly.

Iskur looked at me with bewildered eyes.

"It is like in your life? It is an auto?" He breathed in awe.

Virgil closed his eyes in exasperation.

"Please be quiet."

"Everyone ready back there?" Clive asked.

"Yes we are ready!" I called.

The vehicle roared to life and Iskur jumped. He had the most goofy grin on his face the whole ride to the hospital. I had to try to keep him from smashing his face against the glass like a child to watch the world go past us.

Eventually I sat on Iskur's lap to keep him away from the window as we bumped along the deserted road. The other travelers talked amongst themselves until we arrived at the hospital. The drive felt like it took hours.

"I can come in with you, sweetest ones." Celeste offered as Virgil and Iskur unloaded Travis.

"No, no, we can handle it from here, thank you so much." I hugged her and tried to politely shove her back into the van.

"We'll come back and pick you up. I'm just going to drop Martin and Deena back at the Earthship." Clive sounded particularly final about the situation as he made that decree.

"No, we have already disrupted your evening enough," Virgil said, gritting his teeth to heft the sling onto his shoulders again, "We'll find someplace else to stay."

Deena and Martin laughed.

"Sorry friends, that will be impossible this time of year. There are so many travelers here for the equinox, it will be hard to find a hotel. Is he okay? Sweetie? Isaac?" Celeste moved towards Iskur but I intercepted her.

Iskur was standing transfixed at the illuminated hospital entrance. We were parked right at the door and a pair of paramedics were rushing out towards us.

"He's fine, he's fine, we're good. Really. Please, do not worry about us." I finally maneuvered Celeste away from Iskur and got her back into the van.

"Thank you!" I said, waving.

"We'll be right back." Clive asserted, looking with concern towards Iskur.

Finally, they started the van and drove off into the night. I walked back to Virgil and Iskur. The first two paramedics were loading Travis onto a gurney and a third was approaching Iskur who was still standing dumbfounded and staring at the lights of the building.

"He's fine, he's fine, we're just tired. It's that one you have to worry about." I waved the third paramedic away and hauled on Iskur's arm to get him out of the driveway and onto the sidewalk.

"So what happened?" One of the medics was addressing Virgil.

"The three of us were on a hike and we found him in the desert. He seemed like he was having a really bad trip. We tried to help him get back to town but he got violent."

"You don't know him?"

"We've never seen him before today."

"They know me!" Travis was moaning.

"We really don't." I asserted, trying to sound honest but scared.

"Ari! Stop lying Ari!!!" The doctors were wheeling Travis into the building. Iskur watched the automatic doors open and close. His mouth was hanging open in amazement.

"I don't know any Ari. He keeps saying that name." I said to the medic who was still standing outside with us.

"Okay, did he have any ID on him?" The medic was younger than me, but seemed like he was fed up with drugged out tourists.

"Not that we saw." I said, "But we didn't really look hard."

"Alright, no worries. A John Doe, then." He sighed, "Can I get your names in case the cops have questions for you all later?"

"Sure!" I offered, cutting off Virgil who looked like he was about to protest, "I'm Heather Smith, this is my brother Vee. And my boyfriend Isaac Woods."

The medic wrote some notes sloppily.

"Phone number?"

"Uh...312...area code 312...965...9417." I rattled off the landline I had grown up with.

"Okay great. Thanks, Heather. We should have you three in to get looked at, you look terrible too."

"No no, we are good." Virgil said hastily.

"Look man, I don't give a fuck what you all are on right now. You are all probably dehydrated at least. You didn't eat any plants, did you? Come on in and get an IV and we can make sure nothing's too messed up, okay? At least we can clean those cuts up."

"We'll drink some water and wash up at home," I countered, "I'm sure you have your hands full already."

He snorted in agreement.

"You got that right. You all local?"

"Just visiting. Leaving soon." Virgil said shortly.

"Alright. We'll call that number if the cops have questions. Thanks for helping that guy out. He looks like shit. You all coulda died in the desert. Don't be dumbshits and go back out there tonight." The medic gave us one last suspicious look and walked back inside.

Virgil took off walking with purpose. I drug Iskur along after him.

"Hey, where are we *going?*" I asked as I caught up to him.

"It is *bright*." Iskur said in awe.

"For *fucksake*, Iskur, it is electricity. I taught you about that when Arga first arrived," Virgil snapped. It was the first time I had heard him curse.

"I did not know it would be so bright." Iskur was still trying to turn around to marvel at the hospital.

"Can we please have a plan?" I begged Virgil.

"You are the one who went in without a plan! Making contact with those people! I was not sure they would even be able to *see* us when you went barging out of the cave. They are *humans*, Arga. We are dead! What do you think is about to happen when they find out Travis does not have a heartbeat?"

"Hey! The hospital was your idea!"

"Well how *else* were we going to get rid of him?!"

Iskur had finally returned his attention to Virgil and I. We had made it out of the hospital parking lot and were storming down the side of the road. Iskur let out a low laugh.

"I see why you said he was your brother. It does explain the fighting."

"Shut *up*, Iskur!" Virgil shrilled. I could not help but laugh too.

"This whole thing is absurd." I said, covering the smile on my face with a dusty hand. Once I had started laughing I could not stop.

"You are going to give yourself another seizure," Virgil said, gripping my shoulder, "Stop it."

I took a few breaths and slowed my laughter.

"Mhmhm. Hah. Yeah. Okay. Okay. You are right," I let the manic energy fade away, "Where are we going to go?"

"We should go back out to the desert," Iskur offered, "We can be alone and rest in peace."

"Everyone here is trying to be alone in the desert right now. That's what happens this week." I explained.

"We have no American money. No way to get a hotel." Virgil started walking again. Iskur and I followed dutifully, exchanging glances.

"The ones we met, they have a ship?" Iskur inquired.

"Oh, no, it's like a house. Earthship, you mean?" I asked.

"Yes. Earthship. It is not a ship?"

"No, it's some stupid hippie thing."

"Hippie...?"

"I...nevermind. It's not a boat."

"Mh. But they live in it?"

"Yeah."

"We can go there." Iskur said, smiling as if he had just solved all our problems.

"No, no we cannot," Virgil said tensely, "Because they are going to want to know *why* we are not picking Travis up later. Besides, they are gone. And we are not waiting at the hospital for them."

"Why not?" Iskur frowned.

"Because we do not need to be around humans right now, we need to be alone and to rest and to figure this out."

I watched the two of them argue. Iskur was losing his giddy excitement about the modern world and was growing more enraged with each thing Virgil said.

"We can rest at *their home*," Iskur said aggressively, "They offered it. And one is a Seer."

"She is *not* a "Seer", Iskur," Virgil said with a cold laugh, "There are hardly any seers on Earth at all. And this town will be full of false seers."

"Actually," I said slowly, stepping in between the two of them, "I think Celeste can sense something about us."

"All the more reason to not stay with them- oh for *fucksake*," Virgil growled.

The van was rumbling down the road towards us. Of course it was. It slowed to a halt in front of us and Clive cranked his window down.

"Hello friends! Where are you headed?"

"In search of you." Iskur said, gleefully climbing into the door that Celeste had just opened.

"How is your cousin?"

"He's not well. They are keeping him overnight at least." I got into the van as well, and Virgil followed behind me. I could feel him glaring in rage at my back.

"When he gets released we will cleanse and heal him at our home. We want you all to stay as long as you want. It is an oasis after the pain of your journey so far." Celeste turned in her seat to address us.

"I don't want Travis to come to your house. Honestly, I don't want to continue this journey with him. He's toxic. I think he'll go home after he's out of the hospital." I blabbed.

"Mh. Let us see what tomorrow holds." Celeste said placidly. Virgil clearly took that statement as a threat because he tensed in the seat next to me. I slapped at his leg to get him to snap out of it. Really. Not a single one of us could act slightly normal. Iskur looked like a happy puppy in the van. His head swiveled around to look out each of the many windows.

"How did you make this?" He asked reverently before I could stop him.

"Oh, the seat covers? I crocheted them. You like them?" Celeste said proudly.

"Oh yes they are so pretty." I said quickly, grateful for the misinterpretation of Iskur's question.

I glared at Iskur with my most serious *shut the fuck up* face. Virgil peered around my shoulder to give Iskur the same look. Iskur smiled and took my hand, content to look out at the dark landscape in silence.

# XX.

I t was a short drive to the hippie's house. We arrived as the sky was beginning to brighten with a pre-dawn glow. Iskur nudged me.

"Sunrise." He breathed in awe as we exited the van.

I nodded. He was smiling to himself again, looking utterly pleased. I supposed it would be somewhat pleasing to be back on Earth in his case. It had been eons since he had not been the one in control of the happenings. Night and day and stuff like that. I watched him stare at the sky.

"There's an outdoor shower around back, I'll bring you angels some towels." Celeste was drifting off towards the house.

The structure was made mostly from red clay, with elements of green tile and metal and lots of glass. The whole thing looked like a fairy cottage, sunken into the dirt. The walls were all vaguely curved and it had an organic look to the overall shape of it. Before us there was a low wall a few feet away from the front of the house that opened into a set of steps down to the entrance. The door was framed with sage green metal and opaque stained glass windows. The only angular part of the low, long structure was the roof: it was also made of glass and met at a very steep peak. Ornate metalwork ran along the eaves of the glass roof. Virgil was scowling at the building, but Iskur was still looking East waiting for the sunrise.

"Did you have any belongings with you?" Clive asked awkwardly.

"Uh, no, the airline lost our luggage."

"No carry on?"

"No we just mostly, uh checked bags. I lost my hiking bag earlier today."

"Mine too." Virgil added, not wanting to seem unprepared.

"No worries, no worries," Clive motioned for us to follow him around the back of the house, "I'm sure we can share."

Behind the house was a stone terrace that backed up to a steep red rock cliff. Against the cliff was a wood and tile structure I assumed was the shower Celeste had mentioned. Clive took us to a seating area that was sunken into the ground and strewn with pillows. Above the pit there was a canvas awning with many windchimes and bells hanging from it. They tinkled calmly as we took our seats.

"I like this." Iskur said to Clive.

"Yeah? Celeste did all this herself. She dug it out by hand."

"Wow! It's really lovely." I exclaimed. I admired the tiles and pieces of broken pottery that were inlaid into the stone.

"Yeah, she lives here full time. It is her life's work to welcome travelers to Sedona. I split my time between here and Shasta. I run a self discovery alliance."

"How nice." Virgil said, sounding incredibly sarcastic as he sat on a cushion.

"Mhhmmm. It is nice."

Clive seemed not to notice that Virgil was hating every second of this exchange, especially since we were once again in a conversation pit: his least favorite seating arrangement. Clive, Virgil, and I sat stiffly in silence. Iskur hummed to himself, leaning on two cushions and looking completely at ease.

"There now!" Celeste was floating towards us with a mound of towels and clothes, "I have plenty of linens to share with you sweet angels. Let me show you to the shower, and you all can get your rest."

"Thanks so much." I said, taking the towels and various tie-dyed garments from her.

She led us to the shower and demonstrated its use to us.

"There will not be much for warm water, so you may want to conserve it and share." Celeste suggested.

"*No!*" Virgil and I shouted at the same time.

"Yes, I agree. There is nothing better than a cold shower. So revitalizing." Celeste laughed melodically and waltzed back to the house, "Come in the back door when you are done!"

She and Clive disappeared into the house.

"We are *not* showering together." Virgil asserted as Iskur started to take off his shredded pants.

"Agreed." I rubbed my head. The exhaustion was returning.

"This is something I am just realizing," Iskur paused suddenly, looking between the two of us with suspicion, "Virgil, have we not seen each other-"

"Stop!" Virgil's voice was shrill, "No. Not. We have not and *will not.*"

"But the light form, it is more intimate than being in human form. Human form is just a body. The light form you can see so much more of a person. Who they *really* are. Does it really bother you?" Iskur frowned in thought.

"It is not just a body to most humans," Virgil snapped, grabbing a towel and storming into the shower, "And we must *behave* like *humans.*"

Iskur shrugged and turned to me.

"It would upset you, too?" He inquired as Virgil started the water from inside the wooden shower stall.

"I don't really know what to think right now, Iskur. I'm tired." I sighed, "I don't really want to see anyone naked today."

"No?" He raised an eyebrow with a smirk.

"Please stop."

"I will stop," He winked at me and my face flooded red.

He turned his back to me and busied himself with selecting clothes from the assortment Celeste had brought out. It gave me time to really take in his appearance. He was shorter than in the Otherworld, much closer to my height. But other than that he looked vastly the same. The scars I had given him still laced his skin and glinted in the breaking dawn. Despite being filthy, he looked quite good. Healthy, strong, fit.

"What do I look like?" I asked him.

"Mh?"

"Do I look like I did in the Otherworld?"

He turned to face me.

"You are the same size," He took a step closer to me, "And have the same hair."

Another step closer.

"And your eyes, they are perhaps less bright. But the same color: warm and brown like the bark of our cedars."

He was directly in front of me.

"Stop it." I said, eyes locked with his.

"Arga," He breathed my name out like a playful growl.

"What?" I whispered.

"On Earth it is no different than in the Otherworld," He held out his hand, "I am bound to you in all places."

I took his hand.

"Iskur, I'm just so tired." I said, leaning my head to his chest.

"We will sleep. You must cleanse first."

Virgil emerged from the shower enrobed in his towel. I could see his scars on his arms still, gleaming silvery with the water on his skin. I sighed. Reminders of past and ongoing fuck ups.

I took my shower next, rinsing the grit and grime from my skin and hair. The water went cold just after I began but I did not mind it. The night air was crisp and chilly, but it cleared my head. Iskur showered after me, and was soon done. We all looked ridiculous in the baggy linen tunics and pants Celeste had brought for us. Virgil in particular was irritated about the clothing selection, but didn't say much about it. Until Iskur opted to go shirtless again, at which point both Virgil and I protested on account of the scars drawing too many questions. We had been lucky nobody had mentioned it during the night.

Once inside, Celeste gave us mugs of tea and led us through the cluttered kitchen down more stairs and into a small room filled with pillows and mats.

"This is our meditation space, but you should sleep here. The others will be awake soon and will disrupt your rest if you sleep on the first floor." She explained, giving us blankets and more pillows.

"Thank you, this is so kind of you." I repeated. She was genuinely kind. I liked her.

"It is my honor. Please sleep as long as your bodies require. If I am not around when you wake up, help yourselves to whatever you need in the house. Our home is yours, my friends." She backed out of the room, bowing low, and closed the door.

Once we heard her retreat upstairs, Virgil addressed us solemnly.

"If we regain our powers after we rest, we should try to return to where we first arrived." He said in a calculating voice.

"What if," Iskur countered, flopping onto a pile of cushions and motioning for me to join him, "We take a long rest and do not worry about that part just now?"

I curled up next to Iskur and closed my eyes. Virgil snorted and muttered mockingly.

"Drink the tea, Virgil. It is so soothing. Mint. Good for sleep." Iskur said patronizingly.

I didn't get a chance to hear Virgil's derogatory reply, because sleep took hold of me swiftly.

*Waves crashing.*
*Thunder roaring.*
*Wind blowing.*

To my surprise, I was the first one awake. Both Iskur and Virgil were snoring loudly on either side of me. I knew that I had begun the night tightly entwined with Iskur, but Virgil's proximity surprised me. I smiled after I got over the initial startle of it. The room we were in had two small windows in the ceiling. They were round, made of stained glass that depicted the phases of the moon in one and a caterpillar becoming a butterfly in the other. The sun seemed to be low in the sky, not directly overhead. I guess we hadn't slept too long. Good. I closed my eyes again and breathed in peacefully.

I heard the door crack open and I turned to look at it.

"Oh! You are awake!" Celeste whispered to me, "You poor things. What an ordeal. You must have all been so exhausted."

"What time is it?" I asked.

"Time? Oh, nearly seven."

"I didn't sleep too long then." I mumbled, sitting up and yawning.

"Seven at night, angel. On Tuesday."

"Tues...What?"

"Angel, Heather, we met on Sunday night. You three have slept nearly two whole days." She spoke sweetly, but her eyes were distant and calculating.

"Oh my go-" I smacked Virgil, "Wake up!"

"What?!" Virgil bolted upright in a panic that also awoke Iskur.

"Virgil, stop." He groaned, putting his arm over his eyes, "We can try to see if we have our power back later-"

"Celeste is here." I informed them, extracting myself from our tangle of blankets.

"Who...OH." Iskur sat up and whipped around until he saw Celeste.

"My sweet travelers, it is an honor to let you rest your bodies, but you must know that I have been worried about you all. You have hardly stirred this whole time."

"We...must have been...tired." I smiled, trying to act normal. What did she think of us? We hadn't gotten up for *two days?* Had she been trying to wake us?

"Please, come and eat. I cannot imagine the hunger you must feel."

We followed her obediently, and sat in a variety of mismatched wooden chairs around a long table while she assembled fresh fruit and vegetables for us.

"Clive wanted to call an ambulance for you all at first, but I told him not to worry. He flew out Monday morning. Back to his compound at Mount Shasta. I told him that you are all healing and that I would watch over you. And see? You seem so very healed now. I can sense your energies have balanced. I told everyone else you had departed as they slept, so they would not be disturbed by your lack of waking."

Lying for us to keep the nosy others out of our business? So, she was onto us afterall, wasn't she?

"Where *is* everyone else?" Virgil asked.

"The equinox is completed and our guests have begun to leave. Martin remains, but Deena has left. She was quite fearful for your cousin, so she begged me to remind you all about him. We will go visit him in the hospital once you have eaten."

"No!" I bellowed, "I'm sorry, no, I mean, I told the doctors to call his mom. She's taking care of it. Our aunt. She'll sort it out. I really don't want to see him after all of that."

"Oh well, then that is just perfection. A welcome end to that tumultuous chapter for you." Celeste was staring at us all inquisitively and blinking far fewer times than I was comfortable with.

"Cheers." Virgil raised his glass of orange juice in a mock toast. Iskur nodded with his mouth full of dried figs and vigorously clinked his glass with Virgil's. I couldn't help but smile at their exchange.

"Well sweet travelers, what is your next path?" Celeste started peeling herself an orange.

Iskur leaned back in his chair and tossed some blueberries into his mouth, deferring to Virgil and I to field the question. I stared at Virgil who started opening his mouth with uncertainty.

"Oh, forgive me, let me first say that you are all welcome to stay as long as you like here with me." Celeste said, putting her hand on mine, "I know your plans must have been terribly upset by that ordeal, and you missed most of the equinox festivities with your...*long sleep*. I do not want you to feel that your travels were in vain. It would be such a joy to have you stay. I could guide you and your spirits on a journey of our energetic vortexes."

"*Vortices*," Virgil muttered.

"There are some lovely sites, and you said you all have never been to Sedona before. It would be a shame for you to not get to experience the vortexes. They will change your lives." Celeste went on, completely oblivious to Virgil's flinching at her continued use of the word *vortexes*.

"I think we need to talk about what our path is. We have already used up so much of your hospitality-" I tried to extract my hand from hers.

"Shush! Nothing like that. It is my honor to have you here. Martin is staying another day, and then it will just be me in this lonely rambling home for a few weeks until I host our next spiritual retreat. I would be so overjoyed if you stayed!"

"We will need to talk about it first," Virgil shot me a serious look. Celeste really was growing on me and I was about to agree to staying with her, despite how certain I was that she was on to us.

"Of course, loves."

"It is so kind of you." Iskur said warmly.

He leaned forward and rested his arms on the table thoughtfully. He made very intense eye contact with Celeste for almost a full minute, much to Virgil's horror. I laughed nervously and moved dishes around on the table haphazardly, trying to break their concentration.

"You are a wonder." Celeste breathed, breaking eye contact at last and shaking her head slowly, "All three of you...I feel that our meeting is of deepest importance. I will meditate on this in the garden. Please, make yourselves at home. Martin should be back from taking Deena to the airport in an hour or so. He can help you all get situated in one of the guest spaces. I do not wish to be disturbed."

She bowed deeply and floated out into the garden.

"What the *hell* was that?" I hissed when it was clear she was far from the house.

"She is a Seer," Iskur said, looking very pleased with himself, "And my power is returning."

"What did you *do?*" Virgil demanded.

"I looked at her. She looked at me."

"What did you let her *see?*" Virgil jumped up from his chair in a panic. I caught a bowl of grapes he had sent wobbling off the edge of the table.

"She saw enough." Iskur smirked in an infuriatingly self-satisfied manner.

"*Iskur,*" I seethed, "Stop being cryptic! She is already very *suspicious* that we slept for two entire *days* without eating or doing anything else. What did you show her?"

"What. Did. You. Show. Her?" Virgil said through gritted teeth.

"As you say, she could already sense we are not entirely human," Iskur tossed a plum in the air and caught it, "I gave her a taste that she is right. Nothing specific, just a glimpse of what is ancient, vast, and infinite beneath our surface. I cannot yet do anything so dramatic as display my full depth of power and age to her. Did you hear? I said '*My power is returning*'? But no, it is all '*What did you do, Iskur?*' Not, '*How is your power returning, Iskur?*'"

Virgil was pinching the bridge of his nose and growling at the floor.

"Wait," The snarky statements Iskur was making started to sink in, "Your *power?*"

"At last my love, you appreciate the joy of this moment!" Iskur threw the plum in the air again. Instead of catching it, he made it levitate.

"*Stop that!!*" Virgil snapped in a shrill panic, looking around as if a crowd of humans were going to pop out of hiding any second.

"Please, celebrate for one second? Here," Iskur's mood was buoyant. He snapped his fingers and Virgil's shattered glasses were mended, "Try it yourself!"

Iskur flicked his wrist and sent the plum rocketing at Virgil. Virgil flinched, and held up a hand. The plum stopped in midair. I let out a whoop of joy.

"Shhhhhh!!" Virgil let the plum drop to the floor, but Iskur was already spinning two oranges through the air above his outstretched palms.

"Arga, try it!"

Iskur ignored Virgil's incoherent protests and flicked an orange at me. Like Virgil, I stopped it midair before it smacked me in the face. I cackled with glee, and sent the orange flying across the kitchen in loops. Then another, and another. Fruit was spiraling around us in chaos as Iskur and I laughed with joy.

"SssssstttttooooOOOOOPPPPP!!" Virgil's face was a strange mix of triumph and terror as he waved his arms and all the fruit fell to the floor at his command.

"What is this, a food fight?" At the exact second that the various fruits landed on the floor, Martin walked into the kitchen. That was much less than the hour Celeste had estimated before he returned. All three of us nearly jumped out of our skins.

"*Oh god!* No, haha, you startled me. Uh no, not a food fight, Iskur was juggling poorly, sorry." I scurried to gather up the fruit with Virgil and Iskur.

"Isk...who?" Martin joined the three of us in picking up oranges.

"Isaac! Sorry, it's an inside joke. It's his nickname. It's what I call him. Isaac sucks at juggling. Sorry about the mess." I flushed red. Get the story *straight.*

"So smooth." Virgil muttered so only I could hear it. I glared at him.

"I am just glad to see you three awake and peppy!" Martin and I placed the fruits back on the table, "You were really scaring us for a bit there, but Celeste insisted that we do not call an ambulance. Then you all took off on Monday. Glad you are back!"

"Hah, yeah, yes. Yeah. Yeah, we are good. Just so-so-so tired." I stumbled on my words.

"For sure! I've been there. Once went on a bender and didn't hardly get out of bed for a week. You all didn't have any of what your cousin had, did you?"

"No, no he was the only idiot to have whatever that was." Virgil waved his hand dismissively.

"Deena was sure worried about him. Just dropped her off at the airport. All she talked about on the way there was you all. Have you heard from the hospital?" Martin sat at the table with us.

"Oh he's, uh, his mom is taking care of it. We called her. Our aunt is going to deal with him. I'm done with that ass." I said bitterly.

"I am so sorry that he ruined your experience for the equinox. But did Celeste tell you that she wants you all to stay as long as you like? She is very happy to have you."

Martin smiled broadly revealing a gold tooth. He was a stocky, squat man with dark curly hair and a receding hairline. His eyes were hard but kind, and his hands looked like he worked with them. He was not the lithe willowy hippie that Celeste was, nor the tall hiker type that Clive was. He had a blue collar vibe to him.

"Yes, she made that generous offer to us," Iskur smiled broadly, "We are very inclined to stay."

"That is wonderful! Where is she? I'm sure she'll be overjoyed." Martin stood up.

"She is meditating in the garden and wants to be alone," Virgil said quickly.

"Ah, that's good. She always puts in so much work into these special ceremonies. Her and Clive. But really her. This space is so wonderful and she just really makes folks feel safe. Well, you all know that! Hah!" Martin laughed loudly and slapped Virgil heartily on the back.

"Yes she is so kind." I agreed, "Uh, she mentioned that you could show us to some rooms?"

"Of course! Right this way. Ready to sleep again? Best sleep I get is in this house. Best sleep all year!" Martin set off and we followed dutifully.

He led us out of the kitchen and through a large room towards the front of the house that was filled with plants and pillows. The waning sunlight was filtering in through the glass roof and casting colorful glowing shapes onto us as we passed through. We then went down a long hall absolutely covered with paintings, weavings, stained glass pieces, drawings and photographs. At the end of the hall we came to a large circular room lined with windows that overlooked a side garden. Cacti and desert flowers were clustered around stone and tile sculptures. The room itself was filled with hammocks of various sizes.

"This is one option. You all are young, my back won't let me sleep like this anymore." Martin chuckled, "Celeste has her room down that way. And there are two other smaller private rooms down there as well. I was sharing one with Clive, it's a mess from us still but I'll clean it when I go tomorrow. And Deena already cleaned hers pretty good, I think. Let's look."

Martin took us down a short flight of steps that curved and led us beneath the hammock room. There were three doors along the curved wall at the base of the steps. He went to the one on the far right zed opened it.

"Sure enough. Seems like Celeste got in here and cleaned, too. Fresh sheets and looks like some more extra clothes for you all."

The room featured four beds carved into walls; two on the right side wall and two on the wall straight ahead. Like dug out bunkbeds. There were ladders carved into the walls for the top bunks. On the floor was a plush carpet and, of course, more ornate pillows and cushions. The non-bed wallspaces were decorated with mosaics and tiles of plants. There was no window, as we were underground, but some candles were lit in little alcoves on the walls. The space was cozy and cheerful.

"Would this do? You could have my room when I'm gone tomorrow but my Cpap machine makes an awful din otherwise I'd offer to share with you tonight." Martin was addressing Virgil, assuming that my "brother" would not want to be in the same room as us two lovers.

"This is fine, yes. Thank you, Martin." Virgil said curtly.

"Great! Let's go have some tea." Martin thumped Virgil again and walked us back up to the kitchen.

Once there, he busied himself making tea and filling us in on the history of Celeste and her Earthship home. Virgil kept asking pointed questions, trying to figure out what year it was.

"So, when did she move here?"

"Oh gosh, I don't know. Years ago."

"Mhhh. Yes. Mhh. And when did you meet her? How long have you two known each other?"

"Oh, a few years back, but it feels like a lifetime, you know? Celeste is one in a million. She met me when I was at my lowest. Working a contract out in North Dakota on that pipeline. It was miserable. She was out there protesting and we ended up talking everyday for weeks. She changed my life. Changed my *life*."

Martin got glassy eyed and lost himself in thought as he poured our tea.

"God I guess it was more like, wow I don't know, guess it's been seven years. Feels like yesterday, you know? And a lifetime ago." Martin continued with a quiet laugh, "Yeah. Back in 2016 is when I met her."

"*Twenty sixteen?!*" I shrieked, dumping over my tea as I sprung to my feet.

Martin put his hand on his chest in fear.

"Whoa girl, easy! Heart's not what it used to be! Hah!" Virgil skillfully avoided Martin's hearty backslap that time, "2016 was a rough year for lots of folks. But not nearly as bad as 2020, amiright?"

"Twenty...twenty...?" I was weak in the knees. I slumped back into my chair.

Martin looked at each of us in turn, trying to get a grasp on what my reaction meant. Iskur was unphased, I was hyperventilating, and Virgil was mouthing numbers and counting in a cold sweat while watching me closely in terror. Iskur sipped his tea and took my hand calmly.

"Martin?" Iskur asked sweetly.

"Yeah?" Martin kept his eyes on me while he wiped up the spilled tea.

"What year is it?"

Virgil sputtered and went into a coughing fit.

"Heh...uh...it's 2023." Martin was now regarding us with intense confusion, "Heather? You alright, sweetie?"

I was not alright. Nothing about this was *alright*. I felt a tiny crackle of my destroying energy flare up inside me, but I forced it down. Iskur was pulling me into his arms and cradling me on the floor. I tried to talk to him but couldn't feel my face. The room was spinning and turning black. Sparks flooded my vision and my hearing went in and out. I hear the sounds of oceans and thunder.

"She's having a seizure," I heard Virgil informing Martin in a commanding tone, "Keep her on her side!"

Thirteen years. I had been dead for thirteen years.

Everything went black.

# XXI.

*A train passing overhead.*
*My mother coming home late in her work uniform.*
*Pigeons scuttling across the sidewalk.*
*I was smiling.*
*A tiny apartment that smelled like cigarettes.*
*I was frowning.*
*A small blue bird drinking nectar out of a purple flower.*
*Wind blowing my hair across my eyes.*
*Travis hitting me hard across the face.*
*Iskur touching my cheek gently.*
*Sun shining through the leaves of the fig tree.*
*I was laughing.*
*The world was ending.*

I awoke to the sound of gentle humming and the feeling of cool hands on my forehead. My chest tightened and churned.

"*Mom?*" But no, it wasn't her voice. Where was I? Who was that?

"She's coming back. Sh, sh. It's alright."

"Back up, everyone!" That was Virgil. I knew him. I could picture him. But where were we?

I opened my eyes. I was still on the floor of the kitchen in Iskur's arms. Iskur. I knew him too. He smiled nervously as our eyes locked and placed one of his hands over my face as if to shield me from the overhead light.

"Close your eyes for a moment," He said soothingly, "Just rest. You are here."

"Does that happen often?" Martin was terrible at whispering.

"Yes, it is something she has dealt with all her life." Virgil explained.

"Oh poor angel." That was Celeste, who must have been kneeling on the floor near me, "Did you happen to time it, Isaac?"

"It was a minute and a half active. And she was unconscious for about three minutes total." Virgil again, "A bigger one, but normal."

"Does she have epilepsy?" Celeste asked kindly, placing her hands on my back and gently rubbing.

"No, no it is something else. Hard to diagnose, really."

"Is that why you all are here?" Martin inquired, "For the healing energies?"

"Uh, no? Well, yes. Sort of." Virgil struggled.

"Yes. We all need healing in our own ways." Iskur's hand was still over my face, but he tilted it slightly so he could look at my eyes. He must not have liked what he saw, because he covered them back up quickly.

"I'm so sorry." I murmured. All this attention on me was awful.

"Oh Heather! No! You are not at fault." Celeste was still rubbing my back. Despite my discomfort at the general attention I was receiving from everyone in the room, I had to admit, the rubbing felt really nice.

"Let me get some pillows," Martin offered. I heard his steps retreat.

"Virgil, could you turn off the lights?" Iskur implored, sounding tense, "It is hurting her *eyes*."

The way he emphasized the words made my suspicions grow. My eyes must have turned black.

"Certainly." Virgil obliged. I heard the lights flick off but Iskur did not remove his hand.

I was feeling raw and achy, and a small amount of residual energy was crackling between where Iskur's skin met mine. Could Celeste feel it? Iskur must have wondered the same thing.

"Celeste, could you turn off the lights going down to our room? I will carry her down."

"Of course, of course," She bustled off.

I heard Virgil waylay Martin and redirect him as well.

"Arga," Iskur kissed my cheek, "Can I move you?"

"Yeah, are my eyes black?"

He moved his hand.

"Yes. Still."

I let out a nervous breath.

"It is fine. It will subside. You will need to rest, but it will subside."

"She knows."

"Yes. I believe so."

"Did she see?"

We were talking in clipped, rapid whispers as he stood and lifted me up.

"I think she may have."

"*Fuuuuuck.*"

"Close your eyes." Iskur kissed my cheek again.

I obeyed instantly, overcompensating and squeezing them very tightly shut.

"Are you in pain?" Celeste floated over to us. I could hear her skirt swishing as she moved swiftly to follow Iskur as he carried me out of the kitchen and down the hall.

"No, no, it's not so bad now. I just get so tired. It feels like getting the shit kicked out of you." We were at the steps now.

"Let me know if you need anything at all. Martin and I will be upstairs for some time yet. And you know where my room is?"

"Yes, yes thank you so much." Virgil said to Celeste then followed quickly after us.

Once we were alone in our room, Iskur arranged me comfortably on the floor in a heap of pillows and situated himself with me.

"*Fuck.*" Virgil whispered.

"Agreed." I said with a sigh.

"How are you feeling?" Virgil sat with us and looked at me in the dim light from the candles on the walls.

"Getting better. That one felt like back in the Otherworld. Like the static-y feeling again. The destroying energy."

"I felt it. Yes, it seems like that power returns for you too." Iskur said pensively, rubbing my shoulders.

"Well. Fuck." Virgil was pacing slowly.

"I have to say, Virgil," I laughed hollowly, "I love your new vocabulary."

He shot me an acidic glare.

"My descent into vulgarity is entirely *your* fault." He sounded like he was trying to tease me, but he was a bit too anxious for the sarcasm to come through fully.

"Are my eyes still black?"

"Not anymore. They changed back when we got in here." Iskur smiled slightly, "Do you know what caused it this time?"

"What *caused it?*" Virgil stopped pacing and turned slowly to look at Iskur dumbfounded, "You cannot be serious."

Iskur looked hurt, he frowned.

"It is the year? How short she has been dead?"

"*Short?!?*" I sat up in a flash and regretted it instantly. I got very dizzy and had to steady myself on the nearest pillow. My spine felt like it had been crushed by a giant. I slumped back to the floor.

What terrible thing had happened in 2020 that Martin alluded to? When I had died we had cellphones and internet and television and video games, were there chips implanted in people's heads now? Flying cars? Don't be ridiculous. Had we seen flying cars so far? No.

"You think thirteen years is *short?*" Virgil asked, incredulous.

"Yes? Thirteen years is not so long of a time? No?" Iskur was second guessing himself based on the looks on both Virgil's and my face.

"Iskur, thirteen Earth years is a significant amount of time for humans," Virgil explained slowly.

"I was not sure if she anticipated more time had passed in the Otherworld perhaps?"

"No, Iskur, thirteen years is like...that's not...I just....it did not *feel* like it was that long in the Otherworld." My head was reeling again. I clenched my eyes shut.

"What did you expect?" Iskur looked between the two of us.

"Much less. Maybe five years." Virgil mused.

"*Five?!* You *expected* five?"

"Well, due to Travis being deceased I assumed *some* time had passed on Earth."

"Fuck. Yeah, I forgot he is technically dead too. How did he die?" I rubbed my head.

"Technically? He *is* dead. Actually dead. It is not a technicality, it is a fact." Virgil was sitting in front of me. He pulled my hands away from my face and peered into my eyes.

"Arga, I know it is very hard, but we do need you to get a grip on things."

"Get a *grip?*" I snarled, snatching my hands out of his, "This is all coming as quite a *shock* to me, okay? I have not adjusted to one thing being true the entire time I've been dead before I've been fucking blindsided by the next insane development, okay? I have a pretty fucking good grip all things considered, you smug little *fucker.*"

Virgil looked ashamed and slightly hurt as he slowly stood up. Good. He deserved it for telling me to get a grip. Get a grip. Did I need to list the unbelievable litany of crazy things that had happened to me since I'd entered the Otherworld?

"You are right." He said with a sigh.

"Say it again, asshole." I growled, despite feeling a little bad about berating him.

"You are right." He repeated with sincerity.

"Arga-" Iskur started in a beseeching tone.

"No," Virgil held his hand up to stop Iskur, "No, she is right. I am the asshole in this. This is all incredibly hard for her and I am not making it easier."

"Thank you. Apology accepted," I said sourly, crossing my arms.

"But we all need each other in this. There is no sense in fighting." Iskur leaned around me to look at my pouting face.

"Fine." I grumbled.

"Yes. Agreed." Virgil nodded. He walked to one of the lower bunks and sat on the edge of it.

"We need to figure all of this out." I said, allowing Iskur to pull me back to lean against him again.

"I do not think we can figure it out right now. You need to rest." Iskur said, wrapping his arms around me.

"We just slept for like two whole days without eating or drinking or anything, it's going to seem weird for me to sleep again." I rubbed my temples, which were throbbing.

"Celeste is a Seer. She knows we are something else." Iskur said tactfully, "And after a seize- what is it called?"

"Seizure." Virgil said.

"Yes. Right. After a seizure I do not think it is strange to rest." Iskur looked over at Virgil for agreement. Virgil nodded.

"You just had a gran mal seizure, or whatever the equivalent is for someone who is dead and is not technically occupying a physical body in the human sense. You at least need a short rest. Anything else would be strange. If Celeste or Martin are familiar with seizures they will be astounded how quickly you came back to cognition. Iskur and I can stay awake for a few hours more."

"How do you know so much about seizures, Virgil?" I asked.

Virgil smiled sadly.

"I had a new dead who died of them when I was a Greeter. Long ago, but still. I learned a lot about them. Anyways, Iskur and I will socialize for a few hours then retire to bed."

"Hours, years. This time passing is so strange on Earth. I could not forget how to *breathe* over thousands of years but I forgot entirely how one day feels." Iskur complained with a laugh.

"We will have to adapt, and fast." Virgil frowned thoughtfully.

"Just get a watch." I suggested.

"What?"

"Take watches," Iskur nodded, "Yes, we can take shifts in watching and being awake, interacting with the humans."

"No, not like *military* watches, no, like a clock." I pointed to my wrist for Virgil's understanding.

He shrugged blankly.

"You are an expert on human culture! You know what a gran mal seizure is but have no clue what a watch is?" I cried, "A clock you wear on your wrist!"

"A wristwatch?"

"*Yes.*"

"Oh yes, I am familiar. Yes. I am remembering the invention of clocks. Sundials first, and other structures, then the winding mechanical apparatus, and clocktowers, and they got smaller and smaller eventually. Correct? Becoming on wrists? Oh, and pockets! And walls and stoves? The digital age was a mess of inventions, I sometimes get things confused."

"Yes. That's clocks. Get a wrist watch. Or a pocket watch, that is more your style." I sighed, "What did you learn about if you don't understand watches?"

"The big inventions, mostly. The type that impacted the way humans lived. Clocks certainly, but I learned more about electricity, trains, cars, telephones, blood transfusions, airplanes, telegraphs, and the postal services. Submarines as well. Nuclear bombs. Penicillin. Computers. Syphilis."

"Stop, just stop."Imagining Virgil taking detailed notes on each thing he listed had me laughing.

"I do not know about any of those things." Iskur laughed along with me.

"Oh god, how are we going to convince anyone *he's* a human?" I burst into more manic, anxiety filled laughter. This was going to be impossible.

Virgil started cracking up as well, laughing quietly at first but falling into a fit of uncontrollable hysterics and sliding onto the floor. His hysterics make Iskur and I laugh all the harder. After a few minutes of belly-aching laughter, we began to recover one by one. To my surprise, I was the last to stop laughing. Both Virgil and Iskur were smiling at me sweetly, looking truly glad to see me laugh. How nice. How momentarily nice.

"Alright," I said smirking, "Enough. I do need to rest. But I would feel better if we had a plan first."

"I will inquire about a wrist watch." Virgil said, "And you will rest for six hours."

"I meant after that." I threw a pillow at him, "Hey, how did you time my seizure without a watch?"

"There is a clock on the kitchen wall. It is shaped like a black cat. The eyes move, it is very off-putting." Virgil shivered. "Anyhow, what more of a plan could we possibly make? We need to recover our strength fully before we begin any sort of effort towards returning."

"I think we should stay here for a while, and go with Celeste to the vortexes." I offered.

"*Vortices.*" Virgil corrected.

"Okay, nobody calls them that here, and we *have* to fit in, so get over that. Grammar police. Fuck, Virgil, we have bigger problems." The mirth I had been feeling was rapidly wearing off.

"Easy, easy," Iskur chanted soothingly.

"I, for one, think we should get as far from Travis as possible." Virgil suggested, "But that is neither here nor there if we do not have any means to travel."

"If we can find out if the vortexes are actually powerful, we could perhaps travel back and *not* have to deal with him at all." I countered.

"Hm. Valid point." Virgil considered this for a moment, "Iskur?"

"Yes?"

"Do you have any thoughts on places on Earth that may be better sites to connect with the Otherworld?"

"I recall the places in my land which were easier to speak with the dead, but I do not know how far that is from where we are."

"We are in America, and you lived in Lebanon. So, quite far." Virgil stared up at the ceiling in thought.

"Lebanon? We'd have to fly there." I said.

"Fly?" Iskur shifted so he was looking at me directly.

"Good grief, have you not seen *anything* on Earth in recent years?" Virgil looked horrified at Iskur.

"No, Virgil, you know that." Iskur said sadly.

"No, I do not know that." Virgil squinted suspiciously at Iskur.

"Why didn't you check on how things on Earth were going?" I asked, confused, "Didn't you want to see the world change?"

"I could not see it."

"What do you mean?"

"After I died I could not see Earth like others could. When I went to the vision portals that were opened, the visions were clouded. I could exert my power from the Nameless Ones to make it uncloudy, but the first time I did so the Old Dead were curious what I had done. That portal had opened slightly wider and they were certain it had been me. I convinced them it was not and never tried to look at Earth again. It was agony."

"Why?" I was watching his face become creased at the pain of the memory.

"I could not look for you, Arga. I did not remember who you *were*, but I knew I was missing something. I knew I had left something of great importance on Earth but I could not look. And after my incident, they began closing up the portals and limiting the ways that the dead could interact with Earth. That was when I suggested I be fully isolated. A gesture of good faith to the Old Dead to keep them from caring about me so much."

"All the portals are all foggy windows now." Virgil sighed, "Above all the Old Dead love balance and peace in the Otherworld. The portals to Earth were causing too much involvement between the Otherworld and the daily life of humans. So they began closing them. They are thorough if nothing else."

"Arga, it is like I said, the times when you and I lived it was so much easier to hear and speak with the dead. Many were able. At times the most powerful among the dead would interact directly with Seers on Earth and come among them."

"Yes. And the Old Dead disliked how that was pulling the Otherworld into more and more involvement with Earth events. It was unbalanced." Virgil was thinking deeply again, his brow was furrowed.

"But, you were able to widen a portal, Iskur? You could open it up?" I asked, my mind racing. If he could *widen* a portal...

"From the other side, yes. On the Earth side it took both you and I. And that was before the Old Dead closed the portals more securely."

"But, maybe we could do it together now?"

"We could try." Iskur smiled mischievously.

"I think you are right, Arga. The vortices here may be worth exploring first. Then, if nothing becomes of it, we can figure out how to go to Lebanon."

"Lebanon." Iskur sighed, "It is a pretty word. They did not have that word in my time."

"No. It is a new name. Somewhat. New to *you* certainly." Virgil stood up.

"You should sleep, Arga." Iskur placed his hand back over my face.

I pushed Iskur's hand away only to find that it was not there. I opened my eyes in confusion and realized I was alone on the floor of the room.

"What a rude trick. That dirty-" I growled, rolling onto my side.

"Was it not good sleep?" Iskur was sitting on the floor near the door of our room.

"I don't appreciate you putting me to sleep without my permission." I snapped, sitting up and glaring at him. He held up his hands with a sheepish grin.

"Easy, easy. Apologies. But you needed to sleep."

"*Ask me* before you do that!" I thrashed myself out of the blankets I had been carefully wrapped in and strode to stand in front of him. The vision of him with the Old Dead flitted into my mind:

*"You will have to help in her undoing when she consents to it. It is only you that can deal the final blow."*

"I don't like you powering over me." I put my hands on my hips and glared at him menacingly. He smiled and leaned his head back to look up at me, which unsettled me greatly. My face flooded with heat.

"I will ask next time." He said in a low rumble.

"The Old Dead said you could kill me. Or unmake me or something. I saw them talk to you."

"Ah," Understanding my rage he nodded, "Yes. Our souls are bound, so to unmake you I would need to unmake myself as well. You would have to fully surrender to it. No part of you could resist. But you, my love, you could unmake me without my willingness."

He reached out for my hand and I let him take it. He kissed my palm, then slowly placed it on the top of his head. I stared down at him as he met my gaze with another fiendish grin.

"You could have me at your mercy. You are far stronger than I am."

"I'm not and I-I don't want that."

"Mh." He closed his eyes, "Whether you want it or not, it is the state we are in."

I pulled my hand away, disgusted. My guts churned and my throat went dry.

"Why are you acting like this?" I was being crushed by a boulder.

"I have been reflecting on all that has happened recently." Iskur did not move to stand up, but remained seated on the floor leaning against the wall next to the door.

"And?"

"And you tore a hole between the Otherworld and Earth."

"I didn't mean to."

"But you did it."

"Iskur, what-"

"Arga."

Oh the way he said my name. It was agony and joy all in one and it silenced me.

"Arga," He repeated with a half smile, seeing he had me hushed and fixated, "Your powers are beyond what I ever imagined they would be. I do not think you understand how much I adore and revere what you have become. And what a glorious debt I owe to you. Coming here to Earth, it shows me how truly anointed we are. I am so undeserving."

"*Shut up.*" I whispered hoarsely, "You are only saying that because of the stupid oath."

"No. It is true. Your existence and power are a gift beyond imagining."

"You forfeit your freewill to be subservient to me if you broke the oath, and I made you break it so I could be with you."

The black ball of despair that had started forming in the back of my mind when I had remembered the terms of Iskur's oath was one of the roots of my fear. I hadn't put it to words until that moment, but in saying it I realized how heartbroken I was over that fact. He was enslaved to me. His soul was tied to mine and his love was drawn out through a curse or contract sanctified by an omnipotent being we didn't understand.

"You think that I have no freewill?"

"You don't! '*I vow to prevent her betrothed from killing her, or let my fate be endless servitude to her in this life and the next.*' That's what you vowed!"

"For love and for duty. Loyal. Bound to her. Subservient until my undoing. My oath demands it." He smiled as he finished the vow, "You remember."

"I can't stop thinking about the fact that I have you trapped here and I-"

"Trapped?"

"You can't leave me."

"I *will not* leave you. There is a difference."

"What's the difference? You are stuck."

"Do you want me to leave?"

His brow creased in confusion. He spoke slowly, cautiously.

"If I wanted you to, would you? Could you, even?" I choked back tears, "The beauty of loving someone is knowing that they *choose* to be with you. Not that they are forced to."

Iskur laughed.

"Arga, I made the vow. I made that choice. Thousands and thousands of years ago."

"But you are tainted by it, forced to keep loving me even when I'm a monster-"

"Tainted? Monster? Arga, stop this. I am not tainted and you are not a monster."

"Iskur we *killed* people. We begged for power we don't understand and I don't know how to control it. What if I-" My voice broke.

"You will not do it again. You have such a kind heart. You always have."
He took my hands again and wrapped his hands around them.

"You can't know that!"

"I do know it. And Arga," He brought my hands to his lips, "Arga, I
choose to love you every moment. The oath was not that I would love you.
It was that I owed you a debt. I can be bound to you and hate you. But I do
not. This love? This is the choice. There are marriage vows made less kind
and less loving than the oath I made to you."

I couldn't speak. He put my hands back on his head and breathed deeply.
His eyes were locked with mine. My vision hazed as I refused to blink and
break our stare, giving Iskur a grey aura. Or was he shifting into his light
form?

The oath wasn't some sort of love spell that forced his affections? The
revelation made me giddy. He had freewill to develop his feelings naturally.
I could not deny mine for him.

"Maybe we are both tainted." My voice was breathy.

"Maybe. Tainted and anointed." He drew me down to him.

"Cursed and blessed." His cheek was warm against mine.

"Arga, whatever we are, I am yours."

I closed my eyes and felt the warmth of every sun we had walked under
together. His hands reached up into my hair. I could smell figs and warm
sea air and fragrant cedars.

"You are mine," I whispered, "And I am yours."

I wanted to shift out of my body and be with him. How delicious it
would feel, how safe. The thought had barely formed in my mind when the
door to the room slammed open.

"Well, Celeste would like to- What are you *doing?*" Virgil had breezed
into the room with a jovial stride, but paused mid step upon seeing us
entwined in our human forms.

"Celeste wants what?" No rest for the wicked. No moment of private joy.

Virgil squinted at me suspiciously then glared at Iskur, who flashed him
a devious grin. With a roll of his eyes, Virgil continued:

"Celeste would like to show us the vort-exes," He shuddered at the incorrect pluralization, "Later today if you are feeling refreshed."

"Uh, well, how long have I been asleep?"

"It is seven in the morning. On Wednesday."

"Okay, okay, cool. Good. That's a normal amount of sleep for after a seizure, right? What are Celeste and Martin doing now?"

"Celeste did some sort of sunrise greeting meditation in the back garden several hours ago, which she invited me to as I was awake. And Martin has only recently woken up and is packing to leave."

"What was the ceremony?" Iskur asked, standing up.

"What? Oh that. I do not know all the details. It was a focus on the planet. On the sun rising. On the potential of a new day and the promise that it holds. A very common human tradition."

Iskur smiled pleasantly.

"Sounds nice." He said with a sigh.

"It actually was. Anyways. The vort*exes*. Should I tell Celeste we will accept her invitation?" Virgil shuffled around the room impatiently, "I am beginning to feel anxious for progress."

"Wow, you hide it so well." I said sarcastically.

"Yes, I think it is wise if Arga is feeling well enough to explore." Iskur offered.

"Yeah, I think we should. I feel fine now."

I just wanted to be alone with Iskur for ten to fifteen years to figure each other out, but that wasn't going to happen anytime soon was it? Iskur's intensity before Virgil had joined us had me shaken and longing for more. Add that to the fact of how long I had been dead and all the unanswered questions pressing down on us and I was certainly *not* feeling fine. The skin on my hands and arms was crackling silently, not at all helping me pretend to be calm.

Iskur turned to me slowly, as if I were some rare bird he didn't want to scare away.

"You do not sound fine." He purred.

"Stop, stop, I'm fine." I put my hands up, trying to keep him back and prove that I was fine.

He clasped one of my uplifted hands and raised an eyebrow at the energy he could feel gathering.

"Mh. Fine." He absorbed the energy and smirked at me.

Virgil let out a sigh.

"Arga, you cannot be among humans like this." Virgil said sadly, "What is it that we can do to calm you down?"

"I-I don't know! Stop looking at me!"

They were both so intently staring at me. Iskur had not let go of my hand and I could feel the destructive energy flowing freely from me to him. Fuck. Was I going to scar him again? Was I going to have another seizure? Out of the corner of my eye I saw Virgil lock the door. He didn't shift fully into a blue light form, but his body glowed.

"Look at me." Iskur had gained an inky black aura and his voice was deep and soothing. I looked directly into his black eyes.

I felt myself shift slightly. I could not fully leave my human form, I was much too tied to it here on Earth. There was a limit, like a wall, to the amount I could leave my body. Still, being able to extend into even a slight aura felt so good. It was freeing.

"Arga, yes. Is this better?" Iskur asked. I stepped closer to him and let him put his hands on my face.

"Yes." I breathed.

"Now, count with me."

"What?"

"One hundred. Now you say three less."

"Iskur what-"

"Three less."

His arms were encircling me, my head on his chest.

"Ninety seven?"

"Good. Ninety four."

"Ninety one?"

He kissed my forehead.

"Eighty eight."

"Eighty five." I felt my chest relax further.

"Eighty two."

"Seven....Seventy..." I was lost in his eyes as we sat on the floor together in one fluid movement.

"Seventy nine." Virgil offered quietly from across the room.

"Arga." Iskur's voice was low in my ear, "You are doing so well. I cannot find ways to make you see how proud I am of you. You are so strong and what you carry is so heavy."

Tears were on my cheeks and I choked back a sob.

"I'm dead and I took us all away from paradise."

"Something would have happened eventually." Virgil let out another sigh.

"How did he even find us?" My tears were soaking through Iskur's thin linen shirt.

"You are so powerful, Arga, I think when you shifted forms after seeing the memory I showed you-"

"*Fuck!*" I wailed, "He could track my fit I threw? The meltdown I had?"

"Possibly." Virgil said gently.

"What matters is we are here. The three of us." Iskur held me close, "And we can figure this out together."

I let out a shaking breath.

"Seventy nine." Virgil repeated quietly.

"Seventy six." I whispered.

"Seventy three. Take a deep breath." Iskur smoothed my hair.

I breathed with him and allowed myself to relax even further.

"Seventy. We'll figure this out?"

"Yes. We will figure this out."

Iskur pulled back slightly to look at me more directly at my face.

"Arga I know there are so few things answered, but perhaps we can get some answers from Celeste today." Virgil said gently, trying not to seem impatient.

I looked back at Iskur.

"What does she know?" I asked him.

"She felt the energy you gave off during the seizure, I could not stop that. And before that I showed her that there was depth and age to me. She already knew that though."

Iskur's eyes were still black and his black aura was encircling us as he explained. I wondered how a human would react to seeing him like this. His long, inky black hair flowing behind him, the way he held himself. He was a god. There was no denying it.

"You look like a god." I murmured, entranced.

"Imagine how you look, my love." He crooned back, "Your lightform is golden with flashes of light. It is like the sea at sunrise. Tell her, Virgil. She is radiant."

"Very radiant." He admitted with a smile, "You would terrify the humans."

I laughed awkwardly. Iskur kissed my head.

"There now, see? Much better." He was smiling at me.

"How was I so quick-thinking coming up with our backstory and everything and now I'm falling apart?" I sniffled.

"You were not focused on the negative outcomes, you were rising to the new challenges." Virgil mused, "When you think about our situation too hard it seems to make it impossible for you to function. Which is understandable."

I sighed.

"You two are handling this way better than me."

"There is no better, only different."

"Iskur is right. I mauled your murderer ex-boyfriend and Iskur keeps flipping lightswitches on and off and smiling like an idiot. Not exactly flawless adaptability."

That got me to genuinely laugh.

"Breathe with me and fade back," Iskur instructed sweetly after I stopped laughing.

I obeyed and regathered myself into my human form.

"There now, can we go upstairs?" Virgil was trying his hardest to sound compassionate.

I nodded and we filed upstairs.

# XXII.

In the kitchen, Celeste was embracing Martin warmly. His suitcase was sitting on the floor.

"I'm so glad you came out, are you certain I can't drive you to the airport? Please?"

"No no, you have your hands full here with the return of the Three Musketeers." Martin laughed loudly and pointed to us.

"Oh, I will miss you." Celeste looked at his face, her eyes shining with joy.

I shuffled my feet and tried to extract myself from the room. What a personal moment to intrude on.

"Martin is leaving?" Iskur asked, pushing past me to embrace Martin.

Virgil moved to stop Iskur but it was too late. Martin was clapping Iskur on the back heartily.

"*Stop touching the humans.*" Virgil muttered, pinching his forehead.

Martin came to me next and paused in front of me. I made the move to hug him, despite Virgil's hissing.

"Be good, okay?" Martin said to me while he was shaking Virgil's hand.

"I will."

A car outside beeped.

"That'll be my Uber!"

"Who is *Uber?*" Iskur whispered as Martin hugged Celeste one more time and gathered his things. I had no idea who Uber was, nobody had mentioned him so far. Celeste followed Martin out the front.

"Iskur. Stop touching the humans!" Virgil ordered in an acidic whisper once we were alone.

"It is not going to hurt them." Iskur walked over to the table and picked up an orange.

"It *might!*" Virgil retorted.

He made a violent shushing motion when Iskur was about to retort. Celeste had reentered the house.

"Now, my weary travelers. We are alone." Celeste busied herself pouring tea for us. She floated over to the table and beckoned us to all sit.

"So tell me, exactly, who are you?" Her voice lost a bit of its wispiness, "And where is your cousin?"

"He must have gone home?" I offered, sipping tea, "Like I said, his mom was handling it."

"No." Celeste's gaze was piercing. It made my skin prickle with unexpected goosebumps, "I called the hospital. They had no record of him. And I called my friend who works in the Emergency Room there, she told me a very strange story."

"What story is that, exactly?" Virgil peered menacingly over his teacup.

"That a John Doe got dropped off by three hikers. And that the John Doe was strange. *Very* strange. And that he had been picked up by a team of specialists who whisked him away in the night."

"Specialists? What are you talking about?" My mind was reeling. We *did not* need Travis free and on the prowl.

"That sounds like exactly what you described. A peculiar story. Like Arga said, Travis must have gone home already." Iskur said amicably, peeling an orange and distributing slices among us all.

Celeste's demeanor had shifted slightly. She was not unfriendly, but she was certainly on guard.

"It's Arga, not Heather? You all have different names and are not from here." Celeste looked at each of our faces in turn.

"No. We are from Chicago." Virgil asserted.

"I didn't mean *not from Sedona*. I mean not from *here*." Celeste looked at me meaningfully.

"I don't know what-"

"What do *you* think we are?" Iskur asked casually. Both Virgil and I turned to look at him with our mouths open. Our reaction was probably more damaging than his question, because Celeste let out a knowing laugh.

"Oh, well, I've done a lot of things in my day to impair my judgment and loosen grip on reality, so my thoughts often can't be trusted." She laughed and continued, "Had I met you all alone, I would assume that you weren't really here. But everyone else was so involved in this. I know you are real."

Iskur held out his hand for her. Virgil slapped his own hand into Iskur's and ripped it off the table. Virgil kept holding onto Iskur's hand, his knuckles whitening.

"Do *not*." He growled, glaring at Iskur.

Celeste looked between the two of them.

"So he is your brother and some sort of guard?" Celeste mused, pointing at Virgil, "Chaperone? He is older than you."

Celeste pointed to me.

"But you are the most confusing, Heather. You are new and old all at once. And he," she returned her attention to Iskur with a sly smile, "*He* is ancient."

Both Virgil and I were looking stupidly at Celeste. Iskur was laughing a deep, thunderous laugh.

"She is a Seer, as I said." He ripped his hand out of Virgil's and clasped Celeste's tightly.

"*Do not!*" Virgil shouted, his teacup shattering at the intensity of his demand. Celeste didn't notice, she was too wrapped up in trying to figure us out. Iskur glared at Virgil as tea ran off the table onto the floor.

"I cannot *show* her anything important, Virgil. You are the one scaring the humans."

"I-" Virgil stammered, "You! Stop. Just stop."

Virgil stood up in a huff and started pacing around the room. What was the point in stopping it now? She was onto us.

"You're a Seer?"

"I suppose." She said with a sad smile, "I have been called worse."

"What's it like?" I scooted my chair to face her entirely. Iskur released her hand so she could turn towards me.

"What is *what* like, dear?"

"Seeing? Can you hear things? Voices? Do you get visions?"

"Aren't you a Seer as well?" She tipped her head in confusion.

"I was. At one point."

"She is. The most powerful. She just needs to be reminded sometimes." Iskur winked at me.

"I can tell there is great energy and power in you both. Less so him," she motioned to Virgil who huffed indignantly, "But there is still something different about you three. I do not understand."

"Take my hand again," Iskur offered.

Celeste took Iskur's hand. Iskur moved her hand to his wrist.

"*Feel.*" Iskur said encouragingly.

"What for?"

Virgil stopped pacing.

"Feel for what is *not* there." Iskur had that devilish look in his eyes again.

Celeste focused intently. Virgil and I both realized what Iskur was doing at the same moment.

"Iskur, *no,*" Virgil pleaded.

"I don't feel anythi-"

"Exactly." Iskur said smugly with a triumphant wink at Virgil.

Celeste's eyes opened wide and she withdrew her hand in shock.

"*How?*"

Virgil groaned and pounded his fists on the countertop.

"What is *this* going to solve?" He demanded in an impetuous whine.

"No need for it." Iskur explained to Celeste as they ignored Virgil.

"No need for a heartbeat?"

"Not when you are dead." Iskur winked at Celeste playfully.

Celeste's already wide eyes got even wider.

"*Iskur.*" Virgil growled, "What. Are. You. *Doing?!*"

Iskur waved his hand dismissively at Virgil.

"*Dead?*" Celeste whispered, "How?"

"I died because of my own folly. Virgil died of, what was it? Some disease."

"Tuberculosis." Virgil spat, coming over to the table and leaning on it in front of Iskur, "What are you *doing?!*"

"How did you die?" Celeste looked at me kindly, still utterly shook and distant.

"I uh, I was murdered."

"By Travis." Iskur popped his head around Virgil to deliver that piece of information to Celeste.

"What?!" She shook her head, "He killed you? Your cousin?"

"He is not her cousin. He was her betrothed. That was thirteen years ago, yes?" Iskur looked up at Virgil with a mischievous grin. Virgil was absolutely crimson with rage.

"Thirteen years?" Celeste was hardly keeping up. She kept looking at each of us in turn.

"Stop!" Virgil slammed his fist on the table, making the bowls of fruit clank and clatter.

"Virgil!" I shouted at him as my teacup shattered from the rage energy he was putting off, "Stop it!"

He strode across the kitchen dramatically and leaned against the wall in a pout.

"Fine! Fine. I am not involved. I wanted to go see the vortices and explore this in relative peace and obscurity but no, *nobody* listens to Virgil."

"Stop it, you are being an asshole!"

"What do we need humans for?!" He yelled, waving his arms.

"She's right here! Stop being such a fucking jerk!" I screamed back, standing up.

Iskur was watching Virgil and I fight with mild amusement. Celeste was staring off distantly.

"Iskur, you still have not answered me, *why* are you *doing* this?" Virgil shouted.

"I think we need allies." Iskur said calmly.

"Allies?!" Virgil boomed, "Why for *fucksake* would we need *human* allies?!"

"Because Travis will come back. Soon."

Iskur sipped his tea smugly in the stunned silence that followed his statement.

"What?" I whispered hoarsely. My insides churned. Not another curveball. Not another plot twist. I just wanted something to be simple for a few minutes.

"Can you feel it too?" Iskur stood up and took me in his arms as my destroying energy started gaining intensity.

"I-"

Of course I could feel it. The second Iskur said that, I knew he was right.

"Sh. Focus. Reach out carefully and see if you feel him."

I closed my eyes and let out a shaking breath. I did as Iskur said and tried to reach out. I guessed based on Celeste's gasp I was glowing or something. So much for being normal. I let my focus on the kitchen fall away and tried to feel outside of the house. I was across the road, past the hospital, reaching more and more vast spaces, feeling out across the desert until...there. Yes. I felt Travis' existence. He was distant and detained but pursuing. He was reaching out.

"*Shit.*" I retreated back to the kitchen.

"You saw him?" Iskur asked as I returned to myself.

"Your eyes!" Celeste exclaimed, "Both of you! How-"

"I didn't *see* anything I just felt. He is out somewhere out there trying to reach out for us. For me. Trying to make contact somehow. I think he has been captured though."

"Mh. It is as I said. We need allies." Iskur clasped me tightly, siphoning the anxious energy off of me. I closed my eyes and surrendered to the comfort of his embrace.

Virgil let out an elaborate string of curse words.

"What did you *think* would happen when we left him at the hospital?" He asked with venom, "Obviously the humans would take him away to study him. And of course he would find some way to break free."

"The hospital was *your* idea!" I bellowed, pushing away from Iskur.

"To buy us time! Unfortunately it was not *much* time, I admit." Virgil's eyes were black as he strode over to where Iskur and I stood.

Celeste wasn't safe here. She wasn't safe with *us*. I could picture Travis smashing her beautiful home to pieces to find us.

"We need to go *now*." I urged.

"He is not free yet, is he?" Iskur asked, still calm.

"He didn't seem like he was out."

"Area 51 is almost three hundred miles from here." Celeste muttered, "Once he escaped, will he be on foot?"

"What? Area 51?"

"My friend. At the hospital. She said that they took him away to a secure facility. I would be willing to bet that he went to Area 51."

"The alien place?"

"Yes. I mean, where would you take someone like yourself?" Celeste was moving around the kitchen as if she was in a dream. She was gathering bits of food and putting them in cloth napkins and bags. She started talking to herself as she went about. We all watched her.

"Oranges are heavy. But nice. Nuts, dried berries. Protein powder. Yarrow, dried yarrow. For wounds. Do you bleed?"

She was suddenly addressing me.

"Bleed? What? No, we don't really bleed. It's more like bruising and discoloration."

"Oh, then. The yarrow is only for me." She put a sachet of dried plants into one of the bags.

Virgil was scowling at her.

"Celeste, what are you doing?"

"Well, Travis is after you all, correct?"

"Yes."

"So, you need to leave. *We* need to leave." She considered the broken teacups littering the table, then waved her hand at them dismissively.

"You should not come with us." Virgil said slowly, taking the bag of food she was offering him.

"Oh, so I should stay here? Where a dead murderer will come looking for you? No." She laughed musically, "I'll take you to the vortexes. You can try to escape or whatever you need to do with them. Then I'm leaving."

"But your home!" I walked over to her.

"Just a building." She laughed again, and waved me off, "What is useful for you? Do you need medicine? Weapons? Camping supplies?"

"Uh, well I'm not sure-"

"Things to sleep on are nice. Food is just for pleasure and not needed." Iskur walked out of the kitchen suddenly and called over his shoulder, "Maybe an axe? Some swords?"

"An axe? Oh, I do not have an axe. I might have swords. Or something better." Celeste zipped across the room and grabbed up the bundles of food.

She looked at me, then at Virgil. Opening a cupboard she pulled out a tin of saltine crackers. She took off the lid and pulled out a gun.

"What is that for?!" I demanded, shocked that the tin did not hold the snacks it promised.

"Oh, don't worry sweet soul." Celeste tucked the pistol into the waistband of her skirt and rewrapped her shawl to obscure it from view, "I have experience with murderers."

"Experience with? What-"

I was cut off with a kiss on the cheek. Iskur had slunk back into the room with a pack slung haphazardly on his back.

"I have your things my love, are we ready?"

"She has a gun." I muttered, utterly stunned. We weren't the only ones with problematic secrets, it seemed.

"What is a gun?" Iskur was ushering me out the front door. Virgil was already waiting outside by the van.

"A gun?" Virgil furrowed his brow.

Celeste followed us out, carrying a backpack of her own that she seemed to have already had packed.

"Don't worry about the gun," Celeste took the driver's seat, "The safety is on."

Virgil turned to me, eyes wide in concern. I gave him the same exasperated look back and shook my head.

"I don't know, Virg." I pulled him into the van with us.

# XXIII.

Once we were all situated in the Volkswagen, Celeste addressed us.

"Well now travelers, I know the energy here is unbalanced and we are in a race, but can we take a moment to set our intentions for this journey?" Celeste had swiveled in her seat to face us.

"Our *intentions?*" I repeated in disbelief. This hippie shit was wearing on my last frayed nerve.

"There are many sites we could visit, and I intended to take you to some of the more popular places today before all of this happened. But now, with these beautiful revelations being made, I feel I need to know what your needs are. What is the purpose of your journey?"

The three of us looked at each other. Purpose?

"To get home." I said slowly when Iskur and Virgil did not offer any suggestions.

Celeste considered this for a moment.

"I have so many questions. I hope we will have time for them all." She said with a smile and started the van.

"Where are we going?" Virgil asked.

"I am not sure yet. There are a few places where energy is high in this area, but my intuition is telling me that those aren't the right places to go. We found you close to one of the lesser known sites. A place that I hold dear. If we head to another place that has always been special to me, I wonder if that will be a good place to start."

"Is it far?" Virgil was looking out the window as if Travis was going to appear at any moment.

"It is not too far. But it is a bit of a hike to get to the vortex itself. And we will have to get wet."

Iskur was watching the landscape roll by like a contented puppy, not contributing anything to the conversation. A few moments passed quietly as we bumped along the road.

"How... no, well, I guess I'd rather know *where*. Where are you from?" Celeste was smiling at us in the rearview mirror.

"We are dead." Virgil was still in a brooding mood about Celeste's involvement.

"Well. Where is home? Heather, or what is the name you said before? Arda?"

"Arga."

"So beautiful. Yes. Arga said that you want to go home."

"Dead people do not walk around on Earth." Virgil said coldly, crossing his arms, "We are from beyond this world."

"Really, Virgil. Stop it. Pretend she's new dead. You're a Greeter."

He glared at me.

"I *was* a Greeter." He spat.

I rolled my eyes.

"A greeter?"

"Celeste?" Iskur was looking at her intently all the sudden.

"Yes?"

"Do you hear people who are dead? Their voices?"

"Oh my *fucking-*" Virgil was kneading his forehead with his fists.

"I used to." Celeste said slowly, "As a child. My grandmother mostly. Then others. Strangers. That's something I stopped admitting to people a long time ago. Nothing good came of talking about it to anyone else."

I looked at Celeste as she kept her eyes firmly fixed on the road. She looked like a shell of her bubbly self. The luster was gone from her face. The memory diminished her, somehow.

"So, you know that there is life beyond Earth." Iskur reached forward and put his hand on her shoulder.

She nodded.

"We come from that space. The voices you heard, however faintly or strongly, are not from Earth."

"How are you here?" Celeste asked, reaching up and placing her hand on Iskur's.

"A mistake." I said softly.

Virgil snorted.

"No mistake. Arga saved us." I swung around to look at Virgil. Saved us? That was not at *all* how I interpreted what had happened.

"How did she save you?"

"The hunter came for us, and Arga took us away from the situation. The most powerful among the dead are called the Old Dead. They control the balance of the afterlife. Arga and Iskur are something of an anomaly, and they create unbalance. The Old Dead dislike anything that disrupts balance. They sent a hunter to find Arga after we accidentally ran away from them."

"And Travis was the hunter? And also the one who killed Arga?" Celeste shook her head, "I'm sorry, loves, I know you are in danger, but I'm not sure I follow how it's possible to be in danger if you are already dead? What does this hunter want?"

"To take us back to the Old Dead and make us nothing." Iskur said in a low voice, "To truly end our existence."

Celeste made an understanding noise.

"Why did they send Travis? To torture you, Arga?"

"No, they do not have any sense of irony. Travis was the last person to see Arga alive on Earth, he was her lover, and he was her murderer. The Old Dead sending him was a matter of convenience and power. They had a connection, he would have been able to find her easier."

Hearing it explained made me feel even Virgil looked at me with a sad smile and held out his hand for me. My anxious energy was still under control, but I took his hand anyway.

"Arga and Iskur were contemporaries," Virgil began to explain, back in academic dork mode, "They lived together thousands of years ago. Arga and Iskur were Seers. Arga could talk to the dead. The realm of the dead and Earth used to be much more connected. It was easier to talk.

"Arga and Iskur gained power together. Arga was promised to another man, but he was cruel and evil. So Iskur made a vow to not allow her betrothed to kill her. Things got, how should I say, *complicated.*

"Arga unbound her soul from her body and remained trapped on Earth, Iskur eventually died and went to the afterlife. Then Arga figured out how to live as a human again, lived another full life up to about twenty two years old, and found an abusive man: Travis. She got him to propose to her and..."

Virgil trailed off and looked at me. He had already pieced together what I was too afraid to put into words. I had *wanted* to get murdered. It was the only way to break the oath Iskur had made thousands of years before.

"And Arga made me break my vow." Iskur concluded diplomatically.

"So, how did Travis become your hunter?" Celeste asked thoughtfully after a moment of silence.

"He died, I guess." I said, "But he and I have a connection since he was the last person to see me on Earth. And he was given powers from the Old Dead to hunt me down."

"The Old Dead? Oh, I have so many more questions, but we are here. Let's discuss this later."

I was grateful to be done talking. Celeste pulled over on the narrow shoulder of the road. She put the car in park but did not move to get out yet.

"Should we hide the van?" She asked.

"I can hide it." Virgil said.

The ditch was steep and there was a small path a few yards behind us. Trees and bushes lined the bottom of the ditch and the rest of the landscape. We filed out of the vehicle. The morning sun glinted off the pavement on the empty highway.

"Here's the keys," Celeste handed the keys to Virgil, who did not take them.

Instead, he lifted his hands and closed his eyes. The van shuddered, then levitated slowly. Celeste gasped appreciatively and murmured something about Jedi. Virgil was straining and the van stopped its journey down into the brush.

Iskur walked up and touched Virgil's shoulder. Virgil looked at him, his shoulders tensed and trembling. Iskur winked, did not look away from Virgil, and moved the van easily into the bushes with one hand. He clapped Virgil on the back and sauntered down the hill to obscure the vehicle further with more branches.

"Fucking show off." Virgil spat, wiping his face on his flowy tie dyed sleeve.

"Amazing!" Celeste clutched Virgil's arm and patted it as we all walked down to the trail, "Are you all so gifted?"

Iskur trotted ahead of us and conjured a sprig of basil in mid air. Celeste proclaimed joyfully and accepted it as Iskur offered it to her.

"What are you, a magician now?" Virgil said to Iskur with a sneer.

"It feels good to not hide." Iskur said with another saucy wink.

"*Show off.*" Virgil grumbled.

We walked through some stands of trees in the shade. The air was dry but pleasantly cool where we walked in the shadows.

"What kind are these?" I asked Celeste.

"Juniper, mostly. And some sycamore. There's an enormous juniper across the creek that we will see, it is beautiful."

"How far is the vortex?" Virgil asked.

"Oh, quite some time yet. I typically start to feel the energy once we cross the creek and travel for about twenty minutes."

Celeste hummed to herself quietly as we walked. Virgil was carrying her pack and Iskur had his own. I was unburdened except for a couple of canteens Celeste had demanded we all bring. Celeste also suggested that we find sticks to walk with to make the creek crossing easier, so we paused to look for suitable options. Once we had a stick each, we continued. Hardly any time passed and we made it to the creek.

"Oak Creek!" Celeste proclaimed when we arrived.

"Oaks." Virgil muttered to himself.

Was he smiling a bit? His Otherworld voice came to my mind and a smile played at my lips, too. He was an oak tree, wasn't he? Stubborn. Hard. Vast in its branches. A symbol of knowledge. Maybe oaks were his solace on Earth the same way water had been mine. I missed our voices. I was desperate to hear thunder and wind and waves when we spoke again. I let out a shaky breath. One thing at a time.

We walked to the water's edge. The water was not deep, but was moving swiftly. It made refreshing bubbling noises as it passed over rocks. We took our shoes off and crossed with ease. On the other side we sat for a moment to dry our feet and put our shoes back on. Before we had left the house, Virgil had gotten us all pairs of old hiking boots that Celeste had in her stash. I was grateful for them as I laced mine back up on the other side of the creek. The ground was not something that looked inviting to go across barefoot.

"Onward, travelers." Celeste took up her stick and led us down the path.

We walked on and on. Scrub and cacti overtook the landscape as we continued walking. After about twenty minutes, just as Celeste had said, we came across a giant juniper tree.

"Let us sit in her shade for a moment, friends." Celeste beckoned us to the tree's base, "This is the start of where I often connect with the energy here."

We obliged. Celeste handed us some dried fruit and instructed us to drink water. Virgil tried to explain to her that we did not need the water and were carrying it for her sake. She was not satisfied until we had all at least had a swig each.

"You seem so human it is hard to believe that you won't dry out in the sun!"

"I'm glad we seem human." I laughed, "It has been annoying pretending to be."

"So, what does it feel like, being human again? Or well, what is it like to be on the other side?"

"The other side of what?" Virgil handed Iskur a canteen.

"The other side of the veil, dear one."

Iskur frowned at me in confusion.

"It is a human expression referring to the afterlife. Or the spirit realm." Virgil explained studiously.

"Hard to take you seriously in tie dye, professor." I teased. He gave me a cold glare in return.

"What does it feel like to die? Is that what she is asking?" Iskur was still on the original question.

"Not to die, but to be a spirit. To be part of the great beyond." Celeste clarified.

"We call it the Otherworld." Iskur said.

"Oh that's nice!" Celeste beamed, "I like that."

"It feels somewhat like being human, but also different." I said. Really, what a great way of describing it.

"Different how?"

"Well, uh, I'm the most recently dead so I guess I remember what being a human feels like the most. But once I died I had to learn how to exist in the Otherworld. You have more abilities when you die. Like you can create things, move things, it's really awesome but also hard to master." I struggled putting words to the exact feeling of tension and stress I had felt when faced by my own powers in death.

"Each soul has the ability to create and maintain their own dwelling," Virgil explained, "You have the ability to shape your own paradise."

"How beautiful." Celeste sighed dreamily, "You must be anxious to return."

"Hah....yeah." As much as I longed to hear our Otherworld voices again, I shuddered remembering the voices of the Old Dead.

Iskur took my hand.

"So, you two are...?" Celeste smiled knowingly at Iskur and I while pointing at our hands.

"Yes, we are bonded by a blood oath vow and the weight of powers we stole during our lives as humans." Iskur said casually.

Celeste's look of absolute horror would have been comical if my expression didn't match hers.

"She meant, are you two lovers?" Virgil said through gritted teeth.

"Oh! Yes I would say that we are. Bonded by a vow that extends beyond time and space *as well as* lovers. Yes, Arga?"

Virgil was rubbing under his glasses in irritation.

"Yeah. That would about sum it up." I agreed with an uncomfortable laugh.

I wasn't quite sure I could even explain it myself if I tried. What I felt when I saw Iskur, right back to the very first night, was something so powerful it left me wordless. It was like he said we were: ancient, vast, and infinite. It was something I could not argue against. It was my missing piece and it left me breathless the more I thought about it. How do you tell someone you just met who is on the run with you all of that?

"That's....romantic..." Celeste was eyeing us with mild concern.

"So, why do you have a gun?" I asked abruptly, trying to get the focus off the cosmic weight of our boundless love.

"Oh! When I was younger I made some very poor choices. Youth is a time for experimenting, you know. I grew up Mormon, left home when I was sixteen. I was young, in love, and I moved in with my boyfriend at the time. Well, he chose a career path that led him to being a cocaine dealer. I found that the coke dulled the voices I heard, so it was a convenient way to escape for a time. I lived that life for fifteen hard years. Then I changed my path. But sometimes there are threads from that life that haunt me still." She sighed another dreamy sigh that seemed not to match the horrific story she was telling.

Virgil was staring at her with his mouth wide open and Iskur was making me some violets from the air.

"Should we keep going?" Celeste said sweetly.

Virgil gave me another highly concerned look as Celeste and Iskur walked off on the trail.

"*Why* did we involve her?" He whispered as we walked after them.

"I-I kind of like her." I smiled, "She's pretty awesome."

"*Awesome.* Not the word I would use."

"That's because you are a prude asshole who doesn't like people who fuck up." I regretted what I said when I saw his face. Fuck. Why did I say that?

"That is what I am to you?" His eyes had shifted black and his expression was broken.

"Virgil I-"

He held up his hand.

"No. That is fine. I have always been called these things. Cold. Judgmental. Harsh. Unloving. That is what you see?"

"Virgil, no. I'm so sorry." I stopped walking. He kept going for a few more paces.

With a ragged sigh he stopped, clenched his fists and wheeled around at me.

"Arga, I gave *everything* up for you and Iskur. Never once have you asked what I left in the Otherworld when we fled. Go on, ask me."

I was shaking and my chest was writhing in anguish.

"Virgil-"

"*Ask me.*"

"What did you le-" My voice was breaking.

"*Nothing!*"

Celeste and Iskur stopped walking and turned back to look at us, perplexed.

"I died on Earth alone. I was *nothing* here on this planet. No family, no friends, nobody. Not one person noticed. You know as a Greeter you can go and watch lives after they are over? I watched mine. My body laid in an alley for a *week* before someone found it and threw it in a grave. A week! Nobody cared. I tried to find my parents in the Otherworld and do you know what? They elected to dissipate. So yes. I am cold. Nobody ever cared for me, so I found ways to care for others. Endlessly! I gave the entirety of my afterlife to greet new souls as they died. Finally a purpose! A spark of joy in my pitiful and pointless existence."

"Virgil, I an so sorr-"

"No, no. You *deserve* to feel bad. You might not know who you are or what you are able to do but imagine the hollow, empty feeling of *knowing* you are nothing. Nobody in the Otherworld caring that you existed. No parents, no friends, no lovers, no happy reunions. Being utterly alone and *then* finding a purpose. And *then* realizing that you are good at it. Being trusted by the Old Dead. Getting assigned a highly important task: you, Arga, were that assignment. And then discovering the joy and the purpose and everything else you had felt since dying was built on a *lie*. All a terrible lie.

"I could have turned you two in when I had my earliest suspicions but I did not. I waited. I wanted to be sure. And you know what? The more sure I became the less I wanted to betray you two. Then they gave you your ultimatum and I knew - *I knew* - what you two were. I could have told the Old Dead when we were there before them, but I did not. Why? Because I was willing to give up *everything* I have ever cared about to make sure you two did not meet an unjust end.

"So fine, call me an asshole. Tell me I do not care about people who make mistakes. I have learned a long time ago that no matter what I do, I will be *reviled* and hated by the people I care about most."

I was on my knees in the dirt before him and he towered over me, black eyes glinting in the sun and blue aura looking like a searing hot fire against the sky.

"I'm so sorry Virgil, I didn't think-"

"No, you did not. Nobody thinks about me." His voice was icy and his words stung. I had never given more than a passing thought to what he was experiencing. I had been too wrapped up in my own mystery and stress to care.

Iskur was standing protectively between Celeste and Virgil.

"Virgil, we see you." Celeste's voice was calm and gentle, "We see you and we see your great sacrifices."

"We do." Iskur took a step towards Virgil, "We owe you a great debt."

"I do not want your servitude, your indebtedness." Virgil's voice was breaking, "Do not pity me."

"Virg." I stood up and touched his shoulder, "We love you."

He did not turn to face me.

"You feel bad enough to say that, do you?"

"Stop it. You were the first person I met. You have protected us in ways I didn't understand. I just...I'm so sorry. I didn't mean to take you for granted."

He looked over his shoulder at me. I took his hand and traced the scars that laced his arms.

"The scars you cannot see are the ones that truly hurt." He muttered.

"I know. *I know.* I'm so sorry."

Iskur walked up to Virgil and took his other hand. We stood like that for a few moments before Celeste cautiously joined us.

"You feel it?" She asked.

"Feel what?" Virgil asked with a sigh.

"Balance returning. The power of letting go of your past wounds. This space has a deep healing energy. I always find that I can forgive past hurts so easily on this trail." Celeste was crying. What a scene we four made.

"I don't think that's what's happening here, Celeste." I said with a dry laugh.

"So you don't believe in a physical space having the power to help you surface negativity you are housing, face it, and let it go, but you are dead for over ten years and walking on Earth in a human body?" Celeste raised an eyebrow, "I think you need to reassess what is possible, Arga darling."

A great point. I could not help but laugh at that. Virgil embraced us all in turn.

"You are the only soul who has ever asked how I died." Virgil admitted.

"There's no way. How is that possible?"

"The newly dead have more questions about themselves. I am just a guide to them, not an actual being, I suppose."

He blinked and his eyes returned to their human appearance.

"Should we all explore our grievances in this space and ask for forgiveness?" Celeste suggested.

"No, I think we need to keep moving." Virgil wiped his face on his sleeve.

Iskur handed him a silk hankie that he had produced from nowhere. Virgil broke down and sobbed at the gesture. Celeste would not let us move on until we all repeated a forgiveness incantation after her. Once we had all recovered, we continued walking.

Celeste was definitely right: the energy was becoming more and more pronounced. I felt it first as a tug at my mind a few paces beyond where Virgil had snapped. From there it became like an unseen wind. It felt like the energy was blowing through me, a gentle breeze that took away my anxious thoughts. It was the same feeling as stepping into a shower after being covered in dust and grit all day. An instantly cleansing sensation. I was smiling. This was *nice*.

Iskur walked with Virgil and they were deep in conversation. Their words were cut with the undercurrents of gentle thunder and rustling leaves. My smile widened and I found myself wiping tears from my cheeks. Their voices!

"Do you hear thunder?" Celeste was scanning the horizon as we walked side by side.

"That's Iskur."

"The thunder?"

"He's talking with Virgil. We have this sort of special language from the Otherworld. Virgil sounds like wind in leaves, Iskur is a thunderstorm, and I'm water and waves."

"Wonders never cease." Celeste looked blissful. Her face was placid.

"How do you stay so calm? I need some of those skills."

"Hm?"

"You are so calm about all of this. About us. How do you stay calm with all this happening?" I motioned to the three immortals walking among her. She laughed.

"I am so happy that we found each other." She clasped my hand and pulled me to a stop, "You cannot know the torment of my youth, hearing voices from beyond. To know that there is a beyond, that I wasn't totally crazy. Well, it is a gift. All the suffering has been worth *something* at last."

I wanted to talk to her about my childhood: about feeling a driving, dangerous desire to take myself to ruin. The whispers in my mind at night. Crying every time I heard thunder. I had been haunted by memories that I didn't realize were my own. Haunted by myself. I wondered if Celeste could relate to that. She certainly would understand my doing stupid, destructive things because I felt crazy.

I thought about my mother. Was she still alive? We had never had the best relationship. I could still hear the worst thing she ever said to me in one of her drunken rages:

*"You stole my life! It's your fault I'm like this! You wrecked everything! I was normal before I had you!!"*

Was she right, after all? No, don't think about that right now. I forced the thoughts from my head. Back to Celeste, another woman whose life I'd hijacked.

"You have a good life here now though, right? The house, Clive and Martin and all the guests...that's all good? You'll go back to it once we are gone?"

"Oh, it was good. It was. But that door may be closed to me now. I thought I was building that space to share with as many travelers as I could before I couldn't be a guide anymore. Now I see it was a different path."

"Different how?" I asked as we started walking again.

"My purpose is not what I expected it to be."

I rolled my eyes and sighed.

"Cryptic shit." I said teasingly. Being around her put me at ease.

She laughed melodiously and squeezed my hand.

"You heard voices too, didn't you? When you were alive?"

"You are avoiding my question." I retorted.

"You are avoiding *mine*." She replied.

"How is your purpose not what you expected it to be?" I pressed.

"Oh I expected to serve a great many travelers...not three Great Travelers." She winked, "But I see now, it was all leading to this."

My chest tightened. Guilt again. We had royally derailed her life's plans.

"How can you be so sure that this is your purpose? Anyone could have found us out there that night."

"But who did? Not *anybody*. Specific people."

"I guess."

"Trust me, Arga, I know my purpose now. I have seen it clearly. Now, answer my question. Did you hear voices when you were alive?"

"I must have. But I don't remember it really. My memories are more and more...I don't know, messed up the longer I'm dead."

"How so?"

"Well, I have lived two lives in one soul so parts of it get confused. I used to only know my most recent life, the one that died ten years ago. But when Iskur and I were alive...I remember that life now too. Parts of it. So it's hard to tell what is what sometimes."

"You are a reincarnate?"

"No, she only fully died once." Virgil had drifted back to us just in time to deliver his knowledge, "A reincarnate dies, enters the Otherworld, then re-enters as a new life on Earth. Arga is something different. She did not leave Earth when she died the first time. I suppose it was a partial death. She died and remained on Earth before somehow connecting herself to a new life."

"She is a wanderer." Celeste mused, "A displaced soul."

There was no escaping the questions I had about my mother then, was there? I had to ask some of the questions I was dreading to ask.

"Virgil, did I displace another soul to get my most recent life?" I stopped walking, "Did I kill some baby to come back to life?"

"What? No! Arga." He made a disgusted face at me, "I do not know how you did it, but from what I have figured you became a new life where there was none."

"I don't get it."

Virgil sighed and let out an uncomfortable laugh.

"So, you...well. How do I frame this delicately? You are familiar with the *concept* of immaculate conception, yes?"

"What the fu-"

He put his hands up to stop me.

"Just, wait. Yes? Yes? You understand the *concept* of that, correct?"

I absolutely hated where this was going.

"Yes."

"Well, you know we could discuss this later perhaps." Virgil looked pointedly at Iskur and Celeste who were listening with invested interest.

"No, please go on." Celeste urged, "Did Arga enter her mother's womb as a soul and create a life for herself where no life was beginning?"

"Fuck stop. No, we are done! Nevermind! Shut *up* Virgil!!" He stood and looked both deflated and relieved that he wasn't going to get to explain this. My concerns were being validated and I wanted it to stop.

"I believe so." He said quickly dodging the rock I threw at him.

"Stop! We are done with this discussion! We can talk about you dying alone again if you keep this up!!"

Virgil laughed devilishly and ducked out of the way of the stones I was chucking at him.

"You act like siblings." Celeste said, grabbing my arm to stop me from pelting Virgil.

"They may as well be." Iskur said, picking me up and carrying me over his shoulder up the trail.

To my shock, Virgil filed into line after Iskur and stuck out his tongue at me.

"You think this is funny?" I asked, unable to stop smiling at Virgil's uncharacteristically improper antics. It made my heart soften a bit to see him act out after the emotional breaking point he had just been at.

"I think it is funny that you have one more question you are going to realize you need to ask about all this." He said, dusting off his shoulders dramatically.

"What?"

"You will think of it."

I pouted while Iskur trundled onwards. He was humming happily. After a couple of minutes the horrid realization that Virgil had foretold came over me.

"Wait."

Virgil grinned the most evil grin I had ever seen. If he would have sprouted horns and a forked tongue I would not have been surprised.

"Yes?"

"My mom didn't think it was an immaculate conception."

Virgil cackled as I made retching noises.

"*Why* did you make me think about this?!"

"It was your plan to become human again. Seems like you thought of everything, including selecting a very *active* mother."

"Shut the fuck up!!" I howled in agony at Virgil's continued laughter.

"You are *very* clever!" Iskur offered in consolation.

"Shut up." I muttered, rubbing the bridge of my nose, "I hate this."

"You brought it up. You are welcome." Virgil sauntered past us to take the lead position down the trail.

I sighed into Iskur's shoulder.

"So I did steal her life, didn't I?"

Iskur shifted me so that he could see my face easier.

"Whose life?"

"My mother's. My last mom, the recent one."

Iskur pondered for a moment.

"She did not die. She can always change her path. That is the wonderful thing about being alive on Earth. You only have a limited time so it makes you want to change things quickly."

"Iskur, that is not at all how people act." I sighed again.

"Life is fleeting, no? So you must choose or change your path when you are able to. Like Celeste! She has changed her path with joy."

"Yeah, most people would rather be stuck in a bad situation and complain about it until it kills them then try to be better. At least the people I knew."

Before we could get deeper on the subject, Celeste stopped walking.

"Oh!" Celeste said suddenly, "We are coming to the spot where I always see-"

"*Snakes!!*" Virgil shouted, leaping backwards into Iskur.

"Yes! You see one?" Celeste walked elegantly past the jumbled mess that was Iskur and Virgil and I, to go inspect the snakes.

Virgil was trying to climb up Iskur to evade the reptiles and Iskur, equally unexcited about the serpents, was backing down the trail rapidly. He stumbled and we came crashing down on the red dirt. Virgil and I swore profusely.

"Hmm, there are about seven here along the trail that I can see." Celeste was oblivious to the chaos behind her as she inspected the path forward.

"Get *off* me!" I wailed, pulling myself out of the pile of bodies and packs, "What, you hate snakes too?"

Iskur shuffled to his feet.

"They are *not* my favorite animals." He said.

"Good grief, *move.*" I shoved past the two of them and went to stand by Celeste.

"This is quite a lot all in one place, a bit strange." She said, pointing out the seven she had spied.

"I'll try to move them." I said, closing my eyes and focusing my energy on the snakes.

It was easy to lift them all at once with the extra energy radiating from the Earth. I could focus on each of them at the same time, which shocked me. I was used to focusing on creating or moving one single thing at a time, not several very distinct and very angry things. I opened my eyes and watched them writhe through the air over the grass before I set them down a hundred yards behind us.

"There. Can we continue, please?" I addressed my disheveled companions as Celeste laughed quietly.

"Can their venom harm you?" She asked Iskur.

"No, we are already dead. They are just not my favorite."

"What *is* your favorite?" Celeste asked, handing him a dried fig. She spoke with such genuine interest and kindness that it made me feel warm.

"Hummingbirds." Iskur grinned.

Of course. I smiled stupidly as we walked on.

# XXIV.

The trail left the comfortable shade of the scrub trees where we had met the snakes and opened up into a much more stony and steep path. There was no shade and the heat was intense. Celeste put on sunglasses and a straw hat that she covered with a scarf. Seeing the three of us with no sun coverings distressed her, so she demanded we all take one of her many scarves for our head.

"I'm pretty sure if Virgil got a sunburn it would heal after he rested." I said to Celeste, "Nothing really permanently hurts our forms here. He had bruises all over his hands the night we met from...uh..well...they healed after we rested, anyway."

"You can never be too careful! My mother died of skin cancer."

"Celeste." I laughed, "We're-"

"Yes, yes I know, already dead, but still. Please. It would make me feel better."

"Arga and I were born for the sun!" Iskur wrapped his headscarf with an elaborate flourish and scooped me into a side hug, "Our home is warm and arid, but fertile and rich."

"Where did you live?" Celeste asked as we walked on.

"I lived in Illinois." I muttered.

"That's neither hot nor arid," Celeste said with a laugh.

"Iskur and Arga lived in modern Lebanon." Virgil explained, fussing with his headscarf.

Iskur was so irritated that Virgil could not wrap it properly that he made him stop and did it for him.

"Lebanon! How wonderful! And you don't remember much of it?" Celeste looked at me sadly.

"Uh, no. No. Well, parts of it. A fig tree. And..." I trailed off.

A fig tree and killing a bunch of people.

Celeste nodded amicably. We strode on in silence for a few minutes as the trail became more steep and rocky. We were walking along a rock ledge now, climbing steadily out of the canyon.

As the time passed our steps had to slow to accommodate Celeste. She was not out of shape by any means, but her body was certainly not tireless like ours. At each breather she took, she would beg us to take in the stunning views that were unfolding around us. As far as the eye could see, there was nothing manmade. Red rock and scrub trees stretched out before us. The road we had come in on was no longer visible as we wound our way up towards the top of the mesa we were steadily climbing.

The third time we paused, I noticed Iskur and Virgil's eyes had shifted black. I assumed my own were changed as well. The energy was humming persistently along my skin now, vibrating against me. It felt the way I remembered concerts feeling, the live music at top volume pulsing against my body. Except here, there was no sound. Only the undulating sensation of *something* pushing, then pulling, then releasing its hold on me.

"It feels like wind." Iskur said, holding his arms out, "Like wind where there is none."

"It's like the feeling of being in a place with loud music. But with no sound." I said. Virgil nodded.

"A silent symphony." He murmured.

"Do you feel it?" I asked Celeste.

She smiled and shook her head slowly.

"Not the way you do. For me, it's a silence inside me. Voices grow quiet and my heart grows calm."

"You hear the voices all the time?" I asked, looking at her sadly.

"Not all the time. Much less since you all have arrived. They seem to draw away from you three. But there are still whispers at times. Here there is nothing, and I drink it up like water."

She took a drink from her canteen for emphasis.

We continued up the path for another few miles. As we walked, we fell silent, each in our own thoughts. When we paused for Celeste to rest, we would talk about how the energy felt. Eventually it became a constant, steady thrum. Our auras slowly appeared more and more defined. Iskur's inky black and laced with white, Virgil's bright blue, and mine, white and vaporous. I had been able to see our auras for quite some time when Celeste finally exclaimed about their appearance.

"You could not see them before this?" Virgil asked curiously.

"No! Just now I see them faintly. They are beautiful! I have seen auras before but these are so pure." She moved her hand through Iskur's, giggling warmly with delight.

"Arga, can you see them?" Virgil asked.

"Yes I can *see* them! I've been seeing them for the past ten minutes!" I was offended.

"I was just curious." He mumbled, pacing on and getting lost in his own thoughts again. We filed after him.

At last we reached the summit of the mesa. The vista that spread out around us as we surveyed the land from our height was breathtaking. I could have stared at the view for days and not gotten tired of it. The vibrant blue of the sky, the clouds, the rust-red rock all seemed so pristine. They looked almost fake, like something computer generated and calibrated to the exact maximum of loveliness.

"It is one of the best views in Sedona, I think. Others have different prefer-ences, but I am partial to this one." Celeste put her arm around me.

Virgil was winding the silk hankie that Iskur had given him around his fingers absentmindedly. Iskur was smiling faintly and taking in the views.

"What does it feel like to you up here?" I asked Celeste.

"It is quiet still in my mind, and I feel very grounded to the Earth. I can feel energy coming down from on high, centering me."

I closed my eyes and focused on the sensation. The energy felt like it was pulling me back away from the cliff edges.

"Over here." Virgil called from the center of the mesa.

Celeste released me from her embrace and I wandered over to Virgil.

"Stand right here." Virgil said thoughtfully, "I am curious..."

I looked at him suspiciously. He grabbed my shoulders and pulled me into the spot.

"Feel it?" He asked.

I couldn't answer. The force of the energy had me rooted to the spot and paralyzed. At first it felt like stepping under a waterfall; like a crushing weight was pushing me downward. I struggled against it for a moment, then I felt the pressure bend. I was changing the course of the energy, its flow resisting then folding to my will. I pushed further, feeling the energy comply rapidly. As I gathered the fullness of the power, I felt myself break through the ceiling of my abilities so far on Earth. I shifted forms and rocketed upwards.

I could see everything. Iskur watched me from the cliffside, eyes jet black and scarf whipping against his face. His expression was of deep concern and awe. Virgil gleamed blue beneath me, stepping into the center of the vortex and speeding up in pursuit. Celeste was on her knees with her hands against her face.

Virgil was not gaining on me. He was outmatched by the pure ecstasy that fueled me as I flew upwards into the endless blue of the sky. I surveyed the crimson red landscape that expanded as far as I could perceive from my height. Other vortexes pierced the landscape, I could see them shimmering like holographic whirlwinds as I swooped upwards within this one.

Joy became fury as I felt a tug at my consciousness. Travis. He was reaching out for me. I whipped myself around and tore after the call. Maybe I could push him away. Maybe I could destroy his connection to me. If I could just reach him...

Further and further I reached out, allowing the vortex to enhance my ability to perceive. My awareness sped outward further and faster than it had in the kitchen. I found Travis in an instant. He was still far away, detained. I could feel his frustration and fear. My vision was blurring, becoming horribly distorted and dream-like as I tried to get closer to him. No! Just a little further. Anger clenched flamed up in the core of my being. I zoomed in, straining with the effort. I could finally see him.

He was suspended in a tank, floating peacefully. I surveyed him as if I was looking through a warped, dirty window. It felt like a scene in a movie.

Travis' head snapped upwards, and his eyes locked on where I was perceiving him from. Now that I had his attention, I had no idea what to do. My mind was frenzied with anger I could not control.

"*You killed me!*" I raged, my voice a tidal wave crashing against a cliff.

He laughed a single heartless laugh.

"*You wanted to die.*" His voice sounded like sand hissing in the wind.

My vision was spinning. I tried to gather my destroying energy and focus it on Travis. I wanted to stop him from calling out to me. To hurt him. But I could not gather myself in time. I was being pulled backwards, away from the far reaches I had flung myself to.

"*Where are you, Ari? Come visit in person next time. We should talk.*" His self-righteous smile was the last thing I saw.

I slammed into the ground on top of the mesa in my human form. Virgil drove me into the stone, cracking it around us as we collided with it.

"Virgil!" Iskur exclaimed with a ragged, strained gasp. He was underneath me, wrapping his strong arms around my convulsing form.

I realized I was screaming in belligerent rage. The destroying energy was snapping and crackling. Virgil was still pressing down on top of me, hands against my shoulders clenching violently.

"Let me GO!!" I screamed, "*I had him!!*"

"You did *not* have him!" Virgil said in anguish as my energy lashed him mercilessly.

"We are not him!" Iskur was pleading.

"Arga!!" Celeste's voice was pitched with terror.

"*Let me go!*" I cried.

"You. Need. To. Stop. Fighting. Us." Virgil said in pained breaths.

The rage and anguish was consuming me. I felt myself start to slip away into darkness. The last thing I heard was Iskur's sharp warnings to Celeste to stay back from me.

"Where did you send him?" I demanded, my voice as violent as waves in a storm.

"I did not send him anywhere," My father lied bravely, "He simply left."

"You are lying."

"Did he not tell you he was going?"

"Stop playing the fool," I growled, "And tell me where you sent him!"

My mother stood behind my father, her arms crossed and her face stony. Did she agree with my father on this, or was she on my side?

"He did not say where he was going," My father said, shifting uncomfortably from one foot to the other, "But he said to tell you that he was burdened by Qateel's death and needed to be free of the haunting of it."

"*Liar.*"

"Do you dare to call your father a liar again?" My mother's voice was cold, "After what has been done by your hands?"

My hands. *My hands?* I am bestowed the gift of power from a god and they dare to scold me? I did not mean for Qateel to die when the Nameless Ones came, but my mother was not satisfied. Qateel and Aeylin's mother was her beloved friend. That woman's grief had poisoned my mother's heart and turned her against me.

"I have asked for forgiveness for the death of Qateel, and his family has given it. Aeylin holds no grudge. Is that not *enough* for you?"

"It is enough," My father, ever the diplomat, was trying to appease both his terrified people and his daughter who terrified them, "Is it not right that Iskur should leave to seek peace on his own? He is a man. We are not his people."

"He is *mine* and I am *his*," I snarled, "I am his people now."

My mother sighed.

"Anaid-" She started.

"Arga."

*"Arga,"* She sighed again, "What vow did you make with Iskur in that golden light?"

My stomach lurched. She was always the one who cut directly to the heart of the matter.

"He vowed to protect me from the one you forced on me. The murderer you would have me take for a husband. But," I felt my eyes shift black, "I can protect myself now."

My father and mother bowed reverently at the sight of my power. I smiled. I knew this was only a taste. There was more to be had. I was anointed now, and I would be bestowed greater gifts in the future.

I just had to find Iskur.

***

I awoke inside a dark room. My mind swam as I sat up. Iskur was by my side, half awake. He wrapped an arm around me and pulled me back down onto the cushions beneath me.

"Where are-"

"Our new home." He murmured gently, "A cave we have made more comfortable. You had another seizure. Much worse."

The aches in my body confirmed that.

"Is she awake?" Celeste whispered from across the darkened space. It seemed like she was twenty feet away, perhaps. It was hard to tell, the sound traveled strangely across the cave.

"Obviously." Virgil said softly but venomously, moving towards us from much nearer than Celeste. Virgil walked over, carrying an oil lamp with him.

The light shone warmly, revealing that we were situated in a comfortable alcove set into the stone wall of the cave. It was adorned in Iskur's typical style, with sumptuous pillows on the floor and gauze-like curtains separating the cubby from the rest of the cave. Virgil slipped between the curtains and stood with his arms crossed over his chest.

"Do you remember what happened?"

"Virgil, she just woke up." Iskur threw a pillow at him. Virgil let it hit him and did not break eye contact with me.

"I remember being outside." I offered, the memories and guilt slowly returning.

"What *exactly* did you think you were going to achieve?" Virgil asked slowly, not trying to disguise his deep frustration at all.

"I-I had him. I could have gotten him...maybe?" I said, breaking.

"Sh. Sh. Arga, I know. I know." Iskur said softly, kissing my neck. He glared over my shoulder at Virgil, "That is enough."

"I wanted to stop him." I started to cry as the memory of my flight in the vortex flooded back.

"I know it. I know. Shh."

I certainly had not had Travis. The vortex had bolstered my power and led me to a frenzy that I could not control. Had I given Iskur and Virgil new scars? Would Iskur's black lightform be lashed with more of my silvery white lightning the next time I saw it?

Virgil sighed, pinched the bridge of his nose, and sat in front of us.

"I am so sorry for putting you into that vortex like that. I did not think about how it would affect you. I was too curious." He said, sounding less irritated and more disappointed in himself.

Virgil tugged at his sleeves, trying to better cover the fresh set of silvery lightning bolts I had given him. Fears confirmed: more scars. Seeing them I let out a pained wail and whipped around to see how bad Iskur's were. He tried to dim the light quickly, but he was too slow. I cried belligerently and reached up to trace the bolt that ran from his forehead, over his left eye, to his cheek.

"All I do is hurt you two and fuck things up!"

"That is incredibly unhelpful." Virgil said with a tired snort, "And you are taking credit for a failure which was mine. This is not all about you. Stop being so self-centered."

Iskur held me while I sobbed into his chest.

"Oh, I think that you are both wrong. And I think you are looking at this quite the wrong way." Celeste came to my side and knelt with us, "I think this is a great learning moment."

"We already *knew* that I don't know how to do anything." I said bitterly, shivering and crying.

"Well, we learned how very powerful this vortex makes you." Celeste handed me a chalice of water.

"Yes. We are all able to fully enter our light forms in this place of power. None of us have yet been able to do that." Virgil was still rubbing at his new scars, but his academic tone was back in his voice.

"Does *he* know where we are?" Iskur spoke gently.

"He's still trapped somewhere in a tank of water. I guess? I don't know. He can call to me still though. He's trying to find us." I sniffled, "I felt the pull of him when I was up there, and I followed it. Before I felt him it was so nice. I felt so free. I was so happy. And he *ruined* it."

The grief tore at me. I had felt so strong and so powerful and so *capable* only to have it all come crashing down.

"It is so beautiful to see such honest and raw emotion." Celeste whispered to herself.

"What?"

"It's just so human. It's reassuring that not everything changes after death. That you remember how to *feel*." Celeste sighed, "You have all made me very hopeful."

"You said it seemed like he was still detained, Arga?" Virgil turned the conversation back to the crisis at hand.

"Yeah. He was in a tank of water. Like in a sci-fi movie."

"How far away?"

"I don't know."

"Did it seem like he had more abilities than just being able to call to your consciousness?"

"I don't *know*." I seethed, sniffling still.

"You do not know." Virgil repeated, starting to frown in frustration.

"Virgil if you would have *let* me deal with him I could have known more."
I snapped, "You were the one who yanked me back here!"

"You were out of control, Arga! What were you going to do? Try and zap
at him like this?" Virgil pointed to his arms, "The Old Dead would have
certainly given him their blessing and benefit of greater protection against
you before sending him on the hunt. They surely would not have sent him
out untrained and without skills of his own after you were able to disappear
with me to your own realm. I am trying to determine *exactly* what those
skills and training they have bestowed upon him are. And another thing, it
is unlikely you could have sent any sort of energy across such a great distance
without damaging things between here and there at the very least!"

"I-I was there. I saw him." I mumbled. I had *been* there, right?

"You *saw*. You were not there. You were right here. He is at least three
hundred miles away, as Celeste said. That matches how far I believe we had
to mentally pull you back from." Virgil said. He was irritated and bordering
on angry.

"I..." How could that be? I had traveled across the desert and had seen
him.

"Arga," Iskur's tone was tense, but cautious, "You did not physically
travel there. You reached out along your connection to him. The way you
did to me in your realm."

I sighed and held my head.

"It seemed really real."

"It is real. But it is not *striking distance* real." Virgil explained patronizingly. I glared at him through my tears.

"Can you hurt him?" Celeste asked, "If he was here?"

"Unclear. Arga can strike and wound the dead, as you see here on Iskur
and I, but as of yet she has not been able to control her powers or concentrate on the violent effort."

"She does not *need* to concentrate on the violent effort." Iskur held me
as he sat up, "She needs to learn to be calm and channel her focus to expand
the constructive powers she has, not the destructive powers."

"She," I pushed away from Iskur, "Is right here. And *she* thinks we should stop talking about this before I lose my shit again!"

Virgil sighed as I stormed out into the main chamber of the cave.

"Yes, let us wait until you are a bit more-"

"More what?" I whipped around to look at the three of them huddled in my sleeping area.

"More stable." Virgil said, matching my seething energy, "Arga, I know I made a mistake but this anger, you must control it."

"How? *How?* How am I supposed to control it when every time things seem calm *something like this happens again?!*"

Iskur was at my side in a blink.

"Enough!" His voice was a clap of thunder, "Virgil, there is no reason to be so demanding. Arga has just woken up. Surely you can go write and make notes for a time while she recovers more fully?"

Virgil nodded, to my surprise.

"Another mistake. I am tense as well. I apologize, Arga. I do not mean to antagonize. I will retire." Virgil took the lamp with him and went to another alcove.

I sat on the floor of the cave while Iskur brought over another lamp and lit it.

"Are you using a lighter?" I asked, hearing the clicks as he struggled.

"It is from Celeste. She brought these small lamps and lighters."

I took the lighter from him and flicked it to life.

"Why not just light it with your power?" I asked, catching the wick with the lighter's flame.

"We are tired. And fire is complex." Iskur dropped his voice lower, "You are a very draining adversary to spar with, Arga. Virgil has had the worst of it, that is why he is most cranky."

"He can't make anything?"

"He has not had the strength to try. You know how that irritates him."

Of course I remembered what a crabby prick he was whenever he needed us to make things for him on my island.

"I'm sorry." I rubbed my head.

"No sorry, Arga. None of us knew how you would react in the vortex."

"How did you make this cave?"

"It was mostly here. I only made some small additions. I did not have to battle you as long, only catch you when Virgil got control. Still tired, but not too tired for pillows."

I smiled. Celeste came over and sat with us.

"We need to stay close to this vortex and learn how to channel its energy." I said to Iskur.

"What do you think it will be useful for?" Iskur asked thoughtfully.

"For when Travis gets into striking distance."

I wanted nothing more than to rage and maim and lash out against Travis, but a tiny voice inside me reminded that he wasn't entirely to blame. I dismissed the thought. I could figure that out later, I guess.

"Or," Iskur said, taking both my hands, "We can use the vortex for finding a way to return to the Otherworld."

"Right, because that is where we want to go with the Old Dead still feeling unfavorable towards your existence." Virgil snorted derisively from across the cave.

"Do you have a different plan?" I asked sharply.

"No. Your plan is logical." Virgil took off his glasses and dusted them off on a silk hankie, "As logical as anything is in this disaster."

"Unhelpful!" Celeste chided at Virgil.

I sighed. We needed to remain by this vortex, I knew that, but for what? Virgil and Iskur were both right. Fighting Travis didn't seem helpful, and neither did returning to the Otherworld. But there was something here, something making me feel determined to use the vortex to better control my powers. I rubbed my head. I was exhausted.

"Sometimes," Celeste said calmly, seeing my frustration building, "The purpose reveals itself."

"There is never any time to recover." I said, wiping away the trails from the last few tears off of my face.

"There is time to recover now." Iskur said, ushering me back to where we had been sleeping.

I allowed him to guide me back to the alcove and lay me down.

"How long was I asleep before?" I asked, concerned.

"Hardly two hours." He said, "You have nothing to fear."

I breathed deeply and closed my eyes. Sleep took me without any effort.

# XXV.

*Purple flowers growing in the cracks of rocks.*
*Hummingbirds darting among the flowers.*
*Sunshine on a cliffside.*
*Waves crashing.*
*Thunder rumbling.*
*Wind blustering.*
*I was looking for something.*
*Someone laughing at me.*
*A hazy bar where terrible music played.*
*Voices in my head whispering advice.*
*Purple flowers withering where they grew.*

"What did you mean, when you said there is never any time to recover? Back in the cave?" Celeste asked delicately.

She and I were standing on top of the mesa in the setting sun. After two days of on and off resting, Virgil had given me the all clear to go back up top for a meditation with Celeste. He and Iskur had recovered their strength as well. They were both hanging behind us, standing closer to the center of the vortex and trying to look casual. I knew they were there to stop me from diving into it headlong.

"Since I died I haven't had one relaxing thing happen without another stressful thing happening right after." I explained.

I replayed everything in my head. Becoming conscious on Iskur's floor. The pool. The lessons. Injury after injury I had caused Iskur and Virgil. I felt the panic welling up in me again. The Old Dead. My island. Travis.

"Sweet angel, take my hand."

"No. I...I can't touch you." My voice cracked as I tried to get myself under control.

"Shhhhh, shhh. Then listen to my voice. Close your eyes and listen to me." Celeste's tone was soothing but firm. I obeyed.

"You are feeling a panic attack coming on. That is okay. Your body and your brain are getting you ready for danger. This is a superpower, Arga. Your body and your brain want to keep you safe. Breathe in and recognize it. Name it. It is fear, and it is natural. Say it with me. Fear is natural. I see the fear and I name it."

"I see the fear and I name it." I said shakily. This was stupid.

"Good, good, now let us breathe to ten."

Celeste counted and we inhaled and exhaled together. The tension coiled in my chest like a viper, I felt like I would choke. How was this supposed to relax me?

"Arga, feel where you are. Hear my voice. Smell the air. Ground yourself in what is happening at this moment. Open yourself to the fear that your brain is recognizing. Allow it to unfold. You are in a safe space to experience fear."

"I'm not," I croaked, tension in my chest mounting higher, "I could *kill you* if I let go."

"You will not. I have foreseen it."

"Celeste-"

"Arga, breathe and allow the fear to unfold."

I wrestled for a moment between wanting to stifle the feeling in my chest and the flickering desire to listen to Celeste. Did I want to risk this? Why hadn't Virgil and Iskur intervened? Did they not feel me balancing on the edge of spiraling? But, letting go sounded *so good.* I imagined loosening my grip and, as if imagining was enough, I felt the fear and panic blossom in my chest. There was a sense of relief as it began to unfurl its hideous tendrils and course through my body with its destructive energy. I breathed out and let it go.

The fear rapidly expanded beyond the bounds of my chest. As it grew I saw myself from outside my body. My consciousness hovered over the edge of the cliff, looking back at Celeste and me sitting on the ground. I looked small and scared, but somehow placid at the same time. Celeste looked serene and sure of herself. She glowed rosy pink against the bright blue sky. As I observed Celeste's aura, I saw my human form smile.

The fear was still there, too. I could actually see it spreading like an octopus around me as I meditated. It changed color like an octopus too: first black, then red and orange like fire, then blue like the night sky. The colors undulated and faded into each other slowly, like ink being dripped into water.

I moved my awareness closer to my body and looked at the fear from over my own shoulder.

"You can see it now, can't you?" Celeste said kindly.

"*Yes.*" I wasn't sure if I was speaking or just thinking.

"Observe the fear. Tell it that you are allowing it to exist for now. You are in control."

"*I am in control.*"

The fear flickered white and bright blue like lightning.

"*I allow you to be here.*"

"Good, so good. Arga, yes."

There were sounds now. I could hear waves rushing and fire burning from the cloud of fear that hovered in front of Celeste and I.

"*What are you made of?*"

I reached out with both the hands on my body and with my consciousness, leaning into the cloud.

"Stay curious. Do not judge or react. Observe the fear." Celeste instructed.

The cloud oscillated slightly as I put my hands palm up on my lap. Then it washed over me in a flood.

I saw the golden light and heard the unforgettable sound of the Nameless Ones, pierced by the cries of our comrades being consumed by supernatural flames. I watched them die again, becoming one with the Nameless Ones and leaving only their bodies behind.

The scene shifted. The Old Dead stood before me, towering and horrific. They opened their mouths and Iskur's screams of agony echoed across the nothingness. They dissolved into fire and stone as Iskur's voice faded into distant echoing thunder. And finally, horrible silence.

The empty silence and blackness changed subtly to velvet blue as I tried to understand what I was seeing. Was it a person? People. It was *many* people. They were unclear, blurry and distant. They came rushing into focus and I saw my mother, my grandfather, and everyone I had known in my recent life. They were begging, wailing, crying loudly: all pleading with me in incoherent terror. I watched as each one's face turned from pain and confusion to betrayal and dismay. They turned to dust and blew away before me. I saw myself, a pillar of white light against a ruined world, burning fiercely as a hurricane swelled at my feet. There was Virgil, drowning in waves as my agony and anguish pulled oceans across the land. The waves drowned out all sound, all life. Everything.

My white hot light surged and blinded me in the vision.

"This is fear showing you what it is made of." I was shocked to hear Celeste's airy voice in the white nothingness, "We have observed, but we do not need to accept it as truth. Thank the fear for revealing itself and tell it we do not need it anymore."

I was back in my body, I could feel the warm sun on my skin. My eyes were still closed.

"Let us say it together, Arga. Repeat with me, 'Thank you for revealing this. We do not accept it as truth. Leave now.'"

"Thank you for revealing this. We do not accept it as truth. Leave now." I said softly.

"Again, like you mean it, Arga. This is not what truly *is*. It is only what fear is made of."

"Thank you for revealing this. We do not accept it as truth. Leave now." My voice did not shake as I repeated myself. Celeste made me feel safe and bold after the horrors of what I had seen.

"Fear is real, but what it is made of is not something we need to accept. Say it with strength! Arga, you control the fear."

"Leave now!" I shouted.

Celeste giggled at my sudden ferocity. I heard Virgil scrambling towards us. *Now* he was interested.

"Let us breathe to ten, then you can open your eyes." Celeste said sweetly, then added to Virgil, "It's fine."

We took our breaths and I opened my eyes.

"You are not a monster, Arga." Celeste reassured me.

"Did you see the vision too?"

"See what vision?" Virgil asked defensively.

"No, I could not see what you saw, but I know enough about fear to know how to treat it." Celeste reached over and took my hand, "That's a skill I would have died a long time ago without learning."

Virgil made an impatient noise.

"What *are* you two doing?" He demanded.

"Meditating on fear and anxiety and banishing it." Celeste winked at me.

"Virgil, it was amazing. I'm fine."

My hands were still trembling but I felt clearer than I had since arriving on Earth. I had seen what my fears were, and told them that I would not accept them. And they had gone. They had gone away.

"What was the vision?" Virgil walked in front of me and inspected me suspiciously, "What happened?"

"I saw what I am most afraid of."

"And that is?"

"Things that I won't allow to happen. Things that aren't true."

"Exactly." Celeste nodded reverently.

Virgil shot her an irritated look.

"Arga, your power is somewhat different than a typical human nervous disorder. If you saw something significant..." He looked at my eyes intently.

"Are they black?" I asked, knowing the answer.

"Not anymore."

"See? I'm fine."

"Your eyes being human is not a complete prognosis of being *fine*, Arga."

"Don't spoil this for me, Virgil. I meditated and I feel refreshed, okay?" I stood up and stretched my back.

"What kind of meditation refreshes the mind so fully?" Virgil retorted rudely.

Celeste made an offended noise and flowed into a standing position languidly.

"That is *not* helpful, or kind." She said stonily.

"Arga, what did you *see?*" Virgil rounded on me again. Iskur was walking our way now too.

"Really fucked up shit, Virg. But those things aren't *real*. I don't need to accept them as real. They don't need to be true." I stared at him, irritation rising now that he was destroying my calm.

How could he always find a way to be such an insufferable killjoy? I just wanted to go back to how we all were on my island the night we feasted on the beach.

"That's right, Arga! Your fears cannot control you." Celeste cheered. Iskur came to my side and observed the unfolding bickering.

"Arga." Virgil said softly, "We are running from very real dangers. If you saw something in a vision, it could be *helpful* for us to figure out what we can do to get out of this...predicament."

"*He is genuinely worried,*" I reminded myself. "*He just has an annoying way of showing it.*"

I reached out and dusted his tunic gently.

"Virgil. Trust me, I know these were things from me, not some vision. I saw straight to the root of the fear I've felt since I first used my powers. The fear was just my creation. I was terrified of losing control zed...uh," I struggled to admit the root of the fear aloud, "Ending everything."

His brow furrowed.

"Ending everything. Like an apocalypse?"

"Yeah, but like it being my fault."

Virgil looked at the ground and sighed.

"Celeste is right. You are not a monster, Arga."

My voice failed me. Not a monster? Hadn't he seen how I traded my friends and fellow Seers for a slice of unintelligible power?

"It wasn't a vision." I croaked, a flutter of anxiousness returning.

"No. No. You are right. That is a future that you do not have to accept. That is not the truth." He looked up at me, his eyes black.

"Are mine?" I touched my face.

"Yes."

"Why do they do that when I'm emotional?"

"Emotions are powerful." Virgil smirked and took one of my hands.

We stood in silence and stared at each other. Iskur squeezed my shoulder and walked away. We stood in silence and I tried to send waves of gratitude to Virgil. I couldn't say it. I didn't want to speak and start crying or something. Since the void and my island he had become a great, but sometimes annoying, comfort to me. He smiled, and tipped his head in acknowledgement. I felt a similar spark of gratitude flow over me in return. So much for not crying.

We both discreetly brushed tears off our cheeks. Virgil cleared his throat to display some shred of composure.

"Well, Arga, now that you have banished your fear of killing us all, should we begin training again?"

Joyful fire blazed inside me. The vortex pulled on my mind seductively, I could not wait to explore the power I could unlock in its proximity. I smiled over Virgil's shoulder at Iskur who stood a few paces behind him, beaming at me. He was ready, too.

"I thought you'd never ask."

# XXVI.

"**S**how me what you saw this time," Virgil was pacing anxiously on the other side of the pool from me.

I sighed in exasperation, but obeyed. Shifting into my light form I plunged into the pool and focused on the visions that had played out in my mind during our last training exercise. Fragments of scenes played out for Virgil to see:

Iskur and I entwined beneath the fig tree. The sounds of our companions screaming in horror and anguish as they were consumed by the Nameless Ones. Iskur's Otherworld palace sitting in ruin and abandonment. Sunlight filtering between branches of towering cedar trees. Myself as a child, except the scene kept glitching between me laughing and running down a sidewalk in the neighborhood I grew up in, and me laughing and running down a forest trail in ancient times. A dark night sky and the sound of thunder. A forest full of dead leaves blowing in the wind. The sound of distant waves on the cliffside.

"The last three, those are locations you know?" Virgil asked as I came back up to the surface.

Iskur had been busy over the week that had passed, crafting a serene pool in our cave for us to use for training and bathing. The space overall, while still small, was feeling more and more palatial daily with Iskur's refinements. Virgil was constantly issuing warnings to Iskur about not getting too comfortable here.

"I don't know where those locations are, no. But I know *who* they are." I slipped back into my human form and sat next to Virgil.

"What do you mean, *who* they are?"

"Thunder, wind, sea? The three of us? Thunder and wind in leaves is how you and Iskur's voices sounded to me in the Otherworld, before I could understand you two."

Virgil frowned.

"Hm. And the sea is you?"

"I guess. I always hear waves for myself. And I made the sea rage on my island before we came to Earth."

"Yes. I recall." He rubbed his head, "I do not know what to make of these visions. They are disjointed. Murky."

"Are visions usually clear?" I sighed and started to walk towards the doorway back to the main chamber of our cave.

"Well. Clearer than this." Virgil followed me, still frowning in thought.

Iskur and Celeste were draped languidly on pillows in the conversation pit on the floor.

"Done already?" Celeste looked surprised.

"Nothing useful." I pouted, flopping next to Iskur.

"I think we need to approach this from a different angle." Virgil said, conjuring a chair and sitting at the edge of the pit, "Perhaps we can try the vortex again..." He mused.

"Yes!" I said hurriedly.

"Not all the way in its center, but perhaps a meditation up topside would result in more clear visions." Virgil explained, "You had that very productive one with Celeste last week and nothing so clear since."

"Maybe it's *who* I'm meditating with, not *how* I'm meditating." I snapped, then sighed, "I'm sorry. I'm cranky."

I was tired of waiting to explore the vortex. As much as I appreciated Virgil's vast knowledge and analytical nature in helping us understand some of the complexities of our situation, I hated playing it safe now. Virgil sighed and nodded understandingly.

"We need to understand more of what your arrangement was with the Nameless Ones. How you were able to take on so much of the power to avoid

Iskur's destruction? And how did you wandered countless centuries before becoming human again? You have no memory of either."

"I remembered taking the power after Iskur showed me."

"But that was being *shown* something to remind you. I think we will gain more insight from you remembering the things that Iskur does not know."

Iskur rolled over and started braiding a cluster of violets into my hair. I noticed Celeste was covered in daisies.

"Are you bored?" I asked him, looking around and noticing the abundance of new flowers and plants around the cave.

"I am not bored. I am longing for peace just as you are." He smiled at me, but his eyes were black. I took his hands and made him stop messing with my hair.

"Are you worried about something?"

Iskur did not answer.

"Virgil...could we?" He nodded to the doorway to the small room with the pool.

"Hey, what's going on?" I demanded as Virgil nodded and Iskur planted a kiss on my head and walked off.

"May I please have a moment of private conversation with Virgil, Arga?" He asked charmingly. I was not deterred.

"What are you hiding?" I pried, moving to follow after him.

"Arga, they can have a private chat. Respect their privacy." Celeste took my wrist and kept me with her. I sighed in irritation as they exited the main chamber and sealed over the door to the pool with stone.

"I could break the door down." I muttered, begrudgingly settling in with Celeste.

"But that would be rude." Celeste said, offering me a bowl of grapes.

"Would it?" I took the bowl and ate a couple and let my irritation simmer. Breathe in calm, breathe out all that does not serve me.

In our week of training, I had made great progress in managing my anger, fear, and anxiousness. Even if it didn't seem like it in this moment, I had been very tolerant of the slow pace Virgil demanded we move at with my training that week.

We had fallen into an easy, enjoyable routine: Iskur would spend the mornings working with me on exercising my creative powers. Then we would stop that exhausting endeavor for a short rest, and I would pick up in the afternoon with Virgil for meditation and exploration of my visions.

The time with Virgil was going less well, but I was able to call up images of my past with greater and greater ease. The images were never full scenes, more like jumbled fragments of memories from my most recent and past life. Often they repeated. Virgil had grown used to seeing Iskur and I in various states of romantic engagement, much to my initial horror. But by the third day I had grown to expect it. He was unperturbed by then as well, observing each fractured memory and sleuthing for clues or ways to trigger larger memories. So far we had only unearthed a few happy moments from my ancient and modern childhood. Always shown in parallel, shifting seamlessly between the two lives.

Each day, once Virgil and I had exhausted the visions, we would join Celeste and Iskur for food and stories. Celeste told us about Earth and what had happened since I had died. Iskur loved this time together, I could see it plainly on his face. He listened to Celeste with unwavering attention. Some nights she would ask us questions, which was Virgil's delight. He would explain the Otherworld or our situation to her in as great of detail as he could. Iskur and I would unhelpfully interject with our own questions.

Our very human routine would end with Celeste leading us in an evening meditation and sending us all to bed. We had all adjusted to life in the cave quickly. Celeste surprised me by never issuing a complaint or concern. I did not know how she was so placid in the face of this impossible-seeming situation.

"When was the last time you went outside?" I asked Celeste suddenly.

"Oh, yesterday morning. I do get out of the cave each day. Virgil and I took a walk while you and Iskur did your work together. He is a funny thing. He will not go far from the cave entrance. He just walks for a short distance with me, then watches me as I walk and stretch and do tai chi," She giggled, "It's like he's taking his dog out for a walk in the back yard, but he won't leave the back doorstep."

The mental image made me laugh.

"I'm sorry, this has to feel like a prison. Maybe we can see about all of us going topside tomorrow."

"It's far from a prison, look at this place!" Celeste motioned around her.

"Iskur is really good at making places feel comfortable." I admitted, "You should have seen his dwelling in the Otherworld."

"I'm sure I'll see it someday." Celeste patted my hand.

"I think it's in ruins now." I felt a lump form in my throat at the memory of the recurring vision I had of his palace being destroyed, "But it was really beautiful."

"He'll rebuild I'm sure."

"Yeah well, we have to get back there and deal with the Old Dead first."

"I have been thinking about that."

"What about it?"

"Well," Celeste looked sheepish, "Perhaps I'm being selfish, but what if you three remained here on Earth?"

I stared at her.

"What if we *what?*"

"Remained here? On Earth? I know you would be technically in exile, but does it cause you affliction to stay on Earth?"

"Not affliction, no. Celeste, it's more like we just don't belong here."

She smiled sadly.

"We aren't human anymore. We don't belong and we can feel that very painfully. Not like real pain, just this deep feeling of not being right here. It's not our place."

Words failed me as I tried to explain the gnawing feeling Iskur and I had discussed at length in our morning sessions.

"It's like showing up somewhere but all the signs are in a different language and everyone is acting very differently than you are expecting. Like visiting a foreign land. We can adopt the customs and enjoy a visit, but I don't know. We aren't *supposed* to be here. We aren't at home."

Celeste let out a sad sigh.

"Arga, I get the feeling that you have never truly experienced belonging until you reunited with Iskur."

Her words hit me with a pang of realization and guilt. She was right.

I wanted our long countless hours on my island back. The moments we were alone together, and the moments we shared with Virgil. The night we feasted on the beach and Virgil read us poems of love and loss and joy and pain. Never on Earth had I felt such security and comfort in my adulthood, and never since those moments had I felt as safe and seen and at ease.

"Angel," Celeste swept a tear off my cheek, "I know, I know come here."

She pulled me into a hug.

"I am homesick for something I only had for a second." I admitted, letting out a ragged breath. My chest burned with anguish.

"I understand that feeling." Celeste pulled back to look me in the eyes, "Goodness, your eyes are beautiful when they do that."

"It doesn't freak you out?" I wiped a tear away. I was not sobbing or out of control, just letting grief flow out of me. Celeste had shown me how to be better about being at peace with how my emotions rose and fell. The ebb and flow of my own internal tide.

"The first time I saw it I was concerned, but of course I was still trying to convince myself you were human then. It's less scary when you know you are looking at a God."

I laughed.

"How is it less scary to look at a God than a human?"

"At least with a God you know what you are looking at."

"Do you? I don't know what I'm looking at when I look at myself." I laughed again. I adored Celeste and her complete acceptance of things I was still struggling to comprehend. She breathed an unexpected peace into our trio and I loved it.

"You are looking at power when you are looking at a God. Incomprehensible power. The type of power that would break me if I bore it, so it is best to bow in reverence to the one who bears it."

I shook my head with another laugh.

"Please don't start worshiping us. I'd rather be friends."

"So would I. But you know, I always wanted the higher powers to be like friends. Isn't that what most religions say they offer? Friendship with a benevolent God?"

"I always thought it was more about fear of God's wrath."

"Well, I want friendship. I worship my friends. I built my house as a shrine to friendship and welcoming. Why should our friendship and this cave be any different?"

I pulled one of the violets out of my hair and twirled it slowly in my hands. I still felt so bad about her house. We had been keeping an eye on it from afar in case Travis tracked us there. Virgil had seen that there was an investigation going on since Celeste was a missing person. Clive had been trying to call her house nonstop since we had fled, and had eventually come back to run point on the investigation alongside the police.

"Celeste, what are you going to do when we are gone?" I asked. We had upended her life entirely, a fact I was still plagued with guilt about.

She thought for a moment before answering.

"I will help you however I can until that day comes, and when it comes I will decide what to do next." She said, enigmatic as always.

"*Please* don't make this cave into your permanent home." I teased, trying to make light of my deepening concern for her.

"Well, I'm not going to make *that* promise. Iskur has made some very serious improvements here."

The stone sealing the doorway to the pool dissolved and Virgil and Iskur reentered the room. Their eyes were black and their faces grave. Celeste and I stood up and went to them silently. My insides lurched at the intensity of their expressions. Virgil spoke first.

"Arga, Iskur had a vision."

I looked at Iskur. He was avoiding my gaze.

"What was it?" My voice came out as a hoarse whisper rather than the even calm tone I had hoped for.

"It was our next step. We need to get to Arz ar-Rabb in Lebanon." Virgil sounded confident and cold.

"I don't know where-"

"The Cedars of God." He said softly, "You see them in your visions too."

"Where it happened?" My throat constricted.

"*I accept fear. I allow it to exist. I accept fear but I will not let it control me. It is a visitor here. It will leave when I ask it. It will not tell me lies. It will not control me.*" I mentally repeated the fear mantra Celeste and I had been working on.

"Yes. Where you met the Nameless Ones."

"Iskur, what did you see?" He took my outstretched hand.

"Arga, visions are not confirmations of true futures." Iskur said, still avoiding my eyes.

"Look at me." I commanded, my tone more intense than I had meant it to be. Iskur obeyed instantly. The flash of guilt I felt at commanding him, knowing he had to obey me, was overridden by my need to know what the vision held.

"Arga-"

"I am capable of handling what you saw."

Virgil took my hand away from Iskur. I could feel him searching my emotions delicately.

"You are very well in control," He said, nodding approvingly, "What Iskur says is true, his vision is not a set prediction of the future. No vision is. But they can hold clues as to what we should do next."

"What did he see?" I demanded.

Virgil flinched and withdrew his hand.

"Did you mean to do that?" He asked, examining his palm with bewilderment.

"Are you hurt?" Celeste floated to Virgil's side to look at his palm, "I'm sure she didn't mean to-"

"You made a verbal demand, Arga, but I *felt* it where you were touching me."

I stared at him. He must have missed the part where I had commanded Iskur to look at me a few seconds before. But I wasn't going to bring *that* up. Iskur and I locked eyes momentarily before I was forced to look away.

"I wasn't trying to hurt you, I just want to know what Iskur saw."

We all stood in a silent stare down. I could demand that Iskur obey me, thanks to the oath, but my demands caused Virgil pain. I had to force down the rising concern about my willingness to flex my powers over them. I *needed* to see what was in the vision, so I needed to stay calm. I could deal with my guilt and confusion later. Virgil and I were locked in a contest of wills to see who would look away first. Neither of us blinked, but at last he said:

"I think you should see what Iskur saw."

"Okay. Good." I said, trying to sound confident.

*I accept fear but I will not let it control me.*

"Celeste, it will be best if you remain on the ledge of the cave entrance. If anything happens-"

"I will be *fine*, Virgil." I said as Celeste squeezed my shoulder and glided towards the cave's mouth.

The three of us walked into the pool's chamber. Iskur sealed the door behind us and sent a single orb of light floating to the ceiling of the space. The chamber was hardly ten feet across in all directions, with a six foot diameter circular pool at the center. A few lily pads bobbed happily around the edges.

"Arga," Iskur took my hands suddenly and with a voice full of anguish continued, "Please know that what I saw is not the future set to stone. It is a possible outcome, and also a guide to where we can go from here."

"I know, I know, Iskur, it's fine." I clasped his hands tightly, "See? I'm calm. No destroying energy."

He smiled with a sad sort of pride.

"You grow so strong into your powers here, my love."

Virgil made an impatient noise. Iskur kissed my hand, shifted to his light form, and slipped into the water. The surface of the water remained undisturbed and the floating orb of light extinguished itself. The scene began to unfold on the water's surface.

The scene was flooded with golden light and the voices of the Nameless Ones roared in the chamber. Screams and cries pierced the sound as the golden light became flames. I watched in horror as each of our comrades died and became one with the Nameless Ones, their bodies littering the ground.

My chest tightened and my throat constricted. Dread began to well up within me: I had seen all this before. I did not dare to look at Virgil. I could feel his eyes boring into me.

The scene shifted. The Old Dead towered over us with their horrific animal heads. Their mouths opened and Iskur's dying screams issued from their gaping jaws. The Old Dead dissolved into fire and stone as the screams faded into distant echoing thunder and at last, horrible silence.

My breathing slowed to a stop and my chest burned as the empty silence and blackness in Iskur's vision turned into the blurred forms of distant humans. For a moment I desperately hoped that I would not see their faces again, that Iskur's vision would branch off and stop repeating what I had seen with Celeste. But no, the faces of everyone I had known in my recent life came into focus and began to beg for mercy. I watched again as each one's face went through stages of grief and terror before they turned to dust and blew away.

I was shaking now, trembling from shame, guilt, and anguish. I realized I was mouthing my fear mantra, and that Virgil had edged closer to me.

Then came me in the vision, the ruiner of worlds. A beacon of white light drawing the oceans over cliff sides and covering all that was left with water and waves. I watched Virgil get swept under, the last of the things I loved being destroyed as the world fell silent to my destruction.

My white hot light surged and blinded me in the vision. Then it all faded to black and the chamber fell dim.

"Breathe." Virgil was tender and kind as he said it, his arms around me.

I didn't know at what point he had begun holding me but I was grateful for it. I was terrified, but in control. The destructive energy had not flared despite the fear I was feeling. Iskur was returning to us, gathering himself slowly into his human form.

"You have seen that before." He said, coming to stand in front of me.

"Yeah." I said shakily.

"I thought so." He knelt in front of Virgil and I as he looked at the ground sadly, "Why did you not show me before?"

"I-"

"*When* did you see that?" Virgil inquired, sounding hurt as well. Great. They weren't mad, just disappointed. My favorite. Perfect for increasing my guilt.

"When I meditated with Celeste and banished my, uh...fears." I fumbled, trying to fight the tiny prickle of destroying energy that was building up.

"Breathe," Virgil pulled me closer into him and nodded to Iskur.

Iskur put his arms around both of us. We sat in silence for a moment, breathing together until the prickle died down.

"It does not matter that you did not show us." Iskur said, his eyes gleaming black, "We have all seen it now."

"I'm sorry, I really thought it wasn't anything besides my deepest fears."

"That sort of thing is important. Anything you *see* like that, we must also see it. Are we in agreement?" Virgil unwound himself from our huddle and stood.

"But what does it mean?"

"*Agreed?*" Virgil repeated emphatically.

"Yes, I will show you. But I have not had any other visions that you haven't seen besides that one." I looked at Iskur, who was sitting next to me, tracing the palm of my hand gently, "What does it mean?"

"I think it means what Virgil said. We must go to our holy grove."

"The cedars? Where we..." I trailed off, hearing the screams in my head again.

"Yes, the Cedars of God is what it is called now. It will likely look much different from when you walked among those trees. Much has changed." Virgil looked thoughtful.

"Look different how?" Iskur sounded concerned.

"There are fewer trees." Virgil said flatly.

"Fewer? Why? *How?*" Iskur stood quickly, "Those trees are not plants! They are beacons, they are the portals we used to call the Nameless Ones! They are holy beyond understanding, how are there *fewer?*"

"They were being used to build temples and other holy relics in your time, Iskur. Do not act as if you did not know they could be cut down."

"Cut down? Of course but-"

"They got cut down. Many of them."

"I'm sorry to interrupt this debate but how do you propose we *get* to Lebanon?" I asked, standing as well, "We can't just ask Celeste to buy us plane tickets and forge passports."

"I do not think we will be taking a plane, no. That certainly would be unsafe for you," I gave Virgil a warning look, "Yes, well for all of us."

"I'm in control now." I said, staring at him.

No reason to mention the distress I felt at Iskur seeing my deepest fears as a vision. And no reason to bring up the fact that I was getting more and more comfortable using my commanding power over Iskur to get what I wanted. Stay calm. Breathe. We had to figure this out.

"Of course. But would it not be best to test that in spaces that are not thousands of feet in the air with many humans trapped with us? Hm?"

"You don't have to be such an asshole about it. What's your plan?"

"I do not have one at the moment. I feel very strongly that we need to consider a plan before acting on it."

"There's nothing to consider *or* act on. There's no plan!"

"Enough." Iskur waved his arm and the stone wall unsealed, flooding the space with the ambient light of the lamps from the main chamber, "We will work on a plan first. Then we will argue."

We filed out into the main chamber and stood near the central table. Celeste wandered back in hearing us leave the pool room.

"Is all well, my loves?" She asked in her normal airy voice.

"We need to get to Lebanon." I said flatly, "I don't suppose you can make fake passports?"

"Oh!" Celeste laughed, "I only have a few of my own. I don't suppose I could get ones made for you three on short notice unless I can get in touch with-"

"Arga was joking." Virgil said flatly. We were all used to Celeste's concerning criminal connections at this point.

"I was joking." I confirmed when Celeste looked at me quizzically.

"Oh, well then. No need to call my guy. But you *do* need to go to Lebanon?"

"Yes we do." Iskur was sitting at the table, falling into deep thought.

"No clue how we are going to pull this off." I muttered, sitting with Iskur. Celeste hummed. Virgil paced, murmuring to himself.

"Do you think..." I trailed off, frowning in thought.

When I had pulled Virgil and I to my island I had wanted nothing more than safety and isolation. Someplace we could be unobserved. When I had pulled Iskur to us, I had wanted nothing more than to have him by my side.

"Think what, Arga?" Iskur had taken my hand absentmindedly.

"Uh, do you think that I could take us there? Like I did in the Other-world?"

Virgil stopped pacing.

"Traveling in the Otherworld and traveling here on Earth are very different things, Arga. To travel in the Otherworld, someone who has control of their abilities merely needs to think about their destination and they reach it. It is like nothing. To do that here, however, I fear we will attract unwanted attention."

"The Old Dead would see us do it?" I asked.

"No...well, perhaps. But I meant more like it would be very *disruptive* to Earth for us to do that. Which would in turn alert the Old Dead. Which...well. I am not sure what they would do about it. They do not have much power on Earth. Their power lies in determining who can interact between Earth and the Otherworld."

We had discussed whether or not the Old Dead were aware we were on Earth at length over the past week. The consensus among us was that if they were aware, they would have done something already. It was a fragile comfort that I held onto. They probably thought we were all still in the void. Or, maybe they hadn't even noticed how long Travis had been gone. Virgil always said the Old Dead were funny about time. He had once asked them a question and they responded quickly: one hundred Earth years later. We had barely been gone a second in their eyes.

"You said they can't really see the old cedar grove, right?" I asked Iskur.

"Yes. It is a place of blindness for them." He nodded.

"So, like, if we travel there, they might know we traveled but they wouldn't be able to see where we went maybe?" I stood up and joined Virgil in his renewed pacing. This was something. This felt like it could work.

"Arga, you have yet to successfully make any sort of planned travel that was not the result of a major crisis." Virgil as he slowed his walking.

"She could try some simple travels first." Celeste offered, "Like, go from here to the other side of the cave?"

"Hmmm." Virgil considered this, "We need to get to the cedars, certainly. I do not know what a shorter distance to practice would hurt. I am willing to bet that the energy field here is absurd enough to block any of our smaller experiments from getting too much attention. Interesting, yes."

Virgil looked at me with an inquisitive hunger that made me a little uneasy.

"You have a lot more control now, we *could* try it. But you tell me if you are feeling confident enough in your abilities."

I nodded fiercely. I felt ready. I wanted to get us home.

"I want to try."

# XXVII.

"Focus..." Virgil's voice faded and so did I.

Traveling felt like I was being zipped flat, compressed into a single idea: my destination. It had to be what files felt like being sent across the world on the internet. As I fixated myself on the point we had agreed on and let myself become one with the thought of that spot, I felt the now familiar slip into darkness. For a split second I was speeding through space before unzipping and decompressing myself rapidly in the new location.

"My love! A triumph!" Iskur cheered as I opened my eyes.

"It's been two weeks of this nonstop, it better be a triumph." I snapped.

"Arga," He pleaded, "Patience."

I had successfully traveled from within the cave to where Iskur stood waiting for me on top of the mesa. This was a new record distance for me, and the first time I had gone from inside the cave to outside. I sighed.

"Virgil is still playing small." I grumbled, "I can *do this*. I know I can get us there."

"Arga, we want to be sure. Can you imagine the problems if we end up *not* there on the first try for a longer distance?"

"All it takes is intense focus. I know those trees. I see them in every dream and every vision and every second I'm not practicing this. I *know* I can do it." I complained, shifting into my light form and flitting around the edge of the mesa.

*"Arga, I trust you beyond all else, I will speak with him if you think that you are ready."* Iskur had shifted form and was plying himself with me.

*"Do you think you can take us both into the cave?"* He asked, *"You are so strong now."*

Flattery. I loved it. Without answering him, I locked onto his presence and focused on the center of the cave. We flattened and snapped into existence exactly where I intended us to.

"See?!" I roared, shifting back into my human form and whooping triumphantly in Virgil's face.

"What *are* you yelling about?" Virgil said, then he gasped as Iskur gathered himself into his human shape as well.

"Oh*ho*, that is worth yelling about! You brought Iskur back?" Virgil was beaming, "Well done Arga! Well done indeed!!"

"I can do it, we need to try something longer. Something further. With all three of us." I demanded.

Virgil's smile wavered.

"Further? Arga, we should take it slow-"

"Virg! Come *on*, it has been weeks, man." I moaned, "I can do this!"

"Arga, for this to work we are relying entirely on you." Virgil's face was grave again.

"You have mentioned this before. Do not harp on the fact and steal this victory from her." Iskur huffed.

That fact that neither of them could travel on their own had been a point of distress for both Virgil and Iskur when we had discovered it. No matter how they had tried over the past two weeks, they had not been able to make themselves travel. It was a rough start for me at first, but like using my creative energy, it came easily once I learned how it felt.

"I can do this." I said again.

"Why don't you three travel to my home and back?" Celeste suggested, coming to stand near Virgil, "That is further than you have gone, but not so far that you cannot walk back."

Virgil shook his head.

"There has been an investigation at your house, remember? You are a missing person. Having the three people suspected of kidnapping you suddenly reappear in your home would not be ideal."

"I am still so shocked that people would notice I was gone." Celeste laughed.

We had a near miss when the van had been discovered by some hikers a few days prior. Virgil and Iskur had gone out in the dead of night to destroy it before the authorities could come and investigate the vehicle the following morning.

"We can try somewhere else. But we need to try traveling with the three of us somewhere beyond the reach of the vortex. I want to see if that's the only thing making this easy for me."

"Hm." Virgil mused, looking at me intently, "We should repeat you bringing Iskur and myself over short distances first. But before that, we all need to rest."

A brief argument ensued between Virgil and I, which was broken up by Iskur coaxing me with a swim and Celeste asking to go for a short walk before sunset. We parted ways temporarily.

"Virgil is driving me crazy today." I complained, floating in the pool. Iskur had enlarged the pool a bit, making the chamber around it even more similar to the one in his dwelling.

"You are driving him crazy as well." Iskur observed, wetting his long hair.

"And we are both driving you crazy, I take it?"

"Yes. You in particular," Iskur smiled wickedly, swimming towards me, "Are driving me utterly mad."

I smiled at him.

"I am sorry for the annoyance."

"Not as sorry as you will be if I lose my mind."

"Don't tempt me with a good time." I wanted to shift into my lightform and throw myself across Iskur, but he held up his hand.

"Stop, Arga." He said softly, treading water closer and closer to me.

"What?"

"Do you ever wonder what it is like in the physical?"

I recoiled at the thought. After being with him in our lightforms, physical relations seemed a pale imitation.

"Iskur, you've said it yourself: bodies are just bodies, it's when we are shifted that the connection is more pure."

"Ah well, there are certain things that you can begin like this," he held out his right hand, "And end like this."

He extended his left arm and let that half of his body shift into blackness. I squirmed away, floating on my back.

"I'm not interested in getting caught like that."

"Caught?"

"Virgil and Celeste will be back."

Iskur waved his hand towards the entrance and sealed it off with stone.

"They will not bother."

"Iskur..."

"Say you do not want to and I will not ask again." His eyes were black and his half smile was making it very hard for me to breathe.

But, I did not need to breathe.

I shifted into my light form and doused all the floating orbs above us. The water in the pool churned as I swept across the surface.

*"Resist me then."* I teased, pinning him against the wall of the pool, *"I will make you shift with me."*

Iskur stayed human and closed his eyes in ecstasy. I felt him struggle nobly against my commands, but I wasn't asking very forcefully yet. My mind flicked back to how he had placed my hands on his head in Celeste's house and told me that anything I wanted from him I could have. Anything I asked he would obey. I had power over him and he adored it. And normally, the thought terrified me.

But not right now.

Today, I had brought him with me as I traveled with ease. I knew in my core that I was going to be able to travel with both him and Virgil. I could see the cedars clearly. I could visualize us all going there. We would get there and find clarity and answers. We would solve this puzzle and return to my realm. We would be home. We would be safe. We would be together.

I pressed against him and twirled myself around his neck and wrists and torso. I pulled him upwards and watched him smile his devious smile as he lifted above the water.

"*Join me.*" I demanded, he shook his head.

"You join me." He rebuffed my demand gently, but his request made no impact on me. His will was weaker than mine, or he was purposefully weakening it. I didn't care, I was enjoying myself.

"*Please?*" I begged, "*Shift. Please? I need you.*"

"You are begging now? Command me."

"*Shift with me.*"

Iskur shook his head and began to wriggle out of my constraints.

"Make me."

I channeled actual effort, sending a jolt into the one place I still had contact with him: his right arm. His compliance was startlingly immediate. His face was shocked, but aroused as he faded from human shape.

"*Impressive.*" He flitted out of my grasp.

We left words and thoughts behind as I pursued him through the room. We dipped above and below the water, with my presence making the water crash in violent waves with each pass. He plunged into the pool's depths at its center and I followed.

He was projecting memories as he went down, teasing me with images of the two of us in our past life, in his dwelling, and in my realm on the island. I burned for him, but hated seeing myself from his perspective. Iskur was deepening the pool as he went, driving further and further from my grasp. I paused in my chase and reached out for him with my mind.

It was easy to find him below me. With my mind locked on his, I pulled him back to me. He was laughing, giving no resistance. I felt his mirth and awe as I brought us both to the surface again. I shifted back to human form, my chest a tight knot. The thrill was gone. I sat on the edge of the pool and waved the floating light orbs back to life.

"What is it?" Iskur came to my side, in human form as well.

"I don't like it."

"You do not like what?"

"Iskur, I can make you do whatever I want. It's gross, it's weird, I just…I don't like it."

"Arga, I was not truly putting up a fight."

"But you said before I can easily outmatch you. I could just make you do anything, and then it would just be me controlling you and not anything real. Sorry I don't want it to be like that."

"You *could* outmatch me, yes. And you have. Back in the cave, you made me look at you. I enjoy this."

I was repulsed by myself. How had I liked this s a second ago?

"Arga, I *enjoy* being at your mercy." He repeated for clarification.

My face burned and I felt my skin prickle with nervous energy. I did not know what to say. Iskur slid back into the water and faced me.

"Did you hear me?" I could not avoid his gaze: he was smiling a sly, dangerous smile.

"Iskur."

He had his hands on my lower legs beneath the water.

"I like it when you control me."

"I heard you."

"Then do not be upset about it. Did you not enjoy yourself?"

I could not lie to him.

"It was enjoyable."

"See? We are enjoying ourselves and each other. Please, you will not hurt me."

I glanced at the scar I had given him on his face. Seeing my concern, he pulled me into the water by my legs.

"I wear it with honor," He said as I sputtered, "Now, see if you can make me shift with you again."

It was so easy to give in to the power when he asked me to. It scared me: that darker, more demanding part of me, but when he asked me to go there I could not resist the temptation. It was like the voices in my most recent life, begging me to be bad. Leading me on a path to destruction that led to bliss.

*"Fight me a bit harder this time."* I plunged the room into darkness once more. I could hear his victorious laughter fade into thunder as we dove beneath the waves.

The three of us immortals were sitting in the conversation pit. Celeste had gone to sleep after our evening routine of storytelling and meditation. Virgil seemed less irritated after his walk. And I was certainly more calm after my exploits in the pool. We spoke in hushed voices.

"I think we should try to travel all three of us tomorrow. A short distance first." Virgil said cautiously.

"I agree." Iskur said, handing Virgil a crown made of oak leaves.

Virgil rolled his eyes at the gift but put it on his head nonetheless. His tousled hair encircled the leaves naturally as he settled it on his head. It looked like perfect on him, like it was meant to be.

"How short of a distance?" I asked, adjusting my own crown of violets.

"Across the cave first a couple of times, then below to above." Virgil said after a moment of thought, "I have a theory that effort will tire you significantly."

"I wasn't tired today taking Iskur above to below." I countered.

"Can you make a flower crown for Iskur right now?" Virgil asked, accusingly. I narrowed my eyes at him.

"Exactly. I noticed you did not make anything for dinner this evening. Iskur made yours for you. Nothing escapes my observation." Virgil leaned back on a pillow with a smug expression on his face.

"Just because I don't *want* to make something right now doesn't mean I *can't.*" I retorted.

"I do not think she is tired from the travel, Virgil." Iskur said with a wink.

Virgil rounded on Iskur.

"What are you suggesting?"

"There were other activities that were quite draining of creative energy from our dear Arga."

"Enough!" I waved my hand at them both.

"What activities?" Virgil was in interrogation mode.

"You will deduce it soon enough." Iskur blew Virgil a kiss. I groaned and buried my head in a pillow.

"He's essentially my brother, do you *have* to be like this?"

"How did *that* take up all of her creative energy but not yours, hm?" Virgil was leaning towards Iskur now, going full inquisition, "Is there something she can achieve that you cannot?"

"Oh my *god*. Will you two *stop?!*"

"No I am perfectly capable of achieving-"

I stopped Iskur from finishing that statement by launching myself onto him and covering his mouth.

"I'll be fine once I rest. It wasn't the travel that tired me out. Okay? Okay. Moving on."

"Arga?" Virgil was looking at me with such distressing curiosity. I did not want this conversation to continue.

"What? *What?* What more could you possibly want to know about this?"

"Were you asserting your dominance over Iskur?"

If I wasn't dead already I would have died on the spot.

"Virgil please do not embarrass her about it, we had such a lovely time. It is very healing for her to-"

"*Stoooooppppp!!*" I wailed.

Virgil held up his hands.

"One more question before your shouting wakes up Celeste."

I slammed my head into another pillow and refused to look at him.

"What is it? Just end it now, Virgil." My voice was muffled by the velvet.

"Were you successful?"

I looked up at him slowly.

"What are you asking?" My voice was deadly serious despite Iskur laughing underneath me.

"Could you dominate him? Control his will? I have seen you dominate him in small ways, making him stop moving or making him look at you, but can you *fully* control his will now?"

"Please don't ever say that again, for fucksake Virgil I never want to hear you talk about dominating ever again."

Virgil actually laughed one of his rare, impish laughs at my discomfort.

"I thought it was me who would be the biggest prude in our trio, but no, that title belongs to you," He sighed, struggling to regain composure, "I thought you were an exotic dancer for a while before your murder, were you not?"

"*Virgil.*"

"Sh, sh, my love, you will wake up Celeste." Iskur was still giggling unhelpfully.

"Were you not?"

"*Yes,* I was a stripper but that doesn't mean that I enjoy talking about sex with you."

"Sex? Oh Arga, no I do not care for those details. I was asking if you could impose your will over his."

"She can." Iskur raised his eyebrows suggestively. I shoved him down onto the pillows and out of sight.

"See? See how she powers over me?" He said playfully.

"Stop it!"

"Were you resisting her? In the pool?" Virgil peered over my shoulder at Iskur, who I was trying to shield from his view.

"Not fully, but who could?"

"Good point. She is difficult to resist when she is feeling persuasive." Virgil mused, taking his glasses off to clean them. When he put them back on he saw my disturbed expression and jolted.

"Not like *that*, goodness Arga. Iskur is much more my type than you are," Virgil motioned flippantly to Iskur, who blew him another kiss, "I am asking about your strength and ability to push your will over others. That day in the vortex, it was so hard to put my will over yours and bring you back to us. I am curious how your strength is now. It sounds as if you are gaining in power."

"Well, I did not put up much of a fight in the pool, like I said. But she is stronger." Iskur got himself out from under me and dodged the pillows I was hurling at him.

"If that is the case, I am very curious about how our experiments will go tomorrow." Virgil stood up and began to climb out of the pit.

"Sleep well, you two. Do not waste more energy."

In our sleeping area, I glared at Iskur.

"What?"

"Why did you tell Virgil all of that?"

"Oh Arga, he already knows so much from seeing your visions and memories. What is wrong with honesty between friends?"

"It's weird."

"You are weird. He said you were a dancer? I saw some of the dancing. I was not sure I understood it when Virgil and I reviewed your most recent life. What was the dancing?"

I cursed Virgil for bringing *that* up.

"I was a stripper right before I died. That was my job."

"Stripper?"

"Dancing, while taking my clothes off."

"Ah. Yes. Of course there are always such things happening. You were paid to do this? Like for a king?"

My face burned red at the memory: the humiliation felt fresh. Two years before I had met Travis my life was getting into order. Mom was in AA. I had gotten an office job at the hospital. It was boring data entry and IT support, but it was good pay. The voices hadn't left me alone, though. The calm was too much for me: I craved chaos. I met Travis, we became lovers, and my life went spiraling out of control. I stopped going to work regularly. I became unreliable, unruly. Mom started using again. I yelled at my boss, made a scene and lost my job. I had felt glad about it back then. It had felt like a return to my true nature: destruction and chaos.

There was nothing humiliating about sex work. I had known plenty of pros. Like Iskur said, there are always such things happening. Stripping itself wasn't the shameful thing, the shame came from throwing away a path to salvation. My life had been going well, and it had driven me crazy. I had thrown away progress and security and the sense of safety that I always craved, for what? For a terrible life and a violent death?

But since understanding the oath, I knew that without walking directly into that hell I never would have been reunited with Iskur. The voices that drove me mad were my own ancient voice echoing in my head and driving me towards my deepest desire: to be with him. What would have happened if I had stayed on the *good* path? Kept my job, stayed away from Travis, lived and died a normal boring woman? There was no reason to think about it. It didn't happen.

"Arga?" Iskur, "You worked for a king?"

I came back from my own thoughts and laughed.

"Uh no, not for a king. Just in a club. A building. For whoever wanted to watch."

Iskur snorted.

"That does seem strange that you are so uncomfortable talking about-"

"Just because I didn't get uncomfortable like that in front of strangers does not mean I'm comfortable with everything else being everyone's business!"

"Mh. Yes. I see how that is. It was ...anonymous? This job? You did not know the people who watched?"

"Not really, no."

"So it was not personal. And this feels personal."

"Yes."

"I understand. I will not tease about how we are together."

"Thanks."

I felt strangely touched at how hard Iskur was working to be understanding of how I was feeling. I wasn't even working as hard as he was to understand myself. It was easier to ignore the tension I felt about coming to terms with *wanting* to get killed than to face it head on.

"Of course my love. But if Virgil asks, there may be times we will need to tell him how something has happened. Our three minds must work together to unravel the situation we find ourselves in. Any information we learn we must share."

I sighed.

"I know."

Iskur kissed my hands.

"Does it make you feel upset?"

"Does what make me feel upset?"

"Your strength. Your ability to bend me to your will."

"I'm not upset." A partial lie, " It was fun. I'm just uneasy about going too far."

"You will know when to stop." Iskur waved his hand and doused our lights.

"I'd rather we have a safe word."

"Safe word?"

"Yeah, like you say a certain word and I know I have to stop."

I could tell he was pondering this suggestion.

"Island." He said at last.

"Island?"

"If ever you are going too far in any way I will beg you to think of your island, *our* island, and come back to me."

I smiled.

"Perfect."

We laid down and let sleep take us.

# XXVIII.

"Arga, are you certain you are rested enough?"

Iskur was fussing over me as he and Virgil and I stood in the corner of the cave furthest from the entrance. I had slept embarrassingly long, nearly twelve hours. I hated to consider the conversations that Iskur and Virgil had been having while I was asleep about why I was so fully exhausted.

"Yes, Iskur, I'm sure I am rested enough."

Celeste was sitting along the trail outside the cave out of sight. She called in to us:

"Are you three ready?"

"Yes!" We replied in unison.

"See you soon!" She chimed.

"Alright Arga. This is your first attempt. Do not be distressed if it does not work well." Virgil said flatly.

"Great pep talk." I muttered, closing my eyes and focusing on the mouth of the cave.

I coaxed all three of us into our lightforms. It was more like giving a signal to Virgil and Iskur rather than commanding. They obeyed and put all their attention on me. I locked onto them. My existence flattened, and I compressed Virgil and Iskur along with me. There was only us and the entrance of the cave.

And we were standing in it.

"You did it!!!" Celeste cheered, clapping and rushing towards us.

Iskur and Virgil were letting out exclamations of joy as well.

"See? Watch this!!" Without waiting I snapped the three of us into our lightforms and pulled us to the top of the mesa. Virgil and Iskur gasped for a second, rapidly arranging themselves as humans before I flashed us back to the cave's entrance.

"Arga stop!" Virgil cried, stumbling into human form again and leaning against the wall of the cliffside.

I shifted back into my body and beamed.

"I can do it! See? I told you I could do it!"

Iskur was wheezing behind me.

"Arga, slow down." He joined Virgil leaning against the stone.

"What's wrong?" I frowned, my celebrations dampened.

"I was not ready for the second one." Iskur laughed, "You went so quick!"

Virgil was cleaning his glasses nervously.

"Arga, please do not jump like that without our consent first. That was very painful." He put his glasses back on.

"I'm sorry did it injure you?" My chest tightened up considerably. I had not been thinking that traveling could hurt them.

"No, no." Virgil waved me off, "It was just very disorienting to be forced into my lightform and instantly transported against my will."

I realized then how much it had frightened him. Both of them? Iskur wasn't showing it but now I was suspicious it had scared him as well. Guilt flared up in me.

"I scared you."

"Yes." Virgil said.

"No!" Iskur said unconvincingly at the same time as Virgil.

I rubbed my face.

"Sorry, I just got excited. I know I can do this."

"And the confidence is wonderful, Arga." Virgil took my hand, "Really it is. But you have a history of taking me, in particular, to places very suddenly that I am not intending to go."

"Sorry. Yeah."

"That is something we can empathize with, yes." Celeste nodded fervently, "Virgil is feeling the past trauma and fear of your past lack of control, Arga. You should acknowledge this hurt and make amends."

Virgil shook his head.

"Completely unnecessary," He intoned, walking back into the cave, "Arga's newfound control and confidence is all the atonement I require."

Iskur, Celeste, and I followed him dutifully. He stopped by the dining table.

"Shall we go below to above?" He asked with a smile.

Our next dozen jumps were more meticulous, like the first one. I gave ample warning to Virgil and Iskur that we were about to travel and signaled them to enter their lightforms each time. We went from the cave, to the top of the mesa, to various points on the nearby trail, to the cave, and round again. I was beginning to tire when Virgil suggested we stop and rest for the day.

That night, over a feast to celebrate the successes of the day, Celeste made a toast.

"To progress and forward motion!"

We cheered to that, and drank the wine that Virgil had been pouring all night.

"Tomorrow, I think we should try to jump from this vortex to the next nearest one." Virgil said conspiratorially after we all had our drink.

"Jump vortexes?" I said, raising an eyebrow, "Like from the center of this one to the center of another one?"

"Yes. I think it will be good to see if the energy makes the jump easier for you."

My mood was light and bubbly, I felt more sure of things than I had in a long time. Virgil's suggestion made sense, and I was eager to try.

"Is the nearest vortex somewhere that lots of hikers go?" I asked Celeste.

"Hmmm well…" She thought for a moment, "Yes, you could run into some folks there."

"If we jump during the day." I looked at Virgil with a smile, "What if-"

"No, not right now. You need your rest."

"Oh come on Virgil! I think it's a great idea and I want to try it! I'll go by myself first."

"So what, you can jump and get stuck someplace else and have to walk back in the night?"

"You don't really think I'll get stuck if I jump to another vortex, do you?"

Virgil shrugged.

"That is why it is called an experiment. We will have to try and see. But it will be better to try when you have full strength."

I sighed.

"Iskur, shouldn't I try it now? Don't you want to know how it will go?"

"Of course I am curious, but it is better to try when you are well rested."

"Come *oooonnnnn*," I moaned, "We are getting nowhere, truly nowhere by sitting here and waiting."

Iskur and Virgil exchanged a long look. I frowned at them. Celeste sipped her wine uncomfortably.

"Well?" I demanded.

"Arga," Virgil's voice was laced with rattling leaves, "You can try it."

I started to protest, but then processed what he had said.

"Yeah?" I exclaimed, jumping up from the table and waiting for either Iskur or Virgil to stop me.

"Take us to the top with you here, then I suppose you can try for the next nearest vortex alone." Virgil said.

I snapped us to the top of the mesa perhaps more abruptly than I should have, but I did not want to give either of them a second to confer with each other and back out. I was giddy with excitement and brimming with confidence. I could *do* this.

Virgil adjusted his glasses irritably in the moonlight. Iskur wheezed as he regained human form.

"That was a bit harsh, Arga. Please calm yourself." Virgil said tartly.

"Yes, sorry, yeah fine. Fine. Fine." I said with a stupid grin on my face, "I'm going to try and sense the next vortex."

"It's to the west!" Celeste had taken the trail up to join us at the top.

I shifted forms and reached towards the west. There. It was easy to feel the pull of the vortexes now with my more refined ability to focus.

*"Arga this is the first time you have tried traveling to a place you have not physically been before, it will be more difficult to get there than to return, I suspect."* Virgil's voice buzzed distantly. I sighed and shifted back to human form.

"I *know* that, we've talked about this before."

"It will be a long walk back if you drain yourself too fully. Are you sure you do not want to wait?" Iskur half asked, half begged.

"I'm sure I won't need to walk back. Besides, that vortex is not entirely unfamiliar. It is really close to the cave we hid in that first night here on Earth."

"Oh!" Virgil perked up at that, "Wonderful, perhaps you can fixate on that cave instead and do this exercise in the morning."

I glared at him.

"I'm going now, be right back."

I focused on the exact center of the other vortex. I could feel the familiarity of the first cave we had been in, but the energy flowing from the other vortex was much stronger. As I compressed myself to travel, I locked in on the vortex.

In an instant, I was there. I reopened myself and shifted back into human form in a wide expanse of open desert. The cave we had been in the first night was nearby, at the base of the red cliffside. I checked myself. I felt fine. Utterly normal.

"Hah!" I shouted, "I *knew* it! I knew it! I fucking did it!!"

I flailed and danced around for a moment, before fixing my mind on the top of our mesa and snapping myself back there.

"See?!" I shouted as I burst into my human form.

Virgil and Iskur rushed to me, shouting and laughing victoriously.

"I am so glad you did not overextend yourself." Virgil said with a dry laugh, "That would have been a ridiculous walk."

"My love! I knew you could, this is wonderful!" Iskur was crushing me with a relieved hug that betrayed how concerned he had been that I was not going to be right back.

"My friends," Celeste's voice was a strange quaver. My body went icy.

I pushed away from Iskur and turned to Celeste. She was facing northwest and looking at the sky. I went to her side.

"What is it?" I asked. She was trembling profusely.

"I do not think it is a good thing." Celeste whispered, pointing at a fast moving light on the horizon.

Virgil swore bitterly and he and Iskur left their human forms. I was glued to the spot next to Celeste.

"It's him, isn't it?" I murmured, all joy draining from my body.

"Yes, I do believe it is." Celeste gave my hand a squeeze then began to walk towards the trail, "I think you need to go join your boys, my dear angel."

"Do not come out of the cave unless one of us comes to get you." I commanded, "Trust nothing. Ask us questions only we will know."

Celeste nodded, blew me a kiss, and sped down the trail. I steeled myself and shifted into my lightform.

*"We want to trap and contain. Draw off as much of his power as possible."* Virgil said as I joined him and Iskur in the center of the vortex.

The light was growing rapidly now.

*"Arga, hang back and engage him as little as possible."* Virgil demanded, *"You are weak and-"*

*"Don't tell me I'm weak!"* I let the anger and fear crack like a whip around me, *"This is our chance."*

"Oh, very intimidating. Yes. I see y'all there." Travis was below us, standing in his stupid human shape on the ground.

*"What do you want?"* I snarled, towering over him. Virgil and Iskur grew at my sides. Thunder and wind.

"Ari really. Just come down here. I want to talk."

*"No, murderer."* Rage flared up as my last memories of my most recent life came flooding back. The argument. The feral look in his eyes. The shouting. His hands on me. My nails on his skin. The clawing, screaming, biting, brawl. Him shoving and landing hit after hit. How I laughed at him as the lights finally went out.

"Killed you? Yeah. Sure. I sure did. Sure. You know, the more I learn about you the more I realize how you used me, Ari. You just played me. I was not a good man, but I was not a killer. That night...I play it back in my head over and over. You kept going. You kept fighting. I told you to run, to get out of my face and you pushed me. I walked away and you hit me and yelled and egged me on. You knew juuuusssstt how to do it. So why don't you come down here and talk to me face to face? Huh? Or are you afraid I'll kill you again?" His voice was sarcastic and cruel.

"*What do you want?*" Virgil cut me off before I could reply.

"I want Ari to come down here and talk to me, pencil neck." Travis spat, "I want her to stop manipulating and hurting people for her own gain and admit that she is the problem."

Iskur breezed in front of me, intertwining with my form encouragingly.

"*Of course she used you. She was trying to find a way home.*" Iskur's voice clapped with thunder. Dark clouds were slowly enclosing us on all sides.

My mind was a blur. I could remember the night of my death clearly. I *had* picked the fight. And even before that, I had picked *him*. I had given him my number at the bar. I had come on to him. Seduced him, tested him. At the time I had been torn, I knew he was awful. I knew his habits and violent tendencies after the first argument. But echoing in my head was the deep, unexplainable, insatiable voice. And that had pushed me to stay. It had given me the conviction that all the suffering and mistreatment were the path I needed to be on. I deserved this suffering. I was made for it, because I had made others suffer even worse.

Lightning flashed across the desert.

"You remember it, don't you." Travis' eyes were black pits against the sharpness of his cheekbones. He was gaunt, looking more hollow than before. Despite how worn he appeared, there was an enthusiasm to him that unsettled me even further, "You *made* me do it, didn't you?"

Yes. I had made him do it. My anger wavered for a moment. Travis had just been a tool to me, did it really make sense to be mad at him?

He certainly had a right to be mad at me.

# XXIX.

I could not continue my existential crisis for long, because Virgil struck first. He hurled towards Travis as a hot blue blur. Travis snapped into a blue and rust-red tinted streak of light and stood rooted to the spot. As if there were a wall between them, Virgil was repelled as he came within a foot of Travis. I snarled and pelted at Travis, despite Iskur trying to stop me.

I felt the wall, but did not let it stop me. I shoved every ounce of my being against it and felt it begin to buckle. Travis jolted in shock and took off like a bullet across the sand and stone. I was after him like a whip with Virgil close behind me.

*"Tire him."* Virgil reminded me as we tore across the desert. With a mutual understanding we split apart and sped onward, each taking one side of Travis. Virgil boxed in, pushing Travis closer to me. Iskur was above us now, stretching himself like a wide dark cloud.

I dipped under Travis suddenly and drove him upwards into Iskur. As if we had practiced, Iskur snapped himself around Travis and wrested him to the ground. The sound of them hitting the stone resonated and echoed across the empty landscape like a bomb detonating. Thunder rippled from the clouds that were closing in on us from all sides.

On the ground I wove myself into Iskur, giving him strength to keep his hold on the writhing ball of hot rage that Travis had become.

*"You are an abomination!!"* Travis screamed shrilly as I forced him back into his human form.

Virgil landed next to me and shifted back into his human form. With a furious shout he landed a savage punch on Travis' jaw.

"You are an abomination!!" Virgil's voice was unnaturally loud as he wound up to punch again.

"Stop! *Stop!!*" I commanded, wrapping a tendril of my form around Virgil's upraised arm, "What are you *doing?!*"

Virgil sputtered incoherently and backed away. He looked disoriented and confused. Travis surged and flexed his energy against Iskur and I while I was focused on Virgil. I struggled to keep Travis in his human form.

"You'll get tired before me." Travis sneered, "You were already tired when we started."

Panic rose up in me as I bore down harder yet, causing him to wheeze as he laughed. I was tiring rapidly and I knew Iskur and Virgil could not hold him alone.

"What did the Old Dead give you? What powers?" Virgil demanded.

"Oh these?" Travis raged against us still, "Just wait until I'm fully recovered. Those human fuckers had me exhausted with their tests."

Virgil shifted back into his light form and lent us his strength.

*"Well he looks horrible."* Virgil intoned as he struggled to help us keep Travis in his human form.

"Yeah because that's what's important. Three versus one and you all can barely keep me down. Hah. Just you wait." Travis spat as he writhed bitterly.

*"Now what?"* I demanded.

*"Can you hold him for another minute?"* Virgil asked.

*"Yes."* Iskur affirmed with great difficulty.

Virgil snapped back to his human form and landed another jaw shattering punch on Travis' face. I felt Travis temporarily slow his struggle to break free. Virgil grabbed Travis' face roughly and fixed him with a devilish grin.

"Night night." Virgil waved before hitting Travis brutally, right square in the temple.

As Travis fell unconscious I collapsed into my human form in a panting heap in the dust.

"Fuuuuck." I hissed, looking at Virgil as he stood over Travis.

"What?" Virgil asked, taking off his shirt and ripping it into strips, "It worked last time."

"Last time, he wasn't going to recover his strength immediately upon waking up." I breathed, trying to get to my hands and knees. Iskur was heaving by my side, reaching to take my hand.

"You can overpower him, Arga. You broke through his shield when I could not." Virgil was busying himself tying Travis up.

"V," I panted, "I can't move."

Virgil looked over at me in concern.

"Seizure?"

"I don't kno-" The sky filled with clouds and thunder and everything went black.

Travis was on one knee in front of me. We had only been dating for a year or so, in an on again, off again tempestuous way. He was holding a ring and smiling stupidly at me. I did not feel joyful, but rather victorious.

"Yes!" I exclaimed, snatching the ring greedily.

The voices in my head murmured approval.

This was right.

This was the path.

I was smiling.

He was laughing at me.

"It's a fucking fake I got at the pawn shop, you deserve *nothing* better, babe."

There was only one more step.

I was laughing.

This was how I was going to get home.

"Three minutes. Not so long." Iskur was holding me when I awoke. We were still in the desert. Lightning and thunder was nearly constant around us.

"I'm back." I breathed, feeling just as horrible as I had before the seizure.

"That looked painful." Virgil was kneeling at my side.

"Yeah it fucking sucks, Virgil." I snapped at him, closing my eyes.

"We need to get you back." Iskur's voice was full of concern.

"What about-"

"I can carry him, Iskur will take you." Virgil said curtly, hoisting an overly tied up Travis onto his bare shoulder.

There was no time to protest. Rain was coming down in sheets. Lighting illuminated the shape of our mesa. It was not too distant, but we made horribly slow progress. Iskur took a turn carrying Travis and I trudged alongside Virgil. Soaked and miserable, we made it to the base of the cliffs and groped for our trail.

"Wait," I groaned, dragging Virgil to a stop, "The vortex."

"What about it?" Virgil asked.

"He will pull strength from it if we get him too close. Get a rope, tie him to a tree, then we go." I panted.

"Arga-" Iskur began to protest.

"He's tired. He can't follow right away. He can't track unless he has strength and he can only find us when I do something big. Do the big things now while he can't track. We can get there. We can go." I looked at Iskur and Virgil beseechingly, "We can't wait for him to wake up."

"Arga?"

All three of us snapped our heads towards the sound of Celeste's voice from the cave above us.

"Celeste! Stay there!" I shouted.

She was already rushing down the trail towards us. Virgil tried to shoo her away to no avail. She came down to us swiftly, rain drenching her.

"Arga, my sweet angel, I had a vision. And I want you to know it's okay. It is what is supposed to happen."

"What are you talking about? Celeste, you should go back inside. We have to get him somewhere else and get out of here."

Celeste nodded in agreement.

"Yes. Yes, I already know. You are going to make it. I have seen it. The cedars." Celeste's tears of joy mixed with the rain as she kissed my hands, "It's all happening now."

Her blind joy was infectious, I smiled a half-hearted smile and looked at Travis' limp form on the ground where Iskur had set him.

Travis' head snapped up and he smiled wickedly at me.

My whole body went cold.

# XXX.

I t happened as if in slow motion. Like those nightmares where you know what's going to happen next but there's nothing you can do to stop it. I opened my mouth to scream but he was already a blaze of red light. He snatched Celeste and flew upwards. I rushed after him, terror and rage and the electric whip of my blind, destroying panic propelled me to the top of the mesa.

*"NOOO!!"* I shrieked. Walls of rain converged like waves around us. Travis was halfway between human and light, a demonic blaze of red holding Celeste aloft with disturbing ease.

Virgil and Iskur were at my side, they had shifted to their light forms with great effort. I felt the labor in their beings and the strain with which they maintained their forms.

*"She is innocent!"* Virgil cried.

*"Nobody is innocent who helps her."* Travis spat, motioning to me, *"The Great Deceiver, the most cursed of us all."*

Travis released Celeste and zoomed upwards. Virgil and Iskur flew to catch her. I did not. I followed Travis.

Celeste's body hit the ground with a sickening smack. I didn't watch her fall. I already knew she was doomed when Travis had grabbed her. It was inevitable. I saw it all so clearly now. So clearly.

I pummeled towards Travis and let the white hot whips of scaring, destroying energy lash out ahead of me. He wailed as they met him, and I relished in the thought of the searing pain branding him permanently. At last, a worthy recipient of my inability to control myself. At last, I could hurt without fear of hurting someone I cared about. At last, I could give in to the delicious feeling of letting go of all restraint. Here was someone for me to punish.

He circled above, dancing away from my attacks now that he knew they were coming. He laughed mercilessly. I could not hear Virgil and Iskur, but I was sure they were behind me looking on in horror. I didn't care. I flung myself into the center of the vortex and drank in its power. I channeled the strength upwards and directly into Travis. He screamed to the sounds of fire raging. Rain encircled me as I chased after him into the black clouds above.

Within the clouds, I lost him. Thunder boomed deafeningly. I soared angrily upwards, breaking the tops of the clouds and searching in all directions for a hint of that rust-red flame I was hunting. There was nothing but lightning and thunder and stars. For what felt like a lifetime I searched the sky for a sign of Travis.

I felt the tug of Iskur and Virgil looking for me. My rage receded just enough to give way to enormous waves of grief and fear. The anger fell away from me. With despair, I plummeted listlessly back towards the Earth.

There it was again: my true nature. I tumbled like a ragdoll down, down, down. Travis was right. I let those I love get in the line of fire so that I could get what I wanted.

As I fell, the only thought that made its way through the fog of anguish was unnervingly serene: I saw the cedars around me as if I was walking among them.

Was this it? Had I finally become broken beyond repair? Was I shedding the last pieces of my sanity? I embraced that thought and the peace it gave me.

Rain whipped against my body violently. I was human shaped again, falling falling falling. I didn't care. I didn't try to slow myself. Maybe I was finally going to die. Maybe I should have taken the Old Dead up on their original offer and let myself be unmade.

As I reentered the clouds I smelled rain and sky and warm dirt and decaying wood. The black clouds blinded me, or maybe I had closed my eyes. I knew without question that if I reached out I would feel the bark of tree trunks slowly pass me as I fell. Cold rain gave way to the warmth of moss and soil.

The sounds of thunder and wind receded and everything went silent.

"My daughter," My father was not the type of many who would tremble, but there he was, on his knees in front of me: trembling in the light of the flaming hillside behind me, "Forgive me."

"For what?" My voice was a cruel hiss. I wanted to hear him say it.

"For not believing you. Both of you."

I laughed coldly. Iskur took my hand.

"You believe us now." Iskur said evenly, "That is what matters."

I glared at him. *That* is what matters?

"Yes yes, oh holy ones. I am humbled by your presence."

"Our coming was foretold." I motioned to the Seer who cowered among the crowd of our people, "Though the one who bore the message does little to acknowledge that now."

The events of the last few days had left me bitter and resentful. Somehow, the last couple hours had absolved everyone's guilt in Iskur's eyes. I was not so easily placated.

"We were wrong to ignore the signs. Please, forgive us." My father bent his face to the ground.

"We forgive you." Iskur squeezed my hand, "We know that you will not make this mistake again."

Later, after we extinguished the fire to the combined wonder and horror of the tribe, I took Iskur aside.

"What was that?" I asked in a pained whisper.

"What was what?"

"Forgiveness? After what those monsters did to you? To us?"

"Your family are not monsters. The guilty ones are gone and will never be back."

"More will come." I muttered, kicking a smoldering tree branch. The air was thick with aromatic smoke.

"Would you come challenge us after we brought a god down to smite your betrothed and his warband?"

I smirked.

"He really did look terrified when I stood over him, that stupid Prince Aatazaz."

"Yes he did." Iskur agreed with a laugh, "Your darling betrothed is gone. I would say your wedding is off."

"I still cannot forgive my father. They arrived with a *warband* and he was going to continue with the negotiations as if they had only come with emissaries."

"Arga," He pulled me into him, "They are gone."

"So is Qateel." I murmured, a sudden pang of guilt coursing through my body.

Iskur was silent for a while, then kissed my head.

"We all knew there was risk."

"Yes." I agreed, "We did."

"We need to speak to Aleyin." I added, after a pause.

"In time. He needs to grieve with his family."

"What must they think of us?"

Iskur drew me back to look at my face. I could not get the image of his eyes turning black out of my head.

"Arga, they think their son and brother died to bring a prophecy to fruition. And if they don't, they will depart from here in fear of us."

"You say that like it is nothing."

"Some will leave in the coming days. Some have already fled. Does it bother you?" Iskur searched my face.

"No." It wasn't a lie. I was glad that there would be fewer judgemental faces in the crowd each day. Fewer people who looked at us with fear and hatred rather than admiration.

"Everything is changed now," Iskur put his hand under my chin, "You have changed us all."

"We did this together." I took his hand from my face and kissed it, "Now we have a bond between us unlike any other."

He kissed me then, overcome by the implication of what we had accomplished. Speaking with our ancestors among the dead was one thing. Speaking to a god? Cleaving our souls to each other in the golden light of that great power? Indeed, everything had been changed.

Whispers on the edge of my hearing disrupted my focus on our passionate embrace. I was used to the voices, but these were new. Strangers. I pulled away from Iskur and listened. He waited patiently, accustomed to staying silent so I could decipher the messages from beyond.

"New voices." I breathed, exhilarated by this development, "I need to try to hear them more clearly."

Iskur's eyes were black as the darkest night when I looked at him. He smiled that impish smile I loved so much and took my hand. We raced through the blackened trees, not caring as the lingering smoke clogged our noses and eyes.

# XXXI.

T he air was warm and fragrant with the smell of greenery and the cedars. I knew where I was. I had been here so many times in visions and dreams and my past life. There was no question. I knew *exactly* where I was.

Green grass.

Green grass. Blue sky.

Green grass. Blue sky. Sunlight.

Patchy sunlight. Sunlight filtering through the trees.

*The* Trees.

A slight breeze picked up and sent the branches of the cedar that was towering directly above me rustling. Instinctually, I looked around for Virgil. But this wasn't his sound. His was like dried leaves in the wind. Oaks. These towering cedars were evergreen and sounded nothing like him.

Still.

"Virgil?" I called, my voice hardly carried, the sound was absorbed by the trees.

"Iskur?" My voice was thin and small.

Despite hearing no reply, I smiled. I had done it. I had brought us here. Laughter exploded out of me and I leapt to my feet. I raced along the ancient path and closed my eyes, daring myself to remember each curve. It was instinctual, navigating this place. It was like a homecoming I had not realized how badly I had longed for.

I laughed and whooped and ran and skipped, frolicing along the path though the ancient trees. I stopped to touch one and felt the power within it resonate. It coursed through me and I drank it in. It was more restorative than the power of the vortex, more amplifying than anything I had experienced yet. The land was alive and welcoming me home.

No wonder Iskur had gone to such pains to replicate this sacred grove in his dwelling.

"Iskur!" I cried happily, trotting up the path again. I felt like my chest would burst with joy when I lay eyes on him. Where was he? I could not wait to be here with him, to finally be *here* together. It was the only thing in my mind. My singular desire. I had to find where he was lying and resting.

I shifted into my light form and twined myself around the trunk of one of the larger trees, soaking up its restorative energy. I swirled giddily to its uppermost branches.

Virgil had been right, there were fewer trees now than in my visions. It still felt powerful and magnificent, even in its diminished form. I was delighted to take in the views and lingered in the tree top for a while. Slowly, I lowered myself back down to the ground and returned to human form.

"Iskur?"

I walked slowly down the path, the giddy joy of success wearing off.

"Virgil?"

"They aren't here, Ari."

Not that voice. Not him. Not here. Whipping around, I saw him step out from behind a tree.

"*You.*" My voice was a dry rasp of rage. I stood bolted to my spot, tense and ready to fight as Travis sauntered onto the path.

"It was hard to find you. Sorry, your boys aren't coming."

"What did you *do?*" I saw red. Where were they?!

"Me? No. You left us all behind when you came here. You just left them on the top of that stone with me. And I didn't do anything to them, just took them home."

I shrieked. Birds flew up noisily from the trees and scattered as quickly as they could.

"Ari, you don't want to lose it here. This is your place, right? Your special place? Do you really want to be making a mess of it? I can tell it has some old fucking energy. Let's stay calm and leave no trace, right? Smokey the Bear?"

"Where *are they?*" I seethed, slamming Travis against the base of a tree. I wasn't ready to shift into my light form and destroy him yet. I wanted answers.

He choked out a laugh.

"They want to talk to you."

"Who does?" I bore down on Travis viciously. I would rip him to shreds. I would claw the entire universe to pieces to get to where Iskur and Virgil were being held captive.

"*Who do you think?*" He wheezed.

I let him go and he fell to his hands and knees, coughing. He hadn't shifted to his light form when I had come at him. I bet he couldn't do it here.

"You are weak." I spat.

"This place isn't very friendly to the powers they gave me to hunt you."

"Good."

"You could destroy me if you wanted to." He laughed sadly, "You know that? They told me that you could reduce me to an aimless cloud of dust in this place if I pissed you off too much."

"Should I?" My voice was venomous, "Should I make you into a cloud of dust? Should I feed you to my trees?"

"Honestly? I don't give a fuck now. After all this shit you've done to me, it might be nice to not exist."

"*What?* What did I do to you? Your life was already trash before you met me."

"You don't get to decide whose life is trash. *God damn.* None of us do. Fuck. This whole place is pushing me down, Ari. I'm supposed to get you to reach out to them so they can talk to you. I'm just the fucking messenger now."

"What do they want?"

"What do you think? They have your little boys, they want a trade."

Travis struggled to his feet.

"I fucking hate it here." He cursed, glaring at the trees, "Tell your trees I'm not their fucking enemy."

"You are." I said icily, the memory of what he had done coming back to me, "You fucking killed her. They know you killed her."

I could hear Celeste hitting the ground. The sickening smack. His twisted grin as he had dropped her.

"I did do that." he admitted, "But, I'm not going to do anything to the fucking trees. Make them stop."

"You fucking murderer!"

I pushed him down onto the ground again.

"Get off me, I'm just the messenger now."

"That doesn't make her come back!" I screamed.

"She's fucking *fine* now Ari! She's on the other side."

"You had *no right to end her!!* You hypocrite! Didn't you just say we don't get to decide who has a life that's trash?"

"She was a Seer, Ari! She helped you! You are a twisted, destructive monster and you keep manipulating people into thinking you are innocent!"

"*Fuck you!!*" I roared, soaring backwards away from him in disgust, "You can tell the Old Dead to send Iskur and Virgil here or I will come there and-"

"And what? Ari? Destroy dead people and their paradises? Yeah that sounds real nice. Real 'Good Guy' energy." Travis coughed in the dirt and cursed the trees.

I shrieked in rage.

"Yell all you want. Destroy me. I don't care. They'll end your little fuck boys and come find you and end you one way or another. I can't do anything for you." Travis struggled to stand once more.

I growled and started stomping down the path into the valley.

"Where are you going?" Travis called after me.

"They can't reach me here, I need to go to where I can talk to the dead." I snapped.

"What, no cell service in the trees?"

I shot him a withering look.

"Just fucking leave!" I screamed, "Here, I'll help!"

Travis tipped an imaginary hat at me sarcastically and closed his eyes. I flung an arm at him and without a thought, sent a wave of energy careening towards him. The wave hit him and he was gone.

"Shit." Shock temporarily replaced anger. I was certain I had not destroyed him, but his energy was completely gone from this place. The ease with which I had sent him back to the Otherworld stunned me.

I played with the thought of transporting myself back there and freeing Iskur and Virgil in person, but that would mean leaving the place that was giving me the purest and most potent clarity of power I had ever experienced.

No, they were going to come to me.

The sky was growing dark as I stormed down the path to the valley. I could remember the night after Iskur and I had made our vow. The terror on the faces of the people I loved. The way their expressions had morphed from horror to awe and amazement. The sounds of the new voices in my head.

That night we had gone to the widest part of the valley, to a place where a large stone stood. The voices were always so clear there. That was where I was heading.

It was nearly nightfall when I reached the stone. I had not seen any signs of humans at all since I had arrived. I wondered if anyone lived nearby. What would they be seeing when I reached out to the Old Dead? Would I hurt them if they were close? It was going to take all my effort to open this portal.

Pushing those concerns from my mind, I paced around the stone. I could not hear anything, not like the way the voices would assault me in this place in the past. They used to be so loud here, ancestors and strangers calling to me with wisdom and warnings and messages and poems. But now there was nothing.

"They closed these portals up tight." I muttered to myself.

I climbed onto the rock, pausing to feel the familiar textures. Being back in this valley was awakening all my memories of my first life. I felt like I was opening my eyes after a long, strange nap. Had I not been so distraught over the loss of Iskur and Virgil, it would have been an emotional homecoming. I sat on the top of the rock and closed my eyes.

Iskur and Virgil were with the Old Dead, or so Travis had claimed. I had no reason to doubt him, but I toyed with the thought that perhaps he was lying. What would that mean? That they were still back in Sedona? No, if I had found a way to get here, Iskur would have also found a way. This was his home too, the land would welcome him and ease his journey as it had mine. Only some great power could keep him away from me now that I was here.

A wave of distress washed over me. What if I couldn't reach them?

The Old Dead had my only two friends in all of time and space and Celeste had been killed by my murderer. Just for helping us! Just for being a Seer! My destructive energy was building up. I reached out, pressing my consciousness against the veil.

It was a strange sensation, feeling the barrier between dimensions give way slowly. It didn't feel like a feat of strength, more like coaxing a heavy door to open. It moved slowly at first, then buckled and swayed as I applied more effort. I was getting assistance from the other side. The Old Dead were opening the portal too.

"*We see you.*" The Old Dead spoke as one.

"Where are Iskur and Virgil?" I demanded, seeing in my mind's eye a blurred and hazy vision of their chamber.

"*With us.*"

"Give them back to me."

"*We will not.*"

"You will." My voice crashed like a tidal wave as I shifted out of my body.

The vision cleared and I could see the chamber in detail. It was just as unsettling as it had been the first time, with its illogical structures and cold, ornate decorations.

"*We have no reason to return them to you, as they are not yours.*"

"Ask them if they want to come back to me. They'll come willingly."

"*You have upset the balance long enough. We seek only to retain peace and harmony amongst the dead. You destroy this. You cannot allow you to continue.*"

"SHOW THEM TO ME!!"

The Old Dead snapped into view, in their horrific animal conglomeration.

"You do not scare me. *GIVE ME ISKUR AND VIRGIL!!*"

I shouted the demand with every fiber of my being. I dug deep into the well of power at my core and forced my will onto them. No normal soul would have been able to resist obeying my command, but the Old Dead were not normal souls. I didn't care. I snarled and screamed and radiated my power. They would obey me. They would bend and bow and break and submit to me.

The Old Dead shimmered. Were they weakening? Was that concern on their terrible faces? I felt them begin to force the portal closed.

"*NO!!*" I cried, wrenching it open with all my strength.

The Old Dead made a horrendous sound, like mountains grinding against one another. I braced myself and tried to meet their strength. I begged the trees and grass and air and dirt to help me. I wasn't close enough to where the land gave me the most strength. I felt my grasp on the portal slipping. I had to get the the trees or I would lose my hold.

With a mighty leap, I flung myself off the rock. I was dragging the portal away from the stone, speeding over the valley with it in my grasp. I cleaved myself to the connection between our worlds and roared with the effort to haul it with me as I fled into the trees and up the hill. I would not let go. I would not be shut out.

"*WHERE ARE THEY?!*" I screamed against the discord the Old Dead were making as they fought to close the gap and end our connection, "*I will not let you take them from me!!*"

Black clouds rushed in as I reached the thickest part of the woods. I knew the trail and did not dare to pause in my journey upwards. Among the trees, I could harness their energy to force the portal open further. The Old Dead were in utter chaos, striking back at me with all their strength. Each hit and surge of energy they sent gouged into my being as they tried to close the door. I was in immense pain.

I thought of Iskur.

I would not stop.

I thought of Virgil.

I would not stop.

I thought of Celeste.

I roared and heaved and screamed and I would not stop.

The hill loomed before me and had I been in my human form my face would have been twisted into a wicked grin.

"I am bringing you to the seat of my power, you *will* give them back to me." I shouted to the sounds of tidal waves as I crested the hill.

The clouds encircled the hill as I raged against the Old Dead. Lightning flashed nearly constantly in the cloud that hung above me. Atop the hill, I turned all my energy to opening the portal and staring into the faces of the Old Dead. In the corner of my vision, I saw other figures encircling the portal on the hill with me. There were ten of them, but I knew Virgil and Iskur were not among their number. I didn't need to look to see who it was.

The ones I had gotten killed by the Nameless Ones were adding their strength to my mission.

"*Bring them to me.*" My voice was guttural and unrecognizable.

There was no time for the Old Dead to respond. The cloud above me had transmuted from black to fire-laced gold.

# XXXII.

The light in the cloud seemed to writhe and boil, gathering intensity until I could not ignore it. In a flash there was a golden beam piercing from the cloud to the ground in front of me. It swirled and brightened, blocking everything else from my view. My vision was affixed on the light and the endless shimmering surging power it was gathering.

Galaxies split open in the light's depths, as if a door had been ripped open into the cosmos. The wave of energy that came off of the light slammed into me and caused me to release my hold on the portal to the Otherworld. I shouted in dismay, but felt that the portal did not shut. Something else was keeping it open.

*"You return."* The Nameless Ones voice sent ruinous vibrations through my being. I grasped wildly at the ground. Was I human again? Was I anything? Seeing the raw existence of the Nameless Ones in Iskur's vision had not prepared me for being in their blazing presence once more.

*"I returned."* I gasped raggedly, trying not to get washed away in the flood of power radiating off of them.

*"You took more than you were given and walked the path alone."*

Their voice transcended all known and familiar things in its blend of all sounds from all life. It was at once a song and a threat. Misery and jubilation. All that ever had been and all that would come in the future. Hearing it again for myself I was shaking in disbelief. How could I have *ever* forgotten the sound of their voice? Distantly, against the deafening roar of the Nameless Ones, I heard the Old Dead's incoherent trembling through the portal of the Otherworld.

*"I tried to walk the path."* My voice was a pale whisper.

*"You succeeded."*

A compliment? An observation? It was like standing in front of a furnace, a hurricane, a blizzard, and a sandstorm to be in their presence. I quaked, but kept myself facing their blinding glory in the most upright manner I could.

*"I am honored."* I choked.

*"I need no placations from you. You have done all we asked and more."* The Nameless Ones rumbled. A laugh? I didn't have time to wonder.

The Nameless Ones blazed with a brightness that went beyond color. Calling it blinding wouldn't do justice to the intensity of the light. There was nothing but the light. I felt myself spinning, spiraling, swirling.

I saw everything.

I was ancient. I was vast. I was infinite.

I was a hummingbird among the cosmos. Darting, darting, pausing, and seeing myself laid bare.

I saw it all. I saw myself unmade in the light of the Nameless Ones all those thousands of years ago. I felt the burden of Iskur's portion of our gift on my shoulders as I kissed his face and pulled him back from the brink of destruction. I shed my human form and wound up the tapestry of power that I had been given. I braided it into the only thing I had left: my soul.

I was flying over days and weeks and months until everything blurred into years and centuries and timelines and systems. And I saw it all. Empires falling. Empires rising. Wars, journeys, colonies, rebellions, sicknesses, languages coming and going. The tongue I spoke faded into a thousand new dialects. Our trees were taken for temples and ships and relics. Technologies were birthed and I watched them with interest as I pondered how I could get back to Iskur. When should I try my foolish, selfish plan? When should I be born again?

The years wore on and I watched. I waited. I made my schemes like an invisible spider spinning her delicate web. The time was near. I deposited my precious memories of Iskur and our life together one by one into the deepest depths of my psyche. I wove my power, the gift, the curse, around the memories and tightened the binding. I kept everything out of my own sight except the plan. I had to be born again. I had to get killed by my betrothed. I had to get back to Iskur.

It was a gamble, praying that the Nameless Ones would honor the vow between us that they had sanctified. I could not pass into the afterlife with this burdensome gift of power from the Nameless Ones. I had felt Iskur pass on, but I could not. I had tried. I needed the Nameless Ones to act on the vow and fulfill the terms of Iskur's and my contract. I needed them to bring him to my side and bind him in subservience for eternity. Never to be parted. That was the endgame: get those who had blessed and cursed me to give me one more gift.

The plan became the chaos that drove me. I watched my most recent life unfold at breakneck speed. The plan was always there. I saw my mother, confused and broken when she saw the positive result on her pee stick. I watched my first day of school. I saw our horrible dirty house. I heard the kids tease me. They knew I was different. I had always thought they teased me because of where I lived. Because my hair smelled like smoke. Because my mom was an addict. But no. It was all made clear to me in the clairvoyant ether: I was different because I knew too much. I was different because of the plan.

I knew nothing about science and I hated history class because it made me too sad. I hated learning about anything ancient because it filled me with a boundless grief that other kids loved to mock. I may not have understood why I was the way I was, but I understood systems.

I had watched the first jacquard looms run the first programs as their punch cards informed the patterns in the cloth centuries before I was reborn. Languages were just systems. Math was just systems. Computers? Well. Those were just complex looms, weren't they? All systems.

I was Hollis. And Hollis was stupid about so many things, but she understood complex interwoven programs. Call it the side effect of seeing the rise and fall of societies over several millennia. I watched myself excel and head down a golden path towards a well adjusted life. But, no. That path wasn't golden from my point of view. It wasn't the path in *the plan.* Crank up the voices and don't let myself forget the end goal. I saw myself weeping at thunderstorms, crying myself sick with grief in the night. I was so close.

Failure was success. Lose the job. Get the man. Spiral lower and lower and lower and lower. What you want is just beyond the depths of despair.

I watched myself goad a violent man to cross the line. It hurt to see it all so plainly. But I didn't have time to explore how horrible it felt. The scene blazed white hot again.

Everything flattened into a pinprick of nothingness.

# XXXIII.

I knew I was someplace unbelievable before I opened my eyes. It was the kind of thing you couldn't debate. I knew I had gone somewhere *beyond* and I knew who had brought me there.

Soft ground.

Soft ground. Darkness.

Soft ground. Darkness. Thunder.

Thunder?

No. It wasn't thunder. It was a deep, ongoing rumbling.

I opened my eyes to find myself in a different sort of sacred cedar grove. It wasn't on Earth. It wasn't in Iskur's dwelling. This was someplace no other human had been. My perception of space and time and the rightness of the way things looked was skewed. The trees could have appeared as anything: pillars of light, amorphous colors, buildings, people. Anything. It wouldn't have mattered. I would have *known* they were the trees. Everything was vibrant and deeply saturated. I saw colors I had never seen before. The atmosphere shimmered and gleamed.

There was no wind and no movement anywhere, however the light seemed transient. It was like when the light would hit the glass suncatcher in my grandpa's kitchen window: one of the few things he kept after grandma had run off when my mom was ten. I remembered sitting on the kitchen floor, watching the rainbows shiver when the trains clattered by and shook the windows.

It was also like floating in a seaside cave as the sun shone and blazed against the crystal clear water. Ribbons of light and color danced on the walls and ceiling of the cave as Iskur and I swam and laughed. We were still children, but in the last flush of innocence. There was the bloom of something deeper than companionship making itself known. The reflections dazzled me as I floated on my back.

"*You know yourself now.*"

Their voice did not hold the same horror for me anymore. The Nameless Ones' tone was subdued, but it still reverberated in everything. I stood slowly. I was human-shaped, but barely. I glowed too, letting off a golden light laced with sparks of white. It drifted off of my human form delicately, like vapor.

The rage and panic of fighting against the Old Dead had burned off in my journey to this place. Gone too was my fevered panic about Iskur and Virgil's safety. The calmness and assurance was thrumming within me: I was with the Nameless Ones. What was this feeling? A heartbeat? I breathed the heady aroma of cedar deeply.

"*I have been watching you. You found a cheat code.*"

"A cheat code? What do video games have to do with this?" My voice was a cool stream cutting through the mossy forest.

"*All the building blocks have always been here. Every rock and stick and piece of dust on Earth led Humanity towards creation and creativity. It has all been here the whole time: every piece of technology, every tool, every device was here waiting before you sprouted legs and climbed out of our primordial soup.*

"*Gold, for example. We brought that to you on the backs of asteroids for jewelry and microchips. Shining toys for inspiration. We wanted to see what you would create. And create you did.*"

Hearing the Nameless Ones speak at length was a new experience for me. Why were they being so conversational? They had hardly spoken ten words to me each time we had met before. I looked around for the boiling golden cloud that their voice typically emanated from.

"Where are you?"

My focus got magnetically pulled to the trunk of the largest tree. Perched on the bark was a small, jewel-like emerald green beetle. It throbbed with cosmic light as the Nameless Ones spoke.

"*We have enjoyed watching you, Arga.*"

"You're a *bug?*"

"*We are all things, which makes it hard to choose how to appear.*"

It wavered between a million different breeds of beetles in a millisecond before landing back on its small round green form.

"*Beetles are the average lifeform on Earth. We spent a great deal of time on beetles.*"

What were we doing here? The space continued to dazzle me. I was walking in the most beautiful dream. I was wrapped in a blanket of peace and tranquility. No high had ever come close to this. What was the feeling? Why couldn't I describe it?

"Why not appear human if we are finally going to have this overdue chat?"

They laughed with a sound that could stop famines and flatten cities.

"*We will never be Human shaped.*"

"Why not? Humans are made in god's image, right?"

"*Humans made gods in their image, not the other way around. We serve Humans, they do not serve us.*"

I wanted to keep diving deeper down this rabbit hole, but I wasn't here to debate religious iconography with them. I stepped closer to the tree.

"Where are Iskur and Virgil?" My interest was strong, but not rabid like it had been on Earth. I already knew the answer to my question.

"*They are safe. You will be with them soon. We have much to discuss first.*"

"The Old Dead?"

A rush of wind pushed me backwards. A sigh of exasperation?

"*The Old Dead, indeed. They are in need of an operating system update.*"

I blinked at them. Why were we talking about computers again?

"Operating system?"

"*In your most recent life you inherited faulty databases at work and had to go back and change them entirely. You know what it is like. Frustrating, yes? You chased down glitches and bugs and mistaken rulesets, so you know what we are dealing with. Sometimes old tools need new protocols to help them operate in a new era.*"

*"The Old Dead were our first gardeners: the keepers of peace in the land of the dead. They were Humans we raised up and gave gifts to so that they could do their jobs better. We wanted them to create balance, harmony, and peace among souls, but they took that directive too far. That bred isolation, loneliness, and exclusion. That is not what Humans deserve."*

"So what, we're just one big experiment to you?"

The calm slipped away a degree as what they were saying sunk in. A tiny spark of anger glowed amidst the *thrum, thrum, thrum* of the feeling I could not name in my chest.

*"Ah, sweet one, you are a gift not an experiment. All of Humanity is. But you asked for power that many others had requested. None before you and none since you were able to hold it. And you did not only hold it. You walked with it through the centuries and found a way to trick us. You are Odysseus! You found a loophole to trick god. You got us to oversee your vow and then broke it so that we would fulfill it for you. Clever, Arga."*

The vow. The numb tranquility that had been enshrouding me dropped away entirely.

*"I vow to prevent her betrothed from killing her, or let my fate be endless servitude to her in this life and the next. For love and for duty. Loyal. Bound to her. Subservient until my undoing. My oath demands it."*

The Nameless Ones spoke with Iskur's voice and the tiny spark of anger inside me flared to a bonfire.

"Do *not* use his voice."

*"You are angry."*

"Yeah? You think? Where is he if he's so safe, huh?"

I was leaving behind the comfort of the solace this place had given me and entering back into the searing pain of rage and destruction. Their laughter knocked me to my knees.

*"Love, loyalty, and fixation. You see why we worship you Humans? Everything is so simple to you."*

"What's simple about this?!" My voice was a tsunami, "I got some of your power and I murdered a man and his family because he threatened Iskur and

I! I destroyed myself seeking more power, then I hijacked a woman's life to be reborn! I fought with a man until he murdered me! All for what? What is there to worship about this? Why do you love me?

"You know what I did. You know what I lived with. You know my selfish, nasty, twisted heart. All this knowledge now, how am I supposed to cope? How am I supposed to continue on for eternity feeling this?"

It was a flood. The ground beneath my feet vanished with the tide I was rising.

"*You have done many things with your power.*"

"Evil things."

"*So you say.*"

"Oh what, so killing people is okay now?"

A sigh like a solar flare dried my tears.

"*In each act there is the chance to react.*"

"You know I would do it all the same way again. I would ask our friends for help, knowing they would die. I would shed all that blood again to be with him!"

"*You are being dramatic. You love Iskur and are bound to him. But you love something more. You feel it. You keep feeling it now but you do not understand it. Arga, you lived. You died. You wandered. You lived again. You died again. And you were reunited with your love. All because you were seeking something you thought you would find in him.*"

"Where is he?"

"*You are worried about a problem we have already solved. Worry about your future. What have you craved across all your lives?*"

I wasn't playing their twenty questions game. I sneered as the water around us rose higher yet. What would happen if I reached out and crushed them?

"You think this is all a game? Life? Creation? It's all some fucking toy for you?"

The beetle flicked its wings and turned to face me.

"*All of creation is a toy for you. For Humans. We merely gave it to you as an offering. A gift in service to you. Your existence is a gift back to us. Everything you need or can imagine has always existed and it all mirrors nature. What is nature but a giant program? A system? Just like any software,"* they let out a low chuckle at their own impending joke, *"Sometimes there are bugs."*

"You think this is funny?"

*"A bit."*

I was clawing at my chest. The heartache of thousands of years was all piling on at once. I would *not* beg the Nameless Ones to make it stop. No. I would not stoop so low as to grovel at their feet again. I writhed and snapped like an animal in pain. I gasped for air I didn't need.

"You made everything and you still let people suffer. You could make Earth a paradise and you *won't*. You let me be selfish and cruel and you didn't stop me." Tears poured like lava down my face. There's no hell? This was hell. This was torment. Feeling it all at once in the presence of a complacent and apathetic god.

*"Complacent? Apathetic? No. We take great interest. We provided the stage. Humans write the play. We do not stop them, no. That's what makes it so disheartening to see them discuss god. We do not design car crashes or wars or plagues or choose who receives disease. We are not vengeful or judgmental. We gathered stardust and waited to see what would happen."*

"So life is meaningless? *Is that it?* That's why you brought me here? To show me everything is for nothing? All the evil I inflicted on the world was just a part of your game? That's the big secret?"

*"No, life is not meaningless. Life is what you make it. It is community and connection and making yourself proud. Making mistakes and learning from them. Then there is the afterlife, an extension of what was possible on Earth. We thought we could make it a homecoming and allow Humans to be in our presence. But Humans want each other. You prefer your gods Human shaped and comprehensible, even if you pretend they are impossible to comprehend. So we gave you the Old Dead: our firewall. A legion of human souls duty bound to keep you safe and happy and creative in death. They did a good job. Until they didn't."*

"Why didn't you stop them? Why didn't you stop *us?*"

*"We make mistakes, too. We let it play out too long with the Old Dead. But we never would have stopped you."*

"So then what are Iskur and I to you? Another mistake? Another failed experiment?"

They did not answer, but I knew the answer. Well, the human part of me knew an answer and the other part knew another one. The *thrum, thrum, thrum* of that feeling so foreign felt like it was begging me to return to the divine knowledge my human side was rejecting. I could see the path, but I was resisting it. However, the rage and the water were receding.

I was part of the Nameless Ones. Everything was. I could feel it: the woven coil of gold within me that was my gifted power from them. That power was so easy to use for creation, and so volatile to use for destruction; fragile like a bomb. I breathed deeply, letting tears fall to the moss where they glimmered and shone as the waters of my rage dried up. I felt the gaze of the Nameless Ones on me as I gathered myself.

"*Do you think you are a mistake?*"

"Yes." A human answer.

"*So quick to despair. Your divine self does not think that way.*"

They were right. Breathe in. Breathe out. I felt myself gleam more brightly with the breaths. The cocoon of peace and comfort waited for me, but I didn't accept it yet.

"*You know you are not a mistake. We needed a system update, so we waited for one. The Old Dead were losing efficacy. So we watched and waited for Humans, bold, brave, foolish, creative, flawed Humans to ask for knowledge.*"

"Others must have asked."

"*Some did. None as capable as you.*"

"I'm supposed to believe that in all of human history only I was stupid enough to ask you for your power?"

"*Believe whatever you want. You have the power now. How would you use your power?*"

Their power was knowledge. Understanding. Seeing not only like a Seer, but beyond. A Seer looked at the tapestry in all its parts; the Nameless Ones set the threads onto the loom: warp and weft. They brought the wool, the silk, the linen: all the myriad of colored threads. And humans? We were the pattern makers. Each of our stories dictated the image in our spheres. Some spheres were smaller, some larger. Our Earthly dwellings. Not even the Nameless Ones could predict how things would come out or overlap. New artistry was created with each human life. No, not human...*Human*. We were divine creators, supplied tools and materials by a subservient omnipotence that loved us beyond understanding.

I saw the world in systems now. Crossing wires and threads effortlessly blending into a remarkable history. I had witnessed so many of these things come to pass on Earth, and I saw now how they all built on each other. A child braiding grass, a woman spinning linen, a girl smiling as she sees her friends approach, a grandfather kissing her first grandchild with tears in his eyes, myself running down a forest path. There was beauty in seeing every creative pursuit tied to another in an unending body of Human work.

A strand of nothingness from the pith of a plant is twisted upon itself to make the first thread. Then more threads. Threads plied. A loom, rudimentary and blessed. Then more moving parts, complex fabrics. Silks, wools. Patterns spoken for generations until written patterns were saved. A loom with a memory built in. Punchcards. Repeatable processes. Code breakers. Calculators. Copper and gold wires tied with deft fingers to put a man on the moon. Then more men. More feats of daring. Then home computers and microchips and cell phones and it was all available the whole time. Dust from stars became dirt for plants became strings and threads and wires and networks.

That omnipotence let out a quiet laugh that could deafen a village.

*"How will you use your power, we wonder?"* They repeated kindly. The shroud of peace descended over me as I allowed it to.

"Humans can handle this. More of this. More knowledge of their past, more reverence and connection with their ancestors."

*"Can they?"* They were amused. The beetle scuttled up the tree a bit higher.

"Yes."

*"What is it you crave above all else?"*

That question again. From my tranquil clairvoyance I knew the answer. It was so obvious when I stopped resisting the knowledge that was within me.

"Safety."

The word was a warm tide washing over me. Safety was the heartbeat within me, the feeling I could not name. It was sunlight. It was a star-studded sky. It was being held by someone who loved me so fully I thought I would burst. It was a full night's sleep and a warm meal. It was friends smiling around a fire. It was the woods. It was my trees. It was the feeling I chased after through countless years of exile and waiting.

The Nameless Ones made a noise that sounded like agreement and pride.

All I had ever wanted was to feel safe. Iskur made me feel it, until we were threatened by my fiancé. After my soul had been unbound I had equated Iskur with my deepest desire but it had always been safety. The love we shared was still there, but I was finally seeing the covenant that bound us. More powerful than the bond we made in the light of the Nameless Ones, we upheld the unspoken vow of safety between us. A river of revelations flowed through me.

"And Iskur craves belonging. And Virgil seeks acceptance. Those are portions of safety. We make each other up."

*"You three are perfect. We do not foretell. We cannot see the future, we only see patterns that Humans create. The three of you surprised and delighted us. Do not weep. You have what you are seeking. Nothing can ever harm you, and you have the chance to shape the Human experience, if you so desire."*

The grove of cedars faded away until it was just me and the Nameless Ones and the largest tree in an endless expanse of blackness.

"I see it all now."

*"You do."*

"Iskur and Virgil, belonging and acceptance...those are the parts that make up safety." I repeated thoughtfully. I could see the path.

*"Our system needs an update."*

"No more Old Dead?"

*"They get to be souls again. No more keepers of balance."*

"But," A twinge of unresolved guilt twisted inside me, "I killed people."

*"Humans need to go back to loving flawed gods. It helps them love themselves."*

The Nameless Ones glowed softly while I thought. When I didn't say any-thing, they continued:

*"You never successfully convinced yourself that your actions were okay. You know your own morality despite seemingly being rewarded for being selfish. You did not see the power as a reward in the end, but rather a way to get back to what you were looking for."*

"What if I don't want to be a god?"

*"That's fine. We can wait for another path to reveal itself. You can live as a soul in the Otherworld."*

"I won't be punished?"

*"You need to release this fear of punishment, Arga. You have made yourself suffer enough. Those you killed are safe with us. They did not suffer, and they forgave you long ago. Can you do the same? Can you forgive yourself?"*

Hearing them say those words broke me. I wanted to suffer for all the cruelty and selfishness I had acted out. I wanted to be told I was hateful, evil, vile, wrong.

*"If you wish to extend knowledge and safety to Humanity, you cannot exempt yourself from that. You must accept love unconditionally and stop seeking misery and destruction."*

"What if I can't?"

*"You will learn. There is time to practice. You have already died, there is no limit to your existence now."*

They were right. In my core, I knew what they were saying was true. Making myself into a tortured pariah was an indulgence that no longer served me. I had seen the ten Seers surround me on the hill as I had battled with the Old Dead. They had radiated compassion, understanding, and forgiveness. I could forgive myself, too. I closed my eyes and latched on to the acceptance. I breathed it in and drank it up, willing myself to fuse with this feeling and burn it into my being. I shifted out of my human form.

*"Humans deserve to know their pasts."* I said. I had never been more sure of anything.

*"And who will keep them safe?"*

*"We will."*

I felt the Nameless Ones smiling.

The cosmos splayed out around me and I opened my awareness to it all. The dead cannot predict the future, but we can see all the intricacies of the past. What is done is done, and what will be is shaped by what we do now.

The Nameless Ones shifted forms and I matched them. We were hummingbirds, speeding through chaos and order, life and death, here and there. We were the in-between, the sacred knowledge that had been withheld from Earth for too long.

*"What will you do with your power?"*

*"I am ready to serve our Humans."*

*"Good."*

Everything flattened to a pinprick of nothingness.

I heard thunder.

I heard wind.

I smiled and answered the call.

# XXXIV.

We stood on a windswept cliff overlooking the sea. I smiled and breathed and felt almost human.

Almost.

Iskur took my hand, lost in thought. I traced the silvery scars along the ridges of his bones.

"You could change these now."

It took him a moment to come back to me from his reverie.

"Hm?"

"The scars. You don't need to keep them."

"Why not?"

I raised my eyebrows. Did we have to go over this again?

"What's done is done. We can move on. We have new paths before us."

"Exactly. What is done is done. I cannot change the past," he turned to face me, "I *will not* change the past. Is it not you who says Humans deserve to know their history? How can we lead by example when we erase the memories of our own history?"

I rolled my eyes.

"You don't have to throw my words back at me."

Thunder rumbled in his laugh. The sea answered.

"Are you two ready?"

My smile widened as Virgil came around a bend on the path towards the cliffs.

"I like the oak crown, Virgil. It suits you."

"Do not mock me."

"Don't be bitter, Virg, it's not a good look for a God."

His frown was short-lived as Iskur and I walked to his side. Virgil sheepishly presented me with a crown of violets and Iskur with one of cedar. A beetle chirped appreciatively from a bush.

The weight of the power within me was hardly noticeable when split three ways. We all wore it well, accepting the gift of knowledge with reverence and joy. Our directive was simple yet immense: allow Humanity to get in touch with their ancestors. Without another word between us, we faded into our lightforms and sped off across the rising waves.

We were alive and our eyes were open.

It was the kind of thing you couldn't debate. We knew we had been remade and we knew our purpose.

An ancient shuttle passes over a vast expanse of colored threads and the weaver resets the infinite loom.

[root@otherworld]:> pxe_boot(earth) && download_system_image(otherworld_connection) && run_unattended_install_script(ancient_vast_and_inf inite.xyz) && reboot(earth)